"I thought you might be here," Levi said as he came into the barn. "I need to talk to you about something."

Nicki stopped rubbing the saddle she was cleaning. *Here it comes,* she thought with a lump forming in *her throat. He's leaving. I'll never see him again.* Not trusting herself to speak, she resumed her work. The tack room suddenly seemed very small.

"Looks like we're going to have a bad winter," Levi said.

Nicki looked up at him in surprise. The weather was the last thing she'd expected to discuss with him. "What are you getting at?"

Levi stared at her for several seconds, as though he was unsure how to proceed. "I want to stay," he finally blurted out.

"What?" She couldn't believe her ears. He wanted to stay!

"I know cowhands are supposed to leave during the winter, but if this one is really bad, there'll be too much work for just you and Peter. . . ." As his voice trailed off he moved closer to her. She could have sworn he touched her hair lightly, but the sensation was gone in an instant.

"It's fine with me," Nicki said as evenly as she could. But her heart was pounding so hard, she was sure he could hear it.

Other books in the Cheyenne Trilogy
by Carolyn Lampman

Murphy's Rainbow
Shadows in the Wind

Available from
HarperPaperbacks

Willow Creek

⊷ CAROLYN LAMPMAN ⊷

HarperPaperbacks
A Division of HarperCollins Publishers

HarperPaperbacks   *A Division of* HarperCollins*Publishers*
10 East 53rd Street, New York, N.Y. 10022

Copyright © 1994 by Carolyn Brubaker
All rights reserved. No part of this book may be used or reproduced in any manner whatsoever without written permission of the publisher, except in the case of brief quotations embodied in critical articles and reviews. For information address HarperCollins*Publishers,*
10 East 53rd Street, New York, N.Y. 10022.

Cover illustration by R.A. Maguire

First printing: August 1994

Printed in the United States of America

HarperPaperbacks, HarperMonogram, and colophon are trademarks of HarperCollins*Publishers*

❖ 10 9 8 7 6 5 4 3 2 1

To my very own "Levi."
This one is for you, Bru.

1

March 1886, Wyoming Territory

"Watch it, sodbuster!" The drunk cowboy glowered down at Nicki, or what he could see of her. Only faded dungarees and small booted feet were visible beneath the heavy winter coat and wide-brimmed hat. "Don't you know enough to get out of the way when your betters come along?"

Swallowing a retort, Nicki stepped away from him. The man had blundered right into her as she came out of the mercantile, but the last thing she needed was trouble with three cowpokes from the Bar X.

"Hey, boy," said the man's tall, rangy companion. "You owe Shorty an apology."

Nicki gritted her teeth. She'd rather spit in his face. "Sorry," she mumbled.

"We'd best teach this squatter some manners, Buck," the third man said with a sinister smile. "I say we throw him in the horse trough."

Nicki backed up against the wall and watched the three men warily. She wasn't afraid of a dunking, but such things had a tendency to get out of hand when whiskey was involved, and these men clearly had been drinking a long time. At least they were too drunk to realize they were dealing with a full-grown woman. Barely five feet tall, Nicki was used to people mistaking her for an adolescent boy. Even without her heavy coat, the bulky long johns she wore effectively hid her slender figure.

Suddenly one of the cowhands lunged toward her, and Nicki struck out with a small fist. As her assailant clutched his midsection in pain, the third man grabbed her from behind, pinning her arms to her sides. Struggling wildly, she soon realized it was impossible to escape that way.

She slumped in apparent defeat and waited while the other cowboy approached. When he was a mere two feet away Nicki leaned back and swung her foot up in a vicious kick. Taken unaware, the man holding her stumbled backward as his friend howled in agony when the boot connected with his knee. But it wasn't enough and Nicki knew it.

Her heart thumped wildly in her chest as the two she'd injured picked themselves up and headed for her again. Desperately, she fought the hands that held her, but to no avail. Nothing but a miracle could save her now.

"All right, gentlemen, I think you've had enough fun for one day." The three men froze at the sound of a rifle being cocked. "Let the boy go."

Nicki twisted around in surprise. The voice belonged to a complete stranger. He was well over six feet, and his bulk seemed to fill the doorway of the mercantile. A full beard hid his expression, but his blue-gray eyes glinted dangerously as he stepped forward onto the boardwalk. His appearance was nearly as menacing as the rifle he held pointed at the man restraining Nicki.

"Now, Mister," said one of the cowboys, lifting his hands. "You don't understand what's going on. This here is my little brother. He snuck off to town, and Pa sent my friends and me to fetch him home."

"He doesn't seem to want to go with you."

"That's because he was planning on going to the saloon and gettin' himself a woman," Nicki's captor replied.

Finally Nicki found her voice. "That's not true. I . . ." A hand was clamped over her mouth before she could finish.

The cowboy holding her smiled nervously. "He's a lyin' little brat too." He yelped as Nicki sank her teeth into his hand. "Why you little . . ." He raised the injured hand to cuff his captive and then froze as the rifle barrel jabbed into the underside of his jaw.

"Somehow I find it hard to believe he's your brother," the stranger said. "Now, are you going to let him go, or am I going to have to get nasty?"

Nicki was released, and all three men backed away. "What business is it of yours whether he's my brother or not?" asked another of the cowboys.

"Let's just say I don't like the odds." Her savior patted his rifle. "My Winchester and I even them up." He glanced down at Nicki. "Can you shoot this?"

Nicki took the rifle from his hands and fired it once, making a clean hole in one of the cowboy's hats and sending it flying into the street. She ejected the shell and looked up at him.

He grinned. "That answers my question. Is that your wagon in front of the store?" Nicki nodded again and he squeezed her shoulder. "Good. Keep these sidewinders covered while I go get it."

In a matter of minutes, the wagon rattled to a stop beside Nicki and she felt the large, comforting presence next to her once more.

"Well, son, I've had enough excitement for one day. What do you say we leave these gentlemen to find other entertainment and be on our way?"

With a nod, Nicki handed him the gun. Barely glancing at the big bay mare tied to the back, she climbed into the wagon, picked up the reins, and waited for him to join her. Then, with a sharp snap of the reins across the rumps of the horses, they headed out of town.

"Friends of yours?" he asked.

Nicki snorted. "Not hardly. They're two-bit cow-pokes from the Bar X Ranch." She glanced at her companion. Without the steely glint in his eyes he wasn't nearly as intimidating. "I'm sorry you had to get involved in that."

He shrugged. "Looked to me like you were doing all right. If there'd been one less of them, I'd have probably had to save the other two from you."

She was vaguely embarrassed by the compliment. "Well . . . thanks anyway."

"Glad I could help out. By the way, the name's Levi Cantrell."

"Nicki Chandler."

"Pleased to meet you, Nicki." With a friendly smile, Levi extended his hand to her. The large callused palm felt pleasantly warm as it closed over Nicki's smaller one. In spite of his size, there was something reassuring about this man's ready smile and twinkling eyes.

"It'll be late when we get home. Would you like to stay for supper?" she asked impulsively.

"Maybe you should ask your mother first."

"Don't have one, and I do the cooking," Nicki said sharply, her gaze fixed on the road ahead. "It's the least I can do. Besides, Papa will want to meet you."

"In that case, I accept," he said with a smile. Pulling out his bag of tobacco, Levi glanced back at his companion. He knew all too well what it was like to grow up without a mother. His own had died when he was barely two, and he'd been nearly thirteen before his father remarried.

Levi rolled himself a cigarette, licked the edge, twisted the ends, and stuck it in his mouth. At any rate, a home-cooked meal would be a welcome change from his usual fare of beans over the campfire, even if it meant another cold night under the stars. He reached into his pocket, pulled out a match, and struck it on the wagon seat. With a satisfied sigh, he relaxed and bid an unlamented farewell to his thoughts of a hot bath and soft bed at the saloon.

2

By the time they reached the homestead, the sun was low in the west. Instead of the simple sod shanty typical to the area, the cabin was constructed of peeled logs and built in two sections. Though the smaller addition was separated from the main dwelling by a narrow dogtrot, the roof extended over both. Beyond the house lay a large barn, a fair-sized corral, and several other outbuildings where chickens slowly meandered toward their roost for the night. To the east, a small creek gurgled by several tall cottonwoods, giving the homestead an air of tranquillity.

Nicki jumped down from the wagon and smiled shyly up at her guest. "Come in and meet Papa. He's been sick, and he'll be pleased to have company."

Levi followed her into a small but immaculate kitchen. Well-scrubbed pots and pans hung on hooks by the cookstove, a set of blue dishes lined a shelf, and bright calico curtains hung at the window. The furnishings were simple and Levi's first impression was one of cozy welcome.

"Is that you, Nicki?"

"Yes, Papa." Nicki walked to an open doorway off the kitchen. "We have company."

"Company?" There was a creak of bed ropes. "I didn't hear anybody ride up."

Cyrus Chandler's smile barely faltered at the sight of a stranger. He was fairly tall, but the gaunt frame and unhealthy pallor showed the effects of a long illness.

"Papa, this is Levi Cantrell," Nicki said. "Mr. Cantrell, my father, Cyrus Chandler."

The older man's grip was surprisingly strong as he shook hands with Levi. "It's a pleasure to meet you, Mr. Cantrell. Are you a new neighbor?"

"No, I'm just passing through. Nicki and I met in town, and I was going the same way so . . ."

"We don't get many visitors out here. Will you stay to supper and tell us all the news?"

"Thank you, Mr. Chandler. I'd be pleased to." Levi grinned broadly. "Besides, your son already invited me."

"My . . ." He glanced at Nicki and a flash of comprehension crossed his face. "Ah, well good."

Nicki's face turned red, and she ducked her head. "It's getting late," she mumbled. "I'd better start chores."

Levi stared after her in surprise as she hurried out the door.

Cyrus Chandler smiled. "You'll have to forgive Nicki. Er . . . he's a bit shy."

"He is?" Levi glanced toward the door again with a look of mild curiosity. "Now, that's something I'd never have guessed."

"It comes and goes," Cyrus said drily. "Have a seat." He eased himself into a chair and regarded the man before him with great interest. Nicki had never brought anyone home before, much less a man. She was far more likely to chase them off at gunpoint. "How did you meet Nicki?"

"He was having a problem with three cowpokes from the Bar X," Levi said. "The boy was holding his own, but things were starting to get out of hand. I just evened up the odds a bit."

Cyrus gave Nicki a sharp look as she came back in carrying some of the supplies from the wagon. "Mr. Cantrell tells me you had a run-in with some of Herman Lowell's men."

"They were drunk and looking for a fight. That's all there was to it, Papa. They didn't have the faintest idea who I was."

"That's not the point, Nicki. You need to be more careful. If Mr. Cantrell hadn't come along when he did, you might have been in serious trouble."

"I really didn't do that much," Levi put in. "I think those cowpokes will think twice before they tangle with your son. He hurt them far worse than they hurt him." He shifted his gaze to Nicki. "Why don't I unload the wagon so you can get started on your chores?"

"You don't need to do that."

"Maybe not, but you'll be done that much faster."

"Well, all right," Nicki said reluctantly.

Within a short time Levi had the supplies unloaded and was headed toward the barn. He had just started unharnessing the horses when he heard a stealthy noise behind him. He whirled around and found himself face-to-face with the business end of a double-barreled shotgun. Cautiously, Levi raised his gaze to the man behind the gun.

Though he was several inches shorter than Levi, his stocky build and broad shoulders made any thought of heroics foolhardy. The man's features were indistinct in the dim light of the barn, but the determined set of his square jaw and his unwinking stare were distinctly menacing.

Slowly Levi raised his hands and smiled uneasily. "Just putting the horses away for Nicki," he said. "No harm intended."

Silently, the man continued to stare at him.

"I'll leave if you want." Levi slowly started to move back, but the cocking of the gun stopped him in midstep. "Why don't we just go on up to the house and talk to Mr. Chandler," he went on. The man might have been carved from stone for all the emotion he was showing.

"Peter!" Suddenly, Nicki was between them gesturing wildly. The man looked away from Levi but didn't lower the gun. Watching Nicki's hands, he shook his head and nodded toward Levi.

"Nicki, what . . ." Levi began.

"Mr. Cantrell, please. He's nervous enough." Nicki continued to move her hands, repeatedly linking her two forefingers. "He's a friend, Peter. I brought him home." Nicki reached over and removed the twelve-gauge from Peter's grasp.

Peter looked at Levi again and began moving his hands as Nicki had. With a start, Levi realized they were communicating. The interplay between the two continued for several minutes. Finally, apparently satisfied, Peter retrieved his gun from Nicki and turned away.

"Let's go back to the house, Mr. Cantrell," Nicki said. "Peter will see to the horses."

Slowly Levi lowered his hands and followed Nicki out of the barn. "Your brother?" he asked in a low voice when they were finally outside.

"As far as I'm concerned he is, though I guess he's really my cousin."

"I didn't mean to upset him."

"You don't have to whisper," Nicki said. "Peter can't hear you . . . he's deaf."

Suddenly Levi understood. "So that's why you talked to him with your hands. Your sign language wasn't from any tribe I've ever seen, though. I couldn't understand any of it."

"It's the sign language the deaf speak on Martha's Vineyard in Massachusetts."

Levi raised his brows in surprise. "That's a mighty long way from here."

"I know. My aunt lived in Boston but moved there when Peter lost his hearing. He came to live with us when she died."

"And the sign language is the only way he can communicate?"

Nicki shook her head. "He doesn't speak, but he reads lips pretty well."

"He didn't read mine. I tried to explain, but he wouldn't listen . . . well, I mean he didn't seem to understand."

"It was dark in the barn, and you have a beard. Peter couldn't see your lips. He has suffered a great deal of abuse from people. Because he's deaf and mute, they seem to think he's stupid too."

"So he's leery of strangers. It seems I owe you a big thanks. If you hadn't come in when you did, I'd probably have wound up six feet under." His friendly slap on her back nearly knocked Nicki off her feet. She caught her balance with an uncertain smile and tried to match his long strides as they walked to the house.

"All done?" Cyrus asked when they came in the door.

"Yes." Nicki took off her hat and ran her fingers through her short, curly hair. "Mr. Cantrell took the horses to the barn and ran into Peter. I never thought to warn either of them."

"Did he give you any trouble?"

"A little, but I can't say I blame him much. It must have looked like I was stealing the horses." Levi's eyes unconsciously strayed to the small figure near the stove. Something bothered him about Nicki but he couldn't quite place what it was. He dismissed the thought as he pulled up a chair and turned his attention to Cyrus. "This is a real nice place you have here."

"Thanks." Cyrus smiled with pride. "Ten years ago it was just another patch of sagebrush."

"Ten years?" Levi was amazed. "You've accomplished a lot in a short time."

"We've got plenty of water, the soil's good, and the three of us are willing to work." He took a sip from his coffee cup and glanced out the window. "We settled in Iowa for a few years after we left Massachusetts, but Lady Luck didn't smile on us until we came here. With irrigation, our crops do extremely well. Our cattle even seem to do better than most of our neighbors'."

"That isn't luck," Nicki said. "We just use more common sense than they do. Herman Lowell lets his cows calve out on the open range. Too bad if that happens to be in the middle of a blizzard, or there's a rustler nearby with a running iron." She slammed a stack of dishes down on the table so hard they rattled.

"I'm sick of the 'cattle barons' blaming all their problems on homesteaders and small ranchers. It's their own incompetence that's destroying them," she went on, her disapproval emphasized by each plate as she thumped it onto the table. "When they're gone, people like us will still be here because we plan ahead."

The tirade was obviously not unusual because Cyrus paid no attention but looked at the table in surprise. "The good dishes, Nicki?"

Nicki blushed as she stared down at the blue china in her hands. "We don't have company very often, and I just thought . . ."

Cyrus smiled and patted her back as her voice trailed off. "If company isn't occasion enough to use the good dishes, I don't know what is."

Levi found the entire exchange bewildering. What adolescent boy cared a hoot about what dishes they used? How many even noticed? Nicki Chandler was the damnedest boy he'd ever met.

Cyrus gave Nicki a final pat and turned back to Levi. "So tell me, Mr. Cantrell, what line of work are you in?"

"Call me Levi," he said then paused. "I've always thought of myself as a cowhand but most recently I was a sailor."

"A sailor! I'd have never pegged you for a man of the sea."

"I wasn't one by choice." The blue-gray eyes twinkled. "I chose the wrong tavern to drown my sorrows in. The next thing I knew I was on my way to China with one hell of a hangover and a lump the size of a goose egg on my head."

Nicki eyed him skeptically. "I thought nobody who got shanghaied ever made it back."

"It's a pretty rough life, but it's really no harder than being a cowhand. You're already used to being out in the worst kind of weather and you use the same muscles to work the rigging that you use to throw a steer or pitch hay. Once I got my sea legs and convinced a few hard-bitten sea dogs it was easier to be friends than enemies, I managed."

Nicki raised an eyebrow. "You're a long way from the coast here."

"I had enough of the sea to last me a lifetime. I only stayed with it long enough to get back home."

"You're on you're way home then?" Cyrus asked.

"I was already there. After a couple of months I was ready to leave again." Levi shrugged. "I guess the roving gets in the blood."

Nicki was setting the food on the table when Peter slid silently into a chair. Levi smiled at him in a friendly way but the only response was a cold stare. That stare remained fixed firmly in place all the way through supper.

Cyrus and Levi were soon deep in conversation. Even with the older man's frequent coughing spells interrupting the talk, it didn't take long for Levi to realize a keen mind inhabited the wasted body. Since the food was delicious and the company congenial, Levi was able to ignore Peter's hostile attitude enough to enjoy his meal. Still, he was relieved when Peter finished eating, made some quick signs to Cyrus, and left the cabin.

After another half hour of conversation Levi

uncrossed his arms and scooted back his chair. "I'd best be going. Thanks for supper and a very enjoyable evening."

"Where are you headed?" Nicki asked.

"Don't know really. Right now I'm just going where the wind takes me."

Cyrus coughed painfully and stood up. "Well, it was a good wind that brought you our way. We can't offer you much, but you're welcome to bed down in the barn tonight if you like."

"I'm much obliged. A pile of hay is a whole lot more comfortable than the ground."

"It's the least we can do. And we'll expect you for breakfast in the morning."

"Thanks."

Cyrus gave a satisfied nod and gestured to Nicki. "Give me a hand to bed . . . son. I'm tired."

"I've been thinking," Cyrus began as his daughter helped him into bed. "Maybe it's time we hired a man to help out around here."

Nicki looked at him in surprise. "What for?"

"There's too much work for just you and Peter."

"Oh Papa, you'll feel better as soon as it warms up. Look how much better you are already. Last week you couldn't even get out of bed and tonight you were up for hours!"

Busily fluffing her father's pillow, Nicki missed the sad, almost pitying look he gave her. "Besides who would you hire? Everybody around here either has their own place or they work for the Bar X."

"I was thinking of asking Levi Cantrell if he'd stay for awhile," he said, watching her closely.

"What?" Nicki whirled around, her eyes wide.

"I thought you liked him."

"But we don't know anything about him."

Cyrus shrugged. "We know he's a good man, otherwise he'd have just let those cowboys have their fun with you."

"Oh Papa, you're too trusting. Maybe he's the sort who likes to throw his weight around. Those men weren't really any danger to him. He had a rifle; they were unarmed and drunk besides. For all we know he may be a gunslinger or worse."

"Gunslingers carry six-guns not rifles," Cyrus said. "The fact he's not afraid of a fight is a good reason for him to stay. If we run into trouble with the Bar X outfit, we'll need help. Levi Cantrell is big enough to take care of just about any problem that comes up."

"Peter and I do just fine. We don't need some two-bit drifter to get in our way. Cantrell said himself he's just passing through. What happens when he gets itchy feet again?"

"I suppose he'll leave. We won't be any worse off than we are right now, and we'll probably get some work out of him first."

"Well I don't like it," Nicki grumbled. "There's something about him that makes me nervous."

"You liked him well enough to invite him to supper. What changed your mind?"

"I figured I owed him a meal. I didn't know you were going to ask him to stay!"

"I haven't yet. In fact I haven't made up my mind whether I will or not. I'll sleep on it tonight and see what the morning brings."

"I hope it brings you some sense. It's a stupid idea if you ask me," Nicki snapped.

Cyrus gave a small laugh. "You're afraid of what he'll do when he finds out you're a woman aren't you?"

Nicki glowered at him.

"Nicki, Nicki, you have nothing to worry about. Levi will like you just as well as a woman."

Nicki stomped out muttering, "Maybe that's what I'm afraid of."

But she knew it wasn't Levi that frightened her. It was herself.

As she crawled into bed, Nicki thought of her inexplicable attraction to Levi Cantrell. When Samantha Chandler had run away with a handsome but worthless gambler, Nicki had thought she was free of her mother forever. But as she'd grown older the cracked mirror on her bedroom wall had begun to tell a different story. The day she'd seen her mother's face staring back at her, she cut her hair short and began wearing boy's clothes.

Repeatedly, Nicki had told herself she might look like her mother but she was completely different inside. She had believed it too, until today. From the first second she'd seen Levi Cantrell, she'd been drawn to him like a magnet. She'd convinced herself it was gratitude that made her invite him to supper, but deep inside she knew she had wanted to spend a little time with him.

"Well, you may just get your wish!" she mumbled, punching her pillow in frustration. "But then what?"

There was no answer from the darkness.

As he laid out his bedroll on a sweet-smelling bed of hay, Levi contemplated the family he'd just met. In spite of the boy's almost feminine mannerisms, there was something very appealing about Nicki Chandler. Loyalty and courage like his were rare in full-grown men, let alone a boy who was years from shaving. Levi grinned to himself as he wondered what would happen if Nicki knew that one of the despised ranchers was bedded down in the Chandler barn.

Then he sobered. Without being an expert in such matters, Levi was almost certain Cyrus Chandler was suffering from consumption. It was only a matter of time before Nicki and Peter would be alone. Haunted by a pair of violet eyes and a man old before his time, it was a long time before Levi was able to sleep.

3

Ka-thwok . . . ka-thwok . . . ka-thwok.

Nicki opened her eyes and spent several seconds trying to identify the sound that had awakened her. Sleep still clouded her mind as she rose and walked to the window. The eastern horizon was barely turning pink as she squinted into the half-light of dawn. Then her eyes widened in surprise. Levi was splitting firewood in the early morning chill.

Her gaze followed the line of his back down to his trim waist and long muscular legs while he swung the ax with effortless strength. As the sun peeked over the horizon, rays of light caught tiny glints of red and gold in his hair and beard. Something quivered deep inside her. What was there about this man that made her feel so strange?

Suddenly Nicki was wide-awake. It wasn't even full light yet and Levi was already working while she stood there gawking like a fool. She dressed hastily and hurried to the kitchen to start breakfast.

In the other bedroom Cyrus stood by the window watching Levi. "So he's not afraid of a little work," he said thoughtfully. "I think he might be just what I've been looking for."

"Good morning," Levi said cheerfully, twenty minutes later, as he dumped a huge armload of wood into the woodbox.

"Good morning, Levi," Cyrus responded from his chair at the table. "You're just in time for breakfast."

Levi grinned and patted his flat stomach. "I'm hardly ever late for a meal." He glanced at Nicki dumping flour into a bowl and reached for the empty water buckets. "I'll just fill these first."

"No!" Nicki almost dropped the bowl in her haste to grab the bucket nearest her before Levi could pick it up. "That's my job."

Levi shook his head and gently removed her hand from the bail. "Not this morning it isn't. A man has to do something to earn his breakfast."

"But . . ."

"No buts," he said over his shoulder as he strode out of the house. They could hear him whistling as he pulled the bucket up from the well.

At the sound of a smothered chuckle, Nicki glared at her father.

"I think you may have to swallow your pride on this one," Cyrus told her. "He's only being helpful you know."

"I don't want him to be helpful," she muttered, turning back to the stove. She managed a brittle "Thanks," when Levi set the full buckets next to the stove several minutes later, but she didn't look up from the large bowl of batter she was stirring.

Levi gave her a puzzled look but joined Cyrus at the table without saying a word.

It wasn't long before Nicki slapped a plate of flapjacks on the table in front of him and walked away. Levi glanced up in surprise. Was the boy angry just because he'd given him a hand? How strange. Most boys would be delighted to get out of some of their chores.

As he ate, Levi found himself idly watching Nicki working over the hot stove. Funny how the word pretty kept coming to mind, but there was no other way to describe the combination of delicate facial features, violet eyes, and curly black hair. When Nicki reached up and smoothed a strand of hair back from her face, Levi felt a twinge of something akin to distaste. Someone really should take the boy in hand and explain a few things to him. With that small build and that face he'd need to be very careful of the gestures he used unconsciously. To watch him you'd almost think he was a wo . . .

Levi's eyes widened in disbelief as an incredible idea burst into full bloom. Was it possible? For a long moment he sat there with his fork suspended in midair. At last, he became aware of Cyrus grinning at him from across the table.

Nicki suddenly stopped stirring. "Oh, darn, I forgot to wake up Peter." She hurried out the side door and Levi gazed after her in shock.

Cyrus chuckled. "I take it you just figured out Nicki's little secret."

Levi carefully set his fork back on his plate, too stunned to even put his thoughts into words.

Cyrus's grin broadened until Levi began to think the older man's face would split. "If I were you, I wouldn't let on you know right away. She's mighty sensitive about it for some reason."

"Why?"

"Who knows? I gave up trying to figure out women long ago." Cyrus sighed. "I keep hoping she'll come to her senses, but there's no arguing with her until she does."

Levi nodded silently, his mind still trying to grasp the significance of his discovery. How could he have been so blind? From the first he'd suspected there was something more to Nicki than met the eye, but that was about the only accurate observation he'd made. Levi was a man who prided himself on his ability to see through people, a skill that had been woefully lacking this time. If nothing else, he should have realized Nicki was female by his reaction to her. He'd never be attracted to any boy that way, not even one with beautiful eyes.

"Last night it sounded like you might be looking for work. I've been thinking of hiring somebody to help out around here." Cyrus paused. "I can offer you a roof over your head, three square meals a day, and a decent wage. Are you interested?"

Levi took a bite of his breakfast, trying to bring order to his confused thoughts. "I might be. What kind of work is it?"

"We don't have much in the way of stock, but what cattle there are need to be rounded up and branded. Then there'll be plowing and planting before too long. Other than that, just the usual upkeep, at least until midsummer."

Levi contemplated this as he chewed. Maybe it was time to stop for awhile. "I could use a job, but I'll warn you right now, I'm no farmer. My experience has always been with horses and cattle. Other than putting up hay, I've never done any sort of farm work. I'm willing to learn but I'll be a complete fool where plowing is concerned."

Cyrus chuckled. "At least you're honest. Peter can teach you all you need to know. It isn't really difficult. Between the two of you there shouldn't be any reason for Nicki to do it. I'd like to ease her out of as much of the heavy work as I can."

"Peter hated me on sight."

"If you treat him like a normal human being instead of an idiot, he'll come around."

Levi hardly needed to give the question any further thought. He was needed here. Besides, the backbreaking work of a homestead would leave him too tired to be restless. "My father always said it was impossible for me to resist a challenge," he said with a smile. "You just hired yourself a cowhand."

"Good." A smile spread across Cyrus's face. "You'd better finish your flapjacks before Nicki gets back. The mood she's in, she's liable to think you don't like her cooking."

Levi was just cleaning up the last few bites when Nicki and Peter returned. Peter slid into his place much the same as he had the night before.

"I doubt I'll be able to do much this spring," Cyrus said without preamble. He signed in the same fluid motions Nicki had used and spoke at the same time. "There's too much work for just the two of you, so I've hired Mr. Cantrell to help out until the spring planting is done."

Nicki merely nodded and sat down as though the news was expected, if not particularly welcome.

Though Levi hadn't expected Peter to be overjoyed

by the news, he was unprepared for the intense stare the other man directed at him across the table. Unsure how to respond, Levi returned the look with a steady gaze. The silent battle continued until Nicki set a plate in front of Peter and he turned his attention to his breakfast. Neither was sure who had won the contest, but it left each of them adjusting his idea of the other.

Cyrus and Levi carried on a friendly conversation during the rest of the meal while Nicki covertly observed them. In Levi's presence Cyrus was different somehow, more relaxed, less gloomy. But then she was beginning to think it was difficult to be morose around Levi Cantrell. His infectious, booming laugh and twinkling, blue-gray eyes were an irresistible combination.

"Mighty good breakfast, Nicki." Levi slid his chair back. "What did you have in mind for me to do today, Cyrus?"

"We still haven't cleaned out the spring yet," Nicki put in before Cyrus had a chance to answer. "I'm sure Mr. Cantrell would be very good at that."

Cyrus's eyes narrowed. Then, after a moment, he shrugged and picked up his coffee cup. "I guess today's as good as any to clean the spring. It shouldn't take the three of you more than a few hours."

Nicki glared at her father. By suggesting the worst job on the homestead, she had been hoping Mr. Cantrell might yet change his mind and leave. But Cyrus, with his usual keen perception, had seen through her plan. Angrily, she followed Peter out of the house and strode toward the barn.

Levi shook his head as he picked up his hat. "I don't think your daughter is very happy with any of this."

"Don't worry, she'll come around. She's just used to having everything her own way."

Levi sighed as he put on his hat. "Is that why I feel like Daniel going into the lion's den?"

Cyrus's chuckle was interrupted by a deep wracking cough as he waved Levi toward the door.

During the ride out to the spring, Nicki and Peter were so obvious in their attempts to make him feel unwanted that Levi found it almost humorous. Not once did either of them glance in his direction as they talked back and forth in sign language. It appeared to be a very animated conversation, and he had no doubt he was the topic.

Casting an experienced eye over the landscape, Levi was impressed with what he saw. When Cyrus Chandler had staked his homestead he had chosen well. The land lay in a small valley surrounded by high hills, which offered protection against hard winds and severe weather. Even water, the most precious of all resources in this near desert, was available. Though it was now nearly dry, a tiny stream trickled down through several small fields still showing the stubble of last year's crops.

Levi could see that the natural creek bed had been widened and deepened in order to carry more water for irrigation. It appeared Cyrus Chandler was a shrewd planner with a great deal of foresight.

"Oh no, what happened?" Nicki's dismayed voice drew Levi's attention to the hillside where she and Peter sat looking at a hole in the rocks. It was obviously the spring they had been sent to clean and the source of the tiny stream that ran through the valley. Joining the other two, Levi peered down at the clogged opening.

"Looks like the wind blew it full of dirt and tumble-weeds over the winter," he observed. "Shouldn't be too hard to dig it out."

"Of course it's full of trash. That's why we're up here." Nicki pointed to the thin trickle running over the stones and into a small pool. "The pond is usually three times that size."

Levi dismounted and walked over to the spring. "Did you get much snow last winter?" he asked, studying the opening.

"Only a little now and then." A shadow crossed Nicki's face. "Not much rain last summer either. It's going dry isn't it?"

Hunkering down for a better look, Levi scratched his chin. "Looks like it, but maybe it isn't as bad as it seems." He stood up and surveyed the entire hill.

"That's all you know about it! Without that spring we might as well pack up and leave!"

Levi bent and sifted a handful of the sandy soil through his fingers. "The soil around here is like a giant sponge. Any water that hits it soaks in immediately and keeps on going until it hits bedrock and collects there, kind of like a big underground lake." He pointed to the hole in the hillside. "The top of that lake overflows through this hole but since the water level is lower, hardly any is coming out."

"That was very educational, Mr. Cantrell, but it doesn't solve the problem does it?" Nicki's voice was filled with biting sarcasm.

Levi stood up and dusted his hand against his pants. "No, but if you think about it for a minute, the solution is obvious."

Unwilling to admit that it was anything but obvious to her, Nicki silently watched Levi untie the pickax and shovel from his saddle. What in the world was he planning?

"You'd better tell Peter we're going to dig a little farther down into the hill to enlarge the opening of the spring," Levi said. "We have to get below the level of the groundwater again."

By the time Peter understood what they were going to do and had taken the horses to a flat area nearby, Levi was already breaking up the dirt and rock near the entrance of the spring with the pickax. Grudgingly, Nicki picked up a shovel. Her mind was already searching for ways to assert her authority before Levi took over completely.

It was hard, backbreaking labor, but it wasn't long before the three began to see results. Gradually, the size of the entrance increased, and with it the flow of water.

Nicki stepped back and viewed the resulting stream with a pleased look on her face. "So far so good. Now I think we need to get some of this trash out of the way. Peter, you can start by getting rid of all those tumbleweeds." She said the words aloud as she moved her fingers and Levi realized with a start that Peter was reading her lips as much as her hands. "And you," she said turning to Levi. "Move those boulders and rocks over there, out of the way."

For the next twenty minutes Nicki barked out orders to the two men. Well aware that she was just trying to assert her authority, Levi did as he was told, biting the inside of his cheek to keep from grinning when her demands became outrageous.

By the expressions that chased themselves across Peter's face it was obvious that he wasn't used to taking orders from Nicki. At first he was plainly astonished, then irritated, and finally angry. Watching the muscles bunch in the younger man's jaw with every shovelful of dirt, Levi decided it was time to do something.

While Nicki was studying the slowly filling pool below, Levi glanced up the hill to find Peter staring belligerently at her back. When he waved his hand to get Peter's attention, the younger man's gaze dropped to him in surprise.

Rarely did anyone other than the Chandlers even notice Peter, let alone try to communicate with him. It was impossible not to understand Levi's meaning as he pointed his thumb at Nicki and then nodded toward the pool with raised eyebrows. Peter's face broke into a grin. Not only did Nicki deserve it, but she would not take such treatment lightly. Levi was in for a surprise as well. The next few minutes promised to be quite entertaining.

Peter's smile was all the encouragement Levi needed. He marched over to Nicki, slung her over his shoulder, and strode to the edge of the pool, where he dropped her seat first into the muddy water.

Gasping in shock at the unexpected attack, she glared up at Levi, who stood there calmly returning her look.

"If you're going to be the boss, you'd better start acting like it instead of some petty little tyrant," he said.

"Petty little . . ." Like a striking snake her hand shot out and struck the back of his left knee.

Unprepared for retaliation, Levi's knee buckled and he toppled into the frigid water next to Nicki. He hadn't even come up for air before she was upon him, pummeling him with her small fists.

Levi grasped her slim waist with the crook of his elbow, and pulled her down into the pool next to him. He regretted the action almost immediately as Nicki jerked both hands free and scooped water into his face. Levi lost his hold as she pressed her advantage and continued to inundate him with handfuls of water. Coughing and sputtering, he struggled to his feet in an effort to escape her attack.

Nicki stood up and marched out of the pool in dignified retreat. Dumping the self-assured Levi Cantrell into the mud was a good lesson for him. Her eyes narrowed in disgust as she glanced up the hill at Peter. Instead of coming to her defense, he was leaning on his shovel with a wide grin on his face. She might have known the incident would appeal to his twisted sense of humor.

Angrily, she looked at Levi and saw he too was smiling. How dare they laugh at her! On the verge of telling them both off, Nicki suddenly realized how ridiculous she and Levi must have looked flailing around in the muddy water. Levi started to chuckle and before she could stop herself a bubble of laughter rose in her throat. Animosity forgotten, they laughed together in the early spring sunshine.

It wasn't until cool air began to make Nicki uncomfortable in her wet clothes, that she realized how successfully Levi had thwarted her. Instead of giving further orders she joined the other two in the actual work simply to get the job done faster so she could go home and change clothes.

Glancing at him out of the corner of her eye, she could see no sign of smugness, but she had the uncomfortable feeling that things had pretty much gone the way he'd wanted them to. Apparently Levi

Cantrell was a more worthy opponent than she had first realized.

The cold March air, combined with their damp clothes, had forced Nicki and Levi to return to the house early, leaving a still grinning Peter behind to finish the last of the work. Miffed about her dunking, Nicki ignored her companion and they rode in silence for several minutes.

Finally he spoke. "Will you teach me to talk to Peter?"

"What?"

"I want to be able to talk to Peter. Will you teach me how?"

She stared at him, totally dumbfounded by his request. "Peter doesn't talk."

The irrepressible twinkle in his eyes appeared as he turned to look at her. "Yes he does. I've seen him do it, apparently with great eloquence. I know he reads lips but I can't understand what he says and I can't communicate with him in his own language."

"Why do you want to? So you can make fun of him to his face?"

The twinkle died and was replaced by a frown. "Is that what you think?"

Nicki shrugged uncomfortably, wondering why she suddenly felt so mean and petty. "Ever since I've known Peter, people have either treated him as though he had some horrible, contagious disease or like he was a drooling idiot."

"I'm not like that, Nicki," Levi said. "If Peter and I are going to work together, we need to be able to understand each other. So will you teach me his language?"

"I'm not sure . . . I mean I never . . ." Nicki sighed helplessly. "It's not as easy as it looks you know."

"Are you afraid I can't learn it, or that you can't teach it? Look, Nicki, the worst that can happen is me looking like a fool, and I'm willing to take that chance."

"All right, but don't blame me if it doesn't work." Nicki was rewarded with a warm smile that for some unfathomable reason made her heart pound and her mouth go dry. Grimly she set her jaw and urged her horse on faster. Levi Cantrell was unlike any other man she'd ever known. She'd have to keep a closer eye on him in the future.

4

Nicki was puzzled by the scowl on Levi's face. It was the first time in the two weeks he'd been working for the Chandlers that his good humor had slipped even slightly. He'd been in a fine mood when they'd stopped at the store. Now, he looked as if he'd eaten something extremely nasty. "Is something wrong?" she asked him.

"No," he growled. "Everything is just fine!" With the muscle in his jaw clenching, Levi didn't take his eyes from the road as he guided the team and wagon around a particularly large pothole.

At the unfriendly tone in his voice she cast a side-long glance at him. He had no reason to be mad at her. She'd finally given up fighting him and even let some of her responsibilities rest on his broad shoulders for awhile. Besides, in the last two weeks she had given him many reasons to be angry, and he'd smiled through it all.

Perhaps Peter had done something. He'd been unfriendly since the very beginning. Of course, Levi didn't seem to care, not even when Peter viewed his first attempt at signing with sardonic amusement. Lately even Peter's animosity had begun to fade.

The wagon jolted over a rough spot in the road and Nicki grabbed the side of it to steady herself.

"Good," Levi mumbled under his breath. "Maybe the damn wire will fall out and we'll lose it!"

Nicki glanced back at the rolls of barbed wire they'd picked up in town. Was that what this was all about? "You're mad because Papa sent us right out to string up this fence?"

Levi didn't even bother to look at her as he turned off the road and headed toward the area behind the spring.

Holding on for dear life as the wagon bounced over rocks and sagebrush, Nicki glanced at her companion nervously. "Look, even if you wreck the wagon, we'll still have to put the fence up. You might as well slow down so we get there in one piece."

"I've been driving wagons over worse than this since before you were born. Don't try to tell me how to do it."

"If this is how you've always driven, I'm surprised you're still alive to tell the story," she said acidly.

"I'm sure you could do better."

Nicki felt her temper start to rise. "Yes, as a matter of fact I could! What's the matter with you anyway? You've been acting like a bear in a trap ever since we left town." Only Nicki's firm grip on the side of the wagon seat kept her from tumbling to the ground as they reached their destination and Levi brought the horses to a sudden stop.

He jumped to the ground and went to the back of

the wagon to begin unloading the wire. Nicki scrambled off the seat and followed him, though she might as well have been invisible for all the notice he gave her. Levi dumped a heavy roll of wire on the ground, and reached for the next.

"I asked what's the matter with you. Aren't you going to answer me?"

"Nope."

"Why not?"

"It's none of your business, that's why."

Nicki couldn't believe her ears. "Anything that has to do with this homestead is my business," she said as her temper finally snapped. "You're being paid by my father to do a job, and it's my responsibility to see that you do it. I told him it was a mistake to hire a two-bit drifter but he wouldn't listen. The first time some work comes along that you don't cotton to, you act like a spoiled brat."

"Look who's talking about spoiled brats." Levi dumped the third roll of wire on the ground and looked at her with narrowed eyes. "Ever since I started working for your father, you've made sure everyone was aware of your feelings on the matter. Your father, and I, even Peter, have tiptoed around you like we were walking on eggs, afraid of making things worse. I didn't say a word. Figured if you wanted to be in a perpetually bad mood, it wasn't any of my business. But now I see no one else is to be granted the same privilege."

He reached for the next roll. "For your information, your father pays me for the job I do, not for my attitude." He lifted the heavy wire with a grunt. "I promised to do what was asked of me, so I'll build the fence, but I don't have to like it."

Angry and, curiously, a little hurt by his attack, Nicki watched him lug the wire to the corner post of the fence and drop it. When he returned to get the next one she was ready for him.

"You sound pretty convincing, Cantrell, but the way I see it, you don't like the idea of working that hard."

"You never give up do you?" Levi picked up another roll and headed for the corner post again. He seemed completely unaware of her following behind him, until he dropped the wire. Then he turned to her, his mouth set in a thin line of disgust, his eyes as gray as a stormy ocean. For several seconds they exchanged glares, each waiting for the other to speak. Suddenly Levi's face relaxed, and he leaned his arms on the fence post.

"God, you're as bad as my little brother. Once he gets hold of something he just keeps yammering at you until you can't take it anymore. I'm not going to fight with you, Nicki, so if that's what you're after, forget it."

"You don't want to put out the effort it takes to build a fence."

Levi laughed outright at that. "Good Lord, you and Peter have already done the hard work." He nodded toward the long line of posts stretching out from the corner post in two directions. "Digging the holes and setting the posts is far more strenuous than stringing wire."

"I don't understand then. What's bothering you?"

"There are many things you don't understand," said Levi, purposely ignoring the rest of her question. "You aren't very good at figuring people out, but you're young yet. You may learn."

"And I suppose you, with your advanced years, are so observant you never miss anything," Nicki retorted.

Levi's only answer was a shrug.

To Nicki the gesture was unbearably condescending. "All right, so I can't figure out what your problem is when you suddenly decide to be grouchy, but you've been here two weeks and you still don't know—" Nicki's heart jumped into her throat as she realized what she'd been about to say "—as much as you think you do," she finished lamely.

Levi took off his hat and wiped his brow with one sleeve. "I imagine there are many things that I don't know, but that wasn't what I meant. The reason for a person's bad temper often isn't what it seems. At times, it's better to just let it run its course and ignore it. With a little more experience you'll learn how to tell the difference."

He glanced down at her with a suddenly innocent expression. "Besides it seems to me that I'm the only one who's done any work on the fence so far today. Could it be that you're the one who's dragging his feet and trying to put the blame on me?"

Not surprisingly, Nicki bristled at the suggestion of such an underhanded tactic. "A little hard work doesn't bother me in the least!"

Levi grinned, the twinkle back in his eye as he put his hat back on and headed toward the wagon again. "Well, then you can fetch the nails and hammers while I carry over the last roll of wire. Let's get this job started."

It wasn't until they had stretched the first strand of wire and were attaching it to the second post with the U-shaped fencing nails that Nicki remembered he'd neatly avoided explaining what had put him in such a bad mood.

"Well, are you going to tell me or not?"

Levi looked at her in surprise. "Tell you what?"

"What there is about building this fence that makes you so mad."

His hammer stopped in mid swing as he stared at her in exasperation. "I was wrong about you. You're worse than my little brother. At least it's possible to distract him. You never quit!"

Nicki had a momentary vision of Levi bribing a small boy with a peppermint stick and holding his finger to his lips. She swallowed a smile and reminded herself this was a serious matter. "Well?"

Still holding the hammer, he crossed his arms on top of the post and regarded her cynically. "You aren't going to like it."

"So?"

He sighed and gazed out over the prairie. "When I was a kid, this whole territory was wide open range. People, animals, anything, could go wherever they wanted. There was plenty of room for everybody. But when I came home after four years at sea I hardly recognized the land I grew up in." He drove the claws of the hammer into the top of the post and picked up the wire stretchers. "It started with a few people fencing off their land. Suddenly it wasn't wide open anymore and everyone began getting nervous. The last few years there's been a mad scramble to put fences around everything a man owns."

"But don't you see? We have to fence it off. Last year Herman Lowell's cows ate almost our entire crop, and what they didn't eat, they trampled into the ground. If we don't put up wire, we won't have anything."

"Herman Lowell has been grazing his cows on this range for over twenty years," Levi pointed out. "By his standards you're the trespassers."

Nicki gave him a sharp look. "You sound just like him."

"Can't you see that Herman Lowell might have reason to think this is his land even though you have legal claim to it?"

"Oh I can understand why he thinks it's his, but it isn't. We filed a claim on 160 acres, and made improvements during the first five years we lived here. According to the law, that makes it ours. We even took out the water right on the spring."

She pointed an accusing finger at Levi. "Herman Lowell could have easily done the same thing, but he didn't. Seems to me he gave up any claim he might have had by doing nothing. Besides," she added defensively, "Papa says the cattlemen have nearly ruined the prairie by overgrazing. Whose side are you on?"

Levi knew it was true. All he had to do was look around to see the evidence. Thirty years ago the prairie had been grass as far as the eye could see. Now sagebrush encroached on the grasslands more and more each year. Levi sighed. "I'm not on anyone's side. Both have their points and I don't know who's right. But between the ranchers and the farmers the land is changing, and I'm not so sure I like it."

"Building one more fence isn't going to make that much difference," Nicki said. "I think there's more to your anger than that."

Levi sighed. "I dislike the barbed wire even more than the fences."

"Wire?" She looked at him blankly. "I don't under-stand."

"Not just wire, barbed wire."

"What's wrong with barbed wire?"

"You really don't know do you?"

Nicki was momentarily taken aback by the hostile expression in the eyes that met her own. "N . . . no."

"Have you ever seen what it does to an animal unwise enough to run into it?" Levi didn't wait for an answer. "No, if you had, you wouldn't ask. The barbs work like a dozen little knives, cutting and slicing into the flesh. It's especially bad for horses, I've seen them cut clear to the bone. Even if you get to them in time and can sew up the wound, they usually get an infection and die. I can't tell you how many good horses I've had to shoot because they were wire cut. Cattle have tougher hides, but barbed wire doesn't do them much good either."

Nicki swallowed convulsively, shocked and dismayed by his words.

Levi gave the wire stretchers a vicious tug, his voice bitter. "It's even worse for the wild animals. When a deer runs into a fence they'll jump it, usually with no problem. But occasionally one gets its back legs tangled between the top two wires. The lucky ones become prey for coyotes. The only other alternative is a slow death by starvation. Either way, not a very pleasant end."

Since theirs was the first fence to go up in the area, Nicki had never been around barbed wire before. The image Levi described flashed vividly into her mind. "Oh God, I had no idea!"

The stricken sound of her voice brought Levi back to reality immediately. Belatedly he remembered her youth, and the tenderheartedness of her sex. "I'm sorry," he mumbled. "I shouldn't have told you."

Nicki kicked the roll of wire with her booted foot. "I don't blame you for hating the stuff, it's terrible."

Levi felt a surge of guilt. After all, the situation wasn't her fault. "Look, I'm in a foul mood and I shouldn't have been so blunt. As you already pointed out, this fence is necessary, so why don't we just forget what I said and build the thing?"

"But there must be something we can do to make it safe for all those animals!"

Levi grinned in spite of himself. "The whole point is to keep the animals out, or in, whichever the case may be. If the wire is safe, you've defeated your purpose."

"Maybe so, but the poor deer . . ."

"Eat your crops just like Lowell's cattle," he interrupted. "Besides," Levi said, pointing to the small barbs twisted into the double strands of wire, "this isn't one of the really bad ones. I've seen far worse."

Nicki was still troubled. "I still think we ought to do something."

"I suppose we can ride the fence every day checking for . . ." Suddenly he broke off, staring out over the prairie.

"Well, well," he said softly. "Nicki, why don't you go get my rifle from the wagon. Looks like we've got company."

By the time Nicki returned with the rifle, Levi was once again calmly fixing the wire to the post. Nicki squinted at the two riders approaching from the west. "You think it's trouble?"

"Probably not but it doesn't hurt to be ready." Levi glanced at the riders as he picked up the wire stretchers. "I'm pretty sure the one on the left is a woman."

"A woman! That's strange. I can't imagine who . . ."

"We'll find out soon enough." Levi grunted as he pulled the wire taut across the post. "Are you going to stand there gawking all day or are you going to help me build this fence?"

When the pretty brunette and her escort arrived some five minutes later, Levi and Nicki had progressed to the next post and were just finishing with the first strand of wire.

"Howdy!" Levi said pleasantly, driving the claws of his hammer into the top of the post and taking his hat off to wipe his brow.

"Just what do you men think you're doing?" the woman demanded.

"Well, now, I'd have thought that was fairly obvious," Levi said. "We're building a fence."

"I can see that, you dolt! But why are you building it on my father's land?"

"Look around, Amanda Lowell," Nicki broke in. "This is my father's land, not yours."

Startled, Amanda shifted her gaze to the person she had dismissed as just another cowboy. Her eyes widened in recognition. "Good heavens, Nicole, is that you?"

"Why yes, Mandy, as a matter of fact it is!" Nicki's tone was barely polite as she glared at the other woman.

"I prefer Amanda," the brunette said stiffly. "Mandy sounds so lowbred."

"Well, I prefer Nicki!"

She studied the other girl appraisingly. The three years since they'd last seen each other had wrought changes in her childhood companion. Gone was the slightly gangly adolescent; in her place was a sophisticated young beauty. She appeared to have grown several inches, though it was difficult to tell with

Amanda seated on the pretty little black mare, but the change was far more than that. A very stylish hat was perched atop shiny ringlets and matched her blue velvet riding habit perfectly. Nicki felt an unfamiliar flicker of envy at the way the latter clung to Amanda's graceful curves. Even her voice was different; it was a soft Southern drawl instead of the Western twang she'd grown up with. Only Amanda's cerulean blue eyes, which had always reminded Nicki of the summer sky, remained unchanged and even they seemed to be fringed with longer, darker lashes.

Those eyes now regarded her with frank curiosity.

"I didn't expect to find you here," Amanda said.

"Why not? I live here."

"I thought you and your father would leave after your mother . . ." Amanda shifted uncomfortably in her saddle. "Well, you know what I mean."

Nicki's eyes darkened. "This is our home and nothing is going to change that. It takes more than a little public humiliation to make the Chandlers run. Which reminds me, I thought you went to live with your aunt in Alabama."

"Georgia. Aunt Charlotte passed away two months ago and I came home. We just arrived yesterday." A dark flush stained Amanda's face as she tossed her head. "You'll find I've outgrown the indiscretions of my youth, Nicki. The past is over and I, for one, fully intend to forget it."

Nicki shrugged. "I expect we've both done some growing up. I've never been one to dwell on the past anyway."

The subtle creak of saddle leather reminded Amanda of her companion. "Oh, Charles," she said turning to the young man with a brilliant smile. "Allow me to introduce you. This is Nicole . . . er . . . Nicki Chandler. We used to play together as children you know." She made it sound as though it had been a lifetime ago and not particularly pleasant. "And this," she said proudly as she turned back to Nicki, "is Charles Laughton, Lord Avery's nephew. When Lord Avery discovered I was stranded in Atlanta, he sent a wire to Charles asking him to escort me home since he was coming for a visit anyway."

Though Nicki had occasionally seen Lord Avery, a neighboring cattle baron, she was not overly impressed with the Englishman nor his nephew. It was quite obvious she was alone in her view as Amanda gave the handsome blond man a look of pure adoration.

"How do you do," he said in the bored accents of the British upper class. His perfect eyebrows arched questioningly as he looked at Levi. "I'm sorry, I don't believe I caught your name."

"Levi Cantrell," Levi said with a smile.

"Cantrell?" Charles looked thoughtful. "My uncle bought a horse from some Cantrells over by Horse Creek. Relatives of yours by chance?"

Levi shrugged. "It's possible."

"Levi just got back from several years abroad," Nicki said quickly. "He hasn't had time to look up all of his family yet."

"Oh?" Charles allowed only a faint tinge of disbelief to enter his very polite voice. "Europe perhaps?"

Nicki bristled at the man's supercilious tone. How dare he, a foreigner, come in and look down his polished nose at them! Before she could open her mouth to utter a scathing retort, Levi's good-natured voice interrupted her.

"Nothing so civilized I'm afraid. I was in the Orient, China mostly."

"Good heavens. Practically the ends of the earth. Tell me, is it as interesting as they say?"

"It's worth the trip I think." Levi grinned. "Though I can't say I ever particularly wanted to go myself."

"What brings you over this way, Amanda?" Nicki asked suddenly. "I don't seem to remember you were particularly fond of riding."

"That's not true. It was only that I didn't care to ride the rough-and-tumble way you always did. Since then I've discovered it can be a rather enjoyable pastime when one has a more gentle mount." She patted the little mare's neck. "I was just showing Charles some of my father's ranch." A small wrinkle of concern momentarily marred the perfection of her brow. "Does Daddy know you're building this fence?"

Nicki shrugged. "I haven't the faintest idea. The posts were set last fall, so I imagine his men have reported it to him."

"I don't think he's going to be very happy about it."

Nicki's eyes narrowed. "So?"

Amanda tossed her head. "My father has allowed you to stay here out of consideration for your, er . . ." She paused and blushed slightly. ". . . parents but don't think he'll let you take anything you want."

"We aren't taking a thing that doesn't already belong to us," Nicki said. "And we stayed because it's our land, not because your father let us!"

There were several tense moments of silence as the two women glared at each other. The men watched uneasily, not quite sure how to handle the situation.

Finally Amanda sighed. "Oh, Nicki, things really haven't changed at all have they?"

Nicki gave her a rueful grin. "No, I guess they haven't. We're still fighting the same old fights."

Amanda smiled for the first time. "You know it really is good to see you!"

"I didn't think I'd ever say it, but I'm glad to see you too, Amanda. You're different though. You look so much older, so . . ." As Nicki paused searching for the right word, Amanda's smile began to fade a little. ". . . so beautiful!" she admitted finally.

Amanda's smile returned full force and she preened a little. "Why thank you, Nicki. Coming from you, I consider that a great compliment since I know how little you care about such womanly things yourself."

Though the words were pleasant, Nicki suddenly felt very awkward in her boy's clothes and short hair. She lifted her shoulders with feigned indifference. "I've never had time for such foolishness."

Amanda glanced down at the elegant watch pinned to her riding habit. "Oh my, I didn't realize it was so late. Come, Charles, we must be going if we're going to be home in time for tea. It was good to see you again, Nicki, and it was nice meeting you, Mr. Cantrell." She waved over her shoulder as they rode away.

"We musn't be late for tea," Nicki mimicked sarcastically as she gazed after them. "I'll bet Herman Lowell just loves that."

"A close friend of yours?"

"I don't know as you'd call us friends really. We spent a lot of time together when we were kids. My mother used to take me over there all the time; said I needed to be around someone my own age but we've never had much in common."

All at once her voice faltered and she turned to stare openmouthed at Levi. It had suddenly occurred to her that her secret had been blatantly revealed, but her companion seemed totally unsurprised. "You knew!" she whispered, her tone accusing for all its softness.

He didn't even pretend to misunderstand her. "I knew almost from the beginning. In spite of what you think, you really don't look much like a boy. Besides, some of your gestures would look pretty strange coming from a man."

"Why didn't you say anything?"

"What for?" Glancing up at the sun, Levi lifted his hat and scratched his head. "It doesn't make any difference anyway."

"What do you mean it doesn't make any difference?"

"It doesn't. Boy or girl, you're still the same person."

Nicki thrust her jaw out. "I can outwork most men."

"True."

She eyed him suspiciously. "I carry my own weight, and never ask for special privileges."

"I've noticed that." His lips quirked. "Of course you've been trying so hard to avoid working on this fence that I've kind of been wondering . . ."

"I have not!" Angrily she picked up her hammer and drove a fencing nail home with a few vicious swings. "How can you accuse me of trying to get out of work? You're the one who . . ." Levi's deep chuckle stopped her tirade before it began. She glared at him a few seconds then, unexpectedly, the corners of her mouth twitched. Biting the inside of her cheek to keep from returning his grin, she turned back to her work and pretended to ignore him for the next half hour.

Levi merely smiled to himself as he turned his attention back to building the fence.

5

Spring. The air fairly vibrated with the sounds and smells of it. Nicki inhaled appreciatively, rejoicing in the vitality that thrummed through her veins. Though the spring roundup was not her favorite activity, she was pleased to be outside on such a glorious day.

Even the tedious job of searching out cows with unbranded calves seemed less annoying than usual. The fence was part of Cyrus's plan to keep their herd closer to home, but for now, Chandler's fifty head of cattle spent the spring and summer sharing the open range with the deer, antelope, and the cattle from the Bar X.

Scanning the hills and valleys for the animals took a great deal of time, but it kept her away from the disturbing presence of Levi Cantrell. Whenever Nicki was around him, she was in a constant state of confusion. She should be pleased that he didn't care whether she was male or female, but for some reason his nonchalant attitude bothered her.

Today they were scouring the thick stands of skunkbrush, chokecherry, and willow that lined the creeks. It was not uncommon for cows to seek the cool confines in an effort to escape the heel flies that plagued them incessantly at this time of year. Peter and Levi were working the other, denser side of the small tributary. Occasionally she'd catch a glimpse of one of them through an opening in the brush, but for the most part she was all alone.

The sound of breaking branches split the air as a small heifer suddenly burst from the brush almost directly in front of her. Glancing at the familiar Eleven Bar One brand, Nicki smiled in satisfaction. It was one of theirs for a change.

With a closer look, Nicki realized the young cow had a calf of her own. She peered into the thicket. The calf was probably hidden there, safe and secure. With a sigh, she dismounted, and tied Lollipop to a bush. There was no way she'd find it on horseback.

After nearly five minutes of searching she caught sight of the calf, a darker shadow in the dappled light. Nicki made a quick examination to make sure it was healthy and then nudged the baby to its feet. With a firm grip on the calf's neck and the top of its tail, she guided it out of the brush to where Lollipop stood patiently waiting.

Suddenly a bellow of pure rage echoed around thicket as the mother cow spied her baby and came charging to its rescue. "Ho now, Mama, it's all right," Nicki said as she quickly backed away from the calf. "I won't hurt your little one."

Within seconds the calf was with its mother, who

was glaring at Nicki. She bit her lip in vexation. The calf wasn't more than a few hours old, far too small to travel clear back to the homestead. The only way to get the youngster home was to carry it across her saddle, but an angry mother cow was nothing to mess with. The normally docile creatures could inflict serious injury, and Nicki wasn't about to challenge this one, even if she had been able to lift the fifty-pound baby by herself.

She was still wondering what to do when a voice unexpectedly sounded behind her.

"Look what we got here, Shorty."

"I'll be danged." Shorty's chuckle sounded distinctly menacing. "If it ain't the kid from town. It appears your 'little brother's' rustling Bar X cattle."

Nicki looked over her shoulder and recognized two of the three men she'd tangled with in town. It was obvious from their expressions that they still remembered the last encounter and weren't about to let bygones be bygones. Her heart hammered in her chest as she turned to face them, her features betraying none of her trepidation. "These two don't belong to the Bar X. The cow wears an Eleven Bar One brand."

Shorty swung his squat body down from his horse and untied the rope from the saddle. "Ain't that strange? All I see is Bar X cattle, what about you, Buck?"

"Yup, a whole dang herd of 'em." Buck glanced toward a group of about ten cows the two cowhands had obviously gathered. "Reckon this calf belongs to one of them."

"That's the way I figure it," Shorty said, making a loop in his lariat as he prepared to rope the calf.

Nicki's eyes narrowed. "What do you think you're doing?"

"Just taking what rightly belongs to Mr. Lowell."

"I told you, this calf doesn't belong to him."

"And I say it does," Shorty growled. "Did you see anything with a different brand, Buck?"

"Nope."

"Then you're both blind." Nicki was too angry to consider that she was at a distinct disadvantage. "Its mother is right there, and she belongs to the Eleven Bar One."

"You better watch your mouth, boy," Shorty said ominously.

"Seems to me this boy needs a lesson in manners," put in Buck, glancing around to make sure they were alone. "This time there ain't no drifter gonna come along and interfere."

"Reckon you're right," Shorty said. With the speed of a pouncing cougar, he coiled his rope around the middle of Nicki's body, effectively pinning her hands and arms at her sides. "What do you reckon we ought to do with him, Buck?"

"Get this rope off me right now!" Nicki cried. Buck dismounted and sauntered over to Shorty and Nicki. "We can do just about anything we like." His mouth twisted in a bone-chilling smile. "We've got ourselves a real live cattle rustler. Shorty, tell the boy what they do to rustlers."

"Hang 'em!"

"I'm not a rustler!"

"Don't know what else you'd call it." Buck spit a thick stream of tobacco, missing Nicki's boot by less than an inch. "Caught you red-handed with a Bar X calf."

Shorty rubbed his hand. "Besides we have a score to settle with you. Almost lost my hand to blood poisoning after you bit me, and Buck, here, was crippled up for a week."

"Serves you right." The retort rose to Nicki's lips before she stopped to consider the consequences.

Buck raised an eyebrow. "Talks pretty tough, don't he, Shorty?"

Shorty nodded. "'Specially for someone who's about to get himself hung."

Buck pursed his lips. "Eleven Bar One . . . ain't that the brand of that squatter lives over by the spring?"

"You mean Chandler?"

"Yeah, that's the one. I saw that dummy of his over by the crossing a while ago. You reckon this tadpole's Chandler's kid?"

"Nah." Shorty shook his head. "If I remember rightly, the only other youngun' he's got is a girl about Miss Amanda's age." Suddenly his eyes narrowed. "Come to think of it, our friend here is a mite pretty for a boy." He plucked the hat from Nicki's head so he could see her face. His eyes widened in sudden recognition. "Damn it to hell, Buck. He's a woman!"

"You sure?" Buck peered at Nicki's face. "Well I'll be damned. This is our lucky day, Shorty."

Nicki felt sick inside as the tall, lean cowboy ran a grimy finger down the side of her face. She attempted to kick him, but Buck was ready for her.

"Uh-uh, not this time, sister." He deftly dodged her foot and wound more of the rope down around her legs.

With the rope wrapped tightly around her from the bottom of her ribs to her knees, Nicki was at their mercy, completely unable to move. She closed her eyes, willing the tears prickling behind her eyelids not to fall and add to her humiliation.

"I don't know," Shorty said uneasily. "People tend to get riled up over a thing like this. Most folks don't take too kindly to anybody roughin' up their women."

"Oh come on. We're talking about a cattle rustler," Buck pointed out. "Besides, she ain't got nobody to come after us but a sick old man and a dummy."

"Maybe so, but I'm not sure Mr. Lowell would see it that way. He was mighty partial to her ma at one time."

Buck dismissed Shorty's comment with a wave of his hand. "That was a long time ago. Besides, he won't care who her ma was when he realizes she's the one who's been stealing his cattle."

"But, Buck, she ain't been . . ."

"The squatters are getting plumb out of hand," Buck interrupted, with a warning glance at his companion. "I say we make an example of her, and maybe have a little fun in the meantime. You know what they say, like mother like daughter."

Nicki's eyes flew open and blazed with such fury that Shorty took an involuntary step back. Buck was not so fast. He didn't even have time to duck before Nicki spit in his face.

"You'll have to fight me every step of the way," she snarled, her anger at being compared to her mother overcoming all else. "And I promise you, it won't be easy!"

"Why you little bitch!" Buck's backhanded slap knocked Nicki to the ground. With a low growl he delivered a vicious kick to her ribs before she could roll out of the way. She tried to curl into a ball and gritted her teeth, waiting for the next blow.

Buck and Shorty had made a fatal mistake. With their attention focused on Nicki, they didn't realize they were no longer alone until it was too late.

In the grip of anger such as he'd never known before, Peter launched himself from his running horse. He hardly felt the impact as he and Buck rolled to the ground. It felt good to repeatedly smash his fist into one who'd dared brutalize Nicki. He even smiled in satisfaction as he felt the man's nose give.

Shock held Shorty immobilized. The sound of Buck's nose breaking finally galvanized him into action. He circled around and was nearly in position to jump Peter from behind when a large hand closed around his neck. He didn't even have time to blink before a fist connected with his jaw and everything exploded in a white, hot flash of pain.

Levi paid little attention as the man fell unconscious at his feet. With a cursory glance at Peter and Buck he made his way to Nicki. "Are you all right?" he asked, helping her to sit up.

"Y . . . yes, I think so." Nicki's voice was shaky but controlled. "Suddenly her eyes focused on the scene behind Levi's head. "Oh, my God. Levi, go help Peter!"

Levi slipped a knife from its sheath on his belt and began cutting the ropes that bound her. "Peter doesn't need my help."

"But . . ."

"Nicki, Peter is a man and a man does what he has to. He wouldn't thank me for interfering."

Soon Levi's words proved to be true as Peter began to gain an advantage over the larger, older cowboy. It wasn't long before Peter stood victorious over his beaten adversary. He reached down and jerked the other man roughly to his feet. Buck wobbled back and forth for several seconds while Peter steadied him. At last, when it looked as though Buck could stand on his own, Peter crashed his fist into the other man's jaw. Buck crumpled to the ground like a poleaxed steer. Peter stood for a few seconds, breathing hard, with a satisfied look on his face. Then he turned his attention to Nicki.

Levi was pulling off the last of the rope, as Peter knelt next to her.

His dark brown eyes scanned her face with concern. "Did they hurt you?" he signed rapidly.

"Not much." She shook her head but a grimace of pain crossed her face as she shifted positions.

"We'd better check that side of yours," Levi said. "You may have some broken ribs." He reached under her jacket and gently probed her side, uncomfortably aware of Nicki clenching her teeth against the pain as he did so. "Well," he remarked, pulling her jacket closed, "I don't think they're broken but I can't tell if they're cracked or not. You're bruised pretty badly."

Peter untied the knot in his bandanna and pulled it off his neck as he gestured toward Levi's and Nicki's. "We can bind her ribs if we use these." For the first time he moved his fingers slowly enough so Levi could read the individual signs. "I will get something for a splint."

Levi nodded then reached out and tenderly ran his fingers along Nicki's cheek. It was already turning an ugly purple, and Levi clenched his jaw in frustrated anger. He suddenly felt a flash of intense disappointment that Shorty had gone down so easily. Some of his anger could have been pounded out against the other man's face.

Nicki was trying very hard not to cry, but the combination of her harrowing experience and the pain of her injuries was more than she could handle. Swallowing sobs and fighting back tears, she found Levi's stroking her uninjured cheek with his thumb strangely comforting.

Suddenly she was in his arms, sobbing her heart out against the solid chest. She wasn't sure if he'd pulled her into the shelter of his embrace or if she'd gone there on her own. It didn't matter. She felt safe, protected. The tight rein she usually kept on her emotions broke, releasing a torrent of tears.

Levi had meant to comfort her the way an uncle or an older brother might, but as he held her next to him his feelings were anything but avuncular. The fear that had almost strangled him when he'd first seen Nicki tied and at the mercy of the two cowhands came back in full force. It was all he could do not to crush her to his chest and rain kisses of relief all over her face.

Despite his intense rage, Levi kept his arms around the small form, patting her back and murmuring comforting words to the top of her head. Thank God Peter had reached the scene first. Levi was afraid he'd have killed the one who attacked Nicki before he was through.

At last, the sobs quieted. Her emotions spent, but feeling oddly light-headed, Nicki was perfectly content to stay within the safety of his arms. "Does it look bad?" she asked as she looked up at him.

"You've already got a black eye." Trying to ignore the soft violet eyes staring up at him so trustingly, Levi surveyed the bruise critically. "He really smacked you a good one."

Nicki sighed. "I guess I shouldn't have spit in his face."

"You spit in his face?" Levi was aghast. "The man had you tied up!"

Nicki shrugged. "I didn't like what he said. Besides, he was so mad he forgot all about . . . well what he was planning to do." Her eyes darkened angrily. "I'll never allow a man to touch me that way! I'd rather take a beating any day."

By the time Peter returned with the makeshift splint, Nicki had recovered enough to be embarrassed about her tears, not to mention her reaction to Levi. How could she have melted that way? It was disgusting; she'd acted just like one of those silly women she despised. No man would ever throw himself into a pair of strong arms and dissolve into tears. That she hadn't even thought of throwing herself into Peter's arms did not occur to her.

Determined to wipe her weakness from everyone's mind, including her own, she looked pointedly at the two cowboys, who still lay where Peter and Levi had left them.

"What do we do with them?"

Levi stopped in the process of binding her ribs to glance over his shoulder at the ungainly heap of arms and legs.

"What do you want to do with them?"

"Feed 'em to the coyotes."

"Don't blame you." Levi narrowed his eyes. "Maybe a walk home in their underwear would work just as well. Not much a cowpoke hates more than being without his horse." He grinned. "Or his pants."

Once her ribs were bound, Nicki used the end of her lariat to smack both horses on the rump and send them thundering over the prairie. Then, without a backward glance at the two unconscious men, she turned Lollipop for home. The only concession she made to her injuries during the long ride was to let Peter and Levi deal with the cow and calf. When Levi stopped near the barn to help her down from her horse, she raised her chin and rode on by.

With a shrug, Levi signed the word "women" and rolled his eyes. It was lucky for both of them that Nicki didn't see that or Peter's answering grin.

6

"*Levi,*" Cyrus said as Nicki started clearing the table after supper that night, "I want you and Peter to meet the stage tomorrow morning."

Levi's eyebrows elevated in surprise. "Oh? Why is that?"

"My sister-in-law will be on it, and I want you to pick her up."

"What?" Nicki stared at her father in amazement.

"I've invited your Aunt Emily to come stay for awhile."

"You never said a word about it to me!"

"It's supposed to be a surprise. That's why I didn't tell you until now."

"I don't like surprises like that." Nicki put her hands on her hips and glowered at her father. "Whatever possessed you to invite her anyway?"

"It will be good for you to have another woman around, and Emily's always been fond of you."

Nicki's violet eyes blazed. "Well I'm not fond of her! She's a meddling old busybody."

"Nicki! She's your mother's only sister."

"And that's supposed to make me like her?" Nicki gave a short laugh. "Even my mother couldn't stand Aunt Emily. For once I agree with her!"

"Nicole Chandler, I'm ashamed of you. Emily is a good woman and I won't have you judging her when you haven't set eyes on her in seventeen years."

"Some things don't change with time."

"You're not too old to take over my knee you know." Cyrus pointed a finger at his daughter. "As long as this is my house I'll invite who I want, when I want, without interference from you."

Nicki stood, her fists clenched at her sides, then with a cry she turned and ran out the door.

Cyrus sighed. "I guess I didn't handle that very well."

"Neither did Nicki." Levi gave him a sympathetic look. "I take it she's not fond of her aunt?"

"She was only three last time we saw Emily. I doubt that she even remembers her. If she did, she wouldn't have reacted that way." Cyrus rubbed his forehead tiredly. "My wife didn't get along very well with her sister, and I think she must have poisoned Nicki's mind." He stared at the table unhappily. With the rapid deterioration of his health had come the certainty he'd not long to live. He'd sent for Emily, hoping she'd be able to guide his headstrong daughter through the difficult days ahead. If Nicki wouldn't accept her . . .

"I remember Emily." The words flowed from Peter's fingers. "She was my friend. I'm glad she's coming."

"Good." Cyrus gripped his shoulder. "I just wish Nicki felt the same way."

Peter glanced at Levi, then made several more gestures which Cyrus interpreted.

"He says he thinks somebody should go talk to Nicki. She's had a rough day."

"What about you, Peter?" Levi asked, slowly signing the words he knew.

Peter shook his head violently and held up his hands. "He says she wouldn't listen to him. Besides, you are too big for her to hurt."

Levi laughed and stood up. "Thanks for your vote of confidence, not that it will do me much good. All right, I'll see what I can do."

He found her in the barn brushing Lollipop. Nicki looked up when she heard him, then turned her attention back to the horse. "I suppose you think I'm being unfair to Aunt Emily, too."

Levi sat down on a sawhorse. "I don't have any idea. I haven't met the lady." He crossed his arms over his chest and stared at the stars through the open door. "How are your ribs?"

"Better, I think." She paused in her brushing to touch her side. "It still hurts when I touch it, but otherwise I hardly know it's there."

"Do you feel any pain when you take a deep breath?"

Nicki drew air in through her nose then shook her head. "No, not really."

"Good," said Levi. "Then they're probably just bruised. You should be as good as new in a few days."

A companionable silence fell, broken only by the rhythmic whisk of the brush against Lollipop's side. Finally Levi spoke. "Tell me about your aunt."

"Why?"

"Just curious."

Nicki eyed him suspiciously, but his face revealed nothing. "I don't know very much about her. She's quite a bit older than my mother; my mother said Emily used to boss her around."

Levi chuckled. "My little brother says the same about me. Of course, he never listens, but I keep trying." Levi picked up a piece of straw and began to chew on it. "Kind of like Peter and you."

Nicki smiled in the near darkness. "I suppose so. Still my mother complained about it a lot."

"What else do you know about your aunt?"

"Not much. She spends a lot of time helping sick people. She's never been married, but she does have a daughter."

"Oh?"

"Well, Liana isn't actually Aunt Emily's daughter. Her real mother died when she was born." Nicki ran her hand along Lollipop's neck thoughtfully. "Aunt Emily was the midwife, and nobody else wanted the baby because she was half-Chinese. My mother thought it was horrible for Aunt Emily to take her in, but I really don't know why."

"Maybe your aunt was a trifle more open-minded than your mother," Levi said.

Nicki looked at him in surprise. Such an idea had never occurred to her.

Levi took the straw out of his mouth and stared at it for several seconds. "How did your mother die?" he asked after a few moments.

"She didn't. At least I don't think she's dead. She ran away with a gambler."

Levi's brow furrowed in surprise. "I'm sorry, I had no idea . . ."

"It doesn't matter. I'm glad she's gone."

"Don't you miss her?"

"No. We're a lot happier since Mother left. She was mean to Peter. Called him a dummy and wouldn't even let him live in the house. That's why Papa built the dogtrot with Peter's room on the other side."

"Doesn't sound to me like she was a very good judge of people." Levi watched Nicki's face as his words sank in. "Sure was wrong about Peter."

"And you think she might have been wrong about Aunt Emily, too?"

"It's a possibility."

Levi watched the emotions chase their way across her features as she mulled over their conversation. Hers was more than just another pretty face. There was fire, but also compassion. At times Nicki seemed very young, yet she was willing to fight for what she believed in. The greater the odds, the harder she tried.

The full moon rising above the eastern horizon gilded her black curls in silver, making her a creature of ethereal beauty. Levi felt a tightening in his chest and almost groaned aloud. No, he wasn't falling in love with her. Five long years had passed since that tender emotion had clouded his eyes and played him false. It was only the moonlight. In this romantic setting any woman would affect him the same way. The stirring within was nothing more complicated than lust. It was inevitable; he'd been celibate far too long.

Nicki nodded her head decisively. "You're right."

"What?" For one startled second he thought she'd read his mind.

Nicki put down the brush and smiled at him. "It would be stupid for me to take my mother's word for anything."

"Oh."

"I'm not saying I'll welcome Aunt Emily with open arms," Nicki warned, "but I'll give her a chance." She untied the lead rope and led Lollipop outside to the corral.

Levi had just retrieved his saddle from the tack room and set it on the sawhorse when Nicki came back into the barn.

"It wouldn't take much to fix up the storeroom next to Peter for Aunt Emily. Do you think she'll know how to help Papa get better?"

"I wouldn't be surprised."

"She's probably seen hundreds of people with the same sickness . . ." Nicki's voice trailed off as she noticed the saddle. "Are you going somewhere?"

"I thought I might go to town tonight."

"Oh." A shadow flitted across her face. "Why?"

Levi picked up his bridle. "A man just needs to get away once in awhile, that's all."

"W . . . will you be here for breakfast?"

His teeth gleamed in the dim light. "I can't think of anything that would keep me away from your flap-jacks."

She stood at the door staring at him for several long minutes, as though memorizing his features. "Levi?"

"Yes?"

"Thanks for everything you've done for us."

He turned toward her, surprised at her mournful

tone. The uncertain look on her face spoke more eloquently than words. She didn't think he was coming back. "I'll be here tomorrow, Nicki. I wouldn't leave without saying good-bye."

"I . . . Good night."

He walked to the door and watched her run across the barnyard to the house. "Good night, Nicki," he whispered softly.

7

All the way to town Levi argued with himself. He hadn't forgotten the hurt nor his vow never to let love blind him again. Cynthia Mason—even the name brought an angry twist of pain. She had been beautiful and sophisticated. Fresh from the East, Cynthia was totally unlike anyone he'd ever known before.

His brother had tried to warn him, but Levi hadn't listened, not even when Cole told him Cynthia flirted outrageously. Levi had believed her when she said she loved only him. She had accepted his marriage proposal with a sweet smile and a passionate kiss, then disappeared two days later.

Rumor had it she'd run away with another man, but Levi's broken heart refused to accept it. When the telegram had come from San Francisco, saying she'd been kidnapped, he believed every word. Levi had gone immediately, determined to save her from the monster who held her captive.

But when he arrived he'd discovered it was all a clever ruse, one she and her lover had used many times before to get "ransom" money from unsuspecting men. For the first time in his life Levi had been angry enough to kill. Instead, he'd gone to the first tavern he could find and gotten rip-roaring drunk. The next morning he'd been on his way to China.

Levi sighed as the lights of town came into view. Maybe he should be grateful to Cynthia. His anger had made him mean enough to survive the rigors of shipboard life. If it hadn't been for her, he'd have never seen the world, nor would he have known how much a broken heart could hurt.

He wasn't ready to face that kind of pain again, and he certainly wasn't going to fall in love with someone so much younger than he was. It was pointless to worry about it, anyway. A bottle of whiskey and a friendly saloon girl would take care of his illusions of falling in love with Nicki.

Although Nowood was a small town, the saloon was nearly full. It was a rowdy crowd, and no one paid Levi the slightest attention as he walked to the bar and ordered a bottle of whiskey. He grimaced as the rotgut burned a path down his throat. Good. The worse the whiskey was, the faster it washed away the nasty taste he always got in his mouth when he thought of Cynthia.

He'd downed three shots and was working on his fourth when his concentration was broken by a soft voice at his shoulder.

"Hello, cowboy. Want some company?"

He was pleased to see she was young and not too

bad looking, with the ravages of her profession only starting to show on her face. The brassy red hair met with his approval too—neither blonde like Cynthia, nor dark like Nicki. She'd do just fine to blot out the two women preying on his mind.

"Company is just what I need." He favored her with a slow, lazy smile. "Can I buy you a drink?"

"Why?" She looked pointedly at the bottle. "You planning on drinking that all yourself?"

Levi laughed. "It's hardly the drink for a woman. Wouldn't you rather have something else?"

"Sam'll just give me colored water and charge you for a drink. It'll be cheaper if I share yours."

Levi called for another glass and smiled down at his companion. "The name's Levi Cantrell. What's yours?"

She looked up at him in amazement. It had been a long time since anyone had wanted to know her name, at least when they were sober. "They call me Sally Mae."

"Is that your name?"

Sally Mae shrugged. "Close enough."

"Well, Sally Mae, the night's still young and we've got a bottle to kill."

Levi found Sally Mae to be surprisingly good company, and the more he drank, the nicer she looked. She was far better than what he'd expected when he'd come to the saloon, yet he kept putting off the inevitable. They both knew where it would end, but somehow the images of violet eyes and black curls kept getting in the way.

"You haven't touched your drink." Levi gestured toward the full glass sitting on the bar.

"I don't drink much." She grinned. "Especially not

this stuff. Sam likes us to drink with the customers because he sells more that way. Normally he'd be giving me the evil eye, but you've been putting away enough for both of us."

Sally Mae watched Levi stare into the bottom of his glass. Usually she didn't give the men in the saloon a second thought, but this one was different. With his genuine laugh and twinkling blue-gray eyes, she found herself liking him. "It isn't working is it?"

"What isn't?"

"The whiskey."

He gave her a blank look and she shook her head. "I know when a man comes here to forget. Only it isn't working for you."

"How do you figure that?"

She gave an unladylike snort. "If the whiskey had done the trick, we'd have been upstairs long ago."

"Let's go now."

"If that's what you want." Sally eyed him almost wistfully. "But something tells me you don't, not really."

After several seconds he sighed. "You're right, and I'm sorry." He reached into his pocket and pulled out three silver dollars. "For your time."

"No," she said softly, closing his fingers over the money. "It was nice to just stand and talk for once, to be treated like a person instead of a . . ." she trailed off, but they both knew what she meant.

On impulse she reached up and gently ran her fingers across his cheek. "I hope she realizes how lucky she is."

"Who?"

She smiled wisely. "The one you came to forget."

She patted his arm and strolled away, leaving him to stare pensively into his glass.

What had just happened? He'd come to town looking for someone to slake his lust, a straightforward business transaction with no recriminations and no guilt. Sally Mae was exactly what he'd been searching for. He'd even enjoyed her company. So why hadn't the thought of bedding her appealed to him? He took another drink as he pondered the question. Perhaps it was just a momentary fluke, brought on by Nicki's sad little farewell. Or maybe the memory of Cynthia was responsible. It certainly wouldn't be the first time she'd unmanned him.

"And I say Chandler's been rustling calves all along."

The words pulled Levi out of his self-absorption. He hadn't paid any attention when the two cowboys had sidled up to the bar. Now he was unsurprised to find Shorty and another, vaguely familiar man standing less than ten feet from him. After a moment Levi identified the other man as the third cowboy who had been with Shorty and Buck the day he'd met Nicki in front of the store.

"I figure you're right, Slim, only he ain't man enough to do it himself. He's got his kid and that dummy doing it for him."

The two men were spoiling for a fight, and in Levi's present mood he wasn't averse to accommodating them. In fact, maybe that was just what he needed. The anger from this afternoon still burned in his gut. Finishing what he'd started might feel damned good.

"Did you say something to me?" he asked, turning slightly and leaning an elbow on the bar.

"I don't talk to sod-bustin' scum like you," Shorty sneered.

"That's the first intelligent thing I've ever heard you say. Seems to me you get yourself in trouble every time you open your mouth." Levi turned back to his drink.

"I think you've got him worried, Shorty," the other cowboy said, raising his voice slightly. "He knows we ain't gonna let him get away with what he did to Buck."

Shorty nodded. "That's right, poor old Buck was just doing his job when they jumped him. Stove him up so bad he'll likely be in bed for a week." His eyes narrowed. "I notice you ain't so brave without your dummy friend."

Levi swirled the whiskey in his glass. "People who spend their time abusing children don't scare me."

"Too bad you come along when you did. Buck and I would'a had us some fun with that kid." He smiled nastily. "After you and the dummy taking turns with her, she'd a probably liked some real men for a change."

Before Shorty had drawn his next breath he found himself suspended by his coat lapels, his face just inches from Levi's. "You want to fight, we'll fight, but leave the girl out of it, or so help me God, I'll make you wish you'd never been born!" Levi thrust him away with such violence that Shorty staggered against the bar. Without another look, Levi turned and strode toward the entrance. "We'll finish this outside," he called back over his shoulder.

He had just stepped through the door when a slight sound warned him. In one fluid motion, Levi ducked and turned, catching Slim in the midsection with his shoulder. The bottle in Slim's hand crashed to the ground at almost the same instant Levi's fist connected with his jaw.

The impact pushed Slim into Shorty, and the two stumbled backward into the saloon. Then, with a bellow of rage, they both surged to their feet.

Though the fight was over fairly soon, the crowd that gathered to watch it wasn't disappointed. At first it seemed as though the two cowhands from the Bar X had the advantage, but not for long. Not only was the big man surprisingly quick on his feet, he fought with a calculated determination the other two lacked.

To Levi, it was an outlet for all the anger and frustration that had been building up inside him. He was almost disappointed when the last of his adversaries dropped to the ground unconscious.

Levi shook his head to clear it, as he leaned against the side of the building. The first thing he saw was Sally Mae striding toward him as the rest of the crowd disappeared back into the saloon.

"Turning your back on those two is asking for trouble," she remarked, dabbing blood from the corner of his mouth.

"Thanks for warning me."

"Better get this taken care of before you bleed all over the side of Sam's saloon. It's bad for business."

Levi didn't even notice the many looks of admiration cast his way as she led him through the crowded bar to a small room beyond. She had just finished wiping the blood from his face when the door burst open. It was the saloon's owner, and he didn't look pleased.

"What are you doing?" Sam yelled.

Sally Mae didn't even look up. "What does it look like I'm doing?"

"Since when is this a doctor's office?"

"Since I decided to use it for one." Moving the bowl of reddened water to one side she calmly opened a bottle of iodine and glanced up at the irate bartender. "I figured you'd want to show your appreciation to this man."

Sam's eyes narrowed suspiciously. "Why would I want to do that?"

"He could have busted up the place you know." She turned her attention to the cut above Levi's eye.

"Not my fault he picked a fight," Sam mumbled. "And I don't pay you to play nursemaid to every two-bit drifter that happens by. You got customers out there."

"Don't worry, I'm almost done."

"You'd better be," he grumbled as he turned to go. "Lowell wants to talk to him." He slammed the door behind him.

"My, my," said Sally Mae with a raised eyebrow. "A summons from Mr. Lowell no less."

"Who's he?" Levi asked as though he'd never heard the name before. It would be interesting to see if Sally Mae's opinion of the cattle baron matched Nicki's.

"Herman Lowell?" Sally Mae dabbed iodine on Levi's knuckles. "He's 'bout the richest man around these parts. When he says jump, most folks do it. Not a good man to cross."

"What would he want with me?"

"Well, those were his men you left out there in the dirt. Could be he's not real happy about that." After surveying Levi's hands, she pushed the cork back into the bottle. "There, that should heal nicely."

Levi stood up and flexed his hand experimentally. "Thanks, Sally Mae. I hope I didn't get you in trouble."

"Oh, don't worry about Sam. He's all bark and no bite. You'd best be going. Mr. Lowell doesn't like to be kept waiting."

She bit her lip as she watched him go. If Herman Lowell thought Levi Cantrell was a problem, those blue-gray eyes wouldn't be twinkling around here much longer.

8

Even across the crowded saloon, Levi had no trouble identifying Herman Lowell. Years of battling the elements were clearly etched into his still handsome face, yet no one would dare call him old. He had about him an indefinable aura of power. It wasn't just his tall, lean body, nor his glacial blue eyes, which looked as if they could see into a man's soul. He was obviously a man used to giving orders and having them obeyed, instantly and without question.

Levi strode over to the table and extended his hand. "Levi Cantrell, Mr. Lowell. They said you wanted to see me."

Rising halfway out of his chair, Lowell shook the proffered hand. "Ah, Mr. Cantrell." He indicated a chair on the opposite side of the table. "Have a seat. I've been hearing a great deal about you lately." He crooked his finger to beckon a passing saloon girl.

"Bring us a bottle of my special stock and a glass for Mr. Cantrell." He turned to Levi. "You will join me in a drink, won't you?"

Levi smiled. "Don't mind if I do."

"I noticed your bay when I rode up . . . good-looking animal."

"Thanks. I picked her up in San Francisco last fall." Levi didn't even question how Herman Lowell had identified the mare as his out of all the horses tied outside. Men like Lowell made it their business to notice insignificant details. It gave them the edge. If Lowell was the undisputed ruler of the area, it was because he'd earned it.

"I've done business with some Cantrells over near Horse Creek. Any relation?"

"It's a possibility."

"They have some of the finest horseflesh in the country."

Levi leaned back in his chair. "Oh?"

The girl returned to set the bottle and two glasses on the table. Lowell poured the drinks and then turned his glass idly in his hand. "That was quite a fight earlier," he commented finally. "The most entertainment folks have had around here in a long time."

"If you like fights. Personally, I can think of a lot of things I'd rather do."

Herman Lowell raised an eyebrow. "Three of my best hands put out of commission in one day and you say you don't like fights?"

"Actually I can only take credit for two. Peter was responsible for the one this afternoon."

"You mean the dummy? I find that nothing short of amazing."

"Why? Just because he can't hear doesn't mean

he's blind too. He did what any man would do if he saw his womenfolk threatened."

"Buck and Shorty said she was trying to rustle a Bar X calf."

"Did they also tell you the calf's mother had an Eleven Bar One brand on her side?"

"No, Shorty said there was an Eleven Bar One cow, but there wasn't any way of knowing if the calf belonged to it," Lowell said, never taking his eyes from Levi's face. "A man's got to be careful when he runs his cattle on the open range. How many mavericks are just calves that have been penned up till they forget their mamas? No way to tell who they belong to then and it's legal to slap any brand on them."

"You think Chandler is stealing your cattle?"

"I've known Cyrus Chandler for a long time. He's always been an honest man, but it wouldn't be the first time a man turned to rustling when money was short."

"So what does all this have to do with me?"

"Nothing really, unless Chandler *is* rustling cattle and you're helping him do it."

There was a dangerous glint in Levi's eye as he replied, "Only a fool would do that, Mr. Lowell, and I'm not a fool."

"I didn't think you were." Herman Lowell smiled. "You haven't touched your drink, Mr. Cantrell."

"Neither have you."

"You're a cautious man, Mr. Cantrell. I wonder why."

"I have had two unpleasant run-ins with your men today. After I dumped two of them in the dirt, you offer me a drink from your 'special stock,' and you still haven't told me why you wanted to talk to me."

Lowell laughed and raised his glass in a salute. "I see your point, Mr. Cantrell. However, it's perfectly safe, and I think you'll find it considerably more palatable than Sam's regular whiskey." He drained his glass and refilled it. "Actually I wanted to meet you for a couple of reasons. Not many men could have beaten Shorty and Slim the way you did tonight. I'm curious where you learned how to fight."

"From a younger brother and half a dozen hard-bitten old sea dogs." Levi sipped the amber liquid and smiled. "Yes, a definite improvement."

"You're a sailor then?"

"Was temporarily. You said there were a couple of reasons you wanted to talk. What's the other?"

"I could use a man like you in my operation," Lowell said.

"I already have a job."

"You mean working for Chandler?" Herman Lowell dismissed it with a wave of his hand. "I can pay you twice what he does, and it's the kind of work you're used to, working cattle, not farming."

"What makes you think I'm not a farmer?"

Lowell gave a short laugh. "You're not the type. Somehow I just can't picture you behind a plow."

"You may be right about that," Levi said with a wry grin. "But I think I'll stick with it for awhile anyway."

"Do you mind if I ask why?"

"Don't mind at all. It's something I've never done before, so I thought I'd give it a try. Who knows, I may take out a homestead of my own someday."

Lowell considered this for several seconds then shook his head. "You have the look of a man who's spent most of his time in the saddle. That kind of life is hard to walk away from. How did you wind up farming?"

"I was getting low on money and Cyrus Chandler offered me a job," Levi said with a shrug. "I promised I'd stay at least until the spring work was finished."

"Now why would a drifter prefer working for a down-on-his-luck dirt farmer rather than a spread like the Bar X?"

"For one thing, I'm a man of my word. Besides, the little 'discussion' I had with your men this afternoon left me with a bad taste in my mouth for you and your whole operation."

"I find that very odd," Lowell said. "Surely you understand a man in my position can't be too careful. My men are paid to keep their eyes open, and to protect what's mine."

Remembering what Buck and Shorty had planned for Nicki, Levi's hand tightened around his glass. "Thanks for your offer, but I think I'll stick with the Chandlers."

"Sod busting isn't very safe these days." Lowell's voice held a warning note.

"I'll take my chances."

"The range is pretty short on water this year. If it comes to a fight, it wouldn't be too smart to be on the wrong side."

"I'll keep that in mind." Levi drained his glass and stood up. "It's time I was heading home. Thanks for the drink, Mr. Lowell."

"You sure you won't reconsider?"

"I don't think so."

"Well, the offer's still open if you change your mind."

Levi put on his hat. "I'll remember that. Good night."

Herman Lowell sat pensively staring into his drink long after Levi walked out the door.

"Where's Levi this morning?" Cyrus wondered out loud as he watched his daughter putting breakfast on the table. "Usually he's been up for hours by now."

Nicki glanced toward the door for at least the tenth time and shrugged with feigned nonchalance. "I don't know. He went to town last night; maybe he decided to stay."

Inwardly she was not so calm. Levi's sudden restlessness the night before had been as unexpected as it was unnerving. Unable to sleep, she'd sneaked back to the barn long after she should have been in bed. All his things had been there, with only his saddle and horse missing. He obviously intended to come back, but where was he now?

When the door opened several minutes later Nicki's heart leaped, but it was only Peter. The surge of intense disappointment surprised her. What on earth was happening to her?

"Have you seen Levi, Peter?" Cyrus asked.

Peter nodded and grinned. Putting one hand to his head and the other to his stomach, he made a face of intense suffering.

"He's sick?" Nicki was instantly concerned. "Maybe I'd better go see . . ."

Before she could finish, Peter held up an imaginary glass, downed the contents with a quick flick of the wrist, and grinned once more.

Cyrus chuckled. "Too much of Sam's rotgut whiskey?"

Peter nodded and attacked his breakfast with great enthusiasm. He was just finishing the last of the flapjacks when Levi finally made his appearance.

"You look a little the worse for wear this morning," Cyrus remarked cheerfully.

"I'm sure I don't look half as bad as I feel." Levi eased himself into his chair and sighed. "That stuff Sam sells for whiskey could easily pass as kerosene."

"Appears whiskey wasn't the only thing you ran into last night," Cyrus said. "Your face looks like somebody used it for a battering ram!"

Levi touched his swollen lip tenderly. "Just a small difference of opinion. I convinced them to see things my way."

"Them?"

"A couple of drunk cowboys spoiling for a fight. Wish they'd found somebody else though."

Nicki slammed a cup of coffee onto the table in front of him. "You're too late for breakfast!"

Wincing, Levi looked up at her and smiled wanly. "I know, but I couldn't have done justice to your cooking this morning anyway."

"I hope you don't expect special privileges just because you have a hangover. You don't get paid to spend the night in the saloon drinking and fighting." She turned and stomped back to the stove.

"What's wrong with her?" he asked in a low voice.

Peter's eyes sparkled as he made the sign for women, and rolled his eyes as Levi had the day before.

Levi smiled. "You're right about that!" After another look at Nicki's back, he turned back to his coffee. Somehow her anger made him feel worse than the hangover.

9

Levi was feeling a little better when he made the trip to town several hours later. But when the stage finally arrived, Emily Patterson didn't appear to be on it.

"Are you sure those are all the passengers?" Levi asked, trying to ignore the strong smell of whiskey that surrounded the stage driver.

"Yup. We ain't been here long enough to lose one of 'em." He laughed at his own bad joke and spit a stream of tobacco at a hapless beetle scurrying across the street. "I had three to drop off at Nowood and that's how many got off, unless you count the baby."

Levi glanced over his shoulder at the small group on the sidewalk. A young mother comforted a crying toddler while the grandmother, a tiny bird of a woman, held a small baby. "There was supposed to be another woman. Could she have gone into the store?"

"Nope." The driver dumped a large trunk on the ground and took a swig from his pocket flask. " 'Reckon she could'a got off at the wrong stop."

With a sigh, Levi turned back toward the store. What had happened to Emily Patterson? He and Peter had arrived after the stage and there had been no sign of the lady. Could she have gotten off at the wrong town as the driver suggested?

As the stage rumbled out of town, the two women on the sidewalk were joined by an older couple. After a flurry of welcoming hugs, the younger woman and her children left with them. The remaining woman scanned the street as though looking for someone. She wasn't at all what Levi had expected, but maybe . . .

"Excuse me," Levi said, approaching the woman hesitantly. "Are you Emily Patterson?" He could have sworn her eyes widened in dismay though it was difficult to tell behind the thick lenses of her glasses.

"Y . . . yes."

"I'm Levi Cantrell. Cyrus Chandler sent me to pick you up."

"Oh, my . . . I mean . . . H . . . how do you do?"

Levi knew he wasn't imagining the way her face paled. What ailed the woman? He'd seen his share of nervous females in his life, but this one took the cake. Cyrus actually thought this frail, delicate woman would be able to control Nicki?

Levi wished Peter would hurry up and join them. Maybe he should have taken care of the wagon and let Peter meet the stage.

But when Peter finally arrived he made no move toward Emily. Instead he stood there regarding her with a challenging look.

Emily stared back, puzzled. Suddenly she gasped. "Good heavens, Peter!" Without a second thought about the years that had passed since she last held the sobbing child in her arms, Emily took several quick steps and embraced him.

Levi sighed in relief as Peter hugged her back with a genuine smile on his face.

She stepped back and gazed up at Peter in admiration. "Oh, Peter, I'm so glad to see you. My, how you've changed."

Peter smiled and gave her another hug before he went to pick up her trunk.

"Did you need to get anything in town before we leave?" Levi asked.

"N . . . no, I don't think so. Do we have far to go?"

"A few miles."

"I see." She looked a little ill as she pulled a handkerchief from her reticule and proceeded to clean the layers of dust from her glasses.

"You're not the first Easterner to be a little overwhelmed," Levi said.

"It's not that so much, though it is rather wild out here. I'm not much of a traveler, and the driver hit every hole between here and Cheyenne. The man was a little too fond of his bottle if you ask me." She put her glasses back on and looked up at him. "There, that's better . . . Good heavens, Mr. Cantrell, have you been in an accident?"

Suddenly he remembered what his battered face must look like. No wonder she seemed so nervous around him. "A fight, actually, but don't worry," he said with a smile. "I never hurt women or small children."

*   *   *

"Well, here we are," Levi said half an hour later as he pulled to a stop in front of the cabin. He secured the horses and jumped down to help Emily, but Cyrus was there before him, his face creased in a smile as he held his hands out to his sister-in-law.

"Welcome to Wyoming, my dear, welcome to Wyoming."

Levi pulled the heavy trunk off the back of the wagon, smiling to himself as Emily and Cyrus hugged each other. They were obviously old friends as well as in-laws.

With a few gestures Peter volunteered to take the trunk into the house, and Levi eyed him suspiciously. "Why?"

Peter gave him a look of pure innocence. "To help, of course. She is not afraid of me," he signed.

Levi caught a sparkle of mischief in the brown eyes and realized Peter was actually teasing him. For the first time that day Levi felt good, really good.

Extremely pleased that Peter finally seemed to have accepted him, Levi drove the wagon to the barn and unhitched the team.

After the bright spring sunshine the barn seemed dark to him at first. It wasn't until his eyes began to adjust that he realized he was not alone. Nicki was watching him from a hay pile. "Are you here to make sure I still know how to unharness a horse?" he asked with a slight smile.

"I just wanted to make sure Peter remembered to feed the cow. He got done with his chores awfully fast this morning."

Levi nodded as he unbuckled the traces from the horses. "And did he?"

"Yes." Nicki rubbed her toe on the ground nonchalantly. "How was your trip to town?"

"About the same as usual." Levi knew full well she wanted to know about Emily Patterson but decided to let her stew a little. Silence reigned as he finished removing the harnesses and hung them in the tack room. "I don't blame you for being scared," he said at last as he picked up the currycomb and began brushing the horse. "Your aunt Emily is a frightening person."

"I'm not scared," Nicki began indignantly, then looked at him in surprise. "What do you mean she's frightening?"

"Well, she's about the same size as you are, only older of course, and wears thick glasses."

"That doesn't sound frightening."

"No, but then the trip tired her out, I think. She might be vicious when she rests up. You never know about these tiny women."

Nicki eyed him suspiciously. "I think you're being ridiculous. She's probably a perfectly normal person."

"That's right," he said gently. "So there's no reason for you to hide in the barn is there?"

"I'm not hiding."

"Oh? What would you call it?"

"I came to check on the cow."

"Peter probably hasn't forgotten to feed the cow since he was a kid."

Nicki jumped to her feet and walked to the window. "Look, I'm not hiding. I'm not really sure why I came down here, but I'm not afraid."

Levi glanced up from his work. "Then go meet her. She came two thousand miles to see you. I think you owe her that much, don't you?"

"I guess so." She turned slowly and walked toward the door. Then she paused and looked back over her shoulder. "But remember, I only said I'd give her a chance."

"That's all anybody's asking you to do," Levi said, turning his attention back to the horse.

Nicki could hear excited chatter through the door-way before she even got to the house. *My dear Aunt Emily certainly made herself at home,* she thought resentfully. Wondering how once again Levi had managed to convince her to do things his way, she went inside.

Almost immediately Emily spied her standing by the door and stood up, her eyes widening. "Samantha?" she whispered, then she shook her head. "No, of course not. It's Nicole isn't it? How silly of me."

There was barely time for an indignant, "My name is Nicki!" before Emily enveloped her in a tight hug. A protest died on Nicki's lips as the smell of lavender washed over her. From somewhere deep inside her rose vague memories of loving warmth, and a lump formed in her throat as tears prickled behind her closed eyelids. Swallowing hard against the sudden constriction, Nicki fought the unfamiliar emotion.

"Nicki is it?"

"Yes, Nicki," she repeated emphatically, opening her eyes. To her surprise the other woman didn't appear the least offended.

"It fits you very well," Emily said with approval. "Now let me get a good look at you."

Nicki set her jaw and stared back at her aunt. Emily was much as Levi had described her, short and mid-dle-aged without a speck of her sister's flamboyant beauty. Now the light blue eyes behind thick glasses sparkled. She was apparently pleased by what she saw.

"You resemble your mother a great deal, but I see much of your father in you as well."

Cyrus chuckled. "And she reminds me more of you every day, Emily. Not just because she's small either; she's got a stubborn streak a mile wide."

Emily turned and raised her eyebrows in mock surprise. "Me? Stubborn? Now, if that isn't the pot calling the kettle black. I seem to remember a bit of obstinacy from you on occasion. How about the time . . ."

Half an hour later, Nicki slipped unnoticed from the house. She left her father and aunt still happily reminiscing, while Peter watched in fascination. Confused and uncertain, her steps took her unerringly to the barn, where she found Levi working on the plow.

"Well," he said, glancing up with a smile. "How did it go?"

"Fine I guess. I wasn't rude to her if that's what you mean."

"But you wanted to be?"

"No. Well, maybe at first, but she didn't give me a chance."

Levi laughed. "Good for her."

"I don't think she liked me much."

"Oh?"

"She hardly talked to me at all."

"Maybe she's the quiet type."

Nicki shook her head. "No, I don't think so. She and Papa went on and on about things that happened back in Massachusetts."

"She and your father haven't seen each other for seventeen years." Levi grimaced with effort as he tugged on a stiff nut on the bottom of the plow. "They probably have a lot of catching up to do."

"I hadn't thought of that." Nicki bit her lip. "When she hugged me I felt so strange."

Levi looked up again. "Strange how?"

"As soon as I smelled her perfume I felt funny. Kind of like I remembered being little and someone was holding me."

"Maybe you do remember her," he said. "Or maybe something about her reminded you of your mother."

"No, my mother didn't hold me much. Anyway, she's not much like my mother."

"Were you afraid she would be?"

"Sort of, I guess."

"Why? What's wrong with your mother?"

For a moment Nicki was tempted to tell him, but then the image of a lace curtain billowing out from an open window flitted through her mind. What she had seen inside that room had forever changed her image of her mother. No, Levi must never know what her mother was, never.

"Nicki?" The strange look in Nicki's eyes made Levi feel distinctly uneasy. "What is it?"

She started, realizing she hadn't answered his question. "There are many things I don't like about my mother, but I'd rather not talk about her. What are you doing, by the way?"

"Taking the plowshare off so we can take it to the blacksmith and get it sharpened," he answered, accepting the change of subject. "Your father says it's time Peter and I start the spring plowing."

"Oh." Nicki watched silently as he loosened another nut and removed the bolt. "Do you think I look like my father?" she asked suddenly.

He looked at her in surprise. "I can't say that I ever thought about it. Hmm . . ." He pushed his hat back on his head and gazed at her critically for several seconds. "I guess you do at that, especially your mouth and chin."

"Do you really think so?" Nicki was delighted. "I never realized it until Aunt Emily said so."

It had never occurred to her she wasn't just Samantha's daughter, she was also Cyrus's. Perhaps the taint didn't go as deep as she feared. Maybe she didn't have to wind up like Samantha.

10

"Whoa!" Levi pulled back on the reins, and the two huge draft horses came to a stop next to Nicki at the edge of the field. He smiled as he removed his hat and wiped the sweat from his forehead. "What brings you up here?"

"Some grain for the horses and your lunch." Nicki had a burlap bag in one hand and a basket in the other. "Since you said you weren't coming in at noon today, Aunt Emily fixed you something to eat out here."

"And sent you up with it."

Nicki grinned. "I volunteered. It was either that or muck out the barn."

Levi laughed as he unhitched the team and led them out of the field, down to the creek for a drink. "So I'm the lesser of two evils?"

"Just about anything is better than shoveling manure," Nicki replied as she followed him and spread out the blanket under a small cottonwood tree next to the stream.

"Even bringing lunch to me?"

"Yes, even that!"

Hiding his amusement, Levi secured the team while Nicki laid out the lunch on the blanket.

"Aren't you going to unharness them?"

"No, I'm not going to stop that long."

Nicki paused to frown at him. "Papa says you should give the horses at least an hour rest at noon. They do the hardest part of the work."

"I know, and your father's right." He gestured toward huge clouds billowing up on the western horizon. "But I only have about a quarter of an acre left in this field, and I want to get done before that hits."

"Do you want me to go get the other team?"

"No, it shouldn't take much more than an hour."

Nicki surveyed the field. "An hour?"

"Well, I hope so." He took off his hat and sank down on the blanket with a tired sigh. "Hmm," he said looking over the meal. "Either Emily thought I'd be half-starved or she figured on you helping me eat it."

Nicki picked up a chicken leg. "It so happens I packed this, not Aunt Emily." She took a bite and closed her eyes in appreciation. "Aunt Emily may not be able to make biscuits, but her fried chicken is heavenly."

"You're never going to forget those biscuits are you?" Levi grinned as he picked up a thick slice of bread and butter.

"They were hard as rocks," she reminded him. "Papa even tried dunking one in his coffee and he still couldn't eat it."

"True, but not everyone has your knack with biscuits."

Nicki tried to pretend his compliment meant nothing to her, but she was conscious of a warm glow deep inside. Levi Cantrell made her feel things she was anything but comfortable with. Curious flutterings in her stomach and shortness of breath hit her at the oddest moments when she was around him.

Sometimes, just before sleep overtook her, when fantasies seemed possible, she could almost believe she was like any other young woman who was falling in love. But she recognized the feelings for what they really were, the first stirrings of lust. As Samantha Chandler's daughter she knew there was no such thing as love; it was only an illusion, one created by men to control women. Life had taught her not to trust a man with anything, especially not her heart.

"So," Levi began, taking a piece of chicken and settling back on the blanket, "is it just the forlorn hope that Peter will save you from a nasty chore that brings you out here, or do you have an ulterior motive?"

"I doubt Peter will take my hint about the barn. He was acting like he didn't understand a word I said. I hate it when he does that!" Nicki sighed. "Actually I just came to see how the work was going. Papa wants to know when you think you'll be able to plow the hayfields?"

"That depends. Did Peter finish shingling the barn roof?"

Nicki nodded. "About half an hour ago."

"Good, then if I can get through this field today, we can start tomorrow." Levi paused. "You know, I still have my reservations about this lucerne or alfalfa or whatever it is."

Nicki was immediately defensive. "I suppose you think it won't work. You're just like everybody else around here, refusing to even try anything different."

"Whoa now. I didn't say it wouldn't work. I only meant I have a hard time believing it's possible to have as much as three cuttings of hay in one year. After you harvest prairie grass, it doesn't grow much for the rest of the summer."

She snorted. "Some farmhand you are."

"You're right." He chuckled. "Cowboys don't know a whole lot about farming, and I'm as ignorant as any of the rest. I warned your father the day he hired me."

Nicki was about to make a stinging retort when she remembered how efficiently Levi had handled branding the Chandler's small herd. He had accomplished that job, which had always taken most of the day, before noon. "I guess it's all a matter of what you're used to," she admitted. "Papa says the key to growing alfalfa hay is water. Look, I'll show you."

With a stick, she began to scratch pictures into the dirt. But Levi didn't listen very closely as she explained the system of ditches Cyrus Chandler had devised. Though he tried, the finer points of flood irrigation couldn't hold his attention when the movement of her lips kept distracting him.

For the last two weeks he'd tried to squelch the tender feelings she inspired in him. Usually he was reasonably successful, but not today. When he found himself daydreaming about making love to her there under the tree with the dappled sunlight playing across their naked bodies, he jumped to his feet in alarm.

"We'll plant the alfalfa with a crop of oats. That way we'll have oat hay this year even though the alfalfa won't . . . What's the matter with you?" Nicki asked, startled by his sudden movement.

"Nothing." He grabbed his hat and jammed it on his head. "I have to get going, that's all."

"But you haven't finished eating," she protested. "And the horses aren't rested yet."

Desperately he searched his mind for an excuse to put distance between them. "I know, but I just thought of something I need to do."

"What?"

"I . . . ah . . . I need to walk the part I'm going to plow this afternoon and look for big rocks. We don't need a broken plowshare."

"You don't have to . . ."

"Thanks for bringing my lunch up," he called over his shoulder. "I'll see you at supper."

Nicki stared after him, perplexed. "I wonder what got into him," she mumbled. Irritation battled with disappointment as she gathered the remains of their aborted picnic. She had looked forward to lunch all morning. Other than getting the answer to Cyrus's question, she might have just as well stayed home!

It was good for Nicki's peace of mind that she never stopped to wonder why time alone with Levi was so important to her. The answer would have scared her half to death.

Since the giant thunderclouds passed over without spilling a drop of rain, Levi finished the plowing by early afternoon. He spent the rest of the day working on the machinery and at suppertime announced they could begin plowing the alfalfa fields the next morning.

"Good." Cyrus nodded with satisfaction. "Then Peter can start first thing tomorrow." As with all conversations that took place when Peter was present, Cyrus signed as he spoke.

"That is a good idea," Peter signed back. "Who knows what would happen if you let him try it!" He pointed to Levi and rolled his eyes emphatically.

Though Levi still had some difficulty understanding everything that was said, he was very aware of Peter's slight and he grinned. "If you're referring to my first attempts at plowing, maybe it was the fault of my teacher."

It had been obvious from the beginning of Peter's instruction that plowing was not Levi's cup of tea. Peter had found his struggles highly amusing, but Levi's frustration had mounted until Cyrus suggested he develop his own method instead of using Peter's.

The solution had been as simple as running the reins between his thumb and forefinger instead of knotting them around his waist the way Peter did. With his huge hands Levi was able to control the team and the walking plow with ease.

"Actually," Cyrus said, "I have something else for you to do, Levi."

"Oh? What's that?"

"There's some business I'd like you to take care of for me if you will." Cyrus glanced toward the stove where Nicki and Emily were dishing up supper. "I'll explain later," he said quietly.

Levi frowned, for Cyrus had turned his face away from Peter, and his hands had remained still.

As soon as the meal was over Cyrus scooted back his chair. "Let's go for a walk, Levi." Once outside he seemed ill at ease as they walked slowly toward the barn. At last they reached their destination, and Cyrus leaned on the corral fence, gasping for air as he tried to calm his tortured breathing.

"What was it you wanted me to do?" Levi prompted gently when the worst seemed to have passed.

"If there was any way I could do this myself . . ." Cyrus shook his head as he reached into his pocket and drew out a small leather pouch. He held it indecisively for a moment and then thrust it into Levi's hand.

Curiously, Levi opened the bag and spilled the contents into his hand. For several seconds he stood there, staring stupidly at the gold nuggets that glittered in his palm.

"That's eleven ounces of pure gold. It's worth about two hundred dollars. I want you to ride over to South Pass City and cash it in for me."

"South Pass City!" Levi was startled. "That's a hundred miles from here."

"I know, and it's big enough that strangers go pretty much unnoticed. Besides, it's a gold-mining town. They see dozens of nuggets every day, a few more won't attract any attention."

Levi gave him a considering look. "You seem to be going to a lot of trouble to make sure nobody knows about this. Why?"

"It has to be kept secret." Cyrus ran his fingers through his hair in agitation. "All spring I've kept hoping I'd be able to go myself, but I can barely even walk to the corral anymore. I wouldn't be asking you if I wasn't desperate."

"But you haven't told me anything, have you?" Levi's eyes narrowed suspiciously as he rolled the nuggets around with his thumb. "You're a good friend, Cyrus, but I'm an honest man. I won't break the law, even for you."

"What makes you think I'm asking you to?"

"I've known for a long time there was something strange going on here. There's just too much money for a simple homestead. Your house is made of logs instead of sod, you own fifty head of cattle, three saddle horses, and two damn good teams of workhorses, not to mention the expensive barbed wire fence you just put clear around your whole place. Homesteads, even very productive ones, don't make that kind of money." Levi poured the gold back into the pouch. "Herman Lowell thinks you might be rustling his cattle. I haven't seen any sign of it, but now I'm not so sure."

Cyrus gave a humorless laugh. "No, I'm not rustling his cattle, and he's a fine one to talk about taking what belongs to another man."

"Then where did this gold come from?"

The older man stared at him with bleak eyes for a long moment and then sighed. "It's stolen."

11

"Stolen!" Levi couldn't believe his ears.

Cyrus kicked a small rock and looked up at Levi with regretful eyes. "I've never told anyone the story before, but I guess the time has finally come." He took a deep breath. "We lived in Maryland when the War Between the States began. For the first year my pa tried hard not to take sides, so I was neither a Confederate sympathizer nor a Yankee.

"One night when I was alone, I found a Confederate soldier hiding in our woodshed. He'd been shot several times and was bleeding badly. I did what I could for him, but he was dying, and he knew it. He begged me to hide the strongbox he had with him, and made me promise not to tell another living soul about it. He died before morning. When I broke the lock on the strongbox, I discovered a fortune in gold bullion, all in untraceable bars."

"Where did it come from?" Levi asked.

"I never knew. He died without telling me. I had no idea what to do or where to turn, so I went to my father. Without telling him the exact circumstances, I asked him about keeping promises made to total strangers." Cyrus ran his hand along the corral pole and sighed. "He said an honorable man's word freely given is forever binding, and can only be broken if that promise hurts someone else.

"I decided to keep silent about the gold until I could find the rightful owner. Unfortunately, I didn't have the faintest idea who that was. The soldier might have stolen it from the Yankees for the Confederate cause, or maybe from the Confederacy for himself. I didn't even know if he'd stolen it for sure, or if he was transporting it somewhere. Then I joined the Union Army, and didn't feel right about giving it to the South at all. And when the war was over, of course, there was no South."

Cyrus gripped Levi's shoulder. "I swear to you, I never intended to use it myself, but then my wife started having . . . problems. My business failed, and Peter, well, you can imagine how cruel people were to him. I thought if I could just get my family away from the city, we'd be all right. So I 'borrowed' enough gold to get us a wagon and supplies. The children and I were happy here, but Samantha hated it. She started making impossible demands, hoping I'd pack up and go back East, I suppose. First it had to be a log house, then an addition for Peter so she didn't have to live with him. The list was endless, and eventually she left anyway." He coughed and shook his head. "By then dipping into the gold had become a habit. I only use it to tide us over, but it seems like it's always something."

Levi was quiet for several minutes. Finally he spoke. "The way I see it, that soldier gave you the gold for safekeeping, and that's just what you've done. After twenty-five years, I'd say it belongs to you by default. Any you've used was payment for taking care of it all this time."

Cyrus smiled fleetingly. "I wish I could see it that way."

"You said it was in bars," Levi said. "These are nuggets."

"Bars of pure gold are pretty conspicuous, especially out here. I melted them down and poured the liquid gold into cold, shallow water to make nuggets. Not so different from the way Mother Nature does it herself."

Cyrus was silent for a moment then he looked up at the big man. "I'll understand if you don't want to do this. But consider it a request from a friend."

"Two hundred dollars is a lot of money. Are you sure you trust me with it?"

"If I didn't trust you, I wouldn't have given the gold to you. I hate to send you right now, but I need the money to pay for the alfalfa seed."

"That's an awful lot of seed."

"I know, but I want to make sure Nicki and Peter have enough on hand, in case . . ." he stopped, but Levi knew he was thinking of funeral expenses.

Levi slipped the bag into his shirt pocket. "I'll leave in the morning."

"Be careful how you cash the gold in. Don't give out more than one nugget at a time, and make sure you're in a different crowd for each one. It's not as difficult as it sounds. South Pass City is a big town . . . it would take most of a day just to hit all the saloons."

The irrepressible twinkle appeared in Levi's eye. "My kind of town."

"The only drawback is that it's filled with suffragettes." Cyrus grinned, momentarily distracted. "Ever since they got the right to vote, and that woman Esther Morris was appointed justice-of-the-peace, women seem to think they need to stick their noses into everything."

Levi nodded. "I remember my father saying once they got the vote they'd settle down and we'd never hear anything more from them. That's one mistake my stepmother will never let him forget." He paused. "You haven't told Nicki or Peter about the gold, have you?"

"No. I've wanted to, but the time just never seemed right."

"They'll have to know," Levi said softly.

Cyrus's frail body was wracked by a fit of coughing. "I know," he said when he finally was able. "But they're all I have. I don't want them to know what I've done."

"I think you're underestimating them. They're both intelligent adults. I doubt they'll judge you very harshly for making their lives more comfortable, especially when you haven't really done anything wrong."

Cyrus smiled. "Do you always look at the world so philosophically?"

"I try to."

For awhile neither man spoke, each lost in his own thoughts. At last Cyrus broke the silence with an unexpected question. "What are your intentions concerning my daughter?"

"Intentions? I don't have any intentions toward her at all."

"Oh." Cyrus was disappointed. "I was sure you had a certain amount of affection for her."

"I do. I'm very fond of her; too fond to even consider what you're thinking."

"Why? What's wrong with my daughter?"

"Nothing. If I were ten years younger, or if she was ten years older, it might even work out."

"What's a few years?" Cyrus asked, unconvinced.

Levi ran his fingers through his hair. "Nicki is a beautiful young woman. The last thing she needs is to be tied to a man old enough to be her father."

"And just how old are you?"

"Thirty-two."

Cyrus gave a wry chuckle. "Then unless you were out sowing your wild oats at a very young age, you couldn't possibly be her father." He sighed. "I wish I could see her settled before I die."

"Don't worry. One of these days, some fine young man will come along and sweep her off her feet."

"I doubt it. In case you haven't noticed, she hates men . . . or thinks she does. You're the only one she hasn't beat up, chased off, or spit on since she was twelve years old. That's why I hoped . . ."

"She doesn't see me as a man," Levi cut in. "As far as Nicki is concerned I'm a very safe uncle or older brother. Besides, I don't want a wife, and I think she knows that."

Cyrus smiled ruefully. "Well, I had to try."

Levi returned his smile, and silence fell between them again.

"You know, I'm not really afraid to die," Cyrus said quietly after a few minutes. "In a way I think it will be a relief, but I am scared of what will happen to Nicki and Peter when I'm gone. I brought Emily out here so they wouldn't be alone, but she's no match for Herman Lowell. If he decides he wants them off this place, he'll do it. I don't know how they'll survive if that happens. It's the only home they've ever known."

"Cyrus." Levi reached out and gripped the other man's shoulder with one big hand. "I promise you I'll stay with Nicki and Peter until they don't need me anymore, even if I have to fight them both to do it. You have my word on that."

Cyrus studied his face intently for several minutes. "You're serious aren't you?"

"Never more so."

Slowly, Cyrus smiled. "'The word of an honorable man freely given' . . ." he quoted softly. "Thank you."

Levi left for South Pass City before first light the next morning. Peter noticed Levi's bedroll was missing when he went to milk, and he reported his absence at breakfast.

"He's gone?" Nicki exploded. "We're right in the middle of spring plowing and he's gone?"

"Now Nicki," Cyrus began.

She slammed the plate of biscuits on the table so hard that the coffee cups jumped. "That low-down, lying, no-good, mangy coyote. How could he just up and leave? I told you not to hire him in the first place. I didn't trust him, I never liked him, and he didn't even bother to say good-bye." There was a suspicious catch in her voice on the last word.

Cyrus smacked his fist on the table. "Nicki, for God's sake!"

Nicki ceased her tirade. "What?"

"I asked him to go to Buffalo and check the price of seed," he said, naming the first place he could think of. "He'll be back in five or six days."

"Oh."

"Yes, 'oh.' What's the matter with you?"

"I don't know," she mumbled. How could she explain the sudden, overwhelming pain that had slashed through her when Peter said Levi was gone? Since when did his presence, or absence, mean so much to her? Such dependency was dangerous. How long could you expect a roving cowboy to stay in one place? He'd promised to stay through the spring planting, but that would be done in a few weeks. Surely he'd leave for good soon after that.

It would be for the best, she told herself firmly, ignoring the tightness in her throat. It was only the shock of Peter's announcement that had upset her. When the time came for Levi to really leave, she'd be prepared. It wouldn't bother her in the slightest.

"Why Buffalo?" she asked, squelching her emotions. "That's almost two hundred miles away."

"I thought we might get our seed cheaper there."

"It seems kind of sudden." Her voice still sounded a little peevish.

"True, but then I only just thought of it last night. I didn't expect him to leave until after breakfast, though."

Emily set a plate of eggs on the table and gently turned the conversation to other things. Nicki tried to relax. Actually, it would be kind of nice not to have Levi Cantrell looking over her shoulder all the time. Now things could be just like they were before he came.

Six days her father had said. It seemed an eternity.

12

Good! Maybe it will rain, Nicki thought, eyeing the clouds on the far horizon as she drove into town. Rain would fit her black mood perfectly. For the last five days she'd been grouchy and depressed. She told herself repeatedly that it was just a coincidence that it began the day Levi left.

She entered the store still gloomy, but hoping Mrs. Adams's friendly chatter would help.

"Nicki! Oh good, come give me your opinion."

Nicki's heart sank at the sound of Amanda Lowell's voice. She wasn't in the mood to play one of Amanda's silly games. Noticing Charles Laughton's bored expression as he stood next to Amanda, Nicki had a feeling she wasn't going to enjoy this any more than he was. "What is it, Amanda?" she asked, walking over to the counter.

"I just found the most divine fabric hidden away in Mrs. Adams's storeroom, but now I don't know whether to buy lace or this scrumptious ribbon to go with it. What do you think?" Amanda held up the dusky pink silk and a length of rose-colored ribbon.

"How the devil would I know?"

"Oh, Nicki." Amanda smiled. "Don't be so difficult. All you have to do is tell me which one you'd choose."

"I wouldn't bother with either one myself. I don't spend much time worrying about such silliness."

"That's certainly obvious," Amanda's companion muttered just loud enough for Nicki to hear.

"Don't be rude, Charles," Amanda chided him. "Nicki really doesn't have any use for pretty dresses, you know." She turned back to Nicki. "Charles has spent his entire life in England and Europe. He's never met anyone like you before."

All at once Nicki felt clumsy and unattractive. "I've never met anyone like him either," she mumbled with ill humor as she walked to the other end of the counter to wait for Mrs. Adams. What did she care that Amanda's snooty beau thought she was ugly? She'd be happy if all men did. *Except for Levi Cantrell.* The thought flitted through her mind and she pushed it away in irritation.

Even so, she found herself watching a bit wistfully as Mrs. Adams cut the fabric. Nicki hadn't had a dress for many years. Of course Amanda was right, there wasn't much use for one in Nicki's life. Still, it might be nice . . . She let the thought trail away when Mrs. Adams came to wait on her. Cyrus's order was filled in a short time, and Nicki turned to go, disappointed that the older woman wasn't free for a chat.

"Oh Nicki, I clean forgot," Mrs. Adams said in her fluttery voice. "There's a letter for your aunt."

Nicki took the envelope and looked at it curiously before slipping it into her pocket. Probably another letter from her cousin Liana. She felt another flicker of envy as she thought of the girl three years younger than herself. To be able to read and write well enough to send letters was a dream Nicki had secretly cherished for years.

Samantha Chandler had started to teach her daughter but had never progressed beyond the rudiments before other things distracted her. There had never been time after that, and Nicki had grown up unable to read or write.

Nicki placed her purchases in the back of the wagon and climbed up into the seat. Aunt Emily would probably be more than willing to teach her how to read, but Nicki balked at having to admit she couldn't. She wasn't about to lay her failings out for someone else to see. Besides, she had no more need of reading and writing than she did a new dress.

The depressing thought slid away as the roll of distant thunder caught her attention. She eyed the storm clouds building over the horizon again.

If only they would bring rain this time. With very little snowfall and no spring rains there hadn't been enough water for new grass to grow. Last year's was tall and abundant, but there wasn't much nutrition left in the dried yellow stalks.

By the time she reached home, the storm was upon her. Violent gusts of wind blew dirt into her eyes and drove against the horse and wagon with frightening intensity. Finally she made it to the barn, unhitched the team, and led them into the safety of the building.

Removing the harnesses from the skittish horses proved to be far more difficult than usual. Just as she was about to scream in frustration, Peter appeared. With his familiar, gentle touch, the horses calmed and were soon safe in their stalls.

Peering out into the driving wind, Nicki pulled her coat closer around her. At her side Peter indicated that they should go to the house, but Nicki wasn't so sure. Dirt and bits of tumbleweed flew by, driven into the air with terrifying force. She hesitated while Peter pulled his collar up and headed out into the storm.

The sound of not-so-distant thunder decided the matter for Nicki. With the lightning getting closer by the minute, the house suddenly seemed a much better place to be. Gritting her teeth, she pulled her hat down tightly on her head and followed Peter.

Nicki gasped as she came around the side of the barn and the wind struck her full force. Fighting to stay on her feet, she made her way across the barnyard. Just as her toe touched the porch step she belatedly remembered that the supplies were still in the back of the wagon. With a curse under her breath, she started to turn back.

Before she could complete the movement, a particularly strong gust of wind shrieked past. Nicki watched in astonishment as a section of the barn roof was torn loose and thrown to the ground.

White-faced, Nicki scurried into the safety of the house. "We just lost part of the barn roof," she said breathlessly, pushing the door shut behind her.

"We heard the crash." Concern etched deep grooves around Cyrus's eyes and mouth. "Are you all right?"

"I'm fine, I wasn't anywhere near it." Nicki glanced toward the window where Emily and Peter were watching the storm with fascinated horror. "Thanks to Peter."

"We saw you drive by, and he thought you might need help with the horses."

"Well, he was right." Nicki shrugged out of her coat. "I've never seen anything like this storm before."

"Neither have I." Cyrus joined the other two at the window. "Just look at that lightning."

It snaked out of the heavens, jagged knives cutting the air, sometimes four or five at a time. The thunder became a continuous roll, with increasingly loud crashes resounding after each bolt of lightning. Then there was a white-hot flash and a boom so loud it seemed to shake the house.

"Look!" Emily gasped, pointing to one of the few cottonwood trees growing along Willow Creek. The lightning had neatly split the trunk, laying one half down on its side. Through the window they stared at the destruction, aghast at how close the lightning had come to the house.

Then, as quickly as the storm had come, it was gone. The wind dwindled to a gentle breeze and the sun broke through the black clouds overhead. They could hear the thunder to the east as the clouds moved on.

"All that and not one drop of rain," Nicki muttered in disgust. "Guess I'll go check the horses and see how bad the barn is."

Halfway to the barn, Peter caught up with her. She looked up at him and smiled. "Thanks for coming out in the storm to help me, Peter."

Peter shrugged. "You'd have done the same for me," he signed.

"You think so?" she asked, giving his shoulder a playful punch.

With a grin, he reached over and ruffled her dark curls.

"Well," she said, surveying the section of the roof that lay on the ground. "I guess it could be worse."

Peter nodded. "You're right," he said with a few quick gestures. "The wind could have blown the shingles off it too."

The words and the deadpan look that went with them made Nicki laugh in spite of herself.

"I wasn't talking about that and you know it. I meant . . ." She broke off and followed Peter's suddenly intent gaze. Coming up the road at a fast trot was a riderless horse.

Nicki felt a rush of fear as she recognized Lady and the saddle on her back. There was no mistaking the big bay mare and the L.C. tooled into the leather of the saddlebags. Something had happened to Levi.

Peter caught hold of the bridle and attempted to calm the frightened animal. Eyes wide and breath coming in short hard gasps, the horse tried to jerk its head free, but Peter held firm.

By the time he had calmed Lady and put her away, Nicki was waiting for him with both of their horses saddled.

"I'm going with you," she said, challenging him to disagree.

Peter was not pleased. There was a good chance he'd find Levi seriously injured or dead, and he didn't want Nicki along. But after one look at the belligerent set of her jaw he knew it was useless to argue. With the air of a man resigned to his fate, he swung into his saddle.

Too worried about Levi to realize Peter had given in too easily, Nicki wasn't even suspicious when he indicated she should get Levi's rifle. She was in the process of attaching the scabbard to her saddle before she realized she'd been duped. The minute he saw she was entangled in her task he pointed toward the west.

"We're going west?" Nicki asked in surprise. "But why? Buffalo is east of here."

Peter shook his head, his fingers flying in explanation. "No, you are going west; I am going east. We need to split up in case Levi circled around and stopped in town on his way home." Peter glanced at the sun. "I don't think he is too far away or the horse wouldn't have come here. We still have a long time before dark. Be sure to tell Cyrus what we are doing before you leave." With that he turned away, completely ignoring Nicki's futile attempts to get his attention.

Still fumbling with the stiff leather bindings, Nicki watched in helpless anger as he rode away. "I hate it when you do that!" she yelled after him, though she knew he wouldn't hear her. She considered following him, but realized there was a slight chance that Levi might have done as Peter suggested.

Nicki tried not to contemplate what might have happened to Levi, but worry curled around the edges of her anger at Peter. Levi couldn't have just fallen off his horse; he rode far too well for that. Somebody, or something, had separated horse and rider.

All sorts of disasters flashed through her mind, each more ominous than the last. She saw visions of him with a broken leg, then flashes of him burned like the cow she had once seen struck by lightning, and, most frightening of all, the image of Buck and Shorty ambushing him.

Just as she was picturing an unsuspecting Levi toppling from his horse, his body riddled by bullets, a movement to the northwest caught her eye. With a surge of relief, Nicki saw that it was a man on foot. Though he was quite a distance away, she was sure it was he. Only Levi would be wearing that obnoxious old buffalo coat that made him resemble a bear as much as a human.

What in the world was he doing out here anyway? Cyrus had said he'd gone to Buffalo, which lay almost two hundred miles in the opposite direction. Only Nowood lay to the west for many miles. Jackson Hole was nearly two hundred miles beyond that, and it was over a hundred miles southwest to South Pass City. For the life of her she couldn't think of any reason Levi would have gone either place.

Perversely, now that she knew he was all right, her anger flared. Here she'd been imagining all kinds of terrible things, scared half to death, when all the while he'd been taking a leisurely stroll across the prairie.

By the time she reached him, she had managed to work up a rather respectable rage, fed by her suspicions and a deeper emotion she refused to name.

"Well, well, well, imagine meeting you way out here," she said sarcastically.

Levi just grinned. "I'm glad to see you too. Lady must have found her way home?"

"Yes, and Peter was a tiny bit concerned when she showed up minus her rider." Nicki arched her eyebrows. "What happened?"

"Lady took exception to one very loud crash of thunder, and the next thing I knew I was lying on the ground."

"I see you didn't get the seed."

"What seed?"

"The seed Papa sent you to Buffalo to buy."

"Oh, that seed. No, I didn't get it."

"Why not?" Nicki asked indignantly.

Levi sighed and rubbed the back of his neck. "That's between your father and me."

"Oh is that so?" Nicki sat up straighter in her saddle. "I'll have you know Papa's business is also my business."

"Not this time it isn't." He took off his hat and ran his fingers through his hair. Damn Cyrus for not telling his daughter the truth. "I'm sorry, Nicki," he said softly.

"You'd be even sorrier if I just turned my horse around and rode off. I'd do it too, if there weren't another storm coming in."

"Another storm?" Levi turned in surprise. Somehow the huge grayish white clouds billowing into the air didn't look like thunderheads. Levi studied them for a moment, trying to trap the elusive memory niggling at the back of his mind.

Suddenly, it burst into full bloom. "Son of a . . . Get this horse moving," he yelled as he grabbed hold of the saddle horn and swung up behind a very startled Nicki.

"What . . ."

"The lightning started a goddamned prairie fire!"

Nicki's eyes widened, and her face drained of color. "Which way?" she croaked, fear already constricting her throat.

"Toward the creek."

Willow Creek was only two miles away, but Levi knew they couldn't possibly outrun the fire. A strong wind was blowing northeast, driving the flames before it, so they'd be angling away from the main body of the blaze. If they were very lucky, they might get beyond the eastern edge of the fire before it reached them. If not, their only chance lay in finding protection from the flames and smoke. The creek was small, but it had high banks. It might be enough.

Carrying both Nicki and a man the size of Levi at a high lope would be a severe strain on any horse. Long past her prime, Lollipop was lathered and breathing hard within a very few minutes, but the smell of the fire drove her on.

The trio had raced about three-quarters of a mile when disaster struck. Frightened and worried about Lollipop's growing exhaustion, Nicki didn't sense the danger until it was too late. One minute she was gripping the saddle with her knees, and the next she was flying through the air. She felt a jarring impact . . . then everything went black.

13

"Nicki . . ."

At first she was aware only of the pain in her head and a deep voice calling her name. Gingerly she opened her eyes and found herself staring up into the familiar face of Levi Cantrell.

He sighed with relief. "Thank God. Are you all right?"

"I . . . I think so. My head hurts, and my leg. What happened?"

"Lollipop stepped in a prairie dog hole. You landed on your head, and it knocked you cold."

Nicki struggled to sit up. "Oh no, Lollipop . . ."

"She broke her leg. . . . I'm sorry."

"No, that's impossible. She'd be in pain. I'd hear . . ." Her eyes widening with dawning horror, Nicki jumped to her feet, the pain in her leg forgotten. She pulled away from Levi to stare at the carnage. Lollipop lay on her side, the blood from a single bullet hole in her head soaking into the ground.

"Oh, God," Nicki sobbed, stumbling toward her horse.

Levi stopped her with a gentle hand. "You can't help her now, Nicki. She's gone."

Nicki whirled on him. "You killed Lollipop!" She pounded her fists against his chest. "You shot her like she was nothing more than a sick cow. I hate you. Do you hear me? I hate you!"

Levi gripped her upper arms and shook her. "Nicki, we don't have time for this right now. That fire is going to be here any minute."

She had momentarily forgotten the danger that had sent them flying across the prairie. Now she stopped struggling in his grip and looked to the southwest. A line of smoke and flames was racing toward them impossibly fast. The air was already thick with smoke and a strange black dust. For the first time she noticed the surging mass of animal life streaming past them. Antelope, coyotes, rabbits, insects of every description, even a rattlesnake, all trying to outrun the fire, but there was no escape. Nicki's stomach clenched in terror. "We're going to die aren't we?" She was surprised how unemotional her voice sounded. Inside, she felt like a screaming mass of nerves.

"Maybe not," Levi said, pulling her toward the dead horse. "As hard as that wind is driving it, that fire won't stay in one place very long. With a little protection we might manage."

"I don't unders . . . Levi!" Before she knew what was happening, Nicki found herself lying facedown on the ground, between Lollipop's outstretched legs.

Her indignant cry might as well have fallen on deaf ears, for Levi's only response was to join her on the ground, draping his large body over her much smaller one.

"What in blue blazes do you think you're doing, Cantrell?" She tried desperately to wiggle out from under him.

"An old cowboy once told me he'd survived a fire like this by lying low. It jumped right over him." He raised his voice over the roar of the fire, which was growing louder by the second.

"You think that might happen to us?"

"I don't know. Charlie Hobbs is a good one for telling tall tales, but it's the only chance we've got. Whatever happens, keep your head and stay put. It's natural to panic, but don't let yourself."

"I'm not scared," she said.

"Good, because I sure as hell am."

She stopped her writhing and twisted around to look at him. "You are?"

For once his blue-gray eyes were deadly serious. "Terrified. I'd be stupid not to be." Levi adjusted their positions so that Nicki was forced to face the ground again. Then he spoke into her ear. "There's a leather pouch in my pocket that belongs to your pa. See that he gets it, will you?"

"Give it to him yourself," she yelled, frightened by the unspoken possibility that one or both of them might die. "It's probably none of my business, just like the seed wasn't."

Levi said nothing. With any luck his body would prove to be enough of a shield to protect Nicki from the flames. Her greatest danger was from suffocation. Even now the smoke surrounding them was so thick that it seemed to suck the oxygen from the air. Breathing was fast becoming torturous.

Nicki raised her head and peered at the fire that was now only about fifty feet away. It would be upon them within seconds.

"Get down!" Levi yelled, forcing her head down with his hand as he spoke.

For an instant Nicki felt a light pressure on the back of her neck, almost like a kiss. It was forgotten in a moment as the whole world became a hissing, crackling roar. Somehow, the smells were worse than the sounds. Burning sagebrush, blood, sweat, singeing hair, and a dozen other unpleasant odors mixed together in a nauseating stench that threatened to choke her.

Sweeping relentlessly forward, the blaze spared nothing in its path. Hot and deadly, it roared over them like a runaway locomotive. Nicki bit back a scream as she felt the heat branding her skin. Panic surged through her, and she struggled to free herself. Levi's arm tightened around her waist, holding her immobile while she fought him with every bit of strength she had. Suddenly, the breath was crushed from her lungs as Levi's full weight pressed her to the ground.

"Damn it, stay still!" he growled.

With over two hundred pounds of determined cowboy on top of her, Nicki didn't have much choice. She felt Levi's heart pounding against her back, and heard his ragged breathing. It was unnerving to realize he was just as scared as she was.

Minutes passed, hours, a lifetime, and then suddenly it was over.

They both lay where they were for several seconds.

Then Levi rolled away. "Nicki?" he asked, touching her cheek.

Disoriented and confused, she blinked at him. "Are we dead?"

"No." Propping himself up on an elbow, he surveyed the blackened landscape. "At least, I don't think we are." The fire was already a hundred feet beyond them, leaving a smoking ruin behind as it rushed on. Levi shook his head in disbelief. "And I always thought it was just one of Charlie's stories."

"What?" Nicki struggled to sit up. "You mean you lied to me?"

"Not exactly. I thought old Charlie might have exaggerated a bit, but I figured you'd be safe enough." He removed his hat and contemplated a large smoldering hole.

"Strange, I knew some cinders landed on my back, but I didn't even feel that one."

Nicki looked at him and wrinkled her nose. "Ugh, it smells like you branded your coat."

"Singed buffalo hair." Well aware that most of the burnt-hair smell was coming from the dead horse, he touched a blackened spot on his sleeve. "Dang! This was a good coat too."

"Small loss," Nicki muttered. "It's the ugliest thing I ever saw."

Levi grinned slightly as he stood up and removed the heavy garment. "I'll admit it's not real pretty, but I'm sure glad I had it on today."

"I guess so, but . . . Levi, your leg!" Nicki gasped as she stared at the blood seeping through his pants leg from a gash at the top of his thigh. "What happened?"

Levi looked at the wound his long coat had covered.

"I must have cut it on something when we hit the ground. It looks a lot worse than it is."

The sight of his blood jolted Nicki back to reality. During the terror-filled minutes of the fire, her benumbed mind had ceased to think of anything but survival. It was as though a fog had insulated her brain against reality. Now with a flood of remorse and guilt, she reached out to rub the neck of her horse. "Poor Lollipop. She . . . she was a good horse."

"I know," Levi murmured, squeezing her shoulder. "And I'm sorry."

Swallowing the knot in her throat, Nicki dipped her head to hide sudden tears. "Why didn't you wait until I woke up? I should have been the one to decide."

Levi sighed. "I guess it comes from working with horses most of my life. When I realized her leg was broken I put her out of her misery as soon as I could." He gently brushed a stray curl from her cheek. "Nicki, she was in pain. I couldn't let her suffer."

"But you should have let me do it. You think just because I'm a woman I couldn't do what needed to be done, but I could've. She was my horse, and I was responsible for her. It was my job to sh . . . shoot her, and . . . and . . ." To her dismay, she burst into a flood of tears.

Levi pulled her to her feet and into his arms. "It wasn't necessarily your job, Nicki," he murmured, stroking the back of her head with one large callused palm. As Nicki gave way to her grief, he held her, rocking her in his strong embrace, giving the only comfort he could.

At last the storm was over, and his deep voice intermingled with her last hiccuping sobs. "Years ago

I had a horse I called Frog. He was the first horse I ever trained and he meant more to me than anything else in the world. When I was about eighteen he caught the sleeping sickness and had to be destroyed. Pa offered to do it, but I turned him down. I sorta figured if our positions were reversed, old Frog would have done the same for me."

With one finger under Nicki's chin, he tipped her face up and stared down into her tear-drenched eyes. "That was a long time ago, but I still think of old Frog whenever I have to shoot a horse. At the time I thought it was something *I* had to do, but now I almost wish I'd let Pa be the one to pull the trigger."

She stared at him for a full minute then shook her head. "That's a barefaced lie. You felt sorry for me so you made up a stupid story to make me feel better! If it had been Peter's horse or even your little brother's, you wouldn't have said a word, would you?"

A wry expression crossed Levi's face as he thought of the thirty-year-old "little brother" who stood six-foot-four in his stocking feet. "Probably not, but . . ."

"Why can't you just treat me like you would Peter?"

"Because Peter is usually more reasonable than you are!" Levi snapped, then sighed in exasperation. "Sometimes you make me want to . . ."

"What? Spank me?"

"No, that isn't what I was going to say, but maybe that's not such a bad idea."

"Go right ahead and try it," Nicki taunted. "That is if you think you're man enough to do it."

"It doesn't take much of a man to spank a child," Levi replied, irritated that she thought he'd even consider such a thing. "Especially one who's having a tantrum. Why don't you try acting like a woman instead of a spoiled little girl? Maybe then people will start treating you like an adult."

Nicki's eyes flashed in anger. "And how does the great Levi Cantrell treat an adult? With more threats?"

Levi would always wonder what madness drove him that day. One moment he was arguing with the spitting wildcat in his arms, the next he was kissing her with an abandon he'd never felt in his life. With sudden clarity, he knew the twelve years difference in their ages didn't matter, nor the fact that she was the most aggravating woman he'd ever met. He only knew that his attempts to destroy the feelings he had for her had been unsuccessful. Somehow, against his better judgment, he'd fallen in love.

Nicki was caught completely off guard. Having never experienced a man's kiss before, her body responded in ways she hadn't even imagined. Unfamiliar feelings washed over her in waves, weakening her knees and making her heart pound. Instinctively, her arms crept around Levi's waist, and she melted into his embrace. She gave in to the wildly exciting sensations thundering through her and returned his kiss fervently.

Levi broke it off at last. Gently stroking her cheek with his thumb, Levi smiled down at her. "Sweet little Nicki," he whispered. But when he leaned forward to kiss her again his lips met thin air.

Aghast at how easily she'd fallen into his arms and how readily her own body had betrayed her, Nicki pulled away in alarm. *You enjoyed that kiss,* an insidious little voice whispered inside her. *You're just like your mother.*

"Don't sweet little Nicki me, you . . . you bush-whacker!" Nicki rubbed her mouth with the back of her hand as she struggled out of his arms.

Levi released her and stepped back in surprise. "What's wrong?"

"What's wrong?" she repeated incredulously. "First you shoot my horse, then you manhandle me, and now you want to know what's wrong?"

"It was just a kiss, Nicki."

"Maybe to you, but to me it was . . . it was horrible."

"I'm sorry," Levi said laying his hand on her arm.

"Don't touch me!" she cried, striking out with a small but deadly fist.

Levi grunted in agony as her fist connected with his midsection and drove the air from his lungs.

As she stood angrily rubbing her stinging knuckles, watching Levi's face go from white to red, Nicki unexpectedly felt a twinge of remorse. Perhaps she'd overreacted. He probably hadn't intended to kiss her again anyway. She was starting to toy with the idea of making an apology when his eyes focused on her with an accusing glare.

"Jesus, Nicki, I said I was sorry," he rasped out, still trying to catch his breath.

"You shouldn't have grabbed me. I don't like to be touched."

"I'll try to remember that."

"I guess I didn't have to hit you quite so hard," Nicki admitted.

Levi rubbed his stomach. "You didn't have to hit me at all."

"Well, you started it. I don't know what you had to do a damn fool thing like that for anyway."

Staring at her soot-streaked face, Levi felt a curious sensation in his chest. He could plainly see every place he had touched her, the dark smudges poignant reminders of the kiss they'd shared. Could she really have felt nothing?

"Sometimes a man does stupid things when he has a close brush with death," he said sharply. "Look, let's just forget it happened and head for home."

While Levi bent stiffly to pick up his rifle and unwind the canteen from the saddle horn, Nicki said one last good-bye to Lollipop. Then she stood and resolutely turned toward the homestead. Though there was a lump in her throat, she never once looked back as they made the long trek.

14

"*I was beginning* to think we'd never get here," Nicki said. The last rays of the sun gilded the treetops as the two weary travelers topped the rise above the homestead. "Thank heaven the fire didn't come this way."

They had made the long trip home in relative silence. Nicki was still wrapped in her grief for Lollipop, and Levi was fighting the severe headache and light-headedness that had been bothering him off and on all day. Both tried to avoid thinking of the kiss they had shared, though it was never far from their thoughts.

"Good Lord!" Levi suddenly said, staring in dismay at the gaping hole in the newly reshingled barn. "What happened?"

"The wind blew it off just before the lightning hit the tree," Nicki replied, pointing toward the remains of the old cottonwood. "It was awful. I never saw a storm like that before."

Levi shook his head. "Neither have I, at least not with that much lightning. I expect our fire wasn't the only one today either. We'd better ride the range to see how much graze . . . "

The sound of pounding hooves interrupted his observation, and both turned to find Peter galloping toward them, a wide grin on his usually taciturn face. He swung to the ground almost before his horse had come to a halt, and his fingers fairly flew as he demanded to know what had happened.

By the time the story was told, the three had reached the house. With a glance at the already-darkening sky, Peter went to put his horse away and do chores, leaving the other two to make their explanations to an anxious Cyrus and Emily.

Emily immediately whisked Levi into one of the bedrooms so she could clean and bandage his leg wound. After Nicki's bruised hip had been checked and they had washed off the worst of the grime, Emily set steaming bowls of stew on the table. Peter came in for supper, and Nicki began her description of the trip home all over again.

"I've never seen snakes so riled up. The fire didn't seem to hurt them much, just made them madder than a wet hornet in a sandstorm." She took a bite of stew and pointed her spoon toward Levi. "I almost stepped on the biggest rattler I've ever seen, but he plugged it with that rifle of his. He saved my life."

Levi shrugged. "If I hadn't lost my horse, you wouldn't have been out there in the first place." He reached into his shirt pocket and handed Cyrus the leather pouch. "Here's your money. I couldn't get the seed you wanted."

"Seed?. . . Oh, right." Cyrus accepted the pouch with a grateful look. "Well, I'm sure you did the best you could. Thanks."

Nicki frowned. They were hiding something. A stab of anger slashed across her heart. She felt betrayed. Why would her father trust Levi with information he kept from her? She fixed her stare on the bowl in front of her.

Levi rubbed his hand against his forehead. "It's been a long day. I think I'll go to bed."

"But you haven't finished your supper." Emily glanced at the full bowl in front of Levi and then turned sharp eyes to his face. "Do you feel all right?"

"I'm just not hungry."

"Are you sure that's all? Your eyes don't look good."

"I have a headache, but I think a good night's sleep will take care of it."

"Well, one thing's certain. You can't sleep in that barn tonight. Not with that big hole in the roof." Emily stood up. "I'll just move my things into the house, and you can use my room."

"No, Ma'am. You don't need to do that. The barn will be just fine. Doesn't much matter to me if it has a roof or not."

"You don't mind if I share your bed, do you Nicki?" Emily asked briskly, completely ignoring Levi.

When Nicki looked at her aunt she encountered an intense expression. She shifted her attention to Levi and saw what caused her aunt's concern. His face was gray, and his eyes bleary as he stood and swayed slightly.

"No, I don't mind at all," she murmured. "I'll help you."

Together, the two women soon had Levi moved into the room next to Peter's. That he hardly uttered another protest proved how ill he was. They pulled his boots off and left him sitting on the edge of the bed slowly unbuttoning his shirt.

"Do you think he's going to be all right?" Nicki asked anxiously as Emily closed the door and they walked across the dogtrot into the kitchen.

"I can't really say yet. There's no fever, so it could even be simple exhaustion. We should know by morning." Emily smiled at her niece. "You've had quite a day yourself. How about a bath?"

"That would be wonderful."

"I'm sorry you have to share your bed with me," Emily said as she opened the door and walked into the kitchen. "But I didn't know what else to do. If Levi really is ill, sleeping in the barn could make him worse."

"I don't mind." Nicki was surprised to discover that she really didn't. Somehow over the last month she had lost much of her antagonism toward her aunt. Levi had been right again, a very irritating habit he seemed to have.

It wasn't until she was in her room starting to undress for her bath that she remembered the letter in her pocket. "Mrs. Adams gave this to me when I went in for supplies," she said, coming back to the kitchen and handing it to Emily. "In all the excitement, it completely slipped my mind."

"Oh?" Emily glanced at the envelope and smiled. "It's from Liana." Seating herself at the table across from Cyrus, she ripped open the envelope as though she couldn't wait another minute to find out what her daughter had to say.

Nicki felt an unexpected flash of envy. Had her mother ever felt that way about her? Probably not. Samantha had left her without a backward glance.

"Oh my goodness," Emily said in surprise. "She's coming out here!"

Cyrus raised his eyebrows in concern. "All by herself?"

"No, she says she's traveling as far as Denver with an elderly woman who was a patient of Dr. Bailey's. I left Liana with Dr. Bailey and his sister, you know. Anyway, the lady needed a companion, and he suggested Liana take the job. She'll be coming to Denver with the woman and her family, then north on the stage. It says here she should arrive at the end of June." Emily looked up. "Oh, Cyrus, I hope you don't mind."

"Of course not. Your daughter will always be welcome here. You know that."

Nicki opened her mouth to make a scathing remark about nobody asking her opinion, but a sudden, overwhelming loneliness washed over her. What would it be like to have her cousin Liana as a friend? Not an exasperating older brother like Peter, but a girl she could share her thoughts with. Even as the idea occurred, Nicki pushed it away. She needed a silly female companion about as much as she needed to learn to read. Thoroughly disgusted with herself, she stomped off to take her bath.

Very late that night Nicki awoke and lay staring at the ceiling. As she listened to her aunt's soft snores, Nicki sorted through her confusing dreams, which had forced her awake. The terror of the fire coupled with Lollipop's death had produced nightmarish visions that still swirled through her mind. Afraid to go back to sleep, she tried to dwell on more pleasant thoughts.

Without meaning to, Nicki found herself thinking of Levi. He had saved her life, not once but several times. His coolness had kept her from losing her head during the fire and again when she'd almost stepped on the coiled rattler. Though she'd never admit it, she was even grateful he'd taken the job of shooting Lollipop out of her hands.

And then he'd kissed her. Touching her lips, she closed her eyes. Until today she'd always thought that a kiss would be a mere meeting of lips, pleasant perhaps but not earthshaking.

The reality was frighteningly different. Was she like her mother? Would any man's kiss send the blood screaming through her veins or was Levi something special? Horrified by the first thought, terrified by the second, she turned on her side and stifled a groan.

The image of him sitting on his bed barely able to unbutton his shirt rose in her mind. Never, in the three months he'd been with them, had he ever shown the slightest weakness. What if he was really sick? Suddenly, Nicki sat bolt upright. What if he'd gotten worse and nobody checked on him until morning? What if he died?

She slipped out of bed, tiptoed to the bedroom door, and closed it softly behind her. Dressed only in her cotton nightgown, she walked through the house and across the dogtrot, her bare feet making no sound on the cool floor.

The door to Levi's room squeaked in protest as she pushed it open, but nothing stirred within. Cautiously lighting a candle, she moved over to the bed and peered down at the sleeping man.

He had succeeded in removing his shirt, but apparently hadn't had the energy to shed his pants. By the glow of the candle Nicki's eyes took in the dark curly hair that covered his wide chest and tapered into a line down his belly. She had seen Cyrus and Peter bare-chested before, but this was not the same somehow.

Staring at his seminakedness, she felt an odd little twist in her stomach. In spite of the powerful muscles, he looked strangely vulnerable lying there. It was difficult to resist the unexpected urge to trail her fingers across the broad expanse, as she reached out to touch his forehead. She jumped in surprise when his eyes suddenly popped open. They glittered unnaturally in the candlelight as he stared up at her.

Without warning, his big hands closed around her elbows and pulled her down on the bed beside him. "My sweet little Nicki," he whispered as he wrapped his arms around her, pulling her close. Before her shocked mind even had time to react, his lips came down on hers, destroying all thought of resistance before it even occurred to her. Instead, she opened her mouth to his tender invasion as she sought to re-create the magic she'd discovered in his embrace that very afternoon.

She experienced a moment of panic as he deftly undid the buttons of her nightgown and slipped his hands inside. Then she was distracted by the kisses he was trailing down her neck and onto the exposed skin. The feelings created by his lips were incredible, like nothing she had ever felt before. When his tongue gently caressed one nipple then the other, the first fingers of desire uncurled in the pit of her belly and sent shivers of excitement racing through her veins.

His lips returned to plunder hers once more, as his hands held her snugly against his body. She was beyond rational thought as her hands slipped from his neck and embarked on an exploratory journey of their own. His flesh was warm and vibrant beneath her fingers, his body an exciting contrast of smooth skin, rippling muscles, and wiry hair.

Nicki had only just begun when she felt her nightgown slide from her body. A jolt of sheer pleasure coursed through her as Levi pulled her tighter into his embrace. The curly hair of his hard chest rubbing against her sensitive breasts was exquisite torture. His deep kisses seemed to touch her very soul, feeding the tiny flame of an emotion Nicki refused to acknowledge.

He left her briefly to remove the rest of his clothing, but she was so caught up in the tumultuous upheaval within her that the thought of escape never entered her head. She had barely drawn three ragged breaths before he rejoined her. Feeling his totally naked body so near to hers made her suddenly nervous.

Her unease disappeared as he pulled her into his arms once more. "You're so beautiful, Nicki," he whispered against her neck. "I've dreamed of this a thousand times."

She heard his words, but the delicious sensation of his skin against hers pushed all other thoughts from her already-spinning mind. Ruled only by desire, she sought to touch every part of him, arching against him, searching for an unknown release to her inner torment.

When she had reached her limit and was breathing in short, panting gasps, Levi gently rolled her onto her back and groaned against her shoulder as her legs instinctively parted to accept him.

Nicki hadn't really thought of what was coming next. She was conscious only of Levi's soft soothing words in her ear and her heady anticipation. Suddenly, a terrible, burning pain tore through her. She gasped and tears trickled down her cheeks from tightly squeezed eyelids.

Levi kissed her forehead as he stroked the tears from her cheeks with his thumbs. "Shh. I know it hurts, Love, but it will only last a minute. Try to relax."

She opened her eyes and looked up into his, which were strangely bright yet full of tenderness. Closing her eyes again, she bit her lip, dismayed to be so horribly disappointed that the wonderful feelings had fled with the coming of the pain. She, who had sworn no man would ever touch her that way, found herself wanting more.

Levi started to rain tender kisses across her face and neck. With infinite tenderness, he caressed her until the blood was singing through her veins once again.

When he slowly began to move inside her, the pain receded a bit. Although it never quite disappeared, it was soon all but forgotten as his movements fanned the flames of desire once again. At first Nicki didn't realize it was she making the soft, throaty noises, and then it didn't matter as a raging fire built within.

Just when she thought she might die from the sweet agony, a huge flower of ecstasy burst within her. With a cry, she buried her face in his shoulder as wave after wave of sensation washed over her. Vaguely aware that Levi had joined her at the top, Nicki felt herself once again drifting toward earth.

15

When Nicki awoke, she lay in Levi's arms, her head cushioned against his solid chest, his bandaged thigh resting possessively between hers. It felt wonderful, and she savored the moment with a soft smile on her face.

As her mind cleared, she realized with a start that Levi was shivering. She raised her head and stared at him in the light of the candle she'd left burning on the nightstand. The room wasn't cold, yet he was shaking as though it was the dead of winter, and his skin had an odd bluish tinge. She tapped his shoulder, trying to wake him, but got no response.

Dear God, what was wrong with him?

Aunt Emily! She'll know what to do. Nicki squirmed out of Levi's embrace and scooted off the bed. She covered him with the patchwork quilt that had lain at the end of the bed and bent to retrieve her nightgown from the floor. It was then that she noticed the blood smeared all over the insides of her thighs. She stared at it, aghast, knowing it was too early for her monthly flow. Levi must have hurt her inside somehow. He'd acted as though the pain was normal, but surely a woman didn't bleed every time.

Glancing at Levi, who was shaking even harder now, she decided she'd worry about it later. Right now she had to get Emily. Hurriedly sponging the blood away with a rag and some cold water from the pitcher by the bed, she donned her nightgown. With one last look at Levi, Nicki closed the door behind her and stuffed the bloodstained rag into a hole between two logs in the wall outside.

Emily was easily awakened and grasped the situation immediately. "Get a lantern and all the extra blankets you have. Oh, and we'll probably need one of your father's nightshirts as well," she added over her shoulder as Nicki rushed to do her bidding. Settling her glasses firmly on her nose, Emily pulled on her robe and grabbed her precious black bag from its place by the door.

The older woman was just finishing her preliminary examination when Nicki arrived with the requested supplies. "Light the lantern and set it on the table. We need to get him into that nightshirt and under the blankets." Emily looked up with a worried frown. "I really shouldn't let you help, but I don't think I can do it by myself."

Nicki shrugged. "I took care of Papa all last winter."

"Your papa and a young, unmarried man are two different things," Emily reminded her. "But there's no help for it."

Nicki set the lantern on the table and turned to find

her aunt staring at Levi's leg in shock. A large spot of blood stained the bandage. Nicki froze, her heart pounding in her throat as she remembered the feel of that same bandage against her inner thigh when she woke up. Would Emily know where the blood came from and realize Samantha's depravity had been passed on to her niece?

"Oh dear," Emily reached out and touched the bloodied bandage. "I thought the bleeding had stopped."

Nicki nearly sagged with relief. Aunt Emily didn't suspect a thing. Thank God. Nicki wasn't ready to face the possible consequences of what she and Levi had done. Not yet anyway, and maybe never.

"I think there's another bandage in my bag, Nicki." Emily's deft fingers were loosening the binding even as she spoke. "I'll need that and the powder next to it." As she carefully removed the pad, a look of complete bafflement crossed her face. The cut was clean. Not a drop of blood sullied it or the inside surface of the bandage. Puzzled, Emily touched the spot on the outside of the bandage, and for the first time noticed a similar stain on the blanket. She directed a sharp, suspicious look at her niece.

Searching Emily's bag for the powder, Nicki missed her aunt's scrutiny. By the time she returned to the bed Emily's speculations were well hidden. Working together, the two women soon had Levi rebandaged and dressed in Cyrus's nightshirt.

Nicki eyed the seams straining over the broad shoulders. "It doesn't fit him very well does it?"

"No, but it's the best we can do. He needs the warmth."

Nicki frowned at the violently shaking form on the

bed as she pulled the heavy quilt over him. "What's wrong with him, Aunt Emily?"

"I wish I knew. It could be several different things." She pushed her glasses up on her nose and sighed. "All we can do for now is keep him warm and watch him. Why don't you go back to bed?"

When Nicki started to protest, Emily cut her off. "I'm going to need your help, but you'll be of no use to anyone if you're exhausted. You've had a very difficult day and you're tired. Go get some sleep. Tomorrow will be time enough to help with the nursing."

Nicki was reluctant, but it was a surprisingly short time after she crawled into bed that she fell asleep. She slept dreamlessly and awoke to the sound of birds singing outside her window.

She dressed hurriedly and rushed through breakfast preparations. Cyrus questioned her anxiously when he learned of Levi's illness. Nicki thought she detected a flicker of concern in Peter's eyes as well. Gulping her own breakfast down in record time, she nodded absently while Peter told her he was going to take the wagon to pick up her saddle. Even her grief for Lollipop was pushed aside in her worry over Levi. She didn't stop to wonder why concern for a mere hired hand superseded everything else.

Still chewing her last mouthful, Nicki crossed the dogtrot between the two sections of the house. The rag she'd stuffed into the chinking caught her eye. If anybody else found it, there were sure to be questions. She pulled it from the wall, folded it carefully, and stuck it in her back pocket. It looked like her handkerchief, and she could launder it with the other rags next time she had her monthly flow. Seconds later, she found Aunt Emily adjusting the bedclothes around the sleeping figure on the bed.

"How is he?" Nicki whispered.

"He's stopped shivering, but he's still unconscious. He may be over it, or it may just be a new stage of whatever this sickness is."

"Your breakfast is waiting for you on the stove. Tell me what you want me to do."

Emily stood up and stretched tiredly. "Just watch him. If he should wake up, try to get him to drink some water. I'll be back as soon as I get dressed and have breakfast."

"I'm going to need your help, but you'll be of no use to anyone if you're exhausted," Nicki said in a nearly perfect imitation of her aunt's voice. "You didn't get much sleep last night you know."

Emily smiled. "Very well. I'll be back in a few hours then, but if there's any change, come and get me right away." Without further argument, Emily relinquished her patient to Nicki's care.

Nicki settled into the chair and soon found herself wishing she had thought to bring her mending. Unused to inactivity, the hours stretched before her endlessly. There was nothing to do but think, and that was the last thing she wanted to do right now. Facing what she'd done in this very room seemed even more difficult than facing the prairie fire.

Embarrassment, disgust, and self-loathing swirled through her. How could it have happened? More importantly, how was she ever going to face Levi? To have hit him after a mere kiss, only to behave like a complete wanton in his arms only a few hours later, was unexplainable. She hadn't once tried to stop him. Worst of all, she'd enjoyed it. Even now, with the recriminations and guilt, she felt an unfamiliar warm glow inside.

As the memories of the night came rushing back, she closed her eyes. It wasn't the first time she heard those soft throaty noises which had come so naturally to her.

In her mind she saw a lace curtain billowing out from an open window. The sounds drifting out on the summer breeze had been incomprehensible to the two nine-year-old girls who sat under the window wondering what was happening inside. Curiosity had finally gotten the best of them and they had peeked.

Samantha Chandler and Herman Lowell lay on the bed, their naked bodies entwined. Neither Nicki nor Amanda had really understood what was going on, but they were unable to tear their eyes away. Their parents seemed totally oblivious to everything except each other and whatever it was they were doing.

At last, afraid they'd be discovered, Nicki had tugged on Amanda's arm, and the two little girls had sneaked away. Certain that they would be punished if they ever revealed what they'd seen in Herman Lowell's bedroom, Amanda and Nicki had made a pact to keep it secret. But nothing could ever wipe the scene from Nicki's mind.

Nicki sank her head in her hands now, tears prickling behind her eyelids. In spite of everything she had done to prevent it, she was just like Samantha. For there was no denying she wanted Levi to make love to her again.

She jumped to her feet and took a turn around the room. Though she was filled with self-loathing, she couldn't make herself hate what she and Levi had done. It had been wonderful and had made her feel so special, so utterly feminine, so loved.

In the next moment all her confusion was forgotten as Levi moaned. Nicki laid her hand on his shoulder and gasped in surprise when she felt the heat through the thin material of the nightshirt. Almost fearfully, she moved her hand to his brow. Fever! He was burning up with it.

Nicki hit the kitchen at a dead run. "Aunt Emily, Aunt Emily," she cried, bursting through the door to the bedroom. "He has a terrible fever."

Emily was out of bed in a second and struggling into her robe. "How bad is it?"

"I . . . I don't know, but I've never felt anyone so hot before."

"Well, let's go see."

As she followed Emily back to Levi's room, Nicki felt better. She was certain her aunt would know just what to do.

Emily, however, was not so sure. She considered the symptoms as she poured water from the pitcher into a bowl. First a severe chill and then a high fever. An unusual combination. "Nicki, did Levi complain of not feeling well yesterday?"

"No, but I thought it was kind of strange that he got bucked off, even with the lightning. I mean, Levi could ride a bucking horse until it dropped dead from old age. Do you suppose he was already sick?"

"It's possible. He certainly was when he got here." Emily unbuttoned Levi's nightshirt and began to bathe his chest with a cool wet rag. "I thought at first it might be exhaustion or even smoke inhalation, but the symptoms don't fit. He had a headache and no appetite. Several hours later he came down with a chill followed by a fever." She sighed. "I only know one thing with those symptoms, but it's a disease of the tropics. It would be virtually impossible to catch in Wyoming."

"Could you catch it in China?"

"China? Well, I'm not sure, but you certainly could in other parts of the Orient. Why?"

"Levi said he'd spent the better part of four years there when he was a sailor."

Emily raised her eyebrows. "That does put a different light on things."

"Aunt Emily, what do you think he has?"

The older woman adjusted her glasses. "I'm very much afraid Levi has malaria."

16

Nicki gasped. "Malaria! I . . . is he going to die?"

Emily rose from her chair and retrieved her black bag from the table. "I can't say for sure but probably not. Since he obviously didn't catch it here, this isn't his first bout with it. He's survived it at least once before."

She opened the bag and began to rummage through it. "Now where is that? I'm sure I have some . . . Ah here it is." With a satisfied smile she pulled out a small white packet. "Quinine. I always keep it on hand at home. With all the sailors around, I never know when I'm going to have to treat malaria. It can come back over and over again."

"Will that cure him?"

"If he has malaria, it'll help. We can expect the chills and fever to continue for awhile, but the disease always responds to quinine."

Nicki directed a worried frown at Levi. "What if it doesn't?"

"Then he doesn't have malaria." Emily measured a small amount of the powder and added it to a glass of water. "The problem will be getting him to take it."

Between the two of them, they managed to prop him up in the bed. Then, with Nicki supporting his head and shoulders, Emily attempted to force the liquid down his throat. He obligingly swallowed the first mouthful, but then set his teeth and twisted his mouth away from the bitter draught.

After several minutes of concentrated struggle by the two women, Nicki lost her patience. "Levi Cantrell, if you don't stop acting like a big baby and drink your medicine, I'm going to smack you!" For several seconds nothing happened, then, to the surprise of his two nurses, he obediently opened his mouth and drained the glass.

"That's better." Nicki gently laid him back against the pillows and smoothed his hair back from his forehead.

"She's got a damn nasty right punch," he muttered.

Emily and Nicki exchanged a dumbfounded look, then laughter gurgled from both at the same time. "I don't even want to know how he came by that information," Emily said.

"I only hit him once, but I guess I made an impression." Nicki grinned in spite of the blush she felt creeping up her neck. "At least we got the quinine down him."

"Yes, and I don't need to worry about leaving you alone to watch him while I go get some sleep." Emily smiled as she adjusted the bedclothes. "It's obvious Levi knows who's boss." Her grin faded as she felt his

forehead again. "Keep bathing him with cool water to
hold the fever down. You can expect it to break about
noon or a little after, but I should be back by then.
He'll be due for another dose of quinine around one."

Engaged in the endless task of battling the fever
with cool washcloths, Nicki found little time to dwell
on the night before. Obviously delirious from the heat
burning within, Levi mumbled as he tossed and
turned on the bed.

Over the course of the morning Nicki learned an
amazing amount of information about Levi Cantrell
and the people in his life. She was pretty sure that
Cole, Charlie, Kate, and Pa were his family, and it
was obvious he was very close to them all.

Then there were Cynthia and Stephanie. Cynthia
had hurt Levi badly sometime in the past. First he
talked of how much he loved her. Then he cursed
her over and over. Whatever she'd done had left a
permanent scar on his heart. Nicki disliked Cynthia
intensely.

Stephanie she hated. Whenever Levi mentioned
her, his face would soften. The more he talked, the
less Nicki wanted to hear. Stephanie was beautiful.
Stephanie was kind. Stephanie could ride like the
wind. Stephanie was an excellent cook. Stephanie
had held a cattle rustler at gunpoint. Nicki had to
admit, that one intrigued her. Even so, she refused to
change her opinion of the oh-so-wonderful Stephanie,
particularly when Levi said, "Don't be a damn fool.
She's as close to perfect as you're ever going to get.
Marry her!"

It was probably a good thing Emily chose that
moment to return to the sickroom. She noted Nicki's
clenched fists and grinding teeth with surprise but

didn't ask what had prompted her niece's aggravation. "How's the patient?"

Miserable I hope, Nicki thought. "About the
same," she said aloud. "I think his fever is a little less,
but he's very restless."

Emily nodded. "I imagine he's rather uncomfortable."

"He keeps mumbling things."

"It's not uncommon to be delirious with a high
fever like this." Emily laid her hand on his brow. "I
think you're right, though. He does seem cooler. Did
you have any trouble with him?"

"No."

"Good. I fixed some lunch. Why don't you go eat
with your father and Peter?"

"What about Levi? How do we feed him?"

"I'll make some beef broth when he wakes up, but
that may not be for awhile yet."

Nicki took a deep breath of the warm air as she
stepped outside. It felt good to be out of the sickroom. She decided to take a little walk before she
went to the house.

Enjoying the bright sunshine, she was almost to the
barn before it occurred to her that Levi might say
something in his delirious ramblings that she didn't
want her Aunt Emily to hear.

So far, though he'd mentioned Nicki's name quite
frequently, it was obvious she caused him more irritation than anything else. But what if he said something
about yesterday's kiss, or even about last night? Aunt
Emily was no fool. Even an obscure reference might
be enough to tip her off. Nicki quickly retraced her
steps back to the house, determined to spend as much
time at Levi's bedside as possible.

When Nicki returned in slightly less than an hour, Emily raised her eyebrows in surprise. "What's wrong?"

"Uh, nothing. I just thought I'd come back and see how he's doing."

"Did you eat your lunch?"

"Yes, and then I cleaned up the . . . Aunt Emily he's sweating!" Nicki stared at the beads of perspiration gathering on Levi's brow.

Emily nodded as she sponged the moisture from his forehead. "The fever broke just after you left. I'm afraid it will get considerably worse before it gets better."

Her prediction proved to be true. They changed his nightshirt and the bedding, but within minutes he was drenched again. The second dose of quinine, administered with another terse order from Nicki, went down with ease, and still the sweat poured from him. Whereas Nicki had spent the morning trying to keep Levi cool, now they fought to keep him dry. Twice more they changed his linens only to have them soaked almost immediately.

At long last the deluge seemed to slow, and Emily sat back with a sigh. "I think the worst of it is over." She mopped her own brow and smiled wanly. "It appears that Levi does nothing halfway. I don't remember when I've seen anybody sweat that hard, even with malaria."

It took ten minutes for the two women to change everything yet a fourth time. "Now we have to replace all the fluid he lost," Emily said. "I'd best go make that beef broth. He'll be needing it soon." At the door she paused a moment. "Give him as much water as you can get him to take."

"How? I don't think I can force it down him by myself."

Emily grinned. "I'm not so sure about that, but you won't have to. He could wake up any time."

With that, she was gone, leaving Nicki alone with the last person she wanted to face right now. What would she say to him? Looking down at his sleeping face, she shifted nervously.

Maybe she was worrying for nothing. Levi slept deeply, the first real sleep he'd had all day. He probably wouldn't wake up for hours yet. As soon as Emily opened the door Nicki would make her escape. Relieved, she reached up to wipe his brow once more.

At that precise second Levi opened his eyes and gazed up at her. "Nicki?"

A thousand butterflies danced in her stomach as she stared down into the blue-gray depths of his eyes. "Y . . . yes, Levi, I'm here." Her hand shook slightly as she smoothed the hair back from his forehead.

Levi glanced around the unfamiliar room. "Where am I?"

"Aunt Emily's room. Don't you remember?"

He blinked up at her in confusion. "The last thing I remember is shooting a snake out from under your foot. How did I get here?"

A wave of shock ran through her. He had no memory of their shared intimacy! She rose and filled a glass from the pitcher. "You've been sick. Aunt Emily says you need to drink lots of water."

Obediently he raised his head and drank, then fell back against the pillow in exhaustion. "My God, what do I have?"

"Aunt Emily says malaria."

"The doc said it might come back. How long have I been out?"

"Only since last night." *Last night when you held me in your arms and made love to me,* Nicki thought bleakly. Her secret was safe, and yet she didn't feel the relief she should.

"So tired," he murmured, his eyelids drifting closed. "Nicki . . ." but he was asleep before he could finish.

When he awoke again Emily was sitting next to his bed coaxing him to drink something vile from the glass she held to his lips.

"Welcome back, Levi. I was beginning to wonder when you'd join us again."

"Agh! Are you trying to poison me?"

Emily laughed as she set the empty glass on the nearby table. "Hardly. It's quinine. I realize it's rather bitter, but it won't poison you."

Levi made a face. "How could I have forgotten that nasty taste?" He looked around the room. "Did I just imagine Nicki?"

"No, she needed some rest so I sent her to bed. She spent most of the day taking care of you. You spoke to her several hours ago when you were awake briefly. I imagine you're hungry. I made you some broth, and it won't take but a minute to warm it up for you." She plumped his pillow and adjusted the blankets around him. "You just relax. I'll be right back."

Left alone, Levi tried to separate reality from the fever-induced hallucinations. Everything was cloudy except for one dream. Even now, the vivid images came back to torture him. Nicki was in his arms, responding to his caresses, running her hands lovingly over his naked body. It all seemed so real. He could still smell the scent that was uniquely hers, hear the incredibly sexy little noises she made as he loved her, feel her arching against him in the throes of ecstasy. With a groan he closed his eyes, but the images didn't go away. He even had a realistic memory of what it felt like to take her virginity, for God's sake.

Never had he experienced such a lifelike dream. The sights, the sounds, the sensations were all there, lurking in his memory, haunting him with visions that could never be. Thank God Nicki couldn't read his mind. If she knew the erotic fantasy he had created with her at the center, she'd probably shoot him with his own gun.

17

"Are you about done with the roof, Levi?" Nicki's voice rang cheerfully through the afternoon air. It had been almost a month since the big storm had torn the chunk off the barn roof, but with Levi's illness they had been too busy and shorthanded to fix it until now. Since getting the crops planted took precedence over everything else, Peter had taken only enough time to slap some boards over the hole in the barn roof before turning his attention to the newly plowed fields.

Levi looked down over the edge. "Not even close to it."

"What's taking so long?"

"A hole the size of the kitchen, that's what. Grab a hammer and come give me a hand." There was no answer from below and Levi grinned to himself. So much for harassment from Nicki.

Five minutes later he paused in mid-swing when she appeared at the top of the ladder. "What's this? Don't tell me you're actually going to help me."

"It's that or clean the chicken coop," Nicki said as she climbed onto the roof and then turned to peer down over the edge. "I'd forgotten it's so high."

"Heights bother you?"

"A little," she admitted as she crawled to Levi's side. "Show me what to do."

"This is the last board." He pounded a nail into place and pointed to the shingles stacked nearby. "It's just a matter of putting those on now."

Levi had started fixing the roof this morning and was already more than half-done. Even though Nicki had given him a hard time about not being finished, she was more than slightly impressed with how much he'd accomplished.

Nicki watched closely as Levi tacked a shingle into place and reached for another one. *Nothing to it,* she thought and moved to the other side of the bare spot. It only took her a few minutes to discover that shingling was much more difficult than Levi made it look. If the nail didn't bend, she'd hit her thumb, or the shingle would slide out of place. She was only on her second shingle by the time Levi had worked his way clear across the new board into her area. "How can you do that so easily?" she grumbled, tossing her hammer down in defeat.

"Years of practice." Levi chuckled. "My first attempts were pretty sad."

"Is carpentry another of your hidden talents?"

With three good whacks he finished nailing the shingle she'd been struggling with. "I don't know if I'd call it a talent, but it is something I like." He eyed her frustrated expression. "Why don't you hand me the shingles and I'll do the nailing?"

"It's a deal."

"So you'll brave high places and smashed thumbs to get out of cleaning the chicken coop. Seems to me, you used me as an excuse to avoid mucking out the barn a while back too." Levi kept his eyes on the nail in his fingers, but Nicki could see a grin lurking around his mouth.

"It didn't do me any good then." A mischievous sparkle entered her eye. "But this time is different. I saw Peter headed that way looking for me. When he doesn't find me, he'll have to do it himself."

Levi chuckled and shook his head. At times like this she seemed very young, but he hoped she would never lose the innocent charm that was all her own. They worked companionably side by side, each almost painfully aware of the other, but both pretending not to be.

Watching the play of Levi's muscles under his shirt gave Nicki a curious little thrill. Memories of their night together assailed her at the strangest times. His mouth moving in a certain way as he ate his breakfast, his hands gently stroking the necks of the huge workhorses as he brought them in from the field, the smooth hard line of his body as he rode out of the barnyard, had all stirred her memory.

Levi kept up a casual flow of conversation while they worked, and an unfamiliar emotion welled up within her. Her sturdy wall of defense began to weaken as vague romantic images floated through her mind.

"Did your father tell you I'll be leaving tomorrow?" Levi asked, glancing up at her from beneath the brim of his hat.

Suddenly Nicki felt as if the bottom of her stomach had fallen through the roof and plummeted clear to the ground. "Leaving? N . . . no he never mentioned it."

The rhythm of the hammer continued as he tacked another shingle in place. "With the planting done and the cows out on the range, I figured this was the best time."

Nicki took refuge in anger. "You figured it was the best time," she repeated sarcastically. "Did it ever occur to you Papa might have other things for you to do? You still owe us a couple of weeks for when you were sick, you know."

"Your father is the one who suggested I leave as soon as the barn roof was fixed," he said gently.

With tears blurring her eyes and pain clogging her throat, she blinked down at the board in front of her. "Fine. Then finish it and get the hell out of here!" Flinging the last few shingles away, she was over the side of the barn and down the ladder in two minutes flat.

"Damn," Levi muttered under his breath. He tossed his hammer aside and followed her off the roof, cursing her narrow-minded belligerence. He found her in the barn armed with a shovel and a pitchfork.

"Nicki . . ."

"I have to clean the chicken coop."

He grabbed her elbow as she attempted to brush past him. "Nicki, this is ridiculous."

"The chickens don't think so. If you don't keep it clean, the mites . . ."

He swung her around to face him, gripping her other elbow with his free hand. "I'm not talking about cleaning the chicken coop and you damn well know it. Every time things don't go exactly the way you want them to, you have a tantrum. I'm tired of it. If your father has seen fit to give me a couple of weeks off, I don't see what business you have blowing up and accusing me of not doing my job!"

"A couple of weeks?"

"That's right, two lousy weeks. I have some business to take care of."

"Business?" Nicki carefully lowered the pitchfork and shovel to rest on the floor and looked up at him suspiciously. "What kind of business?"

"It's personal." He released her arms. "I made a promise back in January that I need to keep."

"A promise to whom?"

Levi leaned the shovel and pitchfork against the wall. "A friend."

Stephanie, Nicki thought, but she couldn't bring herself to voice the name aloud. "Wh . . . what kind of promise?"

"Nothing for you to worry about." He reached down and lifted her chin with his finger. "I'll be back, Nicki."

Avoiding eye contact, Nicki tried to pull away from his grasp. "Who cares?"

"I think you do."

"Ha! Don't flatter yourself!" She finally succeeded in jerking her chin away. "I've been waiting for you to leave since the day you got here."

He almost smiled at her defiance but thought better of it. "Then I'm sorry to disappoint you. I said I'd be back and I will. That's a promise."

"And you always keep your promises?" Her tone was sarcastic, yet Levi thought he detected a faint wistfulness there as well.

"If it's humanly possible to do so. Besides I still owe you two weeks."

Nicki blushed, knowing full well what Cyrus's reaction would be if he knew she demanded such a thing. "Maybe I was a bit hasty . . ."

"Maybe you were, but then again, your father did ask me to finish the barn and I'm not doing it." He gave her shoulder a squeeze. "Thanks for your help up there. I'll see you later."

With a smile he was gone, leaving her to stare after him, painfully aware of the conflicting emotions warring within her.

It was the same unsettling feelings that forced Nicki to rise at the crack of dawn the next day in order to see him once more before he departed. With the fresh tang of the morning air came the realization that she had no excuse to be out so early. The last thing she wanted was for Levi to think she'd come specifically to see him off.

"Oh," she said in feigned surprise as she came upon him tying his bedroll onto his saddle. "I thought you'd left already."

It was all Levi could do not to grin at her artificial nonchalance. "Not quite. What brings you out so early? Come to say good-bye?"

"I was going out to gather eggs. We need some for breakfast."

"What a disappointment."

Nicki gave him a puzzled look. "The eggs?"

"No, I was hoping you'd come to say good-bye." He tightened the last set of ties on his bedroll. "I didn't sleep very well last night, just thinking about saying good-bye to you."

"Why?"

"Because I don't think you believe me when I say I'll be back." He gave Lady a final pat and turned to Nicki with the familiar twinkle in his eye. "I think I've come up with a way of convincing you, though."

"Oh, and what's that?"

With the speed of a panther pouncing on its prey, he pulled her into his arms and kissed her, his mouth warm and insistent.

Nicki returned his kiss without hesitation. Eagerly, her arms circled Levi's waist as a delicious warmth spread through her.

Then, as suddenly as it had begun, it was over. Levi released her and turned away. Nicki opened her eyes in time to see him already swinging up into the saddle.

Breathing heavily, Levi stared down at her with an odd expression on his face. "Maybe that wasn't such a good idea after all." He took a deep, steadying breath to clear his head. "Two weeks, Nicki. I promise." Nudging Lady with his heels, he turned and rode out of the yard without a backward glance.

Touching her lips with the tips of her fingers, Nicki stood gazing after him until horse and rider were long out of sight.

Leaning against the side of the barn, Peter had observed them with astonishment. When the big man had pulled Nicki into his embrace and bent to kiss her, Peter waited for the inevitable explosion. He'd watched in wonder as Nicki had melted in Levi's arms.

Isolated on the homestead, and locked in his silent world, Peter knew nothing of romantic love or courtship. He'd never even been around a happily married couple. Now, with a puzzled look on his face, he viewed Nicki's unfamiliar bemused expression with real interest. Whatever had passed between the two of them must have been mighty powerful to throw Nicki into such a pelter.

Over a week had passed since Levi's departure, a scene which Nicki had tried, unsuccessfully, to put from her mind. Over and over she mentally replayed it. He had seemed as moved by the kiss as she, and yet his words had been anything but encouraging. Levi might be attracted to her, but clearly he didn't want to be.

Glumly, Nicki tied the reins to the brake lever and climbed down from the wagon. Liana wasn't expected for several days but Aunt Emily was afraid she might arrive early. Using that for an excuse to get out of the house and away from her thoughts, Nicki had volunteered to meet the stage today. Unfortunately, the long trip to town gave her more time to dwell on the very memories she was trying to forget.

Leaning against the hitching rack in front of the store, she watched the stage rumble into town. Within minutes the only passenger, an elderly man, disembarked. The stage driver delivered the mail to the Adamses' store, and the coach departed in a choking cloud of dust. Unwilling to be alone with her own thoughts again so soon, Nicki sauntered into the store.

"Well, Nicki!" Mrs. Adams looked up from the mail she was sorting with a welcome smile. "Do you have time for a visit this morning? I just baked your favorite cake."

Nicki grinned. "I'd love a visit, but stop trying to fatten me up."

"Humph, it would take more than a few pieces of cake to . . . Why, Nicki, here's one for you."

"A letter? For me?" Nicki stared in disbelief at the white envelope Mrs. Adams placed in her hand. Who in the world could it be from? Nobody had ever written to her before. She hardly heard Mrs. Adams's friendly chatter as she followed her to the parlor directly behind the store. Anticipation gave way to a deep feeling of dread. What if it was from her mother? And if not from Samantha, who?

Her curiosity finally overcame her reluctance to admit that she couldn't read. With a determined sangfroid she handed the missive to Mrs. Adams. "Would you mind reading it for me?"

Mrs. Adams obligingly opened the envelope and scanned the single sheet. "Why, it's from Mr. Cantrell!"

"Levi?" Suddenly, Nicki's heart was pounding in her throat.

Mrs. Adams began to read. "Dear Nicki. I am writing to tell you why I can't keep my promise to return in two weeks . . ." She paused in vexation as the bell on her front door sounded. "Oh drat, I have a customer. It probably won't take long, dear. I'll be right back."

Nicki hardly noticed her leaving. *I can't keep my promise. I can't keep my promise.* Like a litany, the words kept playing over and over in her head. Numbly, she rose to her feet, picked up the letter, and headed for the door. She was vaguely aware of Mrs. Adams calling to her when she walked through the store and out into the deserted street. She climbed into the wagon, fighting the nausea that rose in her throat.

He wasn't coming back. Nicki didn't have to hear the rest of the letter to know what it said. He had thought it over and decided he didn't want to play at farming anymore, or he'd gotten a better job offer somewhere else, or whatever. The excuse didn't really matter. Levi was gone and he wasn't coming back.

With pain such as she'd never known slashing through her, Nicki picked up the reins and started for home. By the time the homestead came into view, the wall around her heart was taller and stronger than it had ever been.

18

"I'll go see if she's on the stage," Nicki quickly signed the words to Peter, then made her escape before he could ask any more questions. With the planting done, there was a lull in the work around the homestead, so Nicki had not been surprised when he'd offered to accompany her to town today. She'd even been grateful. Being alone with her thoughts was the last thing she wanted.

It wasn't long before she realized Peter had only come along to find out why she'd been so unhappy the last few days. Sidestepping his inquisition had been a severe strain on her self-control. Now, after thirty minutes of his constant badgering, she was ready to throttle him. At least she wouldn't have to put up with it anymore. She'd just make sure Peter drove home. With the reins in his hands he couldn't talk.

For the fourth day in a row, Nicki watched the stage lumber into town, wondering why she'd bothered to make the trip. Aunt Emily didn't really expect Liana until tomorrow. Nicki straightened in surprise as the door opened, and a beautiful young woman with almond-shaped eyes stepped down.

It had to be Liana. Her delicate features were a perfect blend of her dual racial heritage, the Oriental and Caucasian melding into exotic loveliness. Her skin was the color of old ivory and a thick, black braid wound around her head beneath a pert little hat. Tall and slender, she moved with willowy grace as she gazed around curiously.

"Liana?"

The young woman turned to Nicki in surprise. Then, quite suddenly, a brilliant smile lit her features. "Are you my cousin Nicole?"

"I am, but my name is Nicki."

"Nicki. Oh, I like that." Liana smiled shyly. "But I hope you won't mind if I slip occasionally. I've thought of you as Nicole ever since I can remember." All her life Liana had adored her older cousin from afar and now she smiled at Nicki hopefully.

Even Nicki couldn't hold out against all that love and admiration shining forth from the seventeen-year-old. She felt an unfamiliar glow as she wholeheartedly returned her cousin's smile. For the first time in her life, Nicki found herself trusting someone immediately.

The two women were jostled just then, as another passenger stepped off the stage. "Damn Chink," he muttered just loud enough for them to hear.

Nicki turned, her violet eyes snapping with fire. "Did you say something to me, Mister?"

"No, Ma'am. Just commenting on the trash you find on the stage and in the streets these days." His gaze raked Liana from head to foot. "It's getting so a man can't get away from it anywhere."

"I've noticed that myself, and most of it seems to be white," Nicki said angrily. "Around here, a gentleman apologizes for bumping into a lady."

"Sorry. All I saw was you and your Chink friend." The man sarcastically doffed his hat and walked away.

Staring after him, Nicki clenched her fists in a burning rage. Gently Liana laid her hand on her cousin's arm. "Never mind, Nicki. It doesn't matter." Over the years Liana had become inured to the hateful comments people made about her Chinese blood. She gave Nicki a quick hug, hoping to distract her. "It's so good to finally be here. My mother didn't come with you?"

"No, she stayed home with Papa. We really didn't expect you until tomorrow."

"Then I'll be able to surprise her," Liana said happily as they turned and walked toward the wagon. "I can't wait to see Uncle Cyrus and Peter."

"Well, you'll get your wish soon enough. Peter's right over there. Don't be offended if he seems standoffish at first. It takes him a while to get used to new people."

You mean trust them, Liana thought to herself. How well she understood the pain and humiliation Peter must have suffered in his life. She had always felt a kinship with the unknown Peter simply because they were both shunned for being different, something they had no control over.

"Here she is, Peter. Liana, this is Peter."

Smiling shyly up at him, Liana had an impression of broad shoulders, beautifully molded lips, and warm brown eyes before his mouth snapped into a forbidding frown. He removed his hat and nodded curtly to her before stomping off to fetch her bag.

"Mama never told me he was so handsome," Liana whispered in an awestruck voice.

"Handsome?" Nicki's eyebrows arched in surprise as she watched Peter walk away. "I hadn't ever thought about it. He's always just been my brother." Looking at Peter in a new light, she couldn't help but wonder what he thought of Liana.

Oddly enough, Peter was wondering the same thing. He'd been expecting a gangly adolescent, not a beautiful young woman, and the reality had stunned him. Then she'd smiled at him with a kind of awe that had twisted his guts in the strangest way. Surely Emily Patterson had told her daughter about his deafness. Why hadn't she reacted with hostility and scorn the way other people did? She would definitely bear watching.

During the ride out to the homestead, Nicki and Liana chattered like two magpies, each more and more convinced she had found a friend in the other. Peter drove the wagon, seemingly oblivious to the other two. Liana's eyes were drawn repeatedly to his square-jawed profile. He hadn't been very welcoming, but at least he hadn't looked at her as if she were some sort of loathsome insect the way most strangers did. It wasn't much, but it was a start.

Over the next few days, to the deep satisfaction of both Nicki and Liana, their friendship began to grow into a closeness neither of them had anticipated. Nicki clung to it in an effort to drive away the pain of Levi's desertion.

Countless times, she'd pulled his letter from her pocket and attempted to decipher it. Though she was able to identify individual sounds, her skills were too limited to unlock the meaning behind the letters. She always ended up frustrated and angry with herself for even trying. She'd even thought of having Emily read it to her, but the fear that Levi's desertion had something to do with their kiss kept her from it. Nicki didn't want anyone to know her wanton behavior had driven him away.

Today, she was hoeing the young beans, an activity that left entirely too much of her mind free to remember and dwell on "if onlys." The wind eliminated the necessity of swatting mosquitoes. Normally, she would have considered it a perfect day for the work she had to do, but she would have rather battled the mosquitoes than Levi's ghost.

"Nicki! Nicki!"

She straightened and smiled to see Liana flying toward her. Then she recognized a frantic quality in Liana's voice. Something was very wrong. Dropping the hoe, Nicki ran, jumping rows of immature beans as she went. They met at the edge of the field, both breathing hard, Nicki wide-eyed with fear. "What happened?"

"Your father's having an attack! Mama says come right away."

Nicki was running before Liana had finished her message. Even so, it seemed to take forever to reach the house. Once inside, she burst into her father's room, gasping for breath and shaking with terror.

Emily was frantically fanning the air, trying to help ease Cyrus's tortured breathing, but it was obviously not helping much. He was fighting for every breath he took in, the agony clearly written in the hands that fiercely gripped the bedclothes. No sooner had the life-giving oxygen entered his body than the muscles in his face and chest strained with the effort it cost to push the used air back out again. It whistled through tightly pursed lips in a frightening cacophony. Blue-tinged lips and fingernails gave mute testimony that his body was losing the desperate battle it was fighting. It hurt Nicki just to watch him.

"Nicki, thank God you're here. Check the teakettle to see if it's boiling. I'll need a big bowl and a couple of extra sheets, too." Emily's voice was steady, but Nicki could sense the urgency lying just below the surface.

Nicki sped to the kitchen, snatched the bowl she used for bread dough off the wall, and ran to her bedroom. Within seconds, the blankets and quilts lay on the floor as she jerked the sheets from her bed and hurried back to the kitchen.

With her heart pounding in her throat Nicki grabbed the handle of the now whistling teakettle and let out a yelp when it seared her hand. Ignoring the pain, she seized a dish towel, wrapped the handle, and hefted the kettle again. This time she made it clear back to the table beside her father's bed before the heat once again burned through to her hand.

Just then, Liana rushed into the room with Peter at her heels. "I found him, Mama. What do you want me to do now?"

Pouring a measure of brown powder into a mug, Emily nodded to the fan she had abandoned on the chair. "Keep fanning him while I get things ready. It doesn't help a whole lot, but it does keep fresh air where he can get it. Nicki, fill this cup with hot water and tell Peter to help your father sit up while we build a steam tent. He must be kept in an upright position, or he won't be able to breathe at all."

With Peter supporting Cyrus, Nicki and Emily quickly erected a tent with the extra sheets. From her medical bag, Emily produced a bottle of camphor, poured some into the bowl, and added hot water. Covering both Cyrus and the bowl with the tent, she let the pungent steam go to work. After five minutes, she pulled the sheet back and Liana resumed fanning for five minutes. Then, back under the sheet for another five minutes. Five minutes in, five minutes out, over and over again.

After half an hour the brew in the cup was ready, and Nicki held it to her father's lips, encouraging him as he drank the herbal tea. Then he went back under the tent. And so it went until, at long last, the worst of the attack seemed to have passed.

Cyrus's breathing was still strained, but he was no longer fighting for every breath. Emily stacked two quilts and every pillow in the house behind him to prop him into a sitting position.

"Didn't think I was going to make it that time," he said in a thin and reedy voice.

Laying his hand out flat, Emily frowned down at it. The fingernails were still a distinct blue rather than the normal pink. "You're not out of the woods yet, my friend. This New Jersey Tea should have had more of an effect too." Picking up the now empty mug, she glared into it as though it were somehow at fault.

Cyrus merely smiled and glanced out the window at the late afternoon sky.

Liana stood and walked to the door. "I'll go start supper."

Startled to discover it had grown so late, Nicki jumped to her feet. "I'd better go do the chores."

Shaking his head, Peter indicated she should stay with her father and started to leave. Then he turned back toward the bed and stood staring at Cyrus for a long moment.

"What is it, son?" Cyrus barely had the energy to lift his hands and make the signs, but it was enough.

With a look of anguish so eloquent that it hurt, Peter hurled himself across the room and knelt by the bed. With his right hand opened wide, he touched his thumb to his forehead twice in the sign for father. Grasping Cyrus's emaciated hand in his own callused palm, he held it to his cheek, silently staring down into the other man's face. His square jaw trembled, his brown eyes blurred, and for the first time since he'd lost his hearing, sound passed between his lips. "I . . . love . . . you . . . Papa."

The words were hesitant and barely understandable, but they were the most beautiful words Cyrus had ever heard. With what little strength he had left, he pulled Peter into a hug.

When the embrace ended, Peter stood up and strode out the door without another backward look.

"God, I didn't even know he could still speak." Cyrus's weak, breathy voice quavered with emotion. "I wish he truly was my son."

"Your sister knew what she was doing when she asked you to take him," Emily said rubbing his hand. "He may not be the son of your body, but he is the son of your heart. Isn't that what's important?"

"The three of us have been a family for almost as long as I can remember, Papa," Nicki said. "As far as I'm concerned, Peter's my brother."

Cyrus smiled. "And together you're invincible." He reached up and touched her cheek. "Ah, Nicki, you're the best daughter a man could have."

"Oh, Papa."

He knew then that he should tell her about the gold before it was too late, but he decided to wait until that night, after Emily went to bed. He wanted no one to know his secret but Nicki.

The herbal tea he had consumed soon had the sedative effect Emily had hoped for, and Cyrus fell into a deep sleep. Sometime during the night the wind began to blow, once again filling the air with invisible poisons. The pollens and dust that had triggered the earlier attack returned to infiltrate his lungs and wreak havoc on his already-weakened body.

Nicki was dozing in a chair next to the bed when the sudden wheezing and gasping awoke her. Grasping the situation instantly, she shook Peter, who had taken up a similar position on the other side of the bed. "Go get Aunt Emily," she rapidly signed. "Hurry!"

Peter was gone almost before her fingers stopped moving. Panicking now, Nicki started fanning Cyrus in an effort to supply him with oxygen. Suddenly his eyes popped open.

"Nicki," he gasped, "can't . . . explain. Levi . . . have . . . to . . . ."

"Papa, don't talk. Save your breath."

"Tell Levi . . . north . . . east . . . corner . . . Peter's . . . bedroom . . . ."

"Papa, please don't waste your breath on it," Nicki begged.

Drawing on the last of his reserves, Cyrus sat up and grasped Nicki's arms in a feverish grip. "NO! This . . . is . . . important . . . tell . . . Levi!"

The pained gasps between each word made Nicki realize her father was trying to tell her something he considered more important than life itself. "Tell me what you mean," she said.

"No . . . time. Promise . . . you'll . . . tell . . . Levi."

"Papa, he's not coming back," she blurted out desperately.

"PROMISE!"

"All right, I'll tell him. Only please don't try to talk anymore." Nicki was frantic. No matter what he thought Levi needed to know, his life was far more important.

With her words, Cyrus sank back against the pillows, apparently satisfied. "He'll . . . be . . . back. Gave . . . me . . . his . . . word." He closed his eyes to better concentrate on breathing.

He never opened them again during the long, long night while Emily, Nicki, and Peter struggled to save him. Emily tried everything she knew to ease his tortured breathing, but he only seemed to slip farther and farther away. Finally, just as the morning sun touched the horizon, he drew one last agonizing breath and then lay still. In the silence that followed, before the grief and feeling of loss could envelop them, the three who were left knew a sudden overwhelming sense of relief that Cyrus would suffer no more. His battle was over.

19

"*Ashes to ashes* and dust to dust." The circuit preacher's voice droned on in the bright summer sunshine.

Nicki knew she should be grateful that he had been passing through and offered to stay an extra day to give her father a good Christian burial, but it was hard to stand there and listen to the flat monotone voice.

The raw earth of the open grave lay right next to the tiny mound marked John Chandler. Today, Cyrus Chandler would join his infant son as he was laid to rest in the shallow, rocky soil. Nicki could hear the vague sound of Willow Creek as it trickled by, its stream bed nearly empty because of the drought. The air was filled with the smell of sagebrush and dust instead of the usual lush odor of growing things.

Numbly, Nicki wondered how much longer the minister would keep the handful of black-clad mourners standing in the hot sun. A trickle of perspiration ran between her breasts beneath her borrowed clothing. Aunt Emily had produced an extra black dress that fit Nicki surprisingly well. She thought she should be crying, but she couldn't. There were no tears left to cry, no more pain left to feel, only a horrible emptiness. A nudge from Aunt Emily brought her out of her reverie to discover that the preacher had finished at long last. She leaned down, scooped up a handful of soil, and dropped it on the pine coffin below.

She turned away and walked to the edge of the cemetery so her friends and neighbors could pay their respects. "Such a nice service . . . If there's anything I can do . . . It's a blessing he doesn't have to suffer anymore . . . I'll miss him . . ." People spewed out meaningless platitudes because they didn't have the faintest idea what to say. The crowd was small, but the receiving line seemed to go on forever. Then the last man stood silently before her.

Nicki looked up into the ice blue eyes of Herman Lowell, and goose bumps rippled over her skin. For the first time, she realized that now only she and Peter stood between Lowell and what he wanted, the Willow Creek spring. A muscle in his jaw flexed as he turned the hat he held in his hands. Nicki wondered if he was going to demand they pack up and leave immediately.

When he finally spoke, his words were a complete surprise. "Cyrus and I had our differences, but he was a damn good man. The world won't be the same without him."

Stunned, Nicki could only stare after him as he walked away.

*   *   *

Finally the day was over. The funeral meal had been
eaten and cleared away. The preacher, undertaker,
and grave digger had been paid, and all the well-wish-
ers had finally gone home. The family sat around the
kitchen table, staring at one another, unsure what to
do now.

"Aunt Emily." Nicki toyed with her cuff. She felt
oddly shy about the request she was about to make,
but a night alone in the empty house was untenable.
"You and Liana must be crowded in the room you've
been sharing. Papa's room is . . . well I was thinking
maybe you'd be more comfortable there."

"Oh no, we're f . . ." Emily caught a fleeting look of
dismay in her niece's eyes and changed her mind.
"You know, that might be nice. Liana snores."

"Mama!"

"I'm sorry, my love, but it's quite true." She turned
to Nicki and Peter with a sad shake of her head. "We
tried to take in a boarder one year, but he couldn't
abide the awful racket at night."

From the sparkle in Liana's eye it was apparent this
was an old joke between them. "Actually it was
Mama's cooking. She baked biscuits the first morning
he was there. He didn't come back for supper."

"No, no, he said it was the snoring he couldn't stand.
Claimed he could hear it right through the walls."

Peter had been following the conversation closely,
but having no concept of the word snore, he was confused. "What does Liana do?" he asked Nicki.

With a few quick gestures she explained Liana was
making noise when she slept, so loud, in fact, that the
sound carried through walls.

After contemplating this for several seconds, Peter shook his head and started to sign.

"It must have been the biscuits that made him leave," Nicki interpreted the words as they flowed from his hands. "I sleep next door and I hear nothing." Peter smiled ever so slightly.

The three women stared at him with identical stunned expressions and then simultaneously burst into giggles. The giggles became guffaws, and soon all four were laughing uproariously, as their souls sought to shake off the despondency. Vaguely aware that Peter's joke hadn't warranted such a high degree of hilarity, they all, nevertheless, felt cleansed and rejuvenated.

Nicki slid back her chair and stretched. "I think I'll go change clothes and then help you switch rooms, Aunt Emily."

Liana and Emily helped with the heartbreaking task of storing away Cyrus's things in an old trunk. The three women had Emily moved in by the time Peter had finished the chores, and life began to take on a new normalcy without Cyrus.

Later that night, Nicki relaxed for the first decent sleep she'd had in several days. Just as her eyes began to drift closed, an odd thought flitted through her consciousness. Even in the horror of the last few days there was some good to be found. Levi Cantrell had hardly crossed her mind at all.

Once again Nicki was hoeing the beans when Liana came to the field. With a feeling of dread, Nicki laid down her hoe and went to meet her cousin halfway. "What's wrong?"

"Mr. Lowell is here to see you. Mama's filling him with chatter and coffee, but I don't think he's here for a social visit."

Nicki's stomach felt heavy as lead. She'd known it was coming; she just hadn't been sure when or how. Suddenly Cyrus's words came back to her. *Together you're invincible.* "Peter's cleaning the ditch on the other side of the creek," she said to Liana. "Will you go get him for me? I'll show you the signs in case he doesn't understand you."

"I knew you'd want him so I practiced all the way up here. I think I know most of them."

Nicki's eyes widened in surprise. "You know sign language?"

"No, I just started learning, but I've been watching very closely, and Peter's been helping me."

"He has?" Nicki was incredulous. Liana had been here less than three weeks and Peter was teaching her to sign? He'd never done anything like that before. "You'll have to tell me sometime how you managed that. All right, show me what you're going to say to Peter then."

Slowly Liana signed the words and Nicki nodded her approval. Only the sign for Herman Lowell was missing. This Nicki provided by placing all five fingers around her nose and then pulling her hand out to a point.

Liana copied the gesture with a puzzled expression. "What does it mean?"

"It's the sign for wolf. I've always thought it was appropriate. The man is cunning and ruthless. Tell Peter to get to the house as fast as he can."

But Nicki didn't hurry as she walked back to the house. Let him wait. Aunt Emily could effortlessly keep up a flow of conversation for hours if necessary, and Nicki needed time to think. For the first time in her life, she stopped to consider the best course to follow before rushing in.

It was important to let Herman Lowell know immediately that they could not be bullied and had no intention of leaving. But how was she to do that? Belligerence only made her appear childish, and threats were useless against a man like him.

What was it Levi had said just before that first shattering kiss? He'd been angry, but perhaps there was a grain of truth in his advice. *Why don't you try acting like a woman, then maybe people will start treating you like an adult.* How did a woman act? She had a momentary flash of her mother in a seductive pose and pushed it away with irritation. For Samantha it had been extremely effective, but Nicki wouldn't resort to such tactics even if she knew how.

Then she thought of Aunt Emily, unfailingly polite but always in control of every situation. Her self-assurance carried her through everything she did. When Emily had first arrived, Nicki had been prepared for an ugly confrontation, one that never materialized simply because Emily never allowed it to. Though Aunt Emily's ways were as foreign to her as Samantha's, Nicki decided to try playing it her way. It might even work.

And so it was a very self-possessed young lady who entered her home a few minutes later and hung her hat on the hook by the door. "It's so good of you to drop by, Mr. Lowell," she said with a smile. She walked to the table and extended her right hand. "Is Amanda with you?"

Lowell had no choice but to rise and shake her hand. "No, my daughter went into town this morning."

"How disappointing. We haven't had a chance to visit since she came home." Nicki sat next to her aunt and nodded toward Lowell's empty chair. "Please sit down, Mr. Lowell." With a glow of satisfaction, Nicki realized she had just put Herman Lowell firmly into the role of visitor. Perhaps there was something to this feminine power. "How nice that Mr. Laughton has time to escort Amanda to town," she said conversationally.

"He left last week."

"Oh, that's too bad. He seemed like a very nice young man."

Lowell's expression darkened. "And about as worthless as teats on a bull," he muttered. Then he blushed. "Pardon me, ladies."

Nicki had a strong desire to laugh out loud at his discomfiture but settled for watching his ears change color. "More coffee, Mr. Lowell?"

"No, thank you." His impatience was beginning to show. "Nicki . . . Miss Chandler, this isn't a social call."

"Oh?"

"No, I came to discuss business, and I haven't got all day, so . . ."

"I'm sorry, Mr. Lowell, but if you want to discuss business, we'll have to wait until my brother Peter gets here."

"Peter? You mean the dummy?"

"No, I don't mean the dummy. I mean my brother Peter. But don't worry, I sent Liana out to the field after him. He'll be here any minute."

Herman Lowell's shock clearly showed in his face. "God, Samantha never told me he was her son."

Nicki's eyes flashed fire. "I can't imagine why you think you should know everything about my family. I'm sure you and my mother didn't spend much time discussing such things."

"I . . . no, we didn't." Herman Lowell had the grace to look embarrassed.

"Nicki, my dear, I believe I'd like some more of that coffee if you don't mind." Emily's hand on her arm and her controlled voice brought Nicki to her senses. Lowell hadn't even begun, and already she was on the verge of losing her temper. That would mean disaster.

In an effort to calm down, Nicki considered how upset Samantha would be if she knew her former lover thought that Peter was her son. She had to bite the inside of her cheek to keep from grinning.

Filling Emily's cup with coffee and getting one for herself allowed Nicki time to rein in her temper. Emily picked up the conversation and carried it almost completely by herself until Peter and Liana finally appeared at the door a few minutes later.

Herman Lowell experienced another unpleasant surprise. Like most people, he had always thought of Peter much as one would an idiot. The young man seating himself across the table was not what he expected. He was clearly wary and angry, but most assuredly not feebleminded. Lowell had seen this same young man affect a slack-jawed blank stare at least a dozen times. It was an act, apparently, for now there was a spark of intelligence in the young man's dark brown eyes and an aura of power about his strong muscular body that Lowell had never even suspected before. No, this man was anything but an idiot.

"Now then, Mr. Lowell. What was it you wished to discuss with my brother and me?" Nicki asked sweetly.

"I want to buy this place."

"I'm sorry, Mr. Lowell." Nicki managed a regretful look. "It's not for sale."

"But you haven't even heard how much I'm willing to pay."

"It doesn't matter." Her fingers flying, Nicki interpreted the conversation for Peter even though she knew he could understand Lowell's words almost as well as she could. "We've spent years building this place. Papa put his whole life into it. It's our home and it's not for sale at any price."

"How do you plan to keep on going here? With only the two of you, I don't see how you possibly can."

"You forget my father was sick for a long time. Peter and I have managed quite well for the last two years. We'll get by the way we always have."

"If you'll pardon my saying so, I think you give yourselves too much credit. First and foremost, your father was the brains behind this operation. Without him, some things he started may be difficult for you to finish. Secondly, you and . . . your brother had a great deal of help this spring, or have you forgotten Levi Cantrell?"

"Mr. Cantrell was merely a hired hand. He'll be easy to replace."

Herman Lowell gave a snort of laughter. "That proves how little you know. Men of Cantrell's stamp are few and far between."

"Oh?" Nicki couldn't quite keep the sarcasm from her voice. "You know him well?"

Sensing that he'd found a vulnerable spot, Lowell pressed his advantage. "You can learn a lot about a man over a good bottle of whiskey. Mr. Cantrell and I spent a congenial evening discussing his coming to work for me."

Nicki felt as though a giant fist had slammed into her gut. "Working for you?" she whispered.

At her stricken look Herman Lowell almost relented. She reminded him too much of the woman he'd loved and lost. "We couldn't come to an agreement, but it appears he took my advice."

"Advice?"

Lowell nodded. "I pointed out what a bad idea it is to be on the wrong side of a range war and suggested he might be smart to move on if the drought got any worse."

It was only the sudden presence of Emily's reassuring hand on her leg under the table that kept Nicki from falling apart. Reminding herself how much depended on her ability to carry this off, she nonchalantly took a sip of her coffee and regarded Herman Lowell over the rim of the cup. "I really don't see what Levi's reasons for leaving have to do with you wanting to buy this place. We still have no intention of selling out."

Nicki was the picture of calm self-assurance, but the pain, oh God, the pain. She had thought nothing could hurt her more than Levi's letter. How wrong she'd been. Then, from somewhere deep inside came a blast of anger so intense it stiffened her spine and hardened her heart.

So Levi Cantrell had walked out of her life forever because of a nebulous threat from a powerful man. So what? She didn't need him. She never had. Self-pity was a luxury she couldn't afford. Even now, the thought of him was distracting her when she needed all her wits about her. She resolutely pushed Levi Cantrell from her mind.

Herman Lowell could tell he'd struck a nerve and was unwilling to give up his advantage. "Without him you'll have trouble keeping up everything you've started."

She carefully set her cup back on the table and looked Herman Lowell squarely in the eye. "What we do or do not do here is our business, not yours."

"I'm not so sure about that." He looked around the room. "This homestead has always seemed a little too prosperous to me."

Nicki frowned. "Just what are you getting at?"

"Somebody's been rustling my cattle, a few at a time."

"And you think we're doing it?" Her anger started to rise but before she could respond to Lowell's accusation, Peter's quick-fingered reply drew her attention. "Peter wants me to interpret for him," she said, but her ill humor was thinly disguised as she repeated Peter's words out loud.

"I know why you think we rustle your cattle. When cows disappear we are the most obvious suspects. Who else is around? That's why we're the last people who would steal from you. This is the first place you'd come to look for the thieves. Our herd is so small you could tell immediately if we had any extra calves, and a cow with a doctored brand would be impossible to hide. We couldn't even butcher them and sell the meat. You have enough men to watch us day and night. We'd never get away with it, and we're too smart to try. I think you know that and . . . Peter!"

Nicki gave Peter an indignant look, then vehemently shook her head. It was obvious she didn't want to finish interpreting Peter's words. It was also clear Peter was adamant she do just that. He kept placing his index finger next to his chin, rolling it away, and then pointing to Herman Lowell with an increasingly determined look on his face.

"Oh, all right." Nicki turned to Lowell, her face a fiery red. "He says he thinks you already know we haven't been rustling your cattle, and you're just trying to make me mad enough to lose control."

It was only years of keeping his thoughts to himself that kept the amazement from showing on Herman Lowell's face. The dummy had read his motives exactly, leaving Lowell with the uncomfortable conviction that he'd underestimated his opponents, both of them. *What now? Reasoning perhaps?* He sighed.

"Look, Nicki, I don't want to hurt you, but I need water for my cattle. All but two of the ponds are gone, three of the five creeks on the range are already dry, and the other one won't last too much longer. Willow Creek is less than half of normal, and you're diverting most of that for your crops."

Nicki could barely control her anger. "Papa took out a water right on Willow Creek four years ago. We aren't taking a drop of water that doesn't belong to us. In fact we're actually entitled to more than we're using. I can show you the legal papers."

Herman Lowell slammed his fist down on the table. "I don't give a damn if you have a hundred documents. For twenty years I've used that spring to water my herds, and now it's suddenly yours? I have two thousand head of cattle that I refuse to let die of thirst because the government gave you a flimsy piece of paper."

He rose to his feet and glared down at Nicki. "If we don't get rain soon, you can bet I'll be back, and it won't be to talk. I'd rather buy you out, but if it's a range war you want, you'll get it." He turned on his heel and strode angrily to the door.

"Mr. Lowell?" Nicki said softly.

He turned to face her.

"You forgot your hat." She held it out to him with a smile. "Be sure to give my regards to Amanda."

He glowered at her for a few seconds before he shoved his hat on his head and walked out, slamming the door behind him.

"Whew!" Nicki collapsed into her chair and wiped her hand across her eyes. "Was he mad!"

"Yes, he was, and probably surprised as well." Emily beamed at her niece and Peter. "Your papa would be so proud of you two. How ever did you manage to keep your temper, Nicki?"

Nicki laughed. "I just pretended to be you. I figured as effective as your tactics were on me, they would surely work on Herman Lowell." She grinned. "I wasn't wrong."

"You pretended . . ." Emily was clearly stunned by her niece's admission. "I'm very flattered, but I don't think I'd have handled that nearly as well as you did, my dear." She sighed. "So what do we do now?"

Peter walked to the window and gazed worriedly after Herman Lowell. "We wait," he signed. "We wait."

20

"*Nicki?*" Emily peered into the barn. "Nicki, are you in there?"

A huge forkful of hay sailed down from the hayloft and landed in the feedbox. "I'm up here." Nicki put down her pitchfork and looked over the edge. "Something wrong?"

"I'm not sure. There's a rider coming in."

Without hesitating Nicki stabbed the pitchfork into a pile of hay, picked up her father's rifle, and scrambled down the ladder. "How far away?"

"Close. He was nearly to the bend in the road when Liana spotted him. She went to find Peter and I came here."

"There isn't much time then. I hope Peter hurries." In fact, by the time Nicki got to the big double doors, the stranger had already ridden past the house and was headed straight for the barn. A second horse followed him, led by a rope.

Squinting out into the bright sunlight after the darkened barn, Nicki had trouble focusing on the rider. Her mouth went dry, and her breath seemed to stick in her throat. Was he just a stranger passing through or a hired gun sent by Herman Lowell to drive them away? With her heart pounding, Nicki readied her rifle and stepped from the barn.

Unaware of her presence, the stranger started to dismount.

The minute the first booted foot touched the ground, Nicki pulled back the hammer. "Freeze!"

He froze with his arms stretched above him, one foot on the ground and the other still in the stirrup.

With catlike stealth, Peter suddenly appeared at her side, and Nicki breathed a sigh of relief. Just knowing she wasn't alone made her feel stronger. "All right, Mister, now back away real slow and keep those hands in the air."

Slowly, he removed his foot from the stirrup and turned. With the sun behind him it was difficult to see his face, but she could tell he was wary as he faced her.

"What do you want, Mister?"

His eyebrows lifted in surprise. "I thought I had a job here."

The familiar, deep voice rolled over Nicki like warm molasses and brought her heart slamming into her throat.

"Levi?" Moving around so the sun was out of her eyes, Nicki took a good look at his clean-shaven face. Without the heavy beard he was almost unrecognizable. He looked ten years younger, and decidedly handsome. There was even the suggestion of a dimple in his firm chin. Something deep inside

Nicki quivered, and pure joy bubbled through her at the sight of him. *God, he's beautiful.* The thought flitted through her mind before she could stop it.

Nicki glanced toward Peter and found him grinning at her, as he leaned his rifle up against the barn. She might have known he'd think it was funny that she hadn't recognized Levi.

Suddenly, intense anger boiled up in her. If Levi thought he could come back after more than a month and expect to pick up where he left off, he was about to find out how wrong he was. "Right, Cantrell, you had a job. Not anymore. You can climb right back on your horse and ride out."

"But I just got here."

"Too bad."

Peter gave her an exasperated look. "Don't be stupid, Nicki," he signed. "We need him."

"No, we don't." Nicki continued to hold the rifle trained on Levi. Peter could just read her lips, she decided angrily. "I can't believe you'd even suggest it, considering what we know."

Peter rolled his eyes in disgust. "What we were told was a lie, and you know it. If you send him away, what will we do when Herman Lowell comes again?"

"Herman Lowell doesn't scare me."

"Then you are empty-headed. He will kill us if he has to." Peter shook his head. "As always, you will do what you want. I can't stop you." He picked up his rifle and walked away, his disapproval obvious.

Levi put his hands down. If Herman Lowell was on the rampage, this hostile reception almost made sense. "Nicki, what's happened?"

"None of your business."

"All right." He turned toward the house. "I'll just go ask Cyrus."

"You can't," she said. "He's dead."

Levi whirled around and stared at her in astonishment. "Dead?" An endless second passed while he digested the unwelcome news. Then he closed his eyes and drew in a ragged breath. "When?"

Nicki toyed with the idea of refusing to speak about it, but Levi and her father had been good friends. "Last week. He had an attack."

Levi took off his hat and ran his fingers through his hair. "I'm sorry, Nicki. I wish . . . God . . . if only there was something I could do."

"You could have been here." She glared at him. "Papa expected you back in two weeks, and you didn't come. He trusted you, and you let him down."

Levi's eyebrows rose a fraction. "But he knew my plans had changed."

"How was he supposed to know that?" Nicki asked sarcastically. "By reading your mind?"

"Didn't you get my letter?"

"Your letter said you weren't coming back."

"No, it didn't." Levi looked confused. "I'm sure I explained . . ."

Nicki stared at him for several seconds then she reached into her shirt pocket to retrieve the letter.

Holding the dog-eared envelope in his hand, Levi felt a rush of warmth. The letter was practically worn out from handling. She must have carried it around with her for weeks. It still retained the heat of her body and he had to resist the urge to hold it to his nose to catch her scent. Carefully unfolding the tattered paper, he read the words he'd written nearly a month before.

Dear Nicki,

I am writing to tell you why I can't keep my promise to return in two weeks. Something unexpected has come up and I must go to St. Louis. I don't know how long my business there will take, but I should be able to complete it in a few days. Barring unforeseen difficulties I'll be back by the middle of June. I should make it in plenty of time for haying. Please tell your father that I haven't forgotten my promise. He'll know what I mean. I'm sorry I have to be away longer than I had planned, but I'll be back as soon as I can.

Yours, L. Cantrell.

When he finished reading, Levi glanced up to find Nicki gazing at him with an expression of total disbelief on her face.

"Is that what it says?"

"Didn't you read it?"

Nicki's neck and face turned a deep red. "N . . . not exactly."

"What do you mean not exactly? Either you read it or you di . . ." Sudden comprehension stopped him in mid-sentence. "You don't know how, do you?" he asked softly. "Oh, Lord, Nicki, I didn't realize . . ."

She looked away in embarrassed silence.

"You thought I wasn't coming back." He reached down and removed the rifle from her slack hold. "I don't even want to know what you've been thinking of me all this time."

"Levi! Thank goodness you're back." Emily was walking quickly across the barnyard, a broad smile on her face.

"Welcome home." She stopped in her tracks as she caught sight of his clean-shaven face. "Well, I declare. You certainly look different."

Levi grinned. "An improvement I hope."

With an inward sigh, Nicki stepped away. Apparently Peter had gone directly to Aunt Emily, and the two of them were determined to keep Levi here at all costs. Knowing she was outmaneuvered, Nicki retreated to the barn, secretly glad to have the decision taken out of her hands.

Torn between joy and dismay, she climbed up into the mow and began tossing hay down into the feedbox. The attraction she felt for Levi was impossible to deny, but she knew she couldn't let it rule her. In spite of everyone else's favorable opinions, Levi Cantrell was still a drifter, plain and simple. For the moment, he was content to stay, but for how long? A few months at most, certainly not beyond the end of the summer.

The pain of the last five weeks had taught her how foolish it was to let herself care for him. She would have to keep him at arm's length. Cool, detached friendship was the safest course to follow. His kisses robbed her of rational thought, and spending another night in his arms was unthinkable.

Less than ten minutes later Levi entered the barn. "Nicki?"

She wanted to run and hide in the back of the haymow, but she had to face him sometime. Reluctantly, she peered over the edge of the loft. "What do you want?"

"I brought you something."

"From St. Louis?"

"No, but I think you'll like this better than anything I might have bought you there."

"My birthday isn't until October."

Levi shrugged. "This isn't a present." His eyes twinkled mysteriously. "It's something I owe you."

Intrigued in spite of herself, Nicki stuck the pitchfork in a pile of hay and climbed down the ladder. "Well?"

"It's outside."

Struggling to hide her curiosity, Nicki followed him out into the sunlight and over to the corral.

"What do you think?"

Glancing around the barnyard she could see nothing unusual. Levi's two horses and Peter's gelding all stood in the shadow of the barn contentedly munching hay. Otherwise, the entire area was deserted. Nicki glanced at Levi questioningly.

He just grinned and leaned on the corral as though waiting for something.

Perplexed, she turned back to the horses. All at once an incredible idea burst upon her. "You mean your new horse?" she squeaked.

Levi chuckled. "Not my new horse. Yours."

Nicki looked back at the dappled gray mare with new eyes. The animal was a graceful combination of delicate bones and sleek muscles. The compact body, proudly arched neck, and small head were unlike any Nicki had ever seen before. The combination was stunning.

"She's beautiful." Nicki's eyes sparkled with excitement. "Where did she come from?"

Levi was pleased with her reaction. "Her dam is the result of a cross we tried using an Arabian stallion."

"We?"

"My . . . friend and I." With a sinking feeling Levi cursed himself for the slip. Now was definitely not the time to tell Nicki he was part owner of a horse and cattle ranch nearly as big as the Bar X. She'd already lost enough trust in him. "This little lady will never be up to my weight. Luckily, I happened to know a young woman who isn't overly large herself."

"Your friend doesn't mind?"

"No. I told him about the fire and he agreed I owed you a mare."

"Charlie?"

Levi was astonished. "How do you know about Charlie?"

"You talked a lot when you were sick. Charlie's name seemed to come up whenever you mentioned horses."

Levi relaxed slightly. "That's not surprising. Horses are his life."

Nicki wanted to protest his generosity, but when she turned back to Levi she froze. He stood there with one foot resting on the bottom pole of the fence, his arms crossed on the top as he contentedly watched the horses. The light cotton shirt was stretched taut over his arms and back, outlining the bulky muscles beneath. Unconsciously Nicki's eyes slipped lower to his slim hips and long muscular legs.

Embarrassed by an unexpected reaction deep within her body, she forced her gaze back up to his face and encountered a profile that set her heart pounding. She swallowed convulsively and turned back to the corral to stare unseeingly at the horses. How in God's name was she going to remain cool toward him when just looking at him made her feel this way?

"You don't owe me a horse," she finally said.

"Don't I?" Levi's expression was gentle as he lifted his hand to rub the backs of his fingers against her cheek. "If it hadn't been for me, you'd still have Lollipop."

Nicki jerked away from his touch as though she'd been burned. "That's ridiculous. Her leg was broken, you just happened to be the one who shot her."

"Neither of you would have even been out there if Lady hadn't come home without me." He hadn't missed her reaction, and it disturbed him. There'd been no recoil after that soul-wrenching good-bye kiss, so why did a mere touch set her off now? To see what she'd do, he reached out to brush a stray curl from her forehead. He frowned when she flinched. "What is it, Nicki?"

"I told you before," she snapped, trying to control her racing heart. "I don't like to be touched."

It was impossible to miss the pain that flashed through his eyes, but it was gone almost as quickly as it appeared. "I forgot. I'm sorry." He decided to change the subject. "The mare's only green-broke, so it's up to you to finish gentling her."

"When can I start?"

"How about now?"

"Really?" Excitement shone from her face as she clambered over the fence.

Levi followed more slowly, feeling a small sting of regret for the generous impulse that had sent him to St. Louis. He had smoothed the path of love for his brother and Stephanie, but at what cost to himself? He wasn't back where he started with Nicki but had suffered a severe setback. At least she'd accepted his gift. For a minute or two, he'd thought she meant to turn it down.

When he joined her in the corral, Nicki turned to him with shining eyes. "What's her name?"

"As far as I know, she doesn't have one yet."

"How about Wildfire?" Nicki laughed as the little mare nuzzled her shoulder. "See, even she thinks it's appropriate."

Silently Levi agreed, thinking how the name fit the owner as well as the horse.

21

The sun beat down on the small cemetery as Levi made his way through cactus and brown tufts of prairie grass. It was a serene place, though not especially pretty. In good years Willow Creek flowed around it on two sides, surrounding the area with chokecherry bushes, willows, and an occasional cottonwood tree.

Glancing around, Levi gave a wry grin. Ever practical, the settlers had placed the graveyard here, where common sense dictated it should be. High enough to be safe from flooding, far too rocky to farm, and covered with grass too sparse for grazing, the land was useless for anything else.

Cyrus Chandler's grave was not difficult to locate. The pile of rocks and freshly dug earth stood out among the handful of older mounds with their covering of Russian thistle and buffalo grass. A bouquet of withered wildflowers lay in the middle of the grave.

Staring down at the sad little offering, Levi wondered where they had come from; so few plants had bloomed this summer.

He'd come to say good-bye to a man he'd called friend and found it unexpectedly difficult to do so. Would it have made any difference if he'd been here? Could he have somehow prolonged Cyrus's life? It was doubtful, and yet Levi couldn't quite push the thought away. At the very least he could have allayed some of the man's fears. Cyrus had died not knowing that Levi fully intended to honor his promise.

Levi had the uneasy conviction he was the only thing between Cyrus's family and one of the most powerful men in the Wyoming Territory. It was not a position he relished, but it was a responsibility he'd never turn his back on. This conflict with Herman Lowell could easily develop into a full-scale range war. How far would Cyrus want him to go? Surely he wouldn't want his loved ones to die defending their land.

They all trusted him to bring them through this, but Levi wasn't sure he could. If Lowell decided to take desperate measures, he'd be lucky to get them out alive.

Then what? He couldn't see Nicki and Peter going back East to live with Emily and Liana. Neither of them would be happy. He wasn't sure either of them could even survive without the freedom that allowed them to be themselves.

Cyrus's gold would assure them of that freedom, but Levi had no idea where it was. He didn't even know where to start looking.

"Levi!"

He turned to find Nicki walking toward him. "I

came to pay my respects," he said when she reached his side. "Cyrus was a good friend."

"I know." She knelt by the grave and replaced the wilted flowers with a fresh bouquet. "He felt the same about you." With her head bowed, she was silent for several minutes. When she finally spoke, her voice was even huskier than usual. "I keep thinking I'll walk in, and he'll be sitting at the table drinking coffee."

Levi nodded. "I do, too."

Surreptitiously wiping her eyes with the back of her hand, Nicki stood up and brushed the dirt from her pants.

"Did you see Stephanie while you were gone?" she asked with feigned nonchalance and almost smiled at the incredulous look on his face. "When you were sick you . . ."

"I know, I talked a lot. What other little odds and ends of my life did I tell you?"

She turned and started back toward the horses. "You talked about your family mostly." Nicki gave him a sidelong glance. "And Stephanie. She's the reason you left isn't she?"

"She's part of it." Levi felt a surge of relief as he untied his horse and swung up into the saddle. If Nicki knew about Stephanie and Cole, she'd understand why he had to give them a push in the right direction. "She'd already left for St. Louis when I got there."

An invisible hand tightened around Nicki's throat as she joined him. "And you followed her?"

"I didn't know what else to do. It took me close to a week to find her, but it was easy enough to convince her to come back to Wyoming."

"She . . . she came back?"

"Not yet, she had some business to take care of first. I expect she'll be free as soon as she can." He shrugged. "We'll just have to see how things progress from there." *If my pigheaded brother has any sense at all, he'll marry her the minute he sets eyes on her again,* he added to himself.

"Is she beautiful?"

"Very. Cinnamon hair, green eyes, she's pretty all right and a good cook, too." *But not nearly as interesting as a little tomboy with violet eyes, black curls, and a spitfire temper.* Knowing full well how angry the words would make her, he didn't dare say them aloud.

"It sounds like she'll make somebody a wonderful wife," Nicki said with a tinge of sarcasm.

"I'm counting on it."

Nicki wanted to slap the self-satisfied smile from his face, but she resisted the temptation. What right did she have after all? He had no memory of their shared intimacy, and his kisses had been those of a friend, at least in his mind. It would make things easier for her, she told herself. Since he belonged to another woman, she should have no problem keeping him at arm's length.

"Who's this?" Levi asked softly, pulling his rifle from his scabbard. A single rider was coming toward them, his horse thundering down the road in a cloud of dust.

"It looks like one of the Donaldson boys," Nicki said after a moment. "I wonder why he's in such a hurry."

"Guess we'll find out soon enough."

Within seconds the boy had reached them and

pulled his horse to a halt. "Nicki, please you've got to help me!"

"What's wrong, Jeremy?"

"It's Ma. The baby's coming too soon. Pa sent me for Dr. Calder, but he's drunk, and Mrs. Adams said your aunt was a nurse, so I come to fetch her." It all came out in a rush, the childish voice quavering pitifully.

One look at the terrified boy decided things for Nicki. "You did exactly the right thing. I'll ride over to your place now and you go with Mr. Cantrell to get my aunt. You'll have to show them the way."

"Wait a minute," Levi protested. "What do you know about delivering babies?"

"That's why you're going to get Aunt Emily."

"You don't have any idea what to do."

She gave him a scornful glance. "Look, I may not be able to do anything for Jeremy's mother, but there are six little Donaldsons I can keep out of the way. Now stop arguing with me, and go get my aunt." She wheeled Wildfire around and was gone.

"We'd better get moving," Levi said with an encouraging smile at his young companion. Turning toward home, Levi couldn't help grinning when he thought of Nicki riding off to the rescue. He doubted she knew any more about taking care of children than she did about delivering babies.

Hours later Nicki and Levi rode into the farmyard. It had been long after dark when they had left Donaldson's, but Nicki had insisted on riding home with him.

She sighed as the outline of the house came into view. "I can't remember when I've been so glad to see home. If I ever mention getting married, remind me what today was like."

Levi chuckled. "You did all right. Mr. Donaldson certainly appreciated your efforts."

"Of course he did. He knows what those little devils are like, and he didn't want anything to do with them. I'll bet he even knew I came home with you instead of staying the night just to get away from the little monsters."

"What? And here I thought you just wanted to go for a ride in the moonlight." Levi's teeth gleamed in the darkness as he grinned at her.

Nicki gave a very unladylike snort. "The sky was already overcast when we started out."

A sudden flash of light split the heavens, and thunder echoed in the distance. Nicki glanced at the sky hopefully. "You don't suppose we'll get any rain do you?"

"We could," Levi said as he dismounted in front of the barn. "But it would have to last for several days before it would do much good."

"I wish Aunt Emily could have come home with us," Nicki said as she slid off her horse. "Do you think the baby will live? It's so tiny."

"Who knows? I think if anyone can save it, your aunt can."

"I haven't been around a baby since Liana."

Levi smiled as he pulled his saddle off and threw it over the sawhorse. "That was a while ago."

"They're kind of scary when they're tiny, and then they turn into . . . well, whatever the little Donaldsons are. I don't think I'm cut out to be a mother."

"I'm sure you'll change your mind when the time comes."

"Don't count on it," Nicki said darkly.

Levi's only answer was a chuckle. For awhile they curried their horses in companionable silence. Nicki's thoughts were on the approaching storm, but Levi hardly heard it. His mind was too caught up in the picture of Nicki smiling down at a tiny dark head pressed against her breast.

A particularly loud crash finally shook him from his preoccupation. "Whew! That one was close."

Nicki glanced outside as another flash lit the sky. "Would you like to stay in the house tonight?" she asked. The storm didn't really scare her, but she found herself strangely reluctant to spend the night alone in the house, especially with lightning flashing all around to disturb her sleep. "You can sleep in the other bedroom."

Levi gave her a questioning look, then accepted her invitation with a slight nod. "It might be nice to sleep in a bed at that."

In reality, it didn't prove to be nice at all. Levi was far too aware that they were alone in the house with only a single wall separating them. He spent most of the night staring at the ceiling, trying not to remember his fever-induced hallucination of an unforgettable night of passion. When he finally did fall asleep near dawn, it was to dream of little curly-haired girls and boys with violet eyes.

Peter awoke, disturbed by the bright flashes of light that zigzagged across the sky. His sleep-dulled senses instantly sprang to life as a movement at the far end of the room drew his eyes. The door to his room was moving, being pushed open by unseen hands. At first he thought he was dreaming, and a familiar sense of loathing ran through him. Many years had passed since he'd had his nightmare about Samantha and her hate-filled eyes, but the memories still haunted him. Another flash of lightning illuminated the room, and all thought of his childhood nemesis disappeared.

Liana stood uncertainly in the doorway between their two rooms, her hands twisting nervously in the folds of her demure cotton nightgown. Peter slid into his pants and got up, wondering why she had come, what she wanted from him. He lit the candle beside his bed and saw her terror-filled eyes for the first time.

"I . . . I'm afraid of storms," she said. "C . . . can I stay here with you?"

Like many of the sounds that filled his world before the illness stole his hearing, Peter had only a vague recollection of thunder. He didn't fully comprehend why she was frightened, but he did understand fear. When he was a child, Emily had often held him in her arms, rocking back and forth as she hugged him to her, keeping his anxieties at bay.

Lightning sizzled through the night once more, and he offered Liana the only comfort he had ever known. Without a second thought, she rushed into his outstretched arms, and buried her face against his naked chest, hands over her ears to block the violence of the storm. Peter closed his arms around her, as though to shield her from the sounds he couldn't hear. They stood like that for many long minutes, shudders wracking Liana's body each time the thunder and lightning crashed.

Eventually, Peter became aware of a dampness against his chest. He placed his finger under Liana's chin, gently tipped her head back, and peered down into her face. With the sight of her tear-drenched eyes, a new awareness struck him. The tickle of the thick black braid, brushing his arm as it fell to her hips, the feel of soft curves beneath the concealing nightgown, the fit of the slim, lithe body against the contours of his own hard muscles, and the sudden painful pounding of his heart all burst upon his consciousness with stunning force.

He could see his own astonishment reflected in her eyes as they gazed at each other in awestruck silence. Slowly, she raised her hand and held it against his cheek, her lips parted in wonder.

Remembering the kiss he'd witnessed between Nicki and Levi, Peter lowered his head and touched his lips to Liana's. Neither of them was prepared for the flood of desire that surged between them, sizzling along their nerves and igniting unexpected fires.

Pulling away at last, they stared at each other in complete amazement. Finally, Peter understood the unfamiliar soft radiance he'd seen on Nicki's face; he felt that way himself right now. Gently, he touched Liana's smooth cheek, sure that her starry-eyed expression was a mirror image of his own.

Though Cyrus had long ago explained the facts of life to Peter, he had never thought to mention the passions between a man and woman. The violent emotions Peter and Liana had just shared were a complete surprise, but instinctively he understood their significance. The two of them had forged a bond that set them apart from others in their togetherness.

Suddenly, the storm they had both forgotten intruded with a blinding flash of light and a nearly simultaneous crack of thunder. With a cry of fear, Liana molded herself against his solid body.

Peter swept her up into his arms, carried her to the rocking chair, and sat down with her tucked safely inside his strong embrace. Gently stroking the back of her head, he felt her relax as the lightning moved away. With her face nestled against his shoulder and her breath whispering across his chest in a feather-light touch, he gave a sigh of pure contentment. He closed his eyes to savor the incredible sensations he hadn't even known existed.

They were still there several hours later when the dawn touched their sleeping faces with the soft, enchanted light of early morning. Liana stirred against his chest and opened her eyes. In a moment of disorientation, she looked up and found herself wrapped in a warm brown gaze. Reaching out with uncertain fingers, she touched his jaw in a kind of hopeful fascination.

The color of his eyes deepened as he brushed a stray lock of hair from her face. The world disappeared for both of them as their lips met in a gentle kiss that reached into their very souls. When they drew apart at last, they smiled tenderly at each other, reassured that the magic hadn't faded in the light of day.

Suddenly Liana sat up and listened intently. With eyes shining, she jumped to her feet and tugged on his hand. "Peter, it's raining!" Practically dragging him behind her, she hurried out the door and down the dogtrot. With hands entwined, they stood watching as the rain fell softly in the early light of dawn. Then Liana caught the sound of an opening door and approaching footsteps within the house. With sudden urgency, she tapped Peter's arm and made the sign for Nicki.

Their gazes met, and a flash of understanding passed between them. The feelings they had just discovered were too new and unexplored to share with anyone else just yet. Peter caressed Liana's cheek lightly, then stepped away.

When Nicki joined them in the entryway she saw nothing unusual in Liana and Peter being there together. "It *is* raining. I couldn't believe my eyes when I looked out my window."

Liana laughed excitedly. "Isn't it wonderful? I'm going to wake Mama."

Nicki shook her head. "Aunt Emily stayed at Donaldson's last night. She sent us home about ten-thirty or so."

Barefoot and rumpled, Levi came through the kitchen side door rubbing his face. With a mighty stretch and a smile he peered out over the heads of the other three. "Now that's a sight worth getting up at the crack of dawn for."

Telling herself that she could resist any temptation Levi Cantrell presented, Nicki turned away from the tantalizing vision of muscular chest and hard flat stomach showing through his open shirt. "At least we won't have to worry about Lowell any more," she said.

She was wrong on both counts.

22

"*When was the* last time you used this?" Levi asked, contemplating the broken-down hay stacker before him.

"Not since we built the barn. We put all the hay in the loft so we didn't need the stacker." Nicki regarded him anxiously. "Can we use it?"

"Not the way it is." He walked around the huge piece of equipment, surveying it critically. "But I'm pretty sure I can fix it. All the moving parts seem to be in working order, so it's just a matter of replacing the broken boards."

"How long will that take?"

"A couple of days probably."

Nicki looked out over the field of waving grass that should have been cut two weeks earlier. "Can't you fix it any faster?"

"What's two days? That hay isn't going anywhere."

Nicki closed her eyes in exasperation. "You just

don't understand about irrigated crops. Look." She pointed to the dull coloration of the grass stalks. "See how dry it is? This field really needs be irrigated again, but if we do it now, we won't get the horses out here for another week."

"If you're in such a hurry, why don't we just put it in the barn like you have every other year?"

"Because we planned on putting the alfalfa hay up there. We don't want to mix it with the grass hay."

Levi rubbed his chin thoughtfully as he walked around the stacker one more time. "Well, if I had help, I might be able to get finished by tomorrow evening."

The idea of spending a day and a half almost exclusively in Levi's company was nearly irresistible. It was also unthinkable. "All right then, you and Peter fix the stacker, and I'll start mowing hay. That way it will be ready to buck and stack by the time you're done."

"Wait a minute. That mower's a dangerous piece of equipment."

"So?" There was a glint in Nicki's eye as she stared up at him.

"So, I wanted to make sure it was ready to go before anybody took it out." Levi mentally kicked himself for putting her on the defensive.

With her hands planted firmly on her hips, Nicki looked at him through narrowed eyes. "You don't think I can handle it, do you?"

"I don't know." Levi shrugged, as though such a thing had never occurred to him. "Can you?"

"Don't be ridiculous. I cut the hay last year." It wasn't strictly true. Peter had done most of the mowing, with Nicki spelling him once in a while. "Besides, Peter does a much better job with a hammer."

Unable to argue with her logic and knowing it was a lost cause anyway, Levi gave in. He and Peter began work on the stacker shortly after lunch, though his eyes kept straying to the far end of the grassy expanse where Nicki was opening the field. The tiny figure sitting on the mower behind the huge team looked even smaller and more fragile than usual. In spite of Nicki's assurances that she could handle the dangerous machinery, Levi's throat tightened every time he glanced her way. All he could think of was the razor-sharp sickle blade that could cut through flesh as easily as a hot knife through butter.

Peter didn't notice Levi's nervousness. He was too busy trying to decide how to ask the most personal question of his life. Since the night of the thunderstorm, he and Liana had grown increasingly bold in their caresses. Lately the temptation to go further had become unbearable, but Peter was afraid to indulge in the activity their bodies demanded.

When Cyrus explained the mechanics of sex, Peter had asked curiously if he and Nicki might someday share the experience. Horrified, Cyrus had made him promise to never even consider such a thing. Peter hadn't understood that Cyrus was worried about intimate relations between first cousins and had gone away from the discussion thinking there must be some sort of danger involved in the sexual act itself.

Peter cared for Liana far too much even to consider doing something that might hurt her, yet the tension was getting to be more than either of them could handle. In desperation, he'd decided to ask Levi for clarification. Unfortunately, he wasn't quite sure how to do it.

Gradually, Levi became aware of Peter studying him with increasingly nervous scrutiny. "Something on your mind?" he asked.

Peter nodded slowly, then hesitantly began to sign. "I want you to tell me about men and women having sex."

Levi was shocked. The last sign was unfamiliar, but the graphic movement made the meaning very clear. Peter wanted to know about the birds and the bees for God's sake! Levi swallowed uncomfortably. How in the world was he going to explain such a thing?

"Cows and horses do it all the time," Peter went on. "Horses even seem to enjoy it."

With a flash of insight, Levi thought he understood why Peter had asked such a question. There was something rather erotic about the violent mating of horses, even to Levi, who had seen it innumerable times. It was natural for Peter to wonder how it related to his vague knowledge of human sex. "It's more gentle with people, but they like it just as much."

"Then why is it wrong?"

"I wouldn't say it's wrong. People just have a lot of rules about it."

Peter nodded. "I know, Cyrus told me. I must love the woman. I must be sure she wants to have sex too, and I can't forget that what we do makes babies. Is there more?"

Levi smiled. "No, I think that pretty well covers it."

"But, does it hurt the woman?"

"The very first time it does, but if you are careful it shouldn't after that."

Peter's eyebrows drew together into a frown. "It always hurts the first time?"

Unbidden, Levi remembered his hallucination. For the first time, he realized he'd even imagined Nicki's pain and the disillusionment in her eyes. How strange. Distracted by the thought, his answer to Peter was pensive. "I think it's possible to make the pain brief and unimportant if you concentrate on giving her pleasure first." Then he shook himself and gave Peter a rueful glance. "Actually, I haven't had much experience with virgins. I think maybe they're better left alone."

Peter had no idea what a virgin was, but he had obtained a satisfactory answer to his question. It wasn't wrong, and if he was very careful, Liana would be in no danger. Pleased, he allowed the subject to drop and went back to work.

Levi breathed a sigh of relief, glad to have been let off the hook so easily. It never occurred to him that Peter's questions weren't just idle curiosity.

That night, Peter and Liana acted on Levi's advice. With loving kisses and tender touches, they undressed each other in the soft moonlight, their explorations creating new heights of passion neither had ever imagined.

When they lay naked in each other's arms, at last, Peter concentrated on Liana's pleasure with a single-mindedness that drove them both to the brink. As Levi had predicted, Liana's pain was brief and soon forgotten in the blaze of glory that enveloped them as they consummated their love. It was a long time before they allowed their satiated bodies to finally relax into sleep.

* * *

If Peter seemed a little preoccupied the next morning, Levi hardly noticed. He was too busy worrying about Nicki working the mower. By the time the two men had the stacker repaired, the hay was nearly all cut. Even so, Levi silently breathed a sigh of relief when Nicki let Peter take over the job of mowing.

She made a mournful face as they left the field and walked toward the house. "I guess I'd better go give Aunt Emily and Liana a hand finishing the laundry. They were going to wash all the bedding today."

Levi grinned down at Nicki. "You don't like doing laundry much better than cleaning the barn do you?"

"No, but they'll need help if we're going to have blankets and sheets on our beds tonight. I wish I could saddle Wildfire and go with you to check the range."

"Don't suppose that will be much fun either in this heat."

"Maybe not, but it's a whole lot better than doing the wash," Nicki said with a sigh.

She joined the other women just in time to help Emily hang a dripping load on the line. Neither of them noticed when Liana surreptitiously slipped the sheet from Peter's bed into the washtub and scrubbed away the telltale bloodstain.

Levi smiled and waved as he rode Lady out onto the open prairie. In truth, he was looking forward to a good ride. What a joy it would be to get away for a few hours and not have to worry about farming. It wasn't that Levi scorned the farmers and the work they did. He just didn't enjoy it. Sometimes he was almost envious of Peter, who obviously loved coaxing the land into fruitful bounty.

Levi's promise to Cyrus kept him bound to the homestead, but he couldn't help wondering what fate had in store. He was no longer able to deny that he loved Nicki, but he knew he had no future with her. She'd never forgiven him for his desertion and the trip to St. Louis. If she'd been angry, he could have waited out the storm, but he had no defense against simple friendship.

The sight of the drought-ridden landscape soon drove all other considerations from his mind. The farther he rode, the grimmer his expression became. The range was in serious condition. Although it had been only ten days since the rain, Levi could see no evidence that the prairie had had so much as a drop of water.

Within a few weeks the cattle would be out of feed, unless drastic measures were taken. No longer would it be a matter of Herman Lowell throwing his weight around. He would be fighting to survive.

Levi's attention was drawn to a flicker of bright blue to the northwest. What in the world would be blue out here? Stranger yet, whatever it was seemed to be lying in the area devastated by the fire. Curious, he turned Lady and headed in the direction he'd seen the flash.

Five minutes later he was still waiting for another glimpse of blue as he rode steadily toward the spot he'd last seen it. There was nothing much around, just some burned-over sagebrush and an occasional anthill. Yet the farther he rode the more uneasy he became. He couldn't shake the eerie feeling that someone was watching him.

He might never have given the gully much more than a cursory glance if a sudden noise hadn't drawn his attention. Pulling Lady to a halt, he peered into the dry gulch. Down there somewhere, somebody or something had sneezed. The gulch seemed to be filled only with singed tumbleweeds. Then he saw it, a patch of blue deep down under the camouflage of weeds. Unsure of what exactly he was dealing with, Levi pulled his rifle from its scabbard and cocked it.

"All right, I know you're there. You may as well come out." His only answer was a muffled whimper and a rustle as his quarry burrowed farther under the protective cover.

Keeping his horse between himself and the gulch, Levi dismounted. Cautiously, he walked to the edge and pushed the debris aside with his rifle barrel. Then he blinked in surprise. Staring up at him with terrified eyes was a beautiful young woman.

"Oh, please don't hurt me," she pleaded, fear lending a quaver to the soft feminine voice. "My father will pay you well if I'm returned safely." Several straggling locks of silky brown hair surrounded her face, and dirt streaked her flawless skin. The blue velvet riding habit was ripped across one shoulder, revealing a vicious looking scratch. She was the epitome of Beauty in Distress. Another sneeze ruined the effect somewhat, but a man would have to be made of stone to be unmoved by her teary blue eyes.

Levi was not made of stone. He eased the hammer back into place and lowered his rifle. "I don't want your father's money." Squatting down next to the gulch, he reached out a hand to help her.

"Nnnooo!" She cringed in terror.

Levi sighed, exasperated with himself for not choosing his words more carefully. "I'm not going to hurt you."

"Y . . . you're not one of them?"

"Who?"

"S . . . somebody shot my horse, and tried to kill me."

"Did you get a look at them?"

"No. I . . . I ran." She struggled to sit up. "I got away, but I don't know how. They shot at me a couple of times but didn't try to follow me. When I saw you, I thought it was them so I hid."

"You're safe now. There's no one around for miles." Levi extended his hand to her once more. "I'll take you home, Miss Lowell."

Reluctantly grasping his hand she gave him a startled glance. "How did you know my name?"

"I work for the Chandlers. We met last spring while Nicki and I were building fence."

"Oh, I remember now. Mr. Quantrell."

"Cantrell. Levi Cantrell."

As if discovering he wasn't a stranger was enough to reassure her, she accepted his hand gratefully and clambered up the steep side of the gully.

"You look different someho . . . ha . . . achoo. Oh drat. Pardon me." She pulled a lace-edged handkerchief from her sleeve and daintily blew her nose. "How I hate these weeds. They always make me sneeze."

"My cousin has the same problem," Levi told her with a slight smile. "Are you feeling well enough to ride behind me?"

"I . . . I'm not sure." She gazed uncertainly at her left wrist. "My arm hurts."

Levi carefully pushed up her sleeve, and frowned at the bruised flesh. "What happened?"

"I think I landed on it when my horse fell."

"Could be broken then. We're only a couple of miles from Chandler's. Nicki's aunt is a nurse, and I think it might be a good idea to have her look at it."

Amanda bit her lip uncertainly. "I'm not sure Daddy would like that. He told me to stay away from Nicki."

"If your arm is broken and you don't get it set properly, there's no telling what will happen. It could heal crookedly, leave a big ugly lump, or even get an infection and have to be amputated."

"Amputated?" Amanda stared at her arm in horror.

Levi shrugged. "It's possible. Seems a shame to take a chance like that."

"Well maybe I'll stay just long enough for Nicki's aunt to take a look at it. Daddy shouldn't mind that," Amanda said petulantly. "I really don't understand this sudden aversion to the Chandlers anyway. He's always said he sort of admired Nicki's father, and he acted positively stupid over her mother. Now it's 'Stay away, they're trouble.'" She stuck out her lower lip slightly in what she obviously thought was an adorable pout. "Daddy's been a grouchy old bear ever since I came home. He doesn't even care that I'm bored to tears."

Levi wondered if Amanda was really so self-centered that she didn't realize what was going on around her or the kind of stress her father was under.

Amanda was aghast when he suggested she ride astride behind his saddle. She insisted such a thing was unladylike and said she'd rather walk. With a sigh Levi mounted his horse, and managed to pull

Amanda up in front of him. He settled her sideways and she snuggled against his chest as though it were the safest, most comfortable place in the world.

Levi wondered how Nicki was going to react when he rode into the yard with Amanda Lowell wrapped around his body like a blanket.

23

"I thought you were going out to check the range, not to drag in strays," Nicki said sarcastically as she gave Amanda a hostile glance.

Emily took in Amanda's dishevelment and pasty white cheeks. "Good heavens. What happened?"

"She probably fell off her horse," Nicki muttered, trying to ignore her jealousy at the sight of Amanda cuddled up to Levi.

Levi slid Amanda to the ground. "No, it was shot out from under her."

"What?" Nicki said in surprise.

"Somebody tried to kill her out there."

"Who?"

"I don't know. Maybe whoever is rustling Lowell's cattle."

With gentle fingers, Emily examined Amanda's injured wrist. "I don't think it's broken, but you do have a pretty bad sprain. I'll wrap it and give you something for the pain. You should rest for awhile before you try to go home."

"Well then," Levi glanced up at the sun, "I guess Peter and I'll go take a look around to see if we can figure out what's going on. We'll be back within the hour."

Emily nodded. "Good. That will give Miss Lowell time to rest."

"You're so kind, Mr. Cantrell." Amanda gazed up at him adoringly. "I just wouldn't feel safe with anyone else taking me home."

Levi swallowed a sigh. There was no way Amanda could stay on a horse by herself, and he really didn't want to ride the five miles to the Bar X with her sitting in his lap. He could still feel the imprint of her eager young body, and it was a difficult temptation for a man to resist.

"We don't need the wagon this afternoon, Levi," Nicki said as though she'd read his mind. "I'm sure Amanda will be more comfortable in that than on a horse." The sight of Levi riding in with Amanda in his arms was not one Nicki cared to see again.

After Levi left Amanda sat at the kitchen table watching Nicki fix a pot of coffee while Emily went to fetch her bag. "We haven't had a good visit since I came home. I never even got the chance to tell you how sorry I was about your father." Amanda's voice held just the right amount of genteel regret.

"Thank you," Nicki murmured, ill at ease with the sympathy.

"Well, at least you aren't alone. You know, I don't remember your mother very well, but your aunt doesn't look much like her, does she?"

"No, not much."

"And your cousin, what's she like?"

"Liana's a little shy but we've become good friends."

"Oh, how delightful," Amanda said brightly. "I can't wait to meet her."

"Yes, you'll have to meet Liana."

"I'm sure I'll love her. Does she look like you?"

Nicki grinned for the first time. "You'll have to tell me if you see a family resemblance."

Just then Amanda saw Levi and Peter ride by the window on their way to the prairie. "Mr. Cantrell is wonderful isn't he? Just like a knight in shining armor."

"A night?" Nicki, whose mother had never bothered to read her fairy tales, was bewildered. "What are you talking about?"

Amanda laughed and patted her arm. "Oh, you know. Those men who lived in castles and spent their time saving damsels in distress. Mr. Cantrell is just like the hero of my dreams. He rode up on his mighty stallion and snatched me from the jaws of death."

"He rides a mare," Nicki pointed out.

Amanda rolled her eyes. "Oh, Nicki, you have no romance in your soul. I suppose you don't even think he's terribly handsome."

"I hadn't noticed."

Amanda shook her head. "You're hopeless. Mr. Cantrell is the most attractive man I've seen in a long time. How could you miss that cute little dimple in his chin and all those lovely muscles?" She gave a delighted shiver.

"I don't know. Maybe I just wasn't interested."

"I'll bet he's connected to the Cantrells over by Horse

Creek somehow," Amanda continued as though Nicki hadn't spoken.

"What Cantrells by Horse Creek?"

"You know, the ones that have the big horse ranch. Daddy says the Cantrell horses are the best in the territory, even if they do cost a fortune."

"Come on, Amanda. If he were one of those Cantrells, why would he be working for us?"

"I don't know. Maybe he needed a job."

"If he had to go looking for work, he doesn't have any rich family connections," Nicki said. "Besides, don't you remember what your father did when he caught you messing around with one of his hired hands?"

"Jim and I weren't messing around," Amanda said defensively. "We were only kissing. Anyway, he can't send me to my aunt's again because she's dead." Amanda suddenly stopped. "Nicki," she whispered. "Who's that?"

Nicki glanced back over her shoulder and saw Liana in the doorway. "Oh, Liana, come and meet my old friend Amanda Lowell. Amanda, this is my cousin Liana."

"How do you do?" Liana said politely. "I've heard so much about you from Nicki." She stood expectantly for several seconds then continued on, calmly ignoring Amanda's silence. "I'm sorry I can't stay to chat, but I must have a word with my mother. It was nice to meet you." She smiled and left the kitchen without a backward look.

Amanda stared after Liana, stunned. "She's Chinese!" she whispered as soon as Liana was out of earshot.

"Good heavens! Are you sure?" Nicki stared at

Amanda with a look of total astonishment. "I wonder why I never noticed that before?"

Amanda looked disgusted. "I hate it when you get sarcastic."

"Well, that was a pretty stupid remark," Nicki said. "And you were more than a little rude to my cousin."

Amanda blushed. "I was surprised, that's all. You could have warned me."

Nicki was about to make a scathing remark when she suddenly realized how unkind her own motives had been. By not mentioning Liana's heritage, she had hoped to shock Amanda. She hadn't even thought of how Amanda's reaction might affect Liana. "I'm sorry, it never even occurred to me. I guess I don't really think about Liana being half-Chinese."

Emily chose that moment to return, her bag in hand. "I'm sorry I was so long. It took a while to find something I could use for a sling."

Amanda's faux pas and Nicki's churlishness were soon forgotten as Emily fashioned a sling for the sprained arm and administered a light dose of laudanum. The sedative qualities of the drug seemed to have little effect on Amanda. She kept up a steady stream of chatter for nearly an hour.

Since most of her talk was of the real and imagined attributes of Levi Cantrell, Nicki found herself gritting her teeth in irritation. "Whatever happened to Charles Laughton?" she finally asked.

The first response was a flash of pain in the other woman's eyes. "Lord Avery asked him to deliver an urgent message to his grandfather, the duke."

"He went back to England?"

"Yes." Amanda suddenly seemed to take great

interest in a small tear in the skirt of her habit. "And . . . and I don't think he's coming back." She looked up defiantly. "Anyway, that's all in the past. I'm certainly not going to waste any time thinking about him."

The conversation was interrupted when Levi walked in with a grim expression on his face. "We found the horse and the place Amanda was ambushed from." He took off his hat and wiped his forehead with the back of his arm. "Still no clue to who did it, though."

"Ambushed!" In a second Amanda was out of her chair and across the room where she clung to Levi's arm. "You think somebody was waiting for me?"

"Sure looked that way. But I don't think they intended to kill you. At that range you'd have been an easy target. Your horse was shot with a single bullet right between the eyes."

"That doesn't make sense," Nicki said. "Why would somebody kill Amanda's horse?"

"To scare her maybe. I thought she might have stumbled onto the rustlers that have been giving her father so much trouble, but we couldn't find any evidence of it."

Amanda stared up at him in wide-eyed terror. "Y . . . you don't think they're still after me do you?"

"I don't know, but I don't think you should ride out alone anymore."

"Oh, I won't. I'm so glad you're here to take me home. I feel so safe with you," she said with a worshipful look.

"Well, I guess we may as well be on our way," Levi said, resisting the urge to step away from her. Amanda Lowell had a way of making a man nervous.

Nicki was tempted to accompany them but couldn't think of any excuse that wouldn't make her seem jealous. She refused to consider how close to the truth that really was as she stood at the door and watched Levi help Amanda into the wagon.

"Good-bye, Amanda. Come back again," Nicki called as the wagon started down the road. "And keep your hands off all those lovely muscles," she muttered under her breath.

She didn't see Emily's grin behind her.

Though a mere five miles separated the Chandler homestead from the Bar X, it was closer to nine by the road. It wasn't long before Levi was wishing there were a more direct route between the two. Listening with half an ear as Amanda chattered on and on about her debut in Southern society, Levi couldn't help comparing her rather silly conversation to Nicki's. Nicki might argue just to be disagreeable. She might be irritating or even irrational, but she was never boring. In spite of the imminent meeting with Herman Lowell, Levi was relieved when the large ranch house came into view.

It was obvious the years of hard work and tenacity had paid off for Herman Lowell. The huge corrals and myriad outbuildings had a look of prosperity, but it was the house that most impressed Levi. Built of logs, it sprawled gracefully at the end of a small valley amid a surprising number of trees. A huge stone chimney at one side and a full porch along the front added a kind of rugged charm to the structure. It was magnificent without being ostentatious.

As Levi drove into the yard, a white-faced Herman Lowell came striding toward them from the barn. He had eyes for nothing but his daughter as he reached into the wagon and lifted her down. "Amanda honey, are you all right?"

"Yes, Daddy. I'm fine."

Her voice was muffled against her father's chest as he enveloped her in a hug. "Buck said he found your horse dead. We were just getting ready to go looking for you." Stepping back, his frown deepened as he saw her injured arm. "What happened?"

"Someone killed Princess and shot at me." Tears gathered in her cerulean eyes. "If Mr. Cantrell hadn't come along . . ."

For the first time Lowell glanced at his daughter's companion. "Cantrell, I thought you'd left."

So much for gratitude, Levi thought sardonically. "Only for a few weeks."

"How did you happen along just when my daughter needed rescuing?"

"I caught a glimpse of her riding habit while I was out checking the range. When I went to investigate, I found her hiding in the bottom of a gulch. She's got a sprained wrist and some bruises, but otherwise seems to be all right. It could have been a lot worse."

"Daddy," Amanda's voice held a convincing quaver, "aren't you going to thank Mr. Cantrell for saving me?"

"I'm not convinced he wasn't the one shooting at you."

"Daddy!"

Levi sighed. "If that were true, why would I go to all the trouble of bringing her home?"

"To make me trust you, maybe?"

"If that was my intention, it certainly worked well didn't it?" Levi said sarcastically as he picked up the reins. "I think I'd spend some time trying to figure out who really was responsible if I were you, Mr. Lowell."

"That's easy to do. Nobody around but you and the Chandlers."

"Daddy, shame on you!" Amanda stepped out of her father's embrace and stamped her foot. "Nicki didn't have anything to do with it, and Mr. Cantrell couldn't have been the one who shot at me. He rode in from the opposite direction. Besides, with all the men you have watching the Chandler place, one of them probably followed him. All you have to do is wait for whoever it was to check in."

"Amanda!" Lowell spoke sharply. "This doesn't concern you. Go to the house."

"But, Daddy . . ."

"I said go to the house!"

She turned to Levi and gave him a sad little smile, calculated to break a man's heart. "I guess this is good-bye, then. Thank you for saving my life. I . . . I'll never forget you." Her voice catching on a sob, she bowed her head and hurried toward the house.

It was all Levi could do not to roll his eyes at such a melodramatic little scene, but Herman Lowell obviously didn't see it the same way.

"I don't know what your game is, Cantrell, but stay the hell away from my daughter. And you can tell Nicki Chandler my offer to buy her place won't last forever. She may find herself wishing she'd sold out while she still had the chance. I won't watch while my cattle die of thirst so she can play at farming." He turned on his heel and walked away in long angry strides. "If I had my way, lightning would strike everybody who ever tried to stick a plow in the ground."

24

"*Easy now, Sam.* That'a girl, Bess." Nicki encouraged the team as they strained against their harnesses, providing the power to run the huge hay stacker. The boards creaked and groaned as the mighty table tipped the heavy load skyward, but the hay was smoothly delivered to Levi, who waited at the top of the stack.

As Nicki backed the horses into position to receive the next load, her gaze wandered to the top of the growing pile of hay. Usually running the stacker was a boring job, but today was different. Today Levi was working the stack. His sweat-dampened shirt clung to his back and arms, emphasizing the strong line of his body as he redistributed the hay with a pitchfork.

Watching all the "lovely muscles" Amanda had so admired the day before, Nicki felt an odd little flutter in her stomach. The enjoyment of watching Levi stack hay all day was not without its price. Nicki felt decidedly strange as the last load of hay was hefted up onto the stack, and she realized Levi would be finished and standing next to her within minutes. Suddenly, she didn't think she could handle that; not with her heart pounding the way it was, and her stomach tied in knots.

Afraid of what would show in her eyes if Levi looked at her, Nicki traded teams with Peter and headed back to the barn early. How did Levi always manage to affect her this way? He was about the only man she'd ever been around except Cyrus and Peter. Would she react the same to anybody?

Dismayed and confused by the feelings swirling through her, Nicki halted the team and unhitched Molly from the buck rake. Levi had said Stephanie would be back in Wyoming by the first of August. When that happened he would surely leave and she'd never see him again.

Nicki unhitched Oscar and reached up to grab the thick leather strap that ran down his back. With a terrified snort, the horse took off at a dead run. Nicki was jerked off her feet as her hands became tangled in the traces. It took her less than a heartbeat to realize she was in serious trouble. Dangling helplessly from the horse's side, she could only hang on and pray as Oscar raced along. One of the tugs was still attached to the buck rake, which careened crazily behind them. If she lost her hold, she'd either be trampled under the huge hooves or impaled on the eight-foot wooden tines.

The garden passed beneath them in a blur. There was a sickening crunch as the buck rake hit a tree by the creek, but the impact caused Oscar to turn back toward the barn. They left other pieces of the rake behind at the well, the woodpile, and the corner of the house. At last, Oscar reached the open barn door, where he stopped, unable to go any farther with what was left of the buck rake wedged sideways into the opening.

Nicki was still clinging to the horse's heaving side, her feet dangling several inches from the ground, when Levi arrived. She wasn't even aware of what he said as he pried her fingers loose. Cradled in Levi's embrace like a baby, Nicki wrapped her arms around his neck and buried her face against his shoulder.

Shaking nearly as hard as Nicki, Levi sat down on a keg of nails and held her tightly, as sobs racked her body. The sight of Nicki bouncing helplessly up and down against the side of the huge draft horse was a horror he would not soon forget.

As her sobs subsided, Nicki gradually became aware of Levi's hand stroking the back of her head while his deep voice crooned soft, meaningless words in her ear. Pressed tightly against his body, the smell of new-mown hay and the not unpleasant scent of a man's sweat before it sours surrounded her. With the awareness came the sudden realization of how very badly she wanted him to kiss her just to assure herself she was still alive.

A wave of self-disgust hit Nicki full force. How could she have forgotten to unhook the tugs? Her preoccupation with Levi Cantrell had almost killed her, and yet here she was lusting after him again.

"Damn it, Cantrell, I'm not a baby!" she said through clenched teeth, as she struggled out of his arms. "If Peter had pulled such a stupid stunt, would you have held him on your lap like a two-year-old?"

"I . . ." Levi stammered, completely unprepared for the unwarranted attack.

"No, you'd probably have yelled at him for not unhooking the tugs first. Why can't you get it through your head I don't want to be treated like some brainless female?"

She whirled around and almost collided with Emily and Liana. With identical expressions of astonishment they watched her stomp past Peter and out the door.

Peter stopped in the middle of trying to calm Oscar and stared after her in surprise. Having missed the tirade that went on behind his back, he didn't know what was going on.

"Why is Nicki mad?" he asked, turning to Levi with a puzzled look.

"I'm not sure. I think she wanted me to yell at her, but I don't have the slightest idea why."

Determined to end this obsession with Levi Cantrell once and for all, Nicki locked herself in her bedroom, vowing not to show her face again until she was over him. She ignored the many bruises and aches that settled in her shoulders. The pain inside was far worse than any of her physical hurts. Most of her life she'd fought the image of her mother, tried to be different. Today she'd discovered it had all been for nothing; she was as lustful as Samantha had been.

Toward dawn Nicki finally realized she might have lost the battle but could still win the war. All it would take was strong determination and total indifference to Levi Cantrell. This decision made, she fell into an exhausted slumber at last.

The next morning, Nicki asked Emily for some liniment for her shoulders but otherwise acted as though nothing had happened. After a quick breakfast, she saddled Wildfire and headed out to the range. Levi's report of the drought had been grim, and she wanted to see how bad it was with her own eyes. It didn't take her long to realize he'd been overly optimistic.

The sound of pounding hooves behind her startled Nicki. Remembering the attack on Amanda, she prepared to make a run for it as she turned in her saddle to see who it was. With a sigh of relief, she recognized Levi's bay mare loping across the prairie. By the time he caught up with her, Nicki's mask of indifference was firmly in place.

"Good morning," he said cheerfully. "I missed you at breakfast."

"I ate early."

"Mind if I ask where we're going?"

"We?"

"After what happened to Amanda Lowell I don't think it's safe to ride alone."

Nicki's lips tightened. "I'll bet you wouldn't have followed Peter out here."

"Then you'd lose. Peter and I discussed it this morning, and he agreed with me. From now on nobody rides alone, nobody." His eyes suddenly twinkled. "Tell you what. Since you don't want me riding with you, how about you riding with me?"

"I'm twenty years old, Cantrell. Stop treating me like a child."

Levi sighed in exasperation. "I've never treated you as anything but an adult, even when you didn't act like one."

"Then what about yesterday?"

"My God, Nicki, you scared me half to death yesterday. What did you expect me to do?"

"When I saw you, I thought I was going to watch you die, and there wasn't a damn thing I could do about it. Do you have any idea what that does to a man?" He rubbed his forehead with one hand. "Maybe I just had to be sure you were all right, or maybe I'm the one who needed to be held. I don't know. But Peter or Emily would have done the same thing if they'd gotten to you first."

"I wasn't paying attention to what I was doing," she said. "I know better."

"So you made a mistake. We all do that. The point is, everything turned out all right, so stop worrying about it."

"I still . . ." She stopped in mid sentence, her eyes widening as they focused on something off to the right. "Levi, look at that."

A dead calf lay right next to the trail. Someone had slit its throat and skinned it, all except for the Eleven Bar One brand.

Nicki dismounted and knelt next to the calf's lifeless body. "It doesn't make sense. A rustler wouldn't leave the meat, and the hide won't be worth two cents with that hole in it. Who could have done this?"

Joining her, Levi shook his head as he looked for tracks in the dust. "I don't know, but whoever it was wanted us to find it."

"Herman Lowell!"

"You don't know that."

"The hell I don't. Who else would do it?"

Levi sat back on his heels and scanned the horizon. "Maybe whoever shot Amanda's horse."

*   *   *

Over the next few days Nicki became more and more convinced Herman Lowell had begun a campaign to destroy the homestead. The dead calf was followed by broken posts and cut wire. It seemed like all Peter and Levi ever did was fix fence.

When it happened for the third time in as many days Nicki looked at Peter in dismay. "Again? We're going to run out of barbed wire if this keeps up."

"Bar X cows are getting thirsty. The fence keeps them from water," Peter signed. "Besides, cutting the wire is easy for Lowell's men, and putting up a fence is hard for us. They know that. We have another problem besides the fence."

"What's Lowell up to now?"

Peter shook his head. "It isn't Lowell. It's grasshoppers."

"Grasshoppers?" The pesky little varmints caused their share of damage, but Nicki had never known Peter to be worried about them before.

When they arrived at the edge of the first oat field Nicki realized immediately why Peter and Levi were concerned. The ground almost appeared to be moving as thousands of insects left the drought-ridden prairie and attacked the only food around.

"Good Lord!" Nicki couldn't tear her eyes away. "Are the rest of the fields like this?"

"This one is the hardest hit, but they're moving into the others fast."

"What can we do?"

"Peter and I figure we haven't got much choice but to cut the hay."

Nicki felt a surge of anger. How dare they make a

decision like this without her? Then she stopped herself. This was no time to be stupid. The important thing was to save what they could of the crop.

"What about the beans?"

"The hoppers haven't touched them so far. Maybe they don't like beans."

Peter squinted up at the sun. "We need to start today if we can," he signed.

"Should be able to," said Levi, "as soon as we get the fence fixed."

"How are we going to pick up the hay without the buck rake?" Nicki asked.

"I think I can cobble it together somehow," Levi replied. "Since Peter works the teams faster than either one of us, he can mow while you and I fix the buck rake. I'm hoping the grasshoppers will leave the hay alone once it's cut and we'll have a little more time."

They headed for the barnyard and the hay mower as soon as they had finished the fence. Within half an hour, they had it ready to go.

"Are you going to start where the hoppers are the worst?" Levi asked Peter as he climbed onto the seat.

Peter shook his head decisively, his hands moving in explanation. "No, if I take their food they will move to the other field. First I cut the places with the fewest grasshoppers. That way we save more of the crop."

Levi looked surprised, then nodded appreciatively. "Good thinking." He smiled. "You know, you just might teach me something about farming yet."

Peter cocked an eyebrow. "You think I can do miracles?"

Levi laughed and gave Peter a slap on the shoulder.

"Sometimes I wonder why I wanted to learn your language. I think I was better off not knowing what you were saying."

Peter just grinned as he snapped the reins against the horses' rumps and headed out to the field.

Levi turned to Nicki. "We'd best get moving, too, if we're going to get that rake fixed."

Improvising, they managed to repair, replace, and wire together enough of the buck rake to make it usable. With only three or four reminders from her conscience, Nicki was able to act coolly aloof toward Levi.

First light the next morning found them all heading for the field. Peter finished mowing while Nicki and Levi bucked the hay that had been mown the day before. Then all three of them stacked it. Emily and Liana had a nourishing meal ready at noon and another at five. Both times, the haying crew ate and then headed straight back to the field.

Finally, at eight-thirty, when it became too dark to see, the exhausted teams and their equally tired drivers plodded into the barnyard. In spite of their fatigue, there was a warm feeling of accomplishment. They had all fought a hard battle and won.

"How much more work do you have left?" Emily asked as the meal came to an end.

"A little more than half a field," Levi said, mopping up the last of his gravy with a slice of bread. "But it will probably take only a couple of hours."

With a yawn, Peter stretched and stood up. "For me it's time to sleep. I will see you all in the morning."

It was only by accident that Levi happened to glance up just as Peter's and Liana's eyes met. The

look they exchanged and Liana's almost impercepti-
ble nod, surprised him. A silent message had certainly
passed between them, and he wondered briefly what
they were up to.

"Oh no!" Nicki cried the next morning as she stared
at the small herd of cattle contentedly eating the hay
left lying in the field. "Get out of there!" she
shouted, running toward the cows and waving her
arms.

With considerable help from the others, the cattle
were herded back onto the prairie, amid a great deal
of cursing from Nicki. "If Herman Lowell thinks he
can drive us away with this constant harassment, he's
dead wrong. Chandlers don't give up, and it's about
time he knew it." She kept up a similar tirade all
morning.

Peter finally got tired of it. "Herman Lowell could
have burned the barn or shot the horses," he signed in
exasperation. "He is just playing with us."

"Oh, is that so? Maybe I should ride over there and
thank him for being so kind." Even her signs were
sarcastic.

"Don't be empty-headed, Nicki. If you make him
mad, he'll bring all his men and we'll have to fight.
We won't win."

"I'm not so sure about that. We're not afraid to
fight, and Lowell won't be expecting that."

Peter rolled his eyes and turned away shaking his
head. Levi wisely kept his opinion to himself.

As Peter predicted, they completed the haying just
before noon. Nicki decided it was a good time to
clean the harnesses. She expected the tack room to be

empty and was surprised to find Levi there, shaving in the light from the single window.

Nicki knew Emily had sent Cyrus's shaving stand and mirror out to the barn when Levi returned, but she'd never given it a second thought. Now, gazing at the dearly familiar looking glass, with its wavy, spotted surface, she remembered how often she'd teased her father about getting a new one.

It was at odd times like this, when she least expected it, that Nicki felt the loss of her father most keenly. Levi's soap-covered face twisted to one side as he grimaced into the old mirror. How many times had she watched Cyrus go through the same contortions? She felt tears prickle behind her eyelids.

"Did you need me for something?" Levi asked as he rinsed his razor in the bowl.

"No, I was just going to clean harnesses. I can do it later."

"Don't leave on my account." He smiled down at her. "In fact I might even help you as soon as I'm finished."

She smiled. "Well, if you insist." Forcing her thoughts away from her father, Nicki walked past Levi, lifted one of the heavy horse collars down from the wall, and began to clean the leather with saddle soap.

A comfortable silence fell, broken only by the scrape of the razor and the sound of the soft cloth upon the collar. As her grief faded back to its normal ache, Nicki studied Levi. With his shirttails hanging over his hips, his sleeves rolled to the elbow, and his shirt unbuttoned nearly to his waist, he looked refreshingly cool in the hot little room. The sunlight from the open window glinted off the golden hairs on his muscular forearms as he lifted his chin to shave his neck.

There was something about watching the man perform such an intimate task that made her feel strange. It didn't send her blood pounding through her veins as did the sight of him stacking hay. This was more a feeling of emotional well-being, of tranquillity. While she pondered the odd sensation, Levi wiped the remnants of soap from his face and took the bowl outside to dump the water.

When he returned, Nicki looked up and found him leaning against the shaving stand, grinning at her while he buttoned his shirt.

"What's so funny?"

"Nothing really. I was just thinking how well you do that."

Nicki gave him a puzzled frown. "Do what?"

"Clean leather."

"Any fool can use saddle soap."

"Not necessarily." Levi pulled a harness down from the pegs and settled across from her on the bench. "A friend of mine nearly ruined a pair of boots with saddle soap. She soaked them in water first and then tried to use it like regular soap."

"What?" Nicki was aghast at such blatant stupidity. "She must be a total idiot."

"No, just ignorant. Stephanie figured it was soap, so it should work like every other soap."

Stephanie again. God, how Nicki hated that name. "Do you suppose she's back in Wyoming yet?"

"Probably. At least, I hope so."

Concentrating on the task before him, Levi didn't notice Nicki's thinning lips nor how viciously she scrubbed the horse collar in her hands. "Nicki, look at this," he said suddenly. "This is probably why Oscar bolted with you. The sharp end must have poked into him when you loosened the traces."

Her eyes widened as she glanced at the metal harness ring in his hand. "It's broken. I wonder why Peter didn't notice it was worn when he checked the harnesses last week."

"It didn't break, Nicki, it was cut."

25

The sound of gunshots the next morning brought Nicki straight up out of bed. Her feet hardly touched the floor as she grabbed her rifle and hurried through the house. She could see Levi already striding across the barnyard as she dashed outside.

The eastern horizon was just beginning to lighten when she reached him at the far edge of the corral. "What's going on?"

"Trouble." His expression was grim as he looked northward.

Though it was difficult to see in the dim light, Nicki gasped as she followed his gaze. About fifty head of cows were running through the bean field, trampling the precious crop beneath their hooves. Three men on horseback rode behind the stampeding cattle, shooting pistols into the air and yelling.

"Those dirty . . ." Grasping her rifle in a tighter

grip, Nicki started forward, fully intending to put an end to the destruction.

Levi grabbed her arm. "No, you'll never stop those cows, not even with a rifle. It's too late to do anything now."

"The hell it is!" She glared up at him. "If you think I'm going to just stand here while . . ."

"Jesus, Nicki, look out!"

Before she had time to react, Nicki found herself swept into Levi's arms and crushed against the poles of the corral as they were enveloped in a choking cloud of dust. Though his big body blocked her view, she could tell from the bawl of the cattle and the thunder of hooves that he'd pulled her out of the path of the stampede.

In less than a minute, the cattle were past. A bullet zinged above them, and Levi tensed, sure that the next one would slam into his back. A rifle cracked nearby and both swiveled their heads toward the sound. Peter stood ten yards away, reloading his gun as the horsemen galloped past the house and out of range. It didn't occur to Nicki or Levi how odd it was that Peter had known there was trouble. They were both too glad he'd chased off the intruders to wonder about it.

Even as she sagged in relief, Nicki became aware of the hard chest she was pressed against. Covered only with dark curly hair, Levi's naked skin felt warm beneath her cheek. He smelled faintly of shaving soap and of the hay he'd slept on, a very nice combination. Far too nice in fact.

"You're not dressed," she said accusingly.

"Neither are you." He released her and stepped back. It was true. Clad only in her thin summer nightgown, she wasn't any more decent than he, who had only taken time to pull on his pants.

"Well, at least we'll have fresh meat for a day or two." Levi sighed. "Too bad the weather's so hot. We won't be able to save much of it."

Puzzled, Nicki followed the line of his gaze and saw the dead cow for the first time. It lay on its side between the house and the barn, apparently the victim of Peter's bullet. Emily and Liana reached the fallen animal just as Peter squatted in the dust next to it. With a look of pure disgust, Peter looked up and gestured for Levi and Nicki to join him.

One glance told the story. "It's one of ours!" Nicki cried as she saw the Eleven Bar One brand on the animal's side. "Those low-down mangy coyotes used our own cattle." Faced with the raiders' perfidy, Nicki was hopping mad, but it was nothing compared to the wrath she felt when she saw what was left of the beans. Only a few broken stems were visible in the churned-up soil. She stared at the wreckage for several minutes, then turned on her heel and headed back to the house.

"Where are you going?" Levi didn't like the look on her face, nor the purposeful way she was moving. If he was reading the signs right, she was about to throw a temper tantrum to end all temper tantrums. He fell into step beside her.

"It's none of your business, but I'm going to get dressed."

"Why?"

"Why do you think?" She glared up at him. "I'm going after Herman Lowell and his men."

"No, you're not."

Nicki didn't even break stride. "Oh yes I am, and you can't stop me."

"Nicki, you're smarter than that. You have no proof it was Lowell."

"I can't prove he's the one who tampered with Oscar's harness either, but I'm going to show him he can't just ride in here and do whatever he wants."

"What are you going to do?"

"I don't know, but if he wants a range war, I'll give it to him."

Levi grabbed her arm and pulled her around to face him. "Nicki, Lowell has a dozen men. If you go over there like this, you'll only get yourself killed. Then they'll come after your family. What about Liana and Emily? How long do you think Peter and I can protect them?"

If looks could do damage, Levi would have withered on the spot. As it was, he felt scorched by the naked rage in her eyes. Without a word she jerked her arms out of his grasp and stomped away.

"Try thinking about somebody besides yourself for a change!" he called after her. "Stop acting like a selfish brat!"

Though she was loath to admit it, Nicki knew Levi was right. She was no match for Herman Lowell, and yet there had to be a way to stop him. Today Lowell's men had destroyed the only money crop there was other than the cattle. Nicki knew the grasshoppers would have eaten it within the week anyway, but that wasn't the point.

After Levi's discovery in the tack room yesterday she knew nothing was safe. What would Lowell do tomorrow, burn the barn? Suddenly, she knew what to do. The plan formed in her mind so

quickly that it was all she could do not to chortle
with glee.

The next morning, gripping her rifle in her hands,
Nicki tiptoed out of the house about an hour before
dawn. In spite of the high temperatures during the
day, nights on the prairie were chilly, and she shiv-
ered slightly inside the coat she was wearing. As she
crept by the barn the horses moved restlessly in the
corral, but Levi apparently slept on undisturbed.

Fifteen minutes later she crawled through the fence
and found a hiding place in the sagebrush. Knowing she
was nearly invisible in the shadows, Nicki settled down
to wait. Shortly before daybreak her vigil paid off.

Unaware that they were being watched, three riders
approached. "Yeah, well I'm the one the dummy
almost killed, and I say let's get even."

"But, Buck," another voice whined in the darkness,
"Mr. Lowell said no bloodshed."

"What Mr. Lowell don't know ain't going to hurt
him." The tall figure stopped next to the fence.
"Besides I didn't say I was going to kill him, just
rough him up a bit next time we see him in town."

The shorter man leaned down off his horse to clip
the wire. "I don't know, Buck, he hurt you pretty bad
when we had the girl that time."

Realizing who the three men were sent a shaft of
anger through Nicki's soul. Instead of waiting until
they'd cut the fence so she'd have the proof Levi
wanted, Nicki rose up out of the sagebrush and fired
her rifle at the nearest cowhand.

With a frightened yell, he went down. "Buck, Slim,
help me! They shot my horse."

Before Nicki could jam another shell into the chamber and fire again, one of the other men had lifted Shorty onto the back of his horse and they thundered off into the darkness, firing several shots wildly as they went. Nicki shot back, but it was more to scare them than with any expectation of success.

Nicki was staring remorsefully down at the dead horse when Levi found her, minutes later. "Damn it, I knew you'd pull a stupid stunt like this!" he yelled, grabbing her shoulders and shaking her until her teeth rattled. "What does it take to get through that thick head of yours anyway? If I thought it would do any good, I'd tan your backside." He yanked her off her feet and practically threw her onto Lady before swinging up behind her. "You're going home and you're going to stay there while I go see if I can smooth things over."

"Smooth things over?" she screeched. "Lowell's the one that's in the wrong here, not us."

"He's also the one with all the power, and only a damn fool would cross him."

"I suppose that makes me a damn fool!"

"If the shoe fits." Levi jerked her tightly against him, as though he knew she would try to jump off. "Herman Lowell is just going to love the news that you've killed one of his horses, isn't he?"

"I didn't mean to shoot the horse." She raised her chin belligerently. "It was dark. I was aiming at the rider."

"Oh, well that's different," he said sarcastically. "I'm sure Lowell would much rather have you shoot his men than his horses."

They had reached the front door by then and Levi unceremoniously slid Nicki to the ground. "Get inside that house and stay there until I get back or, by God, I swear you won't sit down for a week when I get through with you."

Nicki exploded. "How dare you order me around! You're nothing but the hired hand around here. I can fire you any time I want to."

Levi leaned down and stared into her eyes. "Don't push your luck, Nicki," he said softly.

Her caustic reply died on her lips. Never had she seen him so angry. His chiseled features looked as though they were carved from granite and there was a glitter in his eye that brooked no argument. Gone was her kind and gentle friend. In his place was a man who almost frightened her. Without a word, she turned and went into the house.

Levi's anger cooled rapidly as he rode toward the Bar X. He really couldn't blame Nicki for reacting the way she had. It just wasn't her way to sit and wait. Unfortunately, Levi could see the other side as well. Though Nicki had legal claim to the Willow Creek spring, Herman Lowell had been here a good fifteen years before Cyrus Chandler had arrived. Lowell had fought predators, bad weather, and hostile Indians to carve an empire out of the wilderness. He felt he had earned the right to the water. The reception Levi had gotten when he took Amanda home did not bode well for the success of his mission today. Lowell was likely to shoot him on sight.

Levi squinted at the eastern horizon where the sun was rising, and wondered if Lowell's men had returned to the ranch yet. He hadn't forgotten Amanda's slip about Bar X men watching the homestead. Lowell knew their every move, and he'd certainly know their vulnerabilities. So far, Lowell's men had done little more than cause aggravation. Why was the man showing such restraint; what was his strategy? It seemed strange he hadn't done more to remove the Chandlers.

To both the Chandlers and Lowell the water was as precious as gold. Without the water from Willow Creek, Nicki and Peter were sure to lose the new alfalfa fields as well as the pasture that would help see their small herd through the winter. On the other hand, if Herman Lowell didn't get control of the water, thousands of his cattle would perish. Whoever controlled the spring controlled Willow Creek.

If only there were some way for the two sides to share the tiny stream. If only . . . and then, in the blink of an eye, it hit him . . . the answer to all their problems.

26

Two horses stood tied at the hitching rack in front of the house when Levi rode into the yard. Otherwise, the Bar X appeared almost deserted. A movement at a window caught his attention as he cautiously scanned the front of the house. Focusing on the glass panes, Levi waited for the motion to be repeated. Nothing stirred.

As he dismounted at the hitching rack, Levi debated about leaving his rifle in its scabbard. After several seconds, he decided to take it with him. Though Lowell might see the rifle as a threat, it could also prove to be an invaluable asset in an unfriendly confrontation.

Amanda Lowell opened the door the second he stepped onto the porch. Had she been the one watching his approach? Probably. Her shirtwaist was mis-buttoned, as though she'd dressed in a hurry. Levi sighed inwardly, wondering why Amanda appeared to be so taken with him while Nicki was totally unaffected.

Amanda looked a trifle breathless, and her eyes sparkled. "Why, Mr. Cantrell, what a surprise." She stepped out onto the porch and gave him a dazzling smile. "What brings you here so early this morning?"

"I need to see your father."

"My father?" Amanda's face fell, her disappointment obvious. "I think he's in his office." Then she brightened. "Have you had breakfast? You could join me while you wait for him."

"No." He smiled apologetically. "Thanks, but my business is rather important."

Leaning against the porch rail, she ran her beautifully manicured hand up the support and gazed at him with limpid blue eyes. "Maybe some other time," she said. Her ploy was so obvious, Levi was hard-pressed not to laugh. He raised an eyebrow. "Your father?"

"Oh." Amanda blinked and dropped her seductive pose. "I think he's busy, but I suppose you can see him if you really want to." With a toss of her head, Amanda flounced into the house. Levi removed his hat and followed in her wake.

If the house was attractive from the outside, it was even more so inside. Levi took in the polished wood floors, bright throw rugs, and handsome furniture as he followed Amanda through the large, well-proportioned rooms. By the time they reached the heavy door on the far side of the house, Amanda had recovered from the first rejection and turned to Levi once again. "When you and Daddy have finished your business, perhaps you'll join me for a cup of coffee."

Not wanting to offend her, Levi tried to seem regretful. "I'm afraid I won't have time today."

With a sigh Amanda opened the door to her father's study. "Excuse me, Daddy. Mr. Cantrell is here to see you."

Herman Lowell quickly masked his look of surprise as he turned to greet his unexpected visitor. "Well, Mr. Cantrell, what an interesting coincidence. My men were just telling me how they were attacked by half a dozen men over by Chandler's this morning."

Levi snorted. "Actually it was only one very small woman with poor aim. Nicki took exception to them cutting her fence again."

Lowell glanced at the three men who stood clustered around his desk. They shifted uneasily under his scrutiny. Then he turned back to Levi. "Somehow I doubt you came over here just to call my men liars, Mr. Cantrell."

"No. I have a business proposition to discuss with you." Levi never took his eyes off the other man. "Alone."

Lowell eyed the rifle Levi carried and then the expression on his face. "All right." He waved the other three men out of the room. "But I never discuss business at the point of a gun," he said as the door closed behind them.

"Neither do I, so if you'll put yours out where I can see it, I'll do the same."

Lowell pulled his hand out from under the desk and placed a six-gun on its polished surface. "You don't miss much do you?"

"I try not to." Levi followed suit with his rifle, then seated himself in the chair across from the other man.

"I assume you've reconsidered my job offer," Lowell said.

Levi was surprised. "After the last time I was here I didn't figure it was open anymore."

"Ah yes." Lowell looked a little uncomfortable. "It seems I owe you an apology for that day. I misjudged the situation. My daughter has been expecting you for the last several days, but I don't think she's the reason you're here either."

"No. I came to discuss water."

Lowell's face hardened. "Look, Cantrell, I've already told you and that little hellion you work for . . ."

"What if I told you there's a way for you both to share the water without either of you getting hurt?" Levi interrupted.

Herman Lowell frowned. "Why should I care? I can take the spring anytime I want."

"That's true, and I find myself wondering why you haven't. I think there's some reason you don't want to hurt Nicki Chandler. I don't know why, and I don't really care, but there is a way to compromise."

"All right, Cantrell, I'm listening."

"We'll put up a windmill."

"What?"

"May I?" Levi asked, indicating a pen and inkwell on the desk. Lowell nodded and sat forward as Levi pulled the writing materials to his side. Levi quickly sketched the hill from which the spring flowed and put an X at its top. "First we'll dig a well here and hit the groundwater the spring comes from." He continued drawing as he talked. "Then we put up the windmill and pump water across the fence to these horse troughs. The water the cattle don't drink fills up the troughs to these overflow holes. It runs out the holes, down these pipes and back into the creek bed."

"It won't work."

"Why not?"

"Just because there's water there doesn't mean you can dig a well and find it." Lowell shook his head. "Besides, all of that will take time, and time is one thing we don't have much of."

"If your men helped, we could have it done in a few days."

"My men are cowhands, not farmers. If I were stupid enough to tell them to dig a well or build a windmill, they'd quit. I need those men to move my cattle around to the waterholes that are left."

"Without the water from Willow Creek, your men are going to have a tough time finding enough." Levi laid the pen down on the desk and sat back. "You'll have to kill Nicki Chandler to get her off that place. Personally, I don't think you want her blood on your hands. Besides, you won't get to her unless you go through me first. I won't die easy."

Herman Lowell sighed and looked out the window. It was true, of course. The last thing he wanted to do was to hurt Samantha's daughter. She reminded him too much of the woman he'd loved. "All right, Cantrell, you've got three weeks. At the end of that time, I'll have access to the water one way or another."

"Three weeks! But that's . . ."

"Take it or leave it."

Levi knew it was the best he could expect. "I'll take it, but call off your men. We'll never get finished if we have to spend half of every day fixing fence."

"Fair enough."

"And no tampering with our equipment or starting stampedes."

Herman Lowell frowned. "What are you accusing me of?"

"Nothing. I just want to make sure there aren't any more accidents. The Chandlers have had an incredible run of bad luck the last few months."

"If there are any accidents, as you call them, they won't be my doing. You have my word on it."

Just then the door opened, and Amanda came in carrying a tray. "I thought you two gentlemen might like some coffee for your discussion." She gave Levi a sidelong glance and lowered her eyelashes demurely. "I had Cook bake some special cakes yesterday. Perhaps Mr. Cantrell would enjoy some."

Levi stood and picked up his hat and rifle. "Thank you for your thoughtfulness, Miss Lowell, but I was just leaving."

"Oh, but surely you can stay just a few minutes more."

"I wish I could, but I'm afraid I find myself short of time this morning." With a smile, he strode from the room, leaving father and daughter to stare after him.

"I don't think he's interested, Amanda." Herman sighed, quite aware of what a good son-in-law Levi Cantrell would make.

Marriage and Amanda Lowell were the farthest things from Levi's mind as he rode away from the Bar X. Three weeks! How in God's name were they going to build a windmill in three weeks? Would he even be able to get the parts in such a short time?

Instead of heading home, Levi rode straight to

Adams's Mercantile, where Mrs. Adams greeted him with her usual good cheer. "Good morning, Mr. Cantrell. What can I do for you?"

"How long would it take you to order a windmill and get it in?"

Mrs. Adams's thin face broke into a smile. "Well, now it just so happens I've got one stored in the back room. Fred Somes ordered it, then pulled up stakes and left before it came."

For the first time Levi felt hopeful. Perhaps they could make Lowell's deadline after all. "How much?"

"I'd have to look that up for sure, but as I remember it's around three hundred dollars. Course for that much money I'd have to have cash," she added apologetically.

Levi nodded. "I haven't got the money right now, but I think I can come up with it. Will you hold the windmill for me?"

"Sure thing, Mr. Cantrell. Never took it out of its crates, so that won't be no problem a'tall."

"Thank you, Mrs. Adams. I'll be back." Levi gave her a wink and left the store. Three hundred dollars was a lot of money. He briefly considered sending his brother a telegram, then discarded the idea. Cole probably wouldn't have that kind of cash on hand. No, the only way to get the money in time was to find the rest of Cyrus's gold. But where was it? He mulled it over all the way home, but he was no closer to the answer than he'd been before.

Within two seconds of walking through the door, he knew he was in trouble. Nicki took one look at him and stomped out the door.

Emily sighed and set a cup of coffee on the table for him. "She told me to say she isn't speaking to you."

He smiled ruefully and sat down. "That's all? I figured she'd fire me." He took a sip of coffee, then glanced up at Emily. "Were you with Cyrus when he died?"

"Yes, we all were."

"Did he say anything unusual?"

"Unusual? Like what?"

Levi gave her a troubled frown. "I don't know. Maybe something about a hiding place or gold."

"Good heavens! I certainly don't remember anything like that."

Levi sighed. "I was hoping he told somebody, and I figured you were the most likely possibility." It didn't take Levi long to tell Emily the story about the gold and then explain the sudden need for money.

"It has to be some place easily accessible or he wouldn't have been able to get it for you himself," Emily said pensively. "On the other hand, it wouldn't be where someone would come across it accidentally. Surely, between the two of us we can find it."

So the search began, but though they looked everywhere they could think of, their search was fruitless. At last they were forced to quit for the evening.

Levi tried to tell Nicki of the compromise he'd struck with Herman Lowell, but she ignored him. Vowing to make her listen the next morning, he finally went off to the barn for the night.

27

Emily pulled a pan from the oven. "Your biscuits are finished."

"I'm starved this morning. How soon can we eat?" Nicki asked.

"As soon as everyone gets here. Levi came in to get the milk bucket about half an hour ago, but I haven't seen hide nor hair of Liana or Peter yet."

"I'll go get them." Nicki stuffed part of a biscuit in her mouth and headed toward the door. "They both probably just overslept."

As she walked across the dogtrot, Nicki wondered what Levi had been trying to tell her the night before. It probably had something to do with his confrontation with Herman Lowell. He certainly seemed to think it was important. Maybe she'd relent a little today. Not enough to forgive him, of course. He deserved to squirm after the way he'd treated her!

Nicki opened Peter's door and stopped dead in her tracks. Even in the dim light it was impossible to miss Liana's head resting against Peter's naked shoulder. Without opening his eyes, Peter dropped a kiss on Liana's forehead before sighing and pulling her even closer into his tender embrace. Unaware that Nicki stood transfixed in the doorway, he smiled to himself and drifted back to sleep.

In stunned horror, Nicki somehow managed to close the door without waking the two within. She stumbled down the dogtrot and into the open air where she leaned against the log wall gasping for breath. Her knees buckled, and she sank to the ground, fighting the sudden nausea that threatened to overwhelm her. The memories came rushing back, numbing her mind and squeezing her heart.

She had just found the kittens hidden in the haymow when she heard her mother's voice below. Anxious to share her discovery, Nicki crawled to the edge of the loft, bubbling over with excitement. But her mother was not alone. Herman Lowell had entered the livery stable with her.

"Are you crazy, Samantha? A dozen people probably saw us together. Why didn't you just wait until Thursday when you bring Nicki over to play with Amanda?"

"This is too important to wait, Herman."

He sighed. "All right, what's this all about?"

"I'm pregnant."

"What!"

"You heard me. I'm going to have a baby."

"Jesus."

"You don't have to swear."

"You took me by surprise." He hesitated. *"Is there any chance it could be Cyrus's?"*

"Y . . . yes."

"You've been sleeping with both of us?"

"He's my husband, Herman. I can't very well refuse him."

"Why the hell not? My wife turned me away often enough!" Then he sighed. *"I'm sorry, Samantha. That was unfair."*

"What are we going to do?" she asked, putting her arms around him.

Lowell pulled her close. *"I don't think there's much we can do at this point is there?"*

"I could leave Cyrus and we could get married."

"You'd divorce him?"

"It could be done."

"Not very quickly it couldn't. The baby would be born long before we could get married. Think what people would say."

"I don't care what people say. There's nobody in this one-horse town I care about anyway."

"What about the children? Amanda and Nicki would have to bear the brunt of it, not to mention what the baby would have to grow up with."

"Amanda's old enough to go to that boarding school you're always talking about, and Nicki can stay with her father for all I care."

"And the baby?"

"With you as its father who would dare say anything?"

"But what if I'm not the father? You can't take a man's child away from him. Cyrus deserves better than that."

"Cyrus deserves better?" Samantha jerked out of his arms. "Is that all you can say? I've shared your bed for all these years and suddenly you're more worried about my husband's feelings than mine? What about me, Herman? What about what I want?"

"Samantha . . ." he began, touching her arm.

"Don't touch me!" She slapped his hand away. "I thought there was something between us, but I'm only a convenience for you aren't I?"

"That's not true."

"Then why don't you want me?"

"Have you really thought what it would be like to leave your family?"

"My family." Samantha gave a brittle laugh. "All they care about is that homestead of theirs. I'm so sick of it all I could scream. I hate being married to a dirt farmer, and I hate having a daughter who's more interested in horses than what she wears. I have more in common with Amanda than I do Nicki."

"Surely it's not that bad."

"Oh, no? I could walk away from my family without a backward glance. There's nothing there for me."

"I think you exaggerate, Samantha."

"You really don't care do you, Herman? All those sweet loving things you said were lies, weren't they? Fine, I don't need you either." With a quaver in her voice and tears in her eyes, she turned and ran to the open door. "You can just find someone else to warm your bed."

"No, Samantha, wait!" He started after her, but it was too late. She was gone.

*   *   *

On his way in for breakfast Levi found Nicki huddled against the side of the house, sobbing. "Nicki, what's wrong?" He squatted beside her. "Are you hurt?"

Nicki didn't respond then or when the front door opened and Emily came out to help. It wasn't until Levi pulled her hands away from her face that Nicki even acted as if she knew they were there. "Nicki, tell us what's wrong," Levi demanded.

"P . . . Peter," she managed to say at last.

"I'd better go see." Emily hurried down the dogtrot. Seconds later Levi heard the door open and Emily's gasp. "Oh my God!"

Fearing Lowell had gone back on his word and somehow perpetrated another attack, Levi surged to his feet and strode to the open door. The scene that met his eyes was the last thing he expected to see.

Holding Liana's obviously naked body protectively in his arms while she sobbed against his neck, Peter pulled the blanket up to shield her from censorious eyes. Then he just lay there, glowering at Emily and Levi, challenging them to do something.

Levi grasped Emily's arm, and pulled her away from the room before firmly shutting the door. "I think they need a few moments alone. Nicki needs us far more than they do right now."

Emily looked up at him with a bewildered expression. "Liana's only seventeen."

"Yes, but Liana and Peter are adults. They'll work it out. Right now Nicki is in some kind of shock, and we have to help her." Levi dragged her back to Nicki. "Can we move her?"

Emily pulled her uncertain gaze away from the dogtrot and focused on Levi's face. "What?"

"Emily," Levi said sharply. "Can we move Nicki?"

Emily looked down at her niece. Suddenly the confusion seemed to clear from her mind. "Oh God, Nicki. Yes, yes, carry her into the house. I've got something in my bag that will help."

Levi lifted Nicki into his arms and carried her to her bedroom where he laid her gently on the bed and sat down beside her. "Nicki . . . Nicki, listen to me."

But Nicki didn't seem to hear him as she pulled away and continued to sob. Levi sat helplessly watching her, unwilling to touch her for fear he'd somehow make it worse.

At last Emily came in and handed him a steaming cup of liquid. "Will you hold this for me, please?" To Levi's utter astonishment Emily pulled Nicki's hands away and dealt her two sharp slaps. Before he could protest, Nicki blinked in apparent surprise and focused on her aunt.

"Aunt Emily?" Her voice was thin and confused.

"That's better." Emily nodded in satisfaction as she removed the mug from Levi's hand. "Now then, after you drink this tea you'll feel much better."

Nicki obediently sat up and swallowed the herbal concoction. Then she closed her eyes tightly, trying to hold back the tears.

"Nicki," Emily said softly. "Tell me what's wrong."

"Peter hurt her. Liana trusted him and he . . . he," she dropped her head into her hands. "Oh, God, he's just like all the other men."

"What other men?"

"Herman Lowell."

Emily exchanged a worried glance with Levi over Nicki's head. "I don't understand, Nicki. What does Herman Lowell have to do with this?"

"He . . . he and my mother were lovers. Amanda

and I saw them together once just . . . just like Peter and Liana. But when she got pregnant he didn't want her."

Emily was startled. "Johnny was Herman Lowell's child?"

"She . . . she didn't know for sure because she'd b . . . been sleeping with both Mr. Lowell and Papa."

"Nicki, how do you know all this?"

"I heard Mama and Herman Lowell f . . . fighting once. She . . . she said she hated Papa and m . . . me. Li . . . Liana and Peter will hate me too."

"Oh, my love, no." Emily pulled Nicki into her arms. "Liana and Peter care for each other a great deal. You can see it in the way they act when they're together." As she said the words Emily knew they were true and wondered why she had missed it before. "But their feelings for each other won't change their love for you. Just because you fall in love with someone doesn't mean you stop loving everyone else."

"My mother d . . . did."

"Your mother was spoiled." Emily sighed. "And I guess it's my fault as much as anybody's. Samantha was so pretty and sweet when she was little, we all doted on her and gave her everything her little heart desired. By the time she was grown-up she'd come to expect it, and heaven help anyone who crossed her. If she didn't get her way, she threw tantrums. She'd had a bad habit of saying vicious, hateful things she didn't mean."

"She meant it. It all makes sense now. When Johnny was born, she kept saying he was the only thing that made her life tolerable. I didn't care. Johnny was my very own little brother, and I loved him." Nicki blinked back the tears. "I didn't care if Herman Lowell might be his father, but Mama did. One night, when they thought I was asleep, I remember Mama and Papa had a terrible fight about it. Papa said as far as he was concerned Johnny was his son and there was nothing she could do about it.

"A few days later when I got up and went to Johnny's cradle just like I always did, he was cold and stiff. He'd died in the night, and he hadn't even been sick. Mama left right after that."

"Nicki," Emily said. "You weren't responsible for any of it."

"I know, but my mother was. What she and Herman Lowell did was evil and . . . and I'm just like h . . . her." Nicki's voice broke and the tears oozed out beneath her lids.

"Oh, my love, you're nothing like Samantha."

"I . . . I look l . . . like her and I liked it w . . . when L . . . Levi . . . when h . . . he k . . . ki . . . ssed me."

Emily took her niece's hand and pressed it to her cheek. "My poor baby. Of course you liked it when Levi kissed you. Enjoying the kisses of someone you care about is perfectly normal. So is what you saw in Peter's room."

"Then you don't care?"

"Of course I care. I wish it hadn't happened." Emily gave her niece a hug. Vividly she recalled her suspicions the night Levi had been stricken with malaria. If her deduction was correct, Nicki had done more than exchange a few kisses with Levi. The poor girl must have been living in purgatory all this time.

"What Peter and Liana shared is not dirty or evil. It's a very natural thing. When two people care about each other it happens, sometimes almost by accident.

When it does it's a thing of beauty. I wish they had waited, but I don't love either of them any less because of it."

"But my mother was bad." Nicki twisted her fingers together nervously. "And so am I. No matter how hard I've tried, I can't seem to escape it. I always bring out the worst in men, even with my hair cut short and dressed like this. Somehow they know just by looking at me, and they do awful things." Wiping her eyes on the back of her hand, she sighed. "The men from the Bar X realized what I was right away."

"Nicki!" Levi's voice was filled with anguish. "That's not true. It wasn't your fault. Those men would have treated any woman the same."

She raised her head and looked him in the eye. "Oh no? Then what about you?"

Levi felt as though something had hit him square in the chest as images flashed before his eyes. Nicki melting in his arms and then slugging him. Nicki sitting by his bedside hour after hour when he was sick, listening to him ramble on and on about other women. Nicki letting him kiss her good-bye and watching as he rode away. Nicki holding a rifle on him when he returned almost a month late. No wonder she didn't trust him. The last thing she needed to hear was that he had kissed her because he couldn't resist her.

"I didn't kiss you because I thought you were a loose woman. I kissed you because you're very special to me. I value our friendship."

"Friendship," Nicki repeated. Then she shrugged. "If you say so."

Levi sighed. "All right, forget our friendship. In my thirty-two years I've been around all types of women.

There are those that you know are . . . available. They make it very obvious. In all the time I've known you I've never picked up that signal. And do you know why? Because you are not that kind of woman. Believe me, if you were, I'd know."

Nicki got up and walked to the window, where she stood looking out for several moments. Finally she turned around and looked at her aunt. "What are you going to do about Peter and Liana?"

"I . . . I don't really know. This is all such a surprise. . . ."

"Maybe we should just go have breakfast," Levi suggested. "Things usually look brighter on a full stomach."

Relieved, Emily nodded and bustled back to the kitchen. "All I have left to do is cook the eggs. Come along both of you," she said over her shoulder.

They had just started to eat when they heard Peter and Liana out in the dogtrot. The kitchen door was open a crack, and Liana's voice was easily overheard by the three seated at the table.

"I know, Peter, but we can't just tell them to go to hell. That's my mother and Nicki in there. . . ." It was easy to imagine Peter signing to her in the ensuing silence. "Oh Peter, that's not true. We knew it was wrong. We even tried to stop, remember? We'll just have to take the consequences. . . . Uh uh, I'll do the talking. . . . No, you're too mad. You'll only make things worse. . . . Look, we're in enough trouble already. If you . . ."

There was a long silence, and then Liana's voice again, though now it had a husky quality that hadn't been there before. "You don't play fair. You know I'm right but instead of admitting it, you kiss m . . ."

There was an even longer silence and the three inside exchanged glances. The hint of a grin lurked around Levi's mouth, but Emily and Nicki weren't quite sure whether to be amused or not.

Liana's voice was now almost a whisper. "Yes, I know. I love you too."

Seconds later the door opened and the two entered side by side, with their hands entwined. Peter's expression was one of open defiance while Liana looked as though she'd been caught with her hand in the cookie jar.

Emily smiled as though nothing unusual had happened. "Good morning. Come and sit down. Your breakfast is getting cold."

Peter and Liana glanced uncertainly at each other, then moved slowly to their places at the table.

Emily left her chair and went to the stove. "Coffee?"

"Yes, please." Liana stared unseeingly at her plate while Emily filled her cup and Peter's.

"How do you want your eggs this morning?" Emily asked, returning the pot to the back of the range and opening a stove lid to add more wood. "The same as usual?"

The stove lid clattering back into place made something inside Liana snap. "Stop it, Mother!" she cried springing to her feet. "I know what you're thinking, and you're wrong. Peter and I have something beautiful, but we'll never convince you of that, so just tell us what our punishment is and be done with it!"

Emily turned and stared at her daughter. The hurt in her eyes and the slight quivering of her chin were mute testimony to the helplessness she felt.

"I can only think of one punishment for what you

two have done," Levi said finally in a grave voice, "but it's pretty harsh." He took a sip of coffee and watched them over the rim of his cup. "In fact, it's the next thing to a life sentence."

Peter and Liana exchanged an uneasy look.

"Wh . . ." Liana nervously cleared her throat and tried again. "What is it?"

"Well, the way I see it, you two ought to get married, and the sooner the better!"

Marriage! The floor beneath Nicki's feet seemed to drop away as the significance of Levi's words sank in. If he knew about *their* night of passion, he'd feel obligated to marry her. Though she hadn't meant to, she'd be guilty of using her body to trap a man. She thought she might be sick.

28

"Just one more, Liana." Nicki worked the small, satin-covered button through the hole, then stepped back to survey her work. "I still think thirty-two buttons is ridiculous, but you look gorgeous."

Liana ran her hand down the full skirt of her wedding gown and smiled. "It's your mother's dress that's gorgeous."

"Our grandmother's dress," Nicki corrected her, "and it's perfect for you. Nobody would be half as pretty in it as you are."

As soon as the three women started making wedding plans, Emily remembered her mother's dress and wondered what Samantha had done with it. They found it carefully packed away in an old trunk. The satin and lace, now ivory-colored with age, had brought gasps of delight from both Liana and Nicki.

Now Emily finished adjusting the skirt and smiled

up at her daughter. "She's right, my dear. The color is lovely on you."

"Oh, fiddle," Liana dropped a kiss on her mother's cheek. "It'll be just as pretty on you when your turn comes."

"My turn!" Emily laughed. "At my age? Don't be silly."

"What about Dr. Bailey? I still think that man is sweet on you."

"John Bailey is back in Massachusetts. I'm sure he's forgotten all about me," Emily said, studiously avoiding her daughter's eyes.

Liana smiled knowingly. "Yes, and that's why he writes to you every week."

Emily blushed to the roots of her hair, but the door opened before she had a chance to reply.

"Mr. Cantrell and Peter are here . . . Oh, my." Mrs. Adams stopped in the doorway and gaped at Liana and Nicki. "If you two aren't about the prettiest things I ever saw."

When Mrs. Adams had discovered there was a wedding afoot, she had enthusiastically joined in the planning. First she'd insisted on supplying the fabric for Nicki's dress, then she offered her home for the wedding.

Mrs. Adams came into the room and fluttered around Liana. "Such a beautiful bride. Your young man will likely bust his buttons with pride when he sees you." Then she held her clasped hands to her narrow breast as she gazed at Nicki. "And you, my dear, are even more lovely than I imagined you would be."

Nicki grinned. "You're just glad to finally see me in a dress that's all." She twirled around. "It is

pretty, though, isn't it?" Made of the same dusky
pink material that Amanda had rhapsodized over, its
puffed sleeves and flared skirt were a secret delight
to Nicki. Would Levi like it? The traitorous thought
kept surfacing no matter how hard she tried to
ignore it.

Mrs. Adams's eyes sparkled. "I came to tell you the
men are here and waiting with Reverend Botwell. If
you two are ready, we can begin."

Liana and Nicki glanced at each other nervously.
Both had been almost giddy with anticipation as
they'd stowed all their finery in the wagon and left for
town. Now, they were suffering from a major case of
butterflies and last minute jitters.

"We're ready," Emily said, giving Liana a reassuring smile and handing her the small white Bible all
Patterson women carried down the aisle.

"Good. Give me a minute to get to the piano then."

Minutes later, Aunt Emily slid her chair and Mrs.
Adams struck up a sprightly march. Nicki and Liana
hugged each other, then turned to the door.

Nicki could almost feel the impact as Liana's and
Peter's eyes met. The look of love-filled wonder on
Peter's face brought tears to Nicki's eyes, and she
glanced away. Her gaze landed on the circuit
preacher just as his eyes widened, and his mouth fell
open in shock. Even from clear across the room Nicki
could read his lips.

"But she's Chi . . ."

Before he could finish the word, a huge hand
closed around his arm and nearly jerked him off his
feet. With everyone else's eyes on the bride, only
Nicki saw Levi lean over and whisper something in
the minister's ear. The little man turned red, then

blanched white. Peering up at Levi, he swallowed, then nodded anxiously.

It was truly a beautiful wedding. If anyone noticed how the preacher kept wiping the sweat from his brow, they attributed it to the hot weather, not to the nervous glances he surreptitiously cast toward Levi.

Reverend Botwell needn't have worried, for Levi never looked his way again. The big man's attention was riveted on Nicki Chandler. From the moment he saw her standing in the doorway, he couldn't tear his eyes away.

The ceremony passed in a blur. Though he produced the ring at the proper time, Levi was unaware of Liana and Peter exchanging their vows in sign language or of Mrs. Adams and Emily wiping their streaming eyes. He even missed the final kiss that bound the two together for all time.

All he saw was his little tomboy miraculously changed into a beautiful woman. She set Levi's heart pounding in his chest and strange images floating through his mind—images of waltzing with Nicki in his arms, of walking through an orchard hand in hand, and of lying on a picnic blanket with his head in her lap while a bevy of children cavorted around them.

Suddenly the wedding was over, and Levi struggled to focus his thoughts on reality. After congratulating Peter, and kissing Liana, he wandered toward the window where he gazed out at the dusty street. Then Nicki was there, grinning mischievously up into his face. "What did you say to that poor man?"

"Who?"

"Reverend Botwell, of course." She glanced over her shoulder then back to Levi. "Didn't you notice?

He said he couldn't stay for the party and practically ran out of here."

"What makes you think I had anything to do with it?" he asked innocently.

"Don't play games with me, Cantrell. I saw you whisper something in his ear that scared him half to death."

Levi shrugged. "All I did was remind him what the scriptures say about loving thy neighbor."

"That's all you said?"

"Well, I might have mentioned my nasty temper too," Levi admitted.

Nicki laughed out loud. "No wonder he lit out of here like he had a pack of coyotes on his tail!" Her laughter faded to a soft smile. "Thank you, Levi. It would have been awful if he'd refused to marry them." Shifting her glance to the happy couple, she sighed. "I just don't understand why people are so mean. Neither Peter nor Liana would ever hurt anybody, and yet a man of God almost turned his back on them today."

"Prejudice is a funny thing," Levi said. "Kind of like a grudge. After you've had it for awhile you tend to forget what made you feel that way in the first place."

"I suppose you're referring to me not speaking to you all week." Nicki tossed her head. "For your information, I haven't forgotten why I was mad at you. I just decided to forgive you, that's all."

"Why the sudden change of heart?"

"Well, for one thing, you saved Peter and Liana's wedding." She gave him a sidelong glance. "For another I want to know about this windmill you think you're going to build on my land."

Levi laughed. "And I thought you were so busy putting this wedding together, you weren't paying any attention to what I was doing."

"You'd be surprised what I know." Nicki gazed at her outstretched hand as though admiring her fingernails. "You and Peter hit water yesterday, and before that you built some very strange looking horse troughs. I'm also aware of an expensive windmill kit you told Mrs. Adams to hold for you. What I don't understand is why."

He straightened and offered her his arm. "Miss Chandler, I think it's time we had a little talk. Would you care to take a short stroll with me?"

Nicki stared uncertainly at his arm for a moment, then placing one hand upon it, twitched her skirt aside. "Lead the way, Mr. Cantrell."

It didn't take long for Levi to explain his project and its desired outcome. When he'd finished, Nicki looked thoughtful. "I'll have to admit, it's a good idea. I suppose we can even get it built in the two weeks we have left, but how are we going to pay for the windmill?"

"There's a fortune in gold hidden somewhere on the homestead."

Nicki laughed. "Buried treasure? That's a good one."

"Nicki, Cyrus gave me two hundred dollars worth of gold nuggets last spring and sent me to South Pass City to cash them in."

"Where did Papa get a fortune in gold, and why don't Peter and I know about it?"

Levi settled Nicki on a bench in front of one of the town's few buildings and told her Cyrus's story.

In the silence that followed, Nicki remembered her

suspicions after the prairie fire. She'd been right after all. Cyrus had trusted Levi with his secret but not his own daughter. That wasn't the only time he'd trusted the younger man either. On the night he died, Cyrus's last words had been about Levi Cantrell. Nicki could still hear the conviction in her father's voice when he told her Levi would return. He'd been so sure, he'd made her promise to tell Levi . . .

"Oh my God!"

Levi watched as the color drained from her face. "What is it?"

"The night Papa died, I . . . I think he told me where the gold was." Her brow furrowed in concentration. "He said, tell Levi the northwest . . . no . . . the northeast corner of Peter's bedroom." She looked up at him. "Do you think that's what he was talking about?"

"There's only one way to find out." Levi helped her to her feet. "Shall we go on a treasure hunt?"

In less than fifteen minutes Nicki and Levi were on their way. After a few words to Emily and a change of clothes for Nicki, they left.

The trip home seemed to take forever but they arrived at last. Nicki tied Peter's horse to the hitching rack, and followed Levi into Peter's bedroom.

"Are you sure he said the northeast corner?" Levi asked, carefully examining the walls.

"I think so. You think it might be in the wall?"

"If one of the logs were hollowed out. Look for loose chinking."

After ten minutes of thoroughly searching the lower logs from her position on the floor, Nicki sighed in defeat. "Nothing! Where else could it be?"

Levi glanced up. "The ceiling?"

Nicki leaned back, her hands braced against the floor as she watched Levi feel along the ceiling planks. As she shifted slightly, she felt something give beneath her hand. She glanced down to find her finger resting in a knothole. Oddly enough, the knot seemed to have moved down into the hole slightly. She pushed at the small piece of wood with her finger. When it disappeared into the floor, leaving an empty space, Nicki sat up excitedly. "Levi, look at this."

Nicki scooted off the board and inserted a finger into the hole left by the knot. When she pulled up the board it lifted easily, revealing a dark, empty space below. For a second Nicki and Levi stared at each other, then Nicki reached down into the darkness.

"I can't feel anything," she said in disappointment as her hand met with nothing but cool air. "I can't even touch the ground."

"Let me try." Levi reached into the hole. "Cyrus was a tall man. Your arm may not be long enough to . . . aha. I found something. Good Lord . . ." He grunted as he pulled the heavy box up through the hole. "How did Cyrus ever lift this thing?"

"Maybe he didn't," Nicki said. "He could have lain on the floor and opened it, couldn't he?"

"He must have." Levi set a black metal strongbox on the floorboards, and wiped a thick layer of dust from the top. "Well, are you going to do the honors?"

Nicki rubbed her sweaty palms against her thighs and swallowed nervously. "What if it's empty?"

"Then it's the heaviest strongbox I've ever seen."

Nicki smiled and then gingerly reached out and lifted the lid. "Oh!" Her eyes widened as she gazed inside at the glittering nuggets.

Levi was as astonished as she. The box was over three-quarters full of pure gold. Never in his wildest dreams had he imagined there would be so much.

Nicki cleared her throat. "There's more than enough for the windmill, isn't there?"

Levi grinned. "You don't need a windmill anymore. It would be a whole lot easier to just hire an army to protect your place. Hell, you could probably buy out Herman Lowell if you wanted to."

Nicki looked confused. "What are you talking about?"

"You really don't understand, do you?" Levi smiled at her. "Nicki, you're probably one of the richest women in the whole territory."

29

"*How much longer* till we get to South Pass City?" Nicki asked. It had been nearly eight hours since she and Levi had discovered Cyrus's horde. They had been in the saddle for the last seven. Stopping only long enough to gather a few provisions and tell Emily where they were going, they had set off for South Pass City.

Levi glanced toward the setting sun. "I figure we'll hit Lander late tomorrow, so we should be in South Pass City the day after."

"We made good time today." Nicki gazed down at the small, muddy stream. "Is this where we're going to camp tonight?"

"It's as good a place as any. Besides, it's getting dark and the horses are tired."

"Not to mention the riders." Nicki dismounted wearily and led Wildfire over for a drink. "The drought is just as bad here," she said, eyeing the cracked, dried mud that had once been part of the stream bed. "This creek will be dry in another week."

"Looks like it." Levi pulled the saddle from Lady's back. "If it weren't for the spring, Willow Creek would look pretty much the same."

Nicki scuffed her boot against the dry ground sadly, then looked back over her shoulder. "Do you want to take care of the horses or fix supper?"

"I get to choose?" Levi raised an eyebrow.

"I figured we could take turns. We'll switch tomorrow night."

Levi grinned. "Which would you rather do?"

"Horses," she replied promptly and led Wildfire away from the creek.

Levi gave her a wry look. He had a strong suspicion he had been tricked into doing exactly what she wanted him to.

Nicki smiled as she loosened the cinch on her saddle. It felt good to be here with Levi. Not content to let him save the homestead by himself, she had refuted every argument he'd presented in an effort to leave her behind. The twenty ounces of gold they had brought along could be converted to cash in the gold-mining town without raising suspicion, but it would take time. Nicki simply pointed out that two of them could accomplish twice as much in the same amount of time.

Levi recalled her to the present as he led Lady up from the creek. "You know, we could still turn back."

Nicki paused in her work and gave him an exasperated glance. "Look, I told you, I'm not interested in being rich. We'll build the windmill and be done with it."

Levi shrugged. "Well, it's your money."

By the time Nicki had the horses curried, fed, and picketed for the night, the aroma of hot coffee and beans filled the air. She settled herself by the cheerfully crackling fire. "If that tastes as good as it smells, you can cook tomorrow night too."

"Uh-uh. A deal is a deal." Levi handed her a cup of coffee, then went back to stirring the beans. "Besides, you haven't tasted the main course yet."

"I'm not worried."

Levi's eyes twinkled at her over the fire. "You're willing to trust a cowhand to do your cooking for you?"

Nicki gave a very unladylike snort. "Even a one-eyed horse thief can fix canned beans."

Levi laughed as he dished up a plateful and handed it to her. "Don't say I didn't warn you."

Nicki took a bite and closed her eyes in feigned ecstasy. "Mmmm. These are wonderful!"

Levi tasted the beans. "It's impossible to turn my head with flattery," he warned, "and I won't be charmed into taking your turn."

"Oh well, it was worth a try anyway." Nicki grinned and took another mouthful. "It's possible you'll regret this tomorrow night, though. I've never cooked over a campfire before."

Levi chuckled. "'Even a one-eyed horse thief can fix canned beans.'"

Filled with an unfamiliar warm feeling, Nicki finished eating and leaned back against her saddle. Was this what Liana and Peter felt when they sat holding hands? After her talk with Emily, Nicki had watched the two closely and decided their love was a complicated emotion. At times it was soft and warm, at others teasing. There were even times when Peter gave

Liana an intense, hot look that made her smile and blush. Nicki didn't understand it any better now than she did before, but it no longer seemed threatening.

"Liana was a lovely bride wasn't she?"

"All brides are beautiful," Levi said, unwilling to admit he'd spent more time looking at Nicki than Liana.

"I know, but she reminded me of a china doll I had once. It was so pretty I used to just sit and look at it." Nicki sighed wistfully. "Did you see the expression on Peter's face when he saw her?"

"Mmmm," Levi said. "That's the way a man looks at the woman he loves on his wedding day." *And the way I looked at you,* he added to himself.

"You know what I don't understand? Liana's younger than I am, and Peter has seen less of the world than either of us, so how did they know how to do it?"

Levi nearly choked on his beans. "What?"

"How did they know how to fall in love?"

Levi cleared his throat. "Oh, that. Well . . . I don't think you have to know how to fall in love. You just do it."

"Have you ever . . ." With a jolt Nicki suddenly remembered Stephanie and swallowed the rest of her question. She really didn't want to know about Levi's love life.

"Have I ever been in love? Yes, several times. And in answer to your next question, I can't tell you how it feels because every time is different." He stood and stretched. "Now, are you going to help me with these dishes or have you thought up some clever scheme to get out of it?"

Nicki was glad to let the subject drop and the conversation turn to less personal topics. At last the campfire was banked for the night and both were stretched out in their bedrolls. Levi was just beginning to drift off when Nicki's voice broke the stillness of the night.

"Do you really think I have enough money to buy the Bar X?"

"Hmmm?"

Nicki turned on her side and propped herself up on an elbow as she gazed at him over the glowing embers. "You said I could buy out Herman Lowell. Do you truly think I could?"

"Well, if he wanted to sell you could. Why?"

"Oh, I was just thinking. With Peter and Liana getting married it might be time to start thinking about getting a bigger place. I don't guess Lowell would sell, though."

"Probably not, but there are quite a few big places you could buy. Since the cattle prices have dropped, a lot of the English investors are having second thoughts about their cattle ranches in Wyoming."

"I know, but none of them have any water. Besides," she said, flopping over on her back and staring up at the sky once more, "Lowell's house is big but not as fancy as some of the others. I don't think I'd like to live with crystal chandeliers and the like."

"I see what you mean." Levi thought of Lowell's graceful log house set among the pine trees. It was like Nicki, beautiful without being ostentatious. Yes, she would fit in there very well. "If it's a bigger house you want, you could always build one."

"That's true. I thought about starting a second homestead, but Willow Creek isn't big enough to irrigate another farm."

Levi smiled at her simplicity. Nicki had enough money to live in the lap of luxury and she was talking about taking out another homestead. "So you're thinking of becoming a rancher instead?"

"God no! The Bar X has a lot of good ground, and Grass Creek runs right through it. If I owned it, I'd farm it." A thread of disgust tinged her voice. "The only things I hate worse than ranchers are liars and cheats." She pulled the blanket up to her chin and closed her eyes. "I'd just as soon become a bank robber!"

Levi lay awake for a long time, mulling over Nicki's words, dreading the time when she discovered his deception. Once Nicki learned that he'd lied to her and was part owner of the Triple C Bar Ranch, she'd turn her back on him forever.

When he finally fell asleep it was to dream of a violet-eyed beauty in a pink dress. She smiled enticingly as she twirled and danced just beyond his reach.

"Cyrus told me the trick is to make sure you're in a different crowd every time you cash in a nugget," Levi said two days later as they stood on the crest of a hill, gazing down into the bustling streets of South Pass City. "I don't suppose you'll change your mind, and just let me do it?"

Nicki shook her head. "Not on your life, Cantrell."

"Do you realize you always call me Cantrell when you know I'm right, but you're bound and determined to have your own way anyhow?"

"No ı don't. I do it when you forget I'm the boss," she told him. "Now, are we going to stand here all day or are we going to get this over with so we can be on our way?"

Watching her turn toward Wildfire, Levi sighed. At the sound, Nicki stopped and peered over her shoulder at him.

"Don't worry, Levi," she said softly. "I'll be careful, I promise." Her eyes met his. "You take care too."

To Levi, her words sounded almost like a caress. Then she flashed him an impudent grin, swung up into her saddle, and headed down the road into town.

Levi wondered if he'd imagined the whole thing. It seemed so out of character for Nicki, and yet she'd been different the last few days. Feeling like a confused adolescent, he mounted his horse and followed her down the hill.

All day yesterday, there had been a closeness between them that had never existed before. As Levi had predicted, they had reached Lander that night, but they had avoided the town to camp at the foot of the Windriver Mountains, a mere twenty-five miles from their destination.

Amid a great deal of good-natured banter, Nicki had prepared their meal of beans. The evening had passed quickly, with bursts of laughter frequently floating out into the night. That special feeling of closeness had been with them all day today as they rode up the steep mountain road and finally reached South Pass City. Levi couldn't help but wonder what the return trip would bring.

Nicki was tying her horse to a hitching rack in front of the Carissa Saloon when Levi finally caught up with her. "I see what you mean about the saloons in this town." She looked toward the White Swan right next door and the Grecian Bend directly across the street. It was the same all the way down the busy thoroughfare and over onto the next. There were some respectable businesses, but they were far out-numbered by the dance halls, saloons, and gambling dens.

"Now do you understand why I wanted to leave you home?"

Nicki grinned up at him. "I always understood. You don't want me to have any fun."

"Nicki . . ."

"Oh come on, Cantrell. Look around you. There are women all over the place, and none of them seem particularly frightened." She glanced pointedly toward an old woman tottering down the walkway clinging to the arm of a young girl. "How dangerous can it be?"

"It's full of rough miners who get drunk and . . ."

"And pay absolutely no attention to thirteen-year-old boys," she finished for him.

Much as he hated to, Levi had to admit she was right. The way she was dressed in a loose shirt, it was virtually impossible to tell she was a woman. "Just the same don't talk to anybody unless you have to."

"Sure thing, Captain." Nicki snapped a salute then headed toward the nearest store. "Guess I'll start on this side of the street." She didn't see Levi roll his eyes before he walked into the Carissa.

South Pass City was a new experience for Nicki. Though she had been born in the East, she had grown up in the sparsely populated West and had rarely been any place bigger than Nowood, with its one and only store. In order to get cash for the gold she had to buy something with every nugget she had, and oh, the things there were to buy! There were stores and shops she had never even imagined before. At a blacksmith's shop she purchased a supply of harness rings, at the barber's some shaving soap, and the saddle maker sold her an extra pair of saddlebags to carry all of her purchases home.

The millinery store was her favorite, with its incredible collections of hats. After a great deal of deliberation she finally chose a Tuscan straw bonnet for Liana, only to be embarrassed by the clerk who winked knowingly and asked if Nicki was buying for a sister or a sweetheart.

The mercantiles were even more fun than the specialty shops. With a vast array of goods, they sought to supply the needs of anyone who might enter the store. At the first, Nicki bought Emily a shawl, and at the second, a red wool blanket and a new whittling knife for Peter. The last yielded an amazing variety of canned goods that had Nicki grinning to herself as she picked out food for the return trip. Wouldn't Levi be surprised to find the beans replaced by something called sardines! The clerk assured her they'd be delicious with the tin of soda crackers he also sold her.

It was then that the bolts of material caught her eye. A sudden memory of Levi at the wedding rose in her mind. Whenever she'd glanced his way he'd been staring at her with the oddest look on his face. Perhaps it was time for another dress or two.

Ten minutes later she emerged from the store with two dress lengths of fabric, feeling extremely pleased with herself. Across the street, Levi walked out of a saloon, and stood blinking in the bright sunlight. Excited, Nicki started forward, impatient to share the excitement of the day with him, but before she could catch his attention an unfamiliar voice called to him.

"Levi? Good heavens, it is you!" Levi turned toward the sound, and his face broke into a smile. The woman who flew into his arms was one of the most beautiful Nicki had ever seen. She felt as if the world was crumbling around her as she watched Levi sweep the stranger into a bone-crushing bear hug.

Even from across the street it was impossible to miss the thick cinnamon hair swept up into a very becoming style. Nicki knew for certain the eyes gazing so lovingly up into Levi's were green and the tall, graceful woman was none other than the mysterious Stephanie.

A feeling very much like nausea rose in Nicki as the couple talked for a few minutes, then Levi bent down and gave the woman a kiss. Stephanie hugged him again before they turned and walked arm in arm to the Sherlock Hotel, where they disappeared through the doors.

Nicki stumbled blindly up the street, oblivious to the stares she attracted as she pushed past people on the sidewalk. At last she found a deserted corner behind a building, where she sank to the ground and buried her face in her arms. Fortunately, there was no one around to hear the heartbroken sobs and wonder at the boy crying his heart out behind the livery stable.

30

Levi grinned when he caught sight of the slight figure seated on the bench outside the Carissa nonchalantly whittling on a piece of wood. The casual observer would never suspect Nicki was anything but an indolent boy who had escaped his mother's eye for the moment.

"Since when did you take up wood carving?" he asked.

She didn't even look up. "Since you decided to take all afternoon doing God knows what. I got tired of waiting." She eyed the piece of wood critically, then tossed it away in disgust. "To tell you the truth I don't understand what Peter sees in this."

Levi chuckled. "I expect it takes practice. What do you say we try that restaurant down the street? We can get a decent meal and talk about what to do next."

"I don't care what you do. I'm going home." For

the first time Nicki looked up at him, and he was shocked by the combination of anger, hurt, and fear he saw in her slightly reddened eyes. It almost looked as though she'd been crying.

"My God, Nicki, what's wrong?"

"Wrong? Nothing's wrong. I just want to go home. If you've decided you want to stay here, that's fine with me. I can find my way back to Nowood." She slipped the knife back into its sheath and stood up. "If you'll just give me my money, I'll be on my way."

"Nicki . . ."

She put out her hand. "My money?"

Perplexed by the sudden change in her attitude, Levi reached into his shirt pocket, drew out a leather pouch, and handed it to her. "I just figured you might enjoy eating in a restaurant." He pulled a roll of bills from a back pocket and put it in her hand. "Then I thought we might get a couple of rooms at one of the hotels and stay to see the play they're having at the theater tonight." He retrieved the rest of the money from his watch pocket and gave it to her.

"I don't have time for such foolishness. In case you've forgotten we . . . no . . . I have a windmill to build and less than two weeks to do it in." She stuffed the money into the pouch before tying it to her belt and sticking it safely into her pocket. Then she walked over to the hitching rack and untied Wildfire.

"Nicki, what's gotten into you?"

Completely ignoring him, she swung up into the saddle and headed down the street that led out of town.

In spite of his bewilderment, he was secretly relieved that they were leaving. Nicki wouldn't have to meet Stephanie and Cole after all. Levi had been astonished and delighted to discover that Stephanie and his brother Cole had come to South Pass City on their honeymoon.

Levi had thoroughly enjoyed the half hour he'd spent with them, but when he'd thought about introducing Nicki to his brother, he found himself strangely reluctant to do so. He was afraid of how she'd react when she discovered he wasn't the homeless drifter he seemed to be.

Now it appeared that keeping his secret was the least of his worries. Unless he missed his guess, Nicki was off on another of her week-long snits, and this time he didn't have the faintest idea what he'd done wrong. Swearing under his breath, Levi tucked the gift he'd bought her into his saddlebag, mounted his horse, and followed Nicki up the road.

"What do you want?" she asked, when he caught up with her.

"I thought we were going home."

"And I thought you wanted to stay in South Pass City," she said with a tinge of bitterness in her voice.

"Only if you wanted to."

"I don't."

"Obviously. It was just an idea anyway. I figured we'd only be able to travel two or three hours before dark so we wouldn't be losing much time."

"A few hours might mean the difference between making Lowell's deadline and not," she said.

"I doubt it."

"Don't let me stop you from going back." Nicki intended to make it clear he was under no obligation to her, that he was free to return to Stephanie. In spite of her attempt to be nonchalant, her words sounded petulant.

"I have no reason to go back. Besides, as you said, we have a windmill to build," Levi reminded her.

"Peter and I can do it."

Levi sighed in exasperation. "Just how do you plan to do that? I doubt you have the slightest idea how to even start."

"I'm sure there are directions in one of the crates."

Levi resisted the urge to point out that she couldn't read the instructions even if there were any. "It doesn't matter anyway. I said I'd build it and I will."

Nicki shrugged. "Suit yourself." She'd been sure Levi would find some way to remain behind and had planned to make it easy for him. Now a tiny, forbidden hope raised its head. Maybe he wouldn't marry Stephanie after all.

She ruthlessly squelched the idea as soon as it occurred to her. Though her mind shied away from an image of what must have happened in the hotel, it was impossible to ignore the kiss she'd witnessed. How could she have forgotten even for a moment, that Levi belonged to another woman?

After several unsuccessful attempts to draw Nicki into conversation, Levi left her to her thoughts, and they rode in silence for the rest of the afternoon. By the time they reached their previous camping place at the foot of the mountain, it was almost full dark.

"Might just as well camp here." Levi dismounted next to the fire ring they'd used the night before. "Whose turn is it to cook?" he asked, hoping to get a smile out of Nicki.

But she merely shrugged. "Doesn't matter to me."

She missed the defeated look that crossed Levi's face as he watched her walk away.

With her indifference firmly in place, Nicki went through the now familiar ritual of setting up camp while Levi fixed supper. Both were sadly aware of how different their relationship had been a mere twenty-four hours earlier. Each was as miserable as the other, but neither knew how to mend the breach. With very little conversation and no laughter, they ate their supper of beans. At last they retired to their lonely bedrolls on opposite sides of the fire and tried to sleep.

In the darkness, Nicki's anguish could no longer be held at bay and rose up to form a tight knot in her throat. As they'd ridden down the mountain, she'd kept wondering why Levi hadn't stayed with Stephanie. It was sometime during the interminable afternoon that Nicki realized he probably couldn't support a wife. Not on the forty dollars a month she paid him. Though he was with her still, Nicki knew it was only out of a sense of duty that he remained. Once the windmill was built as he'd promised, Levi would surely leave to find a better job and marry Stephanie.

With that thought came a thousand images of Levi. Some were memories of the few stolen moments she'd spent in his arms, but most were of all the things he had done for her. Even now he was riding away from the woman he loved to make Nicki's life more secure.

Such loyalty should not go unrewarded, nor would it. When Levi finished building the windmill, Nicki would give him a generous bonus. Then he'd have enough money to marry Stephanie if he wished. The noble decision didn't bring Nicki the comfort she sought, though. Instead, it started a freshet of unexpected tears that she seemed unable to stop.

On the other side of the fire, Levi heard the stifled sobs and gritted his teeth against the pain that slashed through his heart. His arms ached to hold her, to soothe away the agony, but he knew Nicki would reject any comfort he offered. Worse even than listening to her sobs was the certain knowledge that he had unwittingly caused them somehow. Just when he'd started to penetrate her defenses, Nicki had closed up against him once more. Damn Samantha Chandler and the scars she'd put on her daughter's soul!

They made the trip in record time. Conversation was desultory as Nicki drove them mercilessly toward their destination. The only lightening of her mood came when she produced the sardines for supper the second night on the trail. "I bought something different for supper tonight," she said as she pulled the tins from her saddlebag with a flourish. "The man at the mercantile said they were delicious."

"Sardines!" Levi, who was rather fond of the small, salty fish, greeted the surprise with genuine delight. "I haven't had sardines for . . ." he broke off with a grin as Nicki opened the first can and regarded the oily contents with undisguised horror.

"Ugh." She wrinkled her nose at the strong smell. "You mean to tell me people actually eat these things?"

Levi chuckled at her obvious dismay and took the half-opened tin from her hand. "Not only eat them but enjoy them. You'll find they taste considerably better than they smell."

"They'd have to." Nicki watched uncertainly as

Levi removed a sardine, placed it between two crackers, and consumed it with apparent enjoyment.

Then he fixed another and handed it to Nicki. "Here, try one."

Nicki regarded first Levi then the fish suspiciously. Finally, after watching Levi eat his second, she gingerly took a taste. The flavor was unlike any she had encountered before. It wasn't particularly unpleasant, but then it really didn't taste good either.

Levi grinned. "I guess it's an acquired taste."

"I think you're right." She took another bite. "And I'll bet the man that sold them to me knew it, too. He thought he'd have some fun with a boy still wet behind the ears." The corner of her mouth quirked. "I guess they aren't all that bad. In fact I'm sure I'll come to love them." She popped the rest of the sardine into her mouth and closed her eyes as though savoring it. "Mmmm, delicious."

Levi grinned. "You never let anyone get the best of you do you?"

Nicki opened her eyes and smiled mischievously. "Not if I can help it." As she reached for another sardine and more crackers she suddenly remembered Levi holding Stephanie in his arms. "Not if I can help it," she repeated softly to herself, as the smile faded from her lips.

With a sinking feeling in the pit of his stomach, Levi saw the happiness evaporate from her face as she withdrew behind her wall of defense.

The next morning Nicki roused Levi long before the sun touched the eastern horizon and set off down the trail. He had to hurry to catch up with her and then almost wished he hadn't when he was greeted with a wall of silence.

They reached home just as Peter, Liana, and Emily were sitting down for the noon meal. Amid the welcoming chatter, Nicki presented the gifts she had brought for her family. To Levi she seemed happy for the first time since South Pass City, yet even now there was a fragile quality about her.

As soon as the meal was over, she jumped to her feet. "Let's go, Peter. We have a windmill to pick up."

"Would you mind if I go along?" Liana asked. "I need to get a few things up in town."

"Of course, I don't mind. We'd love to have your company wouldn't we, Peter?"

Levi scooted back his chair and stood up. "I'll go too."

"No!" Nicki said in a rush. "I want you to . . . ah . . . get things ready here so we can start building as soon as Peter and I get back."

"But . . ."

"We'll be back in an hour or so," Nicki called over her shoulder as she headed out the door.

Levi sank back into his chair with a defeated sigh.

"What was that all about?" Emily asked, looking at him over the rim of her coffee cup.

"I wish the hell I knew," Levi said.

"Did something happen on the trip?"

"Everything was fine until we got to South Pass City." Levi rubbed his forehead. "No, it was better than fine. She was bubbly, cheerful, full of mischief, happier than I've ever seen her. Then we split up to cash in the gold. When I found her several hours later, I was almost sure she'd been crying. At first I thought maybe some miner had seen through her disguise and accosted her." He sighed. "But now I'm afraid it has something to do with me."

"What makes you think that?"

"She tried to leave me in South Pass City, for one thing. Then on the ride down the mountain, she wouldn't talk to me, not even to argue. And that night she cried herself to sleep."

"That doesn't necessarily mean you were the cause."

"It happens every time I get close to her. As soon as she starts to respond, she remembers I'm a man and pulls back into her shell again."

Emily thought of the blood she'd found on his bed the night he'd been stricken with malaria, but she could never ask him such a personal question. She watched Levi moodily contemplating the bottom of his coffee cup. "Are you in love with her?"

Levi looked up and stared at her for several seconds before he nodded. "Yes, though God knows I tried to avoid it."

"You tried to avoid it! Whatever for?"

"I'm twelve years older than she is, for one thing."

"Oh pooh." Emily dismissed the idea with a wave of her hand. "I know many happily married couples who have more years between them than that."

"And I hate farming."

"Oh, well that may be a bit of a problem."

"A bit," he agreed with a ghost of a smile. "But that's just a small part of it. About the only thing we agree on is good horseflesh. Everything else is likely to produce sparks." He shook his head wearily. "It's like sitting on a keg of dynamite. I never know when she's going to explode."

Emily smiled. "There's a lot to be said for sparks when they're between two people who care about each other."

"I know, but I'm not sure I'm cut out for that kind of relationship."

"So why do you stay?"

"Because I promised Cyrus I wouldn't go as long as there was any danger to Nicki and Peter." Levi stood up and walked over to the window. "And because I don't think I could stand to leave," he added softly, gazing out at the garden.

"Are you going to marry her?"

"I don't know. My feelings don't matter much anyway. She'll never let me be more than a friend."

"I'm not so sure. It's possible she pulls away from you because she's afraid of the way you make her feel, especially if she finds herself falling in love. Nicki's still very confused about love. She's terrified of following in her mother's footsteps."

Levi gave a short, humorless laugh. "That's about the last thing she'd do."

"I know, but every time she looks in the mirror she sees Samantha." Emily shook her head. "The resemblance is amazing, but it's only skin-deep. Inside they're as different as a mother and daughter can be. It's going to take time for Nicki to understand that."

"And when she finally does?"

"I wish I knew," Emily said sadly. "I wish I knew."

31

"*I still don't* understand why you dug here," Nicki said, standing at the bottom of the nearly completed wooden tower and staring at the pipe sticking out of the ground. "The spring is a hundred feet away."

Levi stepped down off the structure and took the dipper of water she handed him. "And I've told you a dozen times, we put the well here because that's where the water is closest to the surface."

"According to the witching rod," Nicki scoffed.

He drained the dipper and wiped his mouth with the back of his hand. "Same thing. Ask Peter how long we had to dig before we hit water."

Peter held up three fingers then traced the path of the sun with his forefinger.

"Three days. So what? It probably would have taken less if you had started directly above the spring opening."

"I had the same thought when he started walking around with the willow switch," Peter signed, "but he showed me how to do it, and I felt the pull of the water, too."

"Well I still don't believe in water witching." Nicki stomped over to the wagon where Liana and Emily were laying out lunch.

Peter grinned at Levi. "It is good that Nicki was mad at you when we dug the well. We would still be digging," he signed and pointed to the top of the hill, "up there."

Levi grinned. "I have no doubt you're right."

Peter's eyes danced. "Maybe I'll make her so mad she won't talk to me when it's time to clean the barn."

Levi chuckled. "Probably won't work if you want it to. Women are like that."

He sobered as he gazed back up at the top of the windmill where they would soon start building the platform that would enable them to mount the windmill head. There was almost no chance that they'd be finished by Herman Lowell's deadline the next day. "Let's go eat so we can get this thing done."

They ate lunch quickly, as they had all week, and went back to work. Peter stopped long enough to kiss Liana, a bit too thoroughly, Nicki thought with irritation. Then she looked away, ashamed of herself for thinking such a thing. They'd only been married two weeks and Peter had spent most of that time working fifteen hours a day building the windmill.

Levi's deep voice called her attention. "How much longer do you think it will take you to finish putting the windmill head together?"

"I don't know. A few hours at most." She looked up at him. "Maybe less. The framework is all done and we've only got about ten more blades to put on."

He nodded and started to unbutton his shirt. "Good. Shouldn't take us much more than that to get ready for it. If we don't get it on today, we'll be able to tackle it first thing tomorrow and finish up late tomorrow or early the next morning."

Nicki blinked at his bare chest as he sat down to pull off his boots and socks. "Wha . . ." she cleared her throat. "What are you doing?"

Levi stood up and shrugged out of his shirt. "That tower is thirty-two feet in the air. I don't want to take a chance on getting hung up on something up there or . . ." For the first time Levi seemed to notice Nicki's wide-eyed shock. A blush crept up his neck as he rubbed his hand over his bare chest self-consciously. "I got in the habit when I had to climb the rigging on the ship. If it bothers you . . ."

"It doesn't matter to me what you wear," Nicki snapped. "You can go up there stark naked for all I care."

With a shrug, Levi started up the ladder.

There was something about his hard muscles rippling under bronzed skin that was difficult for her to ignore. Nicki didn't even try. Her gaze followed him all the way to the top of the tower. Gradually she became aware of Liana standing next to her, waiting patiently. "Ah, you're finally here," she said, as though she'd been waiting for Liana's arrival.

"I've been standing here since Levi took off his boots." Liana's eyes sparkled mischievously. "You were too busy watching him to notice me."

Nicki flushed. "I was surprised, that's all. It's nothing to me what he does. Let's get back to work."

Liana succeeded in keeping a straight face as she settled down next to Nicki. "By all means."

Time passed swiftly, but the work seemed to go slowly, even after Emily came up to help. If Nicki's eyes strayed rather too frequently to the top of the wooden structure where the men were working, nobody seemed to notice.

The long shadows of afternoon were creeping across the sagebrush as the women hefted the next to the last blade into place. Levi and Peter were just putting the finishing touches on the platform about six feet down from the top. No one noticed the rider approaching from the west until the lilting voice called out.

"Yoo-hoo, Nicki."

As one, the three women looked up to find Amanda Lowell waving at them from the other side of the fence.

Nicki's eyes narrowed suspiciously. "What the devil does she want?"

"Do you suppose her father sent her?" Liana asked.

"Probably." Nicki stood up and dusted off her pants. "I'd better go see what she's up to."

It took her only a few minutes to reach the fence. By then Amanda was staring at the top of the windmill with rapt attention.

Nicki frowned. She didn't even have to glance up to know what held the other woman's interest. "Close your mouth, Amanda," she said peevishly. "You'll catch flies."

"What?" Amanda blinked and looked down at Nicki with a bemused expression on her face. "Oh . . .

I was just . . . ah . . ." Color suffused the delicate skin of her cheeks.

"Yes, I know what you were doing, but I don't think that's what you came here for."

Amanda gave her head a tiny shake, as though to clear her mind. "No, I came to see how things are going and to warn you."

"To warn us?" Nicki's voice was sarcastic. "Don't you mean to spy and deliver another threat from your father?"

"Daddy doesn't even know I'm here. If he did . . ." Amanda sighed in defeat and started to turn away. "Never mind, I see I've wasted my time."

"No, wait." Nicki was dismayed for once by her own rudeness. "I'm sorry, Amanda. I guess I'm just tired. We've been working so hard lately."

"That's what I came to find out." Amanda looked uncertainly to the windmill tower. "Will you be done today?"

"Levi says we should be able to finish up by late tomorrow."

"But Daddy said he was only giving Levi until tomorrow morning before he came over with his men."

"It's only one day."

"I know. But you know Daddy. Once he delivers an ultimatum, he never backs down."

"Can't you talk to him?"

"I can try, although I don't know what good it will do. He's been grumbling for three weeks about how he should never have listened to Levi in the first place. I'm afraid he'll be here tomorrow no matter what anybody says to him." Worry shadowed her limpid blue eyes. "I don't want anybody to get hurt, Nicki."

"Neither do I."

Nicki and Amanda exchanged a glance, then looked at the top of the tower where Levi and Peter had just hoisted the pivot into place.

The last vestiges of light had left the sky by the time the five weary people drove back to the house and trudged through the chores. As soon as they ate the cold supper Emily had prepared, they fell into bed exhausted.

Sunrise the next morning found them just finishing chores before they headed for the windmill once again.

"Are these pulleys big enough?" Nicki asked, presenting the heavy block and tackle for Levi's inspection.

He paused in the process of coiling a thick rope to take a look. "I think so. If it can lift a load of hay into the barn, it should be able to lift the windmill head."

Nicki went to the back of the wagon and started to load the collection of ropes and pulleys. "What are we going to do about Herman Lowell?"

"I guess we'll just have to play it by ear." Levi tossed the rope into the back of the wagon. "Maybe he won't show up today."

"You don't really believe that after what Amanda told me, do you?"

He sighed. "No, but worrying about it isn't going to change things. The way I see it, finishing that windmill is the one chance we've got."

"What if it's not good enough?"

"I don't know, Nicki." He gazed down at her as he

shut the tailgate. "If something happens, promise me you'll keep your head."

"Keep my head? But I haven't lost . . ."

"Look," he interrupted, "for some reason, Herman Lowell doesn't want to hurt you. If the worst happens, you may be able to use that to protect the others. Just remember, your lives are more important than any piece of ground. With Cyrus's gold you can always go somewhere else and start over."

The odd expression on his face as much as his words erased the indignant retort from her lips as a nameless fear began to grow within her. "Wh . . . what about you?"

"Oh, I'll be there too," he said, turning away. "I just wanted to make sure we understood each other."

"Levi?" Nicki's gaze traveled uncertainly to his face. "What is it?"

"Nothing." But when his eyes met hers an unexpected spark of foreboding flashed between them. Levi reached up and tenderly traced the line of her jaw with his thumb. "Nicki, I . . ."

She never knew what he had been about to say for Emily came bustling up to them with a basket of food slung over her arm. "Here I am. I hope I didn't keep you waiting."

Levi dropped his hand. "No, we just finished loading the wagon. Where's Peter?"

"Milking. He said to go ahead without him." She glanced toward the barn. "And here comes Liana now."

Levi nodded. "Guess we'd better get moving."

Traveling in the wagon that morning was almost torture for Nicki. An overwhelming sense of urgency made her want to jump down and race ahead to the hill by the spring. When they finally arrived at their destination, she was tempted to bark orders at her companions, who all seemed to be moving at a snail's pace.

Even with the combined efforts of everyone, it took over an hour to mount the newly completed mill head onto the cumbersome gearbox. At last, it was ready to raise to the top of the tower. Peter had just secured the block and tackle to the top of the windmill when a sharp gasp from Liana drew their attention to the area just beyond the fence.

Herman Lowell and a dozen mounted men spanned the brow of the hill with drawn guns and forbidding expressions.

With apparent nonchalance, Levi picked up his own rifle and headed toward Lowell. Only the look of rock-hard determination on Levi's face gave any indication that he considered this more than a friendly social call.

It was then that Nicki realized what he had been alluding to earlier, and her stomach gave a sickening lurch. Only the promise she'd made him kept her from snatching up her own rifle and running to his side. Instead she placed it across her lap, a position from which she could shoot accurately within seconds if need be.

"Good morning, Mr. Lowell." Levi's deep voice rolled through the morning air. "What brings you here so bright and early?"

"Your three weeks are up, Cantrell." Herman Lowell gestured toward the empty horse troughs. "And I don't see the water you promised."

"The windmill is almost finished," Levi pointed out calmly.

"So you built a windmill. That doesn't mean a damn thing until you prove you can use it to fill these troughs."

"We can. All we need is a little more time."

Herman Lowell almost sounded regretful as he unholstered his gun. "Sorry, Cantrell, your time just ran out."

A hysterical sob rose in Nicki's throat as she watched thirteen rifles rise in unison and point straight at Levi Cantrell's heart.

32

"Now wait a minute, Lowell." Levi held up his hand as though to forestall any action. "The way I see it, we've still got until sundown today."

"What difference is that going to make?" Lowell asked. "Another few hours won't change a thing."

Levi shook his head. "That's where you're wrong. We hit water two weeks ago. All we need to do is put the hardware from the windmill in place, and prime the pump."

For the first time, Herman Lowell looked at the nearly completed windmill. "How long will it take you to get everything where it belongs?"

"We're ready to raise the mill head now. After that it's just a matter of hooking the sucker rods to the windmill and the pump and setting up the troughs. We'll be done tomorrow morning at the latest."

"What if . . ."

"Stop!" The frantic cry split the air and everyone

turned to see Amanda Lowell galloping up the road. She slid to a halt just behind Nicki, jumped from her horse, and ran up the hill. There she threw herself in front of Levi and spread her arms wide as if to protect him as she faced her father. "You can't do this, Daddy!"

"Amanda, what are you doing?" Lowell demanded.

"Levi saved my life. You can't shoot him down in cold blood."

"Amanda . . ."

"No, Daddy, nothing you can say will sway me. I won't let you kill him. You'll have to go through me first."

Lowell's expression was thunderous. "Amanda, for God's sake . . ."

If tensions hadn't been so high, Levi would have been tempted to laugh. As it was, he wanted to wring Amanda's neck. The last thing he needed was her theatrics to complicate things. With one strong arm, he lifted her out of the way. "Excuse me, Miss Lowell, your father and I have some business to discuss."

Amanda was clearly shocked by such ungrateful behavior. "But . . ."

"Amanda," Lowell said between clenched teeth, "if you say one more word, so help me God I'll lock you in your bedroom for a month."

Amanda gave Levi a bewildered look then turned on her heel and flounced over to her horse.

Lowell scowled. "She gets the damndest notions."

"I'm sure she means well." Levi's tone was understanding, as though he dealt with such hysteria every day. "Anyway, as I was saying, if you can just let us have until this time tomorrow, we'll have a working windmill."

"I can't wait until tomorrow. I need the water now. You say it will take the rest of the day for you to finish. How long would it take if you had help?"

For a moment Levi was too surprised to respond. "Well . . . considerably less I'd say."

Herman Lowell was silent for a minute while he contemplated the unfinished windmill. Abruptly, he switched his gaze to Levi and nodded. "All right, Cantrell, you've got your help." He slid his rifle into the scabbard. "Come on men, we've got a windmill to finish."

At first the atmosphere was strained, but eventually everyone was too busy to worry about hostilities. Lowell set half his men to work putting together the sections of pipe that would stretch from the pump to the troughs while the others helped Levi and Peter hoist the mill head and gearbox to the top of the tower. Well before noon everything was in place, and everyone was anxiously waiting to see if the system would work.

At a signal from Levi, Peter released the windmill head from its bonds. Catching the vanes, the wind pulled the head around and the blades started to rotate in the hot summer breeze. With a squeal of protest, the sucker rods began the up-and-down motion that would—Levi hoped—pull the water from the ground.

For several endless minutes nothing else happened. Then a tiny trickle flowed from the end of the pipe while everyone held their breath in nervous anticipation. At last, with a mighty gush, water poured into the trough.

A cheer went up from the watching cowhands who started slapping each other on the back while Liana kissed Peter and Emily shook Herman Lowell's hand as though they were lifelong friends.

Caught up in the excitement of the moment, Nicki threw her arms around Levi and hugged him with all her might. Nearly delirious with relief, Levi swept Nicki high into the air and twirled her around. When their lips met, it was in a kiss of celebration, but it soon became much, much more. The world seemed to disappear. The windmill, Herman Lowell, even the crowd of people around them ceased to exist. All that remained were Nicki and Levi, wrapped in a velvet haze of emotion. Misunderstandings evaporated, walls crumbled, and two hearts rejoiced. Finally the kiss ended as it began, with no conscious effort from either of them.

As they gazed into each other's eyes a thousand words that would never be spoken aloud passed between them. Then Levi smiled, set Nicki firmly on the ground, and slapped her on the back. "We did it!"

The festive atmosphere continued over a lunch thrown together by Emily and Liana and washed down by cold draughts of springwater. Feeling shaken by their incredible exchange, Nicki avoided Levi, afraid of what she might find if their eyes met. It was hard to pretend nothing had happened when her entire universe had just tilted on its side.

Watching Levi turning aside Amanda's blandishments, Nicki fought to regain her equilibrium. Nothing had changed. Levi Cantrell was still a drifter, and now that the windmill was finished he'd be moving on. The beautiful Stephanie awaited him with open arms. For Nicki the celebration was over, and Emily's delicious food tasted like ashes in her mouth.

Every day Nicki expected Levi to break the news that he was leaving, but he seemed perfectly content to stay where he was. When she tried to give him a generous bonus for building the windmill, he not only refused it, he acted as though she'd insulted him by even offering.

Days turned into weeks. August slipped into September, and the nip of fall replaced the sultry heat of summer. Much to Levi's dismay, Amanda Lowell became a frequent visitor. He usually found something pressing to do elsewhere, but she often stayed until he reappeared. Nicki watched her friend with growing disgust.

Though the drought continued unabated, Levi's plan had averted a range war. The water supplied by the windmill wasn't enough for Herman Lowell's needs, but he was well-aware that nothing would be gained by having total control over the Willow Creek spring. The valley settled into a kind of armed truce as man and animal alike prepared for the coming winter.

Once again, Nicki treated Levi with guarded friendship, and he reacted by keeping his distance. The kiss they'd shared at the base of the windmill was never mentioned. In retrospect, it became even more precious, a memory each of them could take out and savor at will.

Daily tasks fell into a familiar routine that continued along smoothly until Nicki realized Peter and

Levi hadn't included her in the plans for the huge fall roundup. Peter was the first target of her ire.

"I don't need to go! What are you thinking of?" Nicki demanded.

"We only need two riders. I think you should stay home," Peter signed. "It's too dangerous."

"Dangerous! Of course it's dangerous, and that's part of the cattle business. Since when has that ever stopped me?"

"It's not the cows he's worried about," Levi broke in, "it's . . ."

"Oh, so it's me then! You think I can't handle myself."

"No, that's not what I . . ."

Nicki glared at both of them. "I'll have you know, I can outride, outshoot and outrope any man there." She turned on her heel and stomped off to the barn.

The two men looked at each other sheepishly.

"We didn't handle that very well, did we?" Levi said. "I suppose she'll calm down, and we can explain later."

Peter raised his eyebrows. "You think she will understand we are afraid the other cowhands will hurt her if they see she is a woman?"

Before Levi could answer, Nicki and Wildfire came tearing around the corner of the barn and streaked past the two men at a high lope. Levi sighed. "No, I don't guess she will at that."

Even the wind rushing past her face and whipping through her hair did nothing to cool Nicki's temper. Men! As though she hadn't proved herself over and over again. The more she thought about Peter and

Levi thinking they didn't need her, the madder she became. By the time she noticed the young coyote she was past rational thought. All she saw was a golden opportunity to show Peter and Levi she was as good as any man.

Before she even considered the consequences, Nicki had made a loop in her lariat and swung it in a wide circle above her head. With a nudge of Nicki's heels, Wildfire instantly moved in on their quarry. An expert flick of the wrist sent the lasso sailing through the air to land around the coyote's neck. A triumphant smile lit Nicki's face as she pulled the loop tight and the animal jerked to a halt. Her elation lasted less than thirty seconds.

Wildfire paid no attention to the snarling captive as she backed up and kept the rope taut as she had been trained to do. Nicki watched with a sense of dread as the gray, furry ball crashed into a sagebrush and bounced over a cactus. The only way to remove the rope was to loosen it and pull it off by hand. She'd done it hundreds of times but never when the animal in question had long, sharp teeth and a nasty temper.

For what seemed like an eternity, Nicki maneuvered Wildfire around, trying to get close enough to get some slack in her lariat and allow the coyote to pull its head free, but it proved to be futile. The frightened coyote continuously jerked on the rope, pulling the noose tighter and tighter until it began to look as though the animal would choke itself to death. At last, in defeat, Nicki turned toward home, dragging her unwilling prisoner behind.

For the most part, the coyote followed like a dog on a leash. Every so often, though, he held back, tugging against the irresistible force that pulled him along. These times were the most trying for Nicki. The rope would jerk, and she'd look back to find the animal dragging along on its side. As soon as she slowed, the coyote would struggle to its feet and trail after the horse and rider once more.

By the time she reached the homestead, Nicki felt almost as desperate as the coyote. During the long ride, a dozen plans occurred to her, only to be discarded as impractical. Wildfire had done very well, but she was decidedly nervous by the time Nicki located Levi piling dirt onto the roof of the root cellar. Even though she was busy trying to control the skittish young mare, Nicki didn't miss the look of astonishment that crossed Levi's face when he spied the coyote at the end of her rope.

Nicki's humiliation was complete when Levi leaned on his shovel and tried not to grin. Before she could think of anything bright and witty to say all hell broke loose.

In a terrified bid for freedom, the coyote darted for what looked like a safe haven, the open door of the root cellar. Startled, Wildfire reared in panic, and Nicki had her hands full trying to calm the frightened mare without losing her seat.

Peter stuck his head out of the doorway to see what was keeping Levi. As the streak of gray fury careened into him, he raised his shovel and smashed it down on the head of the coyote in a reflex reaction. Peter stared down at the crumpled body on the ground then looked up at Nicki.

"You killed him!" she cried.

"What did you want me to do?" Peter signed, his eyebrows rising in surprise.

Nicki shook her head angrily. "I wanted . . . I just . . ." she stumbled to a halt when she realized there was absolutely nothing she could say. She glared at Levi, who was desperately trying to keep a straight face.

"He'll make a nice pair of mittens for you," Peter signed. "I'll skin him as soon as I'm finished with chores."

"Mittens?" Nicki was horrified.

Peter shrugged. "Then we'll sell the hide. It's a prime pelt, so we can get top dollar for it."

Nicki eyed the matted fur doubtfully as Wildfire continued to prance around. "If you say so." A strangled noise from Levi drew her attention. Her lips thinned in irritation. It was obvious the man couldn't contain himself much longer.

With a defiant toss of her head, Nicki turned Wildfire toward the barn. It wasn't until Levi's laughter filled her ears that Nicki realized the rope was still tied to her saddle horn and she was still dragging the coyote. Already embarrassed beyond endurance, she didn't even slow down as she pulled the rope off and threw it aside. She heard the knot hit the wall of the chicken coop and wished she could bounce it off Levi Cantrell's head.

Within the cool darkness of the barn, Wildfire and Nicki both regained a measure of their equilibrium. Wildfire calmed under the ministrations of the currycomb. Nicki chose to ignore Peter when he came in to do the milking. She was embarrassed enough without his twisted sense of humor.

Suddenly the chickens began squawking in apparent terror. Nicki rushed outside and halted in stunned amazement. The coyote no longer lay dead on the ground. Instead it raced back and forth in front of the chicken coop, held there by the rope whose end was wedged securely under the corner of the building.

Without any clear plan in mind, Nicki ran forward but stopped short when she realized she didn't have the faintest idea what to do.

"Well, I'll be damned," Levi's deep voice drawled beside her. "Never thought about him just being knocked out. Almost hate to do this."

Nicki turned just as Levi raised his rifle to his shoulder. As though feeling her horrified stare, he glanced her way. Their eyes met and held for several tense seconds, then he sighed and lowered the rifle. "Oh, all right. I guess we do this the hard way." With a weary shake of his head, he went into the barn.

The minutes ticked by while Nicki waited nervously and the coyote paced back and forth. Levi finally reappeared wearing his buffalo coat and a pair of thick leather gloves. As he walked past her, Nicki caught an acrid whiff of singed hair.

Levi grabbed the rope in one hand, and walked slowly toward the coyote. The lariat ran through his gloved hand as he cautiously approached. At last, when he was within reach, he grabbed the coyote, pinning it to his chest with an elbow and holding the mouth closed with one hand. With a piece of rawhide, he wrapped the canine snout shut, then carefully removed the rope from its neck.

Nicki could see the muscles in Levi's jaw flexing with the effort it cost to keep the terrified animal immobilized as he slowly rose to his feet and walked to an open space away from the chicken coop. I'm going to let him go now," he called back over his shoulder. "Whatever you do, don't get between him and the road out of here." With a quick twist Levi pulled off the rawhide string and tossed the animal away from him. The coyote hit the ground running for the prairie at high speed.

"Do you suppose he'll come back and get into the chickens?" Nicki asked belatedly as the coyote disappeared over the hill.

"I doubt it." Levi chuckled as he coiled her lariat. "In fact I'll bet he doesn't stop running until he hits Dakota Territory!"

33

With a happy sigh Nicki snuggled into the hard warmth and smiled. As her mind cleared, she gradually became aware that she was nestled in Levi's arms, her body exactly fitted to the contours of his and separated from him only by the blankets of their bedrolls. Panic gripped her until she realized he was still asleep. She relaxed, secretly enjoying the sensations the close contact created.

Levi couldn't blame her for this anyway. He and Peter had insisted she sleep between them during the roundup. Privately, Nicki thought both of them were being ridiculous. All the other men just assumed she was Levi's little brother.

With nearly a hundred cowhands from fifteen different ranches working the roundup, staying away from Herman Lowell's men had been easy. So far no one else had given her a second glance. For the most part she'd been ignored, just as she had every other year she'd come on the roundup.

She ought to extricate herself without waking Levi up, she thought sleepily, but it could wait. For now she wanted to drift along in her comfortable cocoon for awhile longer. It wasn't long before sleep once again overcame her.

Sometime later Levi shifted in his sleep and released her without hearing Nicki's whimper of protest.

Nicki awoke just before the sun peeked up over the horizon. She couldn't help thinking there was something very nice about waking up next to a man like Levi Cantrell. She enjoyed studying the firm line of his jaw covered with dark stubble and the thick lashes fanning his cheeks. He was so close she could reach out and touch him if she dared. The memory of being in his arms was almost like a dream, but there would be no embarrassing explanations or apologies. Nicki was free to store it away as though it were a special gift, freely given with no strings attached.

By the time Levi woke up, Nicki was long gone. He knew she'd only ridden away from camp to answer the call of nature without danger of discovery, but for some reason he felt vaguely irritated by her absence. He felt like a grouchy old bear as he crawled out of his bedroll and rubbed his stubbly face. God, he hated his beard when it was this length. It itched. But then everything about the last four days had been annoying, one frustration after another. Roundups like this one had been a part of his life for nearly twenty years, but this was the first one he'd ever seen through the eyes of a homesteader.

Within an hour of arriving, Levi understood where Nicki's negative attitude toward ranchers came from. Even though the three of them worked just as hard as everyone else, the cowhands treated them as though they were somehow lacking. More than once Levi had heard the words "squatter" and "sodbuster" muttered behind his back. Even his mild temper had been ruffled.

He nudged Peter's shoulder with his toe to awaken him, then bent down to roll up his own bed. He'd seen a new side to Peter, too, one he didn't particularly like. The first time Peter affected his slack-jawed, stupid look Levi had been incredulous. He understood it was a strategy the deaf youngster had developed to avoid trouble, but it made Levi downright angry to see the intelligent man hide behind a facade of simple-mindedness.

Then there was Nicki. Trying to keep an eye on her had been a severe strain on him. She was like quicksilver, impossible to pin down. When he pointed out that the cowhands from the Bar X knew she was a woman and were therefore a danger to her, she'd just laughed and said she could outsmart Lowell's flunkies without even trying. After a few well-placed threats, the Bar X crew had given Nicki a wide berth, but Levi still didn't trust them.

As bad as the days were, the nights were worse. With her right next to him, his dreams were often very disturbing. He felt as if he spent all night chasing her. Slinging his bridle over his shoulder, he went to get Lady. Thank God today was the last day of this. The cattle buyer would be here this afternoon, and then they could all go home.

* * *

"Thirty-three dollars a head, and that's the best I can do." The cattle buyer rubbed the side of his nose, and waited as the sounds of disbelief rumbled through the cattlemen.

"That's three dollars a hundred-weight," someone said angrily. "Four years ago it was five dollars."

The buyer shrugged. "That was four years ago. Steers were a lot better quality then, not so thin. Wilson's only offering two seventy-five."

A clipped British voice cut through the grumbling indignantly. "I say, that's doing it a bit too brown don't you think? Two dollars and seventy-five cents? Why, that's absurd!"

"So wait until he gets here and find out for yourself. Anyway, I'll be leaving in the morning. If you want to sell, you know where to find me." He walked to the picket line, mounted his horse, and headed toward town.

Nicki heard more than one rancher say he'd be damned if he'd sell for such a low price. She drew Peter and Levi away from the rest of the cattlemen. "What do you think? Do we sell or not?"

"The price of beef on the hoof has been falling steadily since '82," Levi pointed out. "If it continues, you'll get even less next year."

"But it has to bottom out somewhere," Nicki said.

"Maybe so, but can you afford to wait and see how far it drops first?"

"We don't really need the money," Nicki reminded him. "What do you think, Peter?"

"I think we should sell. We have only enough hay to feed thirty cows all winter."

"He's got a point there." Nicki nodded decisively. "All right, we sell. I'll go tell him."

Peter reached out and grabbed her arm as she turned to go. "No you won't. Levi will go."

"Are you off on that track again? We already had this out, and I won, remember?"

"No." Peter shook his head emphatically. "Levi and I let you come to the roundup, but you didn't win."

Nicki put her hands on her hips indignantly. "Oh really? Then how come you changed your minds?"

"We were afraid you would rope a mountain lion," Peter signed, grinning.

"Very funny!" Nicki gave him a disgusted look but couldn't quite hide the blush that crept up her neck.

"In this case he's probably right," Levi put in gently. "Even if that cattle buyer thinks you're a boy, he's likely to try to cheat you. I stand a better chance of getting the full price for your cattle."

Nicki glared at him for several seconds and then gave in. "Oh, all right. I guess it really doesn't matter who goes. Peter and I'll gather the rest of the cattle and go home. I suppose Emily and Liana will be wondering where we are." She glanced at Peter. "Especially Liana."

Within the hour they were headed for home. Nicki was secretly glad Levi was making the trip to town. The five days of the roundup had been tiring. She was looking forward to a hot bath and her own soft bed.

Today, she decided, she'd indulge herself. On the ride home, she'd think about Levi as much as she wanted to. Then maybe he'd stop popping into her head and she could forget about the strange things he made her feel.

During the next three hours Nicki relived every

close encounter she'd had with Levi over the last seven months. But when it came time to stop she found she couldn't. There was still so much she didn't understand.

According to Emily, it was perfectly natural to feel these uncomfortable yearnings for a man. Even Samantha had done nothing wrong there. It was only when she committed adultery that she stepped beyond what was proper. Nicki herself had not done anything improper.

Her only liaison with Levi, Nicki discounted, since Levi didn't remember it and she had been too naive to understand what was happening until it was too late. Still, there were times—too many in fact—that she dreamed of doing it again.

Over the next few weeks it didn't seem to matter how many times Nicki reminded herself Levi would be leaving soon or that it was simple lust she was feeling; she couldn't quit thinking about him. They harvested the garden and she thought about him. Preparations for the coming winter went into full swing and she thought about him. Peter and Levi went hunting for a week and she thought about him.

Like a badger digging out a prairie dog she kept mulling it over and over in her mind. The thought that she might be in love with Levi she rejected immediately. Liana and Peter were in love and they never disagreed about anything. There was very little she and Levi hadn't fought about at one time or another. Still, when he'd kissed her by the windmill she had felt something happen deep inside, something that had changed her forever.

34

"*I thought you* might be here," Levi said as he swung a leg over the sawhorse and picked up a bridle. "I need to talk to you about something."

Nicki stopped rubbing the saddle she was cleaning and looked up at him in consternation. *Here it comes,* she thought with a lump forming in her throat. *He's leaving. I'll never see him again.* Not trusting herself to speak, she went back to her work. The tack room suddenly seemed very small.

"Looks like we're going to have a bad winter."

She looked up in surprise. The weather was the last thing she'd expected to discuss with him. "What makes you say that?"

"Have you noticed how thick the horses' winter coats are?"

Nicki nodded. Even Wildfire, who was generally quite sleek, was beginning to look almost furry. "Yeah, I guess so."

"I've never seen so much hair on horses before." Levi turned the bridle in his hand, and rubbed his thumb over a buckle absently. "The elk Peter shot on the mountain was the same way, and it had so much fat under the hide, it looked like a milk-fed hog. Kind of strange when you consider how short feed has been down here in the valley."

"What are you getting at?"

"I think we're in for it. Nature has a way of preparing her animals to survive."

"And you think heavy hair and thick fat mean a hard winter." It made sense and Nicki was frightened by the implication. Wyoming winters were always hard. What if the coming one was worse than usual? "What should we do?"

Levi dipped the rag and started rubbing saddle soap into the bridle. "I've never been one for ignoring a warning no matter where it comes from. There's more than enough food, that pile of wood is sufficient to keep a roaring fire going for six months, and your cattle will have plenty of hay. I'd say you're as ready for it as you can get."

"Then why are we having this conversation?" Nicki asked.

Levi stared at her silently for several seconds, as though he was unsure how to proceed. "I want to stay," he finally blurted out.

"What?" She couldn't believe her ears. He wanted to stay!

"I know cowhands are supposed to ride the grubline during the winter," he said, "but if this winter is really bad, there's going to be too much work for just you and Peter."

Nicki just stared at him, her hand frozen in midair.

He didn't want to leave! She'd never even considered that possibility. Of course he'd prefer staying here to riding the grubline, a Western tradition that some had started to question. The big cattle ranchers didn't pay cowhands during the winter months. As a means of survival the unemployed cowboys traveled from ranch to ranch, staying for a week or two before moving on to the next. It was an inefficient system, but it was to the advantage of the big landowners.

"Nicki?" Levi, still waiting for his answer, was watching her intently.

She blinked then turned her attention back to the saddle she was cleaning. "It's fine with me," Nicki said as evenly as she could with her heart pounding so hard he must surely hear it.

"Good, then I'll leave tomorrow."

"Leave?" Bewildered, she let her rag fall still again. "I thought you said you wanted to stay."

"I do, but I have something I need to do before winter sets in." Levi did some quick calculations in his head. He should be able to get to Horse Creek and back in a week and a half. "If I leave tomorrow, I should be back by the second week in November."

Nicki's heart fell. He was going to Stephanie just as he had before. Only this time she was here in Wyoming. Levi thought he'd be coming back but he wouldn't. Rubbing the saddle leather hard, Nicki wondered why he had bothered going through this charade with her.

"Nicki?" When she refused to look up he laid down the bridle and walked over to the shaving stand.

Tears threatened to blind her and she blinked them away angrily. "I've changed my mind, Cantrell. We won't be needing you around here after all."

"Maybe not, but I need a place to stay." He came back to her. His deep voice was gentle, persuasive. She could have sworn he touched her hair lightly but the sensation was gone in an instant. "Would you mind keeping these for me until I get back? I won't need them, and I hate to pack unnecessary weight."

Nicki eyed the familiar articles. "That's your shaving brush and razor."

He nodded. "My grandfather's actually. They mean a great deal to me, that's why I'm asking you to keep an eye on them until I get back. If you still want me to leave then, I will."

Cautiously she looked up at him. What she saw caused her breath to stick in her throat. He was asking her to trust him. The only sound in the tiny room was the soft rustle of fallen leaves brushing the outside wall of the building. Slowly her hand rose to take the brush and razor from him. "Well, I suppose I can do that much for you."

"Thanks." With a smile he settled down across from her, picked up the bridle again, and went back to work.

The two weeks Levi was gone were busy ones for Nicki. Emily seemed delighted with his decision to stay but pointed out that he wouldn't be able to sleep in the barn during the cold winter months. It took very little time to move Levi's meager possessions into the room Liana had deserted when she married Peter. Nicki set up her father's shaving stand and hung his mirror on the wall, but she kept Levi's shaving things on her dresser.

The rest of her energy was spent making Levi a

warm winter coat. She used the red wool blanket she'd bought in South Pass City. Emily accepted Nicki's blithe explanation that she had decided to make the coat because Levi couldn't afford a decent one on what she paid him, and he needed one since his buffalo coat had been ruined in the prairie fire. Nicki didn't admit, even to herself, that she had intended it to be a coat for Levi all along. Sometimes she would stop sewing long enough to wander into her bedroom and touch his shaving brush. Then she would return to her chair, reassured that he would indeed return.

The first blizzard of the year struck without warning. The morning had been beautiful, but by early afternoon snow was falling. As the wind began to howl, Nicki found herself pacing back and forth to the window nervously. She kept telling herself there was nothing to worry about. Everyone was safe inside and it was useless to look for Levi until tomorrow or the day after. Yet something drew her to the window over and over. Once she thought she saw a movement in the gloom, but it wasn't repeated.

Staring out into the thick white mass of swirling snow, a deep sense of foreboding, almost like a premonition, settled over her. So intense was her concentration that when the door swung open, a startled exclamation burst from her lips. A huge snow-covered creature slammed the door against the wind and began to shake the snow from its limbs. When the familiar form of Levi began to emerge Nicki's heart began to beat faster instead of slowing down as it should.

"I wasn't sure I was going to make it home there for awhile," he said, throwing his saddlebags over the back of a chair. "About the time I was starting to get worried I saw the corner post by the gate. Didn't think I'd ever be so glad to see a barbed wire fence." He glanced at the overflowing woodbox. "Looks like you've got plenty of wood. What about water?"

"Peter brought in three buckets just a little while ago," Emily said, bringing the broom to brush the snow from his legs and feet. "You must be half-frozen. I'll get you a nice bowl of hot stew." She brushed snow from the back of the old buffalo coat with her hand. "Let's get those wet things off before you catch your death."

Shrugging out of his coat, Levi caught Nicki's eye and smiled uncertainly. "You're still mad at me, aren't you?"

"Mad?" Nicki gave him a blank look. "I'm not mad at you. What made you think I was?"

"All of my things are gone from the barn."

"Oh. That was Emily's idea."

Levi looked from one woman to the other. "Emily's mad at me?"

"Certainly not!" Emily swept the snow into a pile and dumped it in the pail next to the door. "We thought you'd be more comfortable in the house, that's all. You're in the room next to Peter and Liana's."

"But you won't be sleeping there tonight, I'm afraid," Nicki said, turning to the window again and lifting the curtain. "Papa always brought the cot into the main house for Peter whenever we had a blizzard. It's too cold in the other part." She dropped the curtain. "Liana and Peter can have my bed and I'll bunk with Aunt Emily. We'll bring the cot in for you, Levi."

"Shall we start moving things now, or do you want

to eat first?" Liana asked from the stove, where she was stirring the stew.

Peter shook his head emphatically. "No, we can eat later. If the wind shifts, the dogtrot will fill with snow."

"I'll go get started on the cot then." Levi put his coat back on.

It wasn't until Nicki went to get the nightclothes from her bedroom that she remembered Levi's shaving things. For some reason it seemed very important that she not wait to give them to him. Donning her coat, she scooped them into her hand and followed Levi across the dogtrot to his new bedroom.

She found him just standing there, staring down at the red coat that lay across the bed.

"Oh, I forgot to tell you about that. I didn't think your old buffalo coat would make it through another winter so I made you a new one," she said.

"You made me a new one?" He looked at her with incredulous eyes. "And with the blanket you bought in South Pass City."

"I figured if you owed me a horse, I owed you a coat."

"It's not the same thing."

"Oh, it is too," she told him brusquely, laying the shaving brush and razor on the stand. She walked over to the bed, picked up the coat by the shoulders, and shook it out. "Here, try it on."

"I hope it's big enough," she went on as he shrugged out of his old coat and put on the new. "I used that old shirt you left behind for a pattern." Stepping back, Nicki observed the effect with a pleased smile on her face. "It's a perfect fit. The color looks good on you too."

"I don't have to worry about getting lost," Levi told her with a grin. "You'll be able to see me for miles." Then he sobered and ran his hand up the sleeve. "I've never had such a beautiful coat."

"Not for a long time, anyway," she said, glancing at the shaggy buffalo coat on the bed.

Levi gave a mock frown. "Before you say something rude, I'll have you know I traded Pa's mule for that coat when I wasn't much more than a kid." He picked it up and hung it on a wall peg.

"You traded a perfectly good mule for it?" Nicki gave an unladylike snort.

"Always figured I got the better end of the deal too. I hated that mule and the buffalo hunter I traded him to was almost as ornery as he was."

"Your pa must have been madder than a grizzly bear in a wolf pack. I'll bet you had trouble sitting down for a good long time."

Levi grinned. "He wasn't any too pleased, but my punishment was far worse than a whipping."

"What could be worse than that?"

"He sold my horse. As I remember, it was very effective." His smile softened. "Thank you, Nicki. No one has ever done anything like this for me before."

"Oh fiddle." She tried to ignore the warm glow it gave her as she walked over to the shaving stand. "What I really came in for was to return these to you." She ran her finger down the handle of the shaving brush as she had so many times over the last two weeks. "Of course you won't need them till spring."

"Probably not, but thanks for keeping them for me."

"No problem. Well, guess I'd better go . . ."

"Wait. I have something for you too." Levi looked

around in confusion. "There was a small package wrapped in brown paper . . ."

"It's in the top drawer of the dresser." Nicki watched curiously, as Levi located the package and handed it to her with a flourish.

"What is it?"

"Something I picked up in South Pass City for you."

Removing the paper Nicki found a small book inside. She stared at it blankly then raised regretful eyes to Levi.

"But I don't . . ."

"Read. I know. That's what this is for." He reached over and flipped it open. "It's a McGuffey reader. You can learn to read with this."

She ran her hand over the cover. "Truly?"

"Truly. It looks like we're going to have plenty of time this winter. We can even start tonight if you want."

"I . . . I don't know what to say." Nicki fought tears at his thoughtfulness. He didn't even know how badly she'd always wanted it. "To learn to read . . ."

"You may not feel that way by spring." He lifted his hand and traced the line of her cheek with the backs of his fingers. "It's going to be hard work, and I have the next two books in my saddlebags."

The color of her eyes deepened as she gazed up at him. "We weren't expecting you for a couple of days yet. I'm glad you made it back."

"Me too."

"I missed you. Peter's no fun to fight with since he got married."

Levi grinned. "Well it's nice to know I'm appreciated for something important." He dropped his hand regretfully. "Now where's this cot?"

"Hmmm? Oh, it's right over here."

The moment was lost but the memory of it lay soft and warm between them.

Most people would remember that winter as a nightmare of week-long blizzards, subzero temperatures and fifty-foot drifts. With lampblack around their eyes to protect them from snow blindness, Peter and Levi spent at least an hour every day chopping holes through the ice so the cattle could drink from the creek. They used the hay wagon, which had been converted to a sled, to deliver hay to the small herd. Some days the weather was so bad, they were unable to take the hay rack out. There was nothing they could do except follow the ropes they had strung between the house and the barn to feed the farmyard stock and pray for the others.

There was a good side to that winter too, at least to the five people who shared the Chandler cabin. Winter was the only point in a homesteader's life there was any time for leisure, and this winter was no exception.

When the work was finished for the day there were reading instructions for Nicki and later Peter, who decided he should learn too. A good-natured rivalry developed between them, to see who could read clear through the beginning book first. Even though the lessons had a tendency to involve a great deal of teasing and laughter, Levi was amazed at how swiftly his pupils progressed. In the end, it was Peter who finished the first book but Nicki won on the second book.

In the evenings the women sewed while Peter and

Levi worked with wood. Levi spent hours smoothing and shaping the spindles, arms, and rockers of a chair while Peter worked on a carving he said was a wedding present for his wife. As he watched the beautiful face of Liana take form in the wood, Levi began to realize the incredible talent the younger man possessed.

It took quite a little persuading, but Peter finally brought out the carvings he had made over the years. Levi was stunned by the sheer beauty the man had captured in wood. His first attempts were of fish and seabirds. As his technique improved there were horses, cows, coyotes, bears, and deer. Then there were the people. Though some were unfamiliar to Levi, there were several of Cyrus, and half a dozen of Nicki. There was even one of Herman Lowell and another of Mrs. Adams.

The carving Levi kept returning to was one of a much younger Nicki. By depicting Nicki's dancing eyes and gap-toothed grin, Peter had captured the essence of the child who still lived in the woman. It was the same image Levi carried in his heart of the woman he loved.

35

"I don't care if these little January 'thaws,' as you call them, usually come before a storm." Hands on hips, Nicki glared at Levi as he calmly sipped his morning coffee. "That's all the more reason we should take advantage of it and go to town before the weather breaks again."

Levi knew it was useless to argue with Nicki when she was in this mood, but he thought maybe he could make her see reason for once. "Just how do you plan to get there? The snow's too deep for the wagon and too soft for the sleigh."

"So we ride and take Sam along as a packhorse. Look, Cantrell, I know it's dangerous, but this is the first time it's warmed up since November. If we don't go in for supplies, we may never get another chance."

"We'll come home in a blizzard," he warned. "That is, if we make it home."

"That's what you said yesterday, and today is even

nicer." Nicki pointed at the window. "There's even water dripping off the roof. What more do you want?"

Levi threw his hands up. "All right, I'll go. But only because I know you'll go by yourself if I don't." He stood up and walked to the door with a purposeful stride. "Let's get moving."

With a gleeful skip, Nicki scurried after him.

The trip to town proved to be even more difficult than Levi had predicted. The snow was belly-deep to the horses in many places and they had to go around drifts piled far over their heads in others.

The warm sun had only made things more treacherous, with the top layer of snow melting and the water catching in pools that had no place to go. It took almost four hours to reach town, a trip that was normally accomplished in less than thirty minutes.

After buying a sack of flour, another of sugar, a bag of coffee beans, and a few other odds and ends, they were on their way again. Nicki didn't even want to linger for a visit with Mrs. Adams. Small dark clouds were scudding across the sky, and within an hour of their departure the temperature began to fall.

Nicki glanced at the sky. "How long do you think we have before it starts to snow?"

"It's hard to say." Levi turned to look at her. "Losing your nerve, Nicki? You're the one who wouldn't listen to reason and insisted on coming. There's no going back now."

"Who said anything about going back? I just asked when you thought it might start to snow." She was stung by his tone. "You've been telling us all week what the weather was. I just figured you'd have an opinion, that's all."

Levi turned back around, satisfied he'd made her angry enough that she wouldn't panic if they got caught in a blizzard. He glanced back at the sky and prayed the snow would hold off until they got home.

Fat snowflakes were just beginning to fall as they rode into the barnyard. Peter greeted them at the door, relief evident in his face. "We were afraid we would have to come out after you."

"Don't be ridiculous!" Nicki swept by him as though she were the queen of England. "It's only a few snowflakes, nothing to be worried about."

"Maybe not yet," Levi said, "but I was right about the storm."

"Yes, but we got to town and back before it hit. Just remember that the next time you have a cup of coffee and a piece of fresh bread."

Peter rolled his eyes at Emily and Liana. "Neither one can say I told you so," he signed, "and now both of them are mad!"

Though the storm turned out to be a small one, it brought low temperatures. On the homestead the cold was a minor irritation, but on the open range it proved to be disastrous. The water produced by the thaw froze into a hard, icy sheet locking all beneath it. Unable to get even a few blades of grass, range cattle faced certain starvation. They drifted, roaming in an endless search for food and water.

In some places, where the crust was not so thick, their hooves broke through with every step, the sharp edges scraping at the animals' legs until they bled. Many wandered down into gullies and canyons where the drifts were the deepest, others were stopped by fences. Unable to go farther, they huddled together, waiting for death.

The pitiful bawling and moaning of the starving cattle pressed against the fence was almost more than the residents of the homestead could stand. Day in and day out, night after night, the sound beat at them until they all felt like screaming. But it was almost worse when the sounds stopped, for they knew death had claimed the wretched beasts. All would be quiet until another bunch would wander down to the fence.

Peter was unaffected by the sound, but he saw the living skeletons every day when he and Levi went to feed their own small herd. His face took on the same haunted quality as those who could hear.

"Oh God. I can't stand it anymore!" Nicki cried one night, holding her hands over her ears, trying to block out the hideous bawling of the range cattle. "Why can't we just feed them?"

Levi put down the chair leg he was sanding and looked at her sympathetically. "You know the answer to that, Nicki. It's only the middle of February and we've already used all of the hay in the field stacks. If the winter lasts much past the first of March, we're going to run short for your own stock. We just can't take the chance."

"Oh, I know." She rubbed her elbows and took an agitated turn around the room. "But it seems so cruel to just sit here, and we aren't even responsible for it. I wish all the ranchers would starve. They deserve to die a slow death for what they've done."

"Nicki!" Emily was aghast at such an unchristian sentiment.

"Well, it's true, and I hate them all."

A muscle in Levi's jaw jumped. "No one intended this to happen, Nicki."

"No, of course they didn't. People like Herman Lowell wanted everything to go on just the way it always has. Nobody cares that there's a limit to how many cattle the range can support. Any fool could see where it was headed, but that didn't make any difference. This winter would have been a disaster even if it had been a mild one."

"Not all ranchers are to blame."

"Every single person who didn't grow hay and then turned stock out on the prairie is to blame." Nicki kicked the wall angrily.

Realizing it was useless to argue with her, Levi lapsed into silence. Her attitudes might be somewhat narrow-minded, but she did have a point. He went back to smoothing his chair leg.

The evening passed slowly, and everyone seemed relieved when it was finally time to go to bed. Everyone but Levi. Nighttime had become a torture for him. Alone in the dark, his mind turned to Nicki as it almost always did.

Lately he had come to realize what he'd been searching for when he left his home. It was that special relationship that existed between his brother and Stephanie and now between Liana and Peter. Levi wanted that kind of closeness with Nicki. He knew she didn't share his feeling—not yet, anyway.

But, God, she was driving him crazy! He desired her in ways he had never desired another woman. Forbidden images floated through his mind only to be violently pushed away in dismay. He was still trying to put the whole subject from his mind when his concentration was interrupted by the soft feminine sighs and rhythmic squeak of the bed ropes that were a nightly occurrence in the room next door. Levi almost groaned aloud with frustration. Having Peter and Liana around all the time certainly didn't help matters.

That night the nightmares began. They were dreams born of a reality so long ago, Levi's conscious mind had all but forgotten. Once again he was a terrified two-year-old, huddling unnoticed in the corner of the room. Wind and rain lashing against the darkened windowpane were nearly drowned out by the loud, demanding cries of the newborn child.

Levi's big, strong father knelt by the bed, his head touching the cold, white hand that lay so still. Jonathan Cantrell, the man who feared nothing, was crying unashamedly, tears coursing down his face, as he begged forgiveness, blaming himself for the death of his beloved wife.

Most frightening of all was the blood. It was everywhere, on the floor, the blanket, and especially on the bed surrounding the one who lay there unmoving. Though the small boy didn't fully understand what was happening, he knew something had gone very, very wrong in his safe little world.

The nightmare of Levi's mother's death recurred every night for the next few. Then, gradually, it began to change. Levi became the man by the bed, and Nicki, the wife who had died in childbirth. The first time he saw Nicki's face surrounded by blood, Levi woke in a cold sweat. Sitting up in the half-light of dawn, he crossed his arms and sank his face onto his bent knees with a stifled moan.

At last he understood why he'd been having the same dream over and over. Levi was a big man, larger even than his father, and Nicki's tiny body was too small to bear his children. He could never marry her. He'd rather be without her than responsible for her death. At that moment he felt as hopeless as the cows by the fence outside.

By the time the sun had risen above the horizon that morning, Levi had accepted the fact that he would soon have to leave. The drought was obviously over, and so was the threat of Herman Lowell. When spring arrived, with his promise to Cyrus fulfilled, Levi would be free to go.

Tired of the endless winter, everyone looked forward to the coming of spring. For Levi, the days with Nicki were bittersweet and poignant, because he knew they were numbered. He stored it all away, every smile, the sound of her husky voice, the flash of her violet eyes, each hoarded against the day when memories were all he would have.

On the fifth of March, a warm Chinook wind finally broke the iron fist of winter. Sweeping down from the mountains, it brought the long-awaited spring to the beleaguered land. Like children released from a schoolroom, Liana, Peter, Nicki, Levi, and even Emily tumbled outside to romp in the melting snow.

Nicki pelted Levi with a snowball, and he immediately returned fire. Before long everyone was involved, with Peter and Levi delivering their missiles far more accurately than their adversaries did.

Suddenly, amid flying snowballs and girlish laughter, Levi found himself tackled and pushed down in the snow. After having his face thoroughly washed with cold, wet slush by three determined women he lay there, helplessly laughing, while Peter received the same treatment from them.

Chinook winds continued to blow unabated for the next few days. At first they were gloriously welcome, but the warm weather brought its own kind of horror. Fast-melting snow, unable to soak into the still-frozen ground, filled creeks and gullies to the point of overflowing.

For the first time in Nicki's memory, Willow Creek overflowed its banks, washing away the garden plot and coming up almost to the house. For nearly a week, the winter-ravaged land suffered under the onslaught of spring.

At last, the floodwaters receded, and the mud began to dry up. Suffering from a severe case of spring fever, Nicki decided she'd been housebound long enough. Using the excuse that it was high time they check the range, Nicki had an easy time coaxing Levi out into the bright spring sunshine with her.

Their lovely ride soon turned into a nightmare neither of them would ever forget. Littered with hundreds of dead cattle, the prairie looked like something straight out of hell. Most lay where they had fallen, dead of starvation and thirst, but some floated by in the still heavy spring runoff.

The farther Nicki and Levi rode, the worse the carnage. They came to a small stream where the bodies were so thick they could have walked on them for a quarter of a mile without ever touching the ground. The smell of rotting carcasses was nearly overwhelming in some places, and Nicki had to fight the urge to gag more than once.

*

She was torn between the desire to scream in rage or cry hysterically. Levi, as sickened as Nicki by the senseless waste and destruction, rode in complete silence, hands gripped so tightly on the reins that his knuckles showed white. It seemed as though nothing had survived the disaster. Suddenly the unexpected bawl of a calf split the air. Nicki turned startled eyes to Levi, and then searched the surrounding area for the animal.

She finally located the calf standing on a stone out-cropping on the other side of a deep gulch. Before Levi could stop her, Nicki was off her horse and scrambling down the side of the gully, completely oblivious to the strange roaring noise that suddenly filled the air.

At first Levi couldn't place where he had heard that sound before. Then he knew. Vaulting off his horse, he hit the ground running.

"Nicki!" But his bellow was drowned out by a wall of water eight feet high.

36

One minute Nicki was clambering up the steep bank toward the calf, the next she was trapped in a terrifying maelstrom. Icy water surrounded her on all sides, choking and strangling her, stealing the air from her lungs as it tugged at her with incredible force. Only Levi's iron-hard grip around her waist kept her from being swept away.

The crest passed in less than two minutes, but it seemed a lifetime to the two people dangling from the side of the ravine. Gulping great lungfuls of air, Nicki clung to Levi's arm, afraid he wouldn't be able to hold on to her. His other hand, which gripped a large sagebrush, and the negligible protection of the outcropping were all that kept them from being engulfed in the deluge. Nicki wondered how·much longer he could stand the incredible strain.

Levi felt as though his arm was being jerked out of the socket. White-hot pain shot through his shoulder and down his back. With every ounce of strength he had, he tried to haul them both up the embankment, but the pull of the water was too much for him. Then he felt Nicki move, her legs bracing against the bank in an effort to help him. With a mighty heave, Levi used their combined leverage to lift them up out of the flood.

For several minutes they both lay there on the ledge, gasping for breath.

"Can . . . Cantrell. A . . . are you all . . . right?"

"Y . . . yes."

"Th . . . then m . . . move. You . . . you're killing me . . ."

With his arms still around her, Levi rolled onto his back, hugging her to his chest as though he were afraid to let go. For a long time, Nicki stayed there, taking comfort from his closeness. Gradually their panting ceased and their hearts slowed. It was only when Nicki started to struggle that Levi released his hold and sat up. He watched her crawl over to the calf, who had remained above the flood.

She rubbed its neck. "It's all right, little one. You're safe."

"That's more than I can say for us." Levi stared out over the raging torrent. "Our horses are on the other side."

"Don't worry, we're safe too."

Levi gave her an unreadable look. "In case you haven't noticed, we're soaking wet. I figure we've got about half an hour before we're in danger of freezing to death."

Nicki just smiled enigmatically and crawled along the ledge again. She stopped beside a rock that leaned against the cliff wall. With both hands, she pushed it aside, revealing the opening of a small cave. "Peter and I found this when we first came to Wyoming." She grinned over her shoulder at him. "Welcome to the hideout."

Though not tall enough for Levi to stand in, the cave was surprisingly roomy. Over a foot shorter than he, Nicki moved about it with ease. She lit a candle, then went to the back of the cave and began rummaging through an odd-looking box.

Levi glanced up at the smoke-blackened crack in the ceiling that had obviously been used as a chimney. "I don't suppose you have a flint."

"Of course I do, and there's dry kindling over by the woodpile." She tossed him the flint and went back to the box.

Levi set to work building a fire, paying little heed to the sounds behind him. A tiny flame was just starting to take hold when Nicki came up beside him.

"Here. It's a little scratchy, but you won't have to worry about freezing."

Levi's glance took in the blanket she held out to him, then followed her arm up to the naked shoulder. Nicki had removed her wet clothing and wrapped a blanket around her body, securing it under her arm. Wordlessly, Levi accepted the blanket from her and watched in tongue-tied silence as she went to pick up her discarded clothing. The firelight gilded her damp, curly hair and cast a mellow glow over the smooth skin of her shoulders. Feeling as though a heavy weight had slammed into his chest, Levi swallowed hard. He thought he'd never seen anyone so beautiful.

She paused in the process of laying her clothes by the fire to dry and looked at him. "Well, go change. I won't peek."

Not trusting himself to speak, Levi nodded and crawled to the back of the cave. By the time he had struggled out of his boots and pulled off his outer clothing, the fire was burning brightly. His long johns were cold and clammy, but he didn't even consider taking them off. There was only so much temptation a man could resist. The blanket was itchy, but its warmth welcome as he joined Nicki by the fire. He arranged his pants and shirt self-consciously before he sat back and contemplated the smoke going up the natural chimney.

"This is a pretty amazing place."

Nicki nodded. "Peter and I always thought so. We used to come here when Papa and Mama . . . When we wanted to get away. Peter stopped coming when Mama left, but I still use it sometimes." Nicki looked toward the entrance. "This is the first time I've ever been trapped here. Where did the water come from?"

"Probably a big drift up the gulch somewhere. I've seen it happen before when there's a fast thaw. The water builds up behind an ice dam until it finally breaks through. My pa always called them gully washers."

"I thought gully washers were from cloudbursts."

Levi nodded. "They usually are. Whatever causes them, they hit without any warning."

"I never realized how dangerous that gulch was." Nicki frowned. "I guess I'll have to be more careful."

"Do you come here often?"

"Not so much anymore, but I used to come a lot." Nicki sighed. "Now it's mostly when I want to be alone, or I need to think."

The image of a small animal going to a safe place to lick its wounds rose in Levi's mind. "This is where we were headed wasn't it?" he asked gently.

Nicki stared unseeingly at the fire for several minutes. "Yes," she finally whispered brokenly, covering her face. "Oh God, Levi, there were so many." Her voice caught on a strangled sob. "They starved to death, damn it. What a horrible way to die."

"I know, Nicki, I know." Levi put his arms around her and buried his face in her hair. The image of dead cattle piled up like so many pieces of wood was strong in his mind too.

They clung to each other as if to reassure themselves that life still flowed through their veins. At first they touched to give comfort, and then because they couldn't quit. Emotions too-long suppressed surged to the surface in a flood of desire that neither could have stopped, even if they had wanted to.

When their lips finally met, the kiss had a desperate quality to it, as though this moment would evaporate like all the rest. Then Nicki's arms swept up around Levi's neck and her lips opened beneath his. The world disappeared, and they gave in to the heady sensations overwhelming them. Trailing featherlike kisses across Nicki's face, Levi pulled his blanket around her until it enclosed them both in a warm, safe cocoon.

With a sigh Nicki settled against him and gently pushed him to the floor of the cave. His lips found hers and she was pulled down into a whirlpool of desire. All of her inhibitions seemed to dissolve. Even her blanket gapping open didn't break through her cloud of euphoria. When she started to undo the buttons that ran down Levi's chest, he sucked in his breath.

"This thing is wet," she murmured, tugging at the damp fabric. She slipped her warm fingers inside to the chilled skin of his chest, and snuggled closer. "Why don't you take it off?" she whispered against his neck.

Levi groaned as an exquisite shudder ran through him. Together they peeled off the offending garment, and he tossed it aside. Their bodies molded together in a perfect harmony of contrasts, cold against warm, rough against smooth, man against woman. With hands and mouths they explored each other, reveling in the differences, delighting in the intoxicating arousal.

It was like nothing Nicki had ever experienced before. The first time, she had been innocent and unsure. Now she had certain expectations, but found that they didn't even come close to the ecstasy Levi was creating in her. He seemed to know her body better than she did herself. With lingering kisses and tender caresses, he sent devastating tremors rippling through her until she was a quivering mass of desire.

Rolling her onto her back, Levi cupped her face in his hands and gazed down into the beautiful violet eyes, smoldering now with passion. "I'll be as gentle as I can, love," he whispered, stroking her cheek with his thumb.

"I know." Nicki shifted to accommodate him and sought his lips in a drugging kiss, bracing herself for the pain. But the agony never came, only rolling waves of glorious sensation, rushing higher and higher in a wild symphony of passion. His name was on her lips as they reached the explosive crescendo, and she fell back to earth in trembling, throbbing, wonder.

Afterwards Levi lay beside her with her head nestled against his shoulder, their breaths mingling as their hearts slowed. Curled up the way she was, she reminded him of a well-fed kitten. He could swear she was almost purring. Savoring the moment, he closed his eyes and pushed away the questions he knew he would have to ask.

He was nearly asleep when Nicki's screech brought him up off the floor into a defensive crouch. His heart pounding, he thrust Nicki behind him and found himself face-to-face with the calf they'd left on the ledge outside. Still breathing hard, he looked questioningly over his shoulder.

Nicki stood there wide-eyed, her blanket clutched to her chest. "I didn't know she was there until she put her cold, wet nose on my back," she said defensively. "It startled me."

"Well, you scared the hell out of me!" He turned back to the calf with a disgruntled look. "Now what do we do with you?"

"I'll take her back outside," Nicki said, tucking her blanket securely around her as she walked around him. "You might want to put your blanket on again." She flashed him an impudent grin as she held her fingers out to the calf. "It's a nice view, but it's a little chilly don't you think?" The hungry calf began to suckle her fingers, and she led it outside.

By the time she'd situated the rock so the calf couldn't get back in, Levi's blanket was in place around his waist. He put another piece of wood on the fire and settled back against the wall with a gleam in his eye. "A little chilly is it?"

"I was afraid you'd catch cold."

"Then come here and warm me up." Levi reached up and pulled her down onto his lap. His arms went around her as hers circled his neck. They kissed once again, touching and tasting each other with unhurried curiosity, as though they had all the time in the world. Finally, breathlessly they broke apart, and Nicki laid her head on his chest, a satisfied smile on her face.

All was quiet for several moments as Levi ran a loving hand down the line of her back. "It wasn't the first time, was it?" he asked finally.

"Hmmm?"

"We've been together like this before."

Nicki tipped her head back and looked at him silently. She wasn't going to tell him a thing.

He kissed her forehead then trailed gentle fingers down her cheek. "When I was sick last spring, I woke up with a vivid memory of making love to you. Until today I thought it was just a dream."

"What makes you think it wasn't?"

He pushed a stray curl back from her face. "Because I couldn't possibly have imagined it so closely. Why didn't you tell me?"

Nicki regarded him mutely for a long moment, then pulled out of his embrace and sat staring at the fire. "What was I supposed to say?" She wrapped her blanket tighter around her body and rose. "I was glad you didn't remember, because I wasn't very proud of myself. It wouldn't have made any difference anyway."

Levi looked at her in total amazement. "Wouldn't have made . . . Jesus, Nicki! I took your innocence."

"So?" Nicki threw another piece of wood on the fire. "It's not like you could have given it back if I told you. Anyway, you didn't take it. I gave it to you." There was a tiny catch in her voice as she turned her head away. "I didn't even try to stop you."

"Nicki, don't." He grabbed her hand, rubbing his

thumb across the palm when she tried to pull it away. "If you only knew how often I've thought of that night, wishing it were real. I didn't think it could happen that way." Watching her carefully averted profile in the firelight, Levi felt his heart tighten painfully. God, he loved this woman. "Marry me, Nicki."

Her head snapped up, and she stared at him. "Marry you?" Nicki jerked her hand away. A knot formed in her throat as she remembered Levi's insistence that Peter and Liana marry. She'd been afraid this would happen if he ever learned the truth. "Don't be ridiculous."

"I'm not. I love you, Nicki, and I think you love me."

"Are you crazy?" There was a suspicious prickling behind her eyes as she shook her head. Why did his sense of guilt make him say things like that? "I don't love you."

"I think you do," he insisted. "What we just shared was incredible. It can only happen that way when two people love each other."

Nicki gave a brittle laugh. "What you mean is, it can only happen when two people lust after each other."

He gave her an incredulous look. "You think that's all there is between us, lust?"

"No, I also think we're friends."

"Friends? Damn it, Nicki, I'm thirty-three years old. I want a wife, not a friend."

"That's your problem. The last thing I need is a husband and a bunch of runny-nosed brats. Now, I'm going to get some sleep."

Levi didn't even watch as she rolled herself into her blanket and lay down on the other side of the fire. Her words stabbed into his heart. *I don't love you.*

He'd known it ever since he came back from St. Louis, but today he'd dared hope. With a defeated sigh he rubbed his hand across his eyes as Cynthia's image rose in his mind. He'd thought she loved him, too. Why was his love never returned? Was he doomed to a solitary life?

When Levi noticed Nicki shivering, he crawled over to her side of the fire and pulled her into his arms, telling himself it was only to warm her. When he closed his eyes he saw the haunting images of his nightmare. Her reference to children had served to remind him of the inadvisability of their marriage.

Sick at heart, he realized it was time for him to make his break. Nothing would change if he stayed around another month, except the probability that he'd make love to her again. Holding her close, he lay thinking about his broken dreams as the roar of water outside gradually ceased.

It was the lack of warmth that awakened Nicki. She sat up to find herself covered with both blankets and Levi gone. "Levi?" she called uncertainly, looking around the cave.

"Good, you're awake," he said, crawling back inside. "It's time to leave."

"It is?"

Busily putting out what was left of the campfire, he nodded. "The water is way down, but it may come back up in the morning." He tossed her her clothes and turned his back while she dressed.

"What time is it?"

"Probably around midnight. Luckily, there's a full moon. We shouldn't have any trouble finding our way home." He ducked through the entrance and called back over his shoulder, "Bring the blankets along. It's pretty cold out here."

Within a few minutes they were on their way. The sides of the gulch were slippery and hard to navigate. The calf made things even more difficult, but Nicki refused to leave her behind. All three were liberally covered with mud by the time they climbed out on the other side. Once there, Nicki gave a piercing whistle and waited, but Wildfire didn't appear out of the darkness.

"The horses probably went home." Levi glanced at the moon. "Guess we better get going. We've got a long walk ahead of us."

"Not really. It's only a couple of miles. We came the long way around yesterday." She grinned up at him. "This will be just a nice little moonlight stroll."

The darkness hid the horrors of the previous day, with only the occasional stench of a rotting carcass to remind them of what lay hidden in the night. The calf followed along behind, apparently thinking Nicki was her mother. In a little less than two hours the lights of the homestead came into view.

"Oh, dear. I never thought about how worried they must be." Nicki bit her lip. "You don't suppose Peter is still out looking for us, do you?"

"He probably came home when it got dark." Levi stopped a few yards from the door. "Nicki," he said softly. "Come here."

Without a second thought, she walked into his arms and offered her lips to him. Levi reached down into her soul with his kiss, branding her heart with the heat of his love. When it finally ended, Nicki felt weak and breathless. She closed her eyes and leaned into his solid warmth.

"I love you," he whispered against her temple. He held her a long time, memorizing the feel of her, the smell of her hair, the way her tiny body curved to fit his large one. Finally he kissed her forehead and stepped away. "You go on inside and put everyone's mind at ease. I'll check to make sure the horses are back."

Nicki was still asleep the next morning when Levi announced that he was leaving. Emily, Peter, and Liana did their best to try and change his mind, but he was adamant, saying it was high time he moved on. When he refused to let them wake Nicki, Emily and Liana accompanied him out to his horse to say good-bye.

Emily looked up at him beseechingly. "Is there some place we can contact you if we need to?"

The urge to tell her was strong, but he shook his head. "No, not really." If Nicki didn't love him after what had passed between them yesterday, she wasn't likely to change her mind. He'd go back to his family's ranch, and she'd soon forget all about him. It was better that she never know who he was. "Well, guess I'd better get going. Tell Nicki good-bye for me."

"Wait," Liana said, putting her hand on his horse's neck. "Peter said not to let you leave before . . . Good, here he comes now."

When Peter reached them, he stuck a small cloth wrapped bundle in the saddlebag. There was genuine regret in his brown eyes as he looked up at Levi for the last time. "Good-bye, friend," he signed.

Levi repeated the gestures then reached down and gripped the other man's hand in a farewell shake.

It wasn't until he stopped to camp for the night that he remembered Peter's gift. He pulled the parcel out and carefully unwrapped it. His jaw clenched in pain as he gazed down at the carving in his hand. It was of a young girl with a gap-toothed grin and the devil in her eye.

37

"Oh drat!" Nicki threw her wrench down in disgust and glared at the nut on the broken plowshare. Try as she would, she couldn't get the stubborn thing to budge. It had looked so easy when Levi did it last spring.

Levi! Damn, she'd done it again. Nicki sank her head down on her bent knees with a groan. She'd sworn she wouldn't think about him anymore, but he kept popping into her mind at the oddest times.

The pain was even worse than it had been a month ago when she'd awakened to find him gone. Over and over she kept remembering the way he'd kissed her and said he loved her. How could he do that, and then leave the very next day without even saying good-bye?

Maybe because you threw it back in his face and said you didn't love him, the niggling little voice of her conscience reminded her.

But she didn't love him . . . did she? Somehow she

wasn't as sure as she once was. A gentle touch on her back made her look up in surprise.

Peter sat down next to her. "What's wrong?" he signed.

She pointed to the plow. "I can't get the broken plowshare off."

He nodded his understanding and moved over to the plow. With the discarded wrench he yanked on the offending nut several times before it finally loosened up enough to twist off.

When he was finished, Peter wiped his hands and ambled back to her. "I don't think the plow is your problem." He sat down and looked at her with speculation in the dark eyes. "You've been unhappy since Levi left," he signed.

"Don't be silly, I. . ." Nicki began indignantly, but Peter's raised eyebrow stopped her. "Oh, all right. So I miss him, so what?"

"No, it's more than that. Did you fight?"

Nicki shook her head. "We didn't fight, not really. The only time we disagreed was when I said I didn't love him."

Peter's eyebrow rose another notch. "You lied to him?"

"No," she said crossly. "I don't love him."

Peter stared at her, then shook his head in amazement. "How can you be so empty-headed? Emily, Liana, me, we all knew you loved him. We saw it every day."

"That's impossible." She glared at him in disbelief.

Peter rolled his eyes. "If he walked into a room, your face would shine like the sun," he signed. "You watched him whenever he was near. He made you smile."

"But he also made me very angry. We fought all the time, Peter. How can that be love?"

He grinned. "That's one way he made you happy. You like to fight."

"I don't see you and Liana fighting very much," Nicki said pointedly.

"We are not the same. It is easier for us."

"Well, even if I did love him, Levi doesn't love me."

"He loves you."

"And just what do you base that on?"

"He stayed all winter."

Nicki frowned. "Where else would he go?"

"Wherever he went last fall."

She was puzzled. "You mean when he was gone for two weeks?"

"I think there was someone he had to see. People he didn't want to worry about him."

Stephanie, of course. The thought flashed into Nicki's mind, but this time she wasn't so sure. If he'd gone to see her, would he have come back? Her attention was recalled by the movement of Peter's fingers.

"Liana and I were sure you would marry him."

"He asked me, but he didn't mean it."

There was a long moment of surprised stillness, then Peter's fingers once again began to speak. "Levi is not one to say what he doesn't mean."

"Well, I told him I had no interest in getting married."

He gave her a troubled look. "So he left. Are you sure that's what you want?"

"I don't know what difference this all makes anyway," she said testily. "I have no idea where he went."

"It might be hard, but we could find him. He

wasn't trying to cover his tracks." Peter stood up and gripped her shoulder comfortingly. "Think about it."

For the next two weeks she thought about little else.

Were the unsettled feelings Levi had created in her love? In retrospect she realized their act of love had been more than a mere joining of their bodies. They had communicated on every level of their beings without embarrassment or self-consciousness. It had seemed so natural and right that Nicki still felt no shame. What she did feel was pain, deep and agonizing. It was as though a part of her soul was missing, as if Levi had taken it with him.

It was the agony that finally convinced her it was indeed love she felt for Levi. With this insight came the conviction that she needed to find him. Typically she would have made plans to depart as soon as the decision had been made, yet she found herself putting it off. Feeling strangely lethargic, she never seemed to have enough energy left at the end of the day to do more than drop into bed. She attributed the uncharacteristic exhaustion to the many sleepless nights she'd spent thinking about Levi.

It wasn't until she was violently ill for the third morning in a row that she began to suspect another cause. After emptying her stomach in the chamber pot, Nicki lay very still, willing the nausea to go away as she tried to remember when she had last had her monthly flow. There hadn't been one since the Chinook, almost seven weeks ago.

Fighting panic, she closed her eyes and attempted to recall what Emily had told Liana when the younger woman had thought she might be in a family way. Tender breasts, nausea in the morning, and, most damning of all, the absence of her monthly flow; Nicki had them all. She pressed her fist to her mouth, struggling with the certainty that she was going to have a baby.

There was no way she could go after Levi now. If he knew of her pregnancy, he'd surely feel obligated to marry her, and that was why she had refused his proposal in the first place. A tear squeezed its way out from under her eyelid, and she brushed it away angrily. This was no time to feel sorry for herself. What was done was done, and she'd soon have someone else to worry about.

By the time her stomach finally settled, Nicki still hadn't made any firm decisions about the future. As she pulled herself carefully out of bed, she reasoned she had plenty of time. No one would even notice her impending motherhood for several months yet. Determined to keep her secret from Aunt Emily's sharp eyes, Nicki ran a brush through her hair, washed her face, and pinched some color into her cheeks. With a final look in the mirror she turned to face the day.

About mid-morning she noticed two riders coming up the road. Nicki recognized Amanda Lowell's chestnut, and set her shovel aside without any real regret. Surprisingly, Levi's absence hadn't stopped the vivacious brunette's frequent visits. Some of Amanda's inconsequential chatter would be welcome today.

As the riders drew nearer, Nicki noticed that the figure on the other horse seemed to be wavering in the saddle. With rising alarm, she ran to the kitchen door.

"Aunt Emily, come quickly. Someone's hurt." She dashed back outside and nearly collided with Liana. "Liana, thank goodness you're here. Go find Peter. We may need him."

"Nicki! Oh God, Nicki, please help me!" Amanda's sobs bordered on hysteria as she rode into the yard clutching the reins of the other horse. "Daddy's been shot."

"Shot!" Nicki's horrified glance took in Herman Lowell's slumped form and the bloodied saddle. Sheer willpower had kept him on his horse, but when the steady motion ceased, he began to sag. Peter arrived just in time to catch Lowell as he slipped off the horse.

"Carefully now," Emily cautioned. "He's lost a lot of blood. Let's get him in the house." Nicki signed the words to Peter, and he nodded his understanding.

"It was Buck and Shorty," Amanda babbled tearfully as she followed them into the house. "Daddy caught them red-handed, and they shot him."

"Wait a minute," Nicki said, becoming more confused by the second. "You mean your father was shot by two of his own men?"

"Yes. They're the rustlers, the ones who shot at me last summer. W . . . we saw them ch . . . changing the brands on some Bar X cattle. Daddy was going for the sheriff, but they heard us and . . . and they shot him."

It took several minutes but Nicki finally pieced Amanda's semicoherent story together. Father and daughter had only managed to escape by doubling back and hiding in the brush until the two miscreants had thundered past in search of them. Desperately, Amanda had brought her injured father to the only place she could be sure was safe. Nicki prayed that her friend's faith wasn't misplaced.

When they laid Herman Lowell gently on Nicki's bed, there was a gasp of dismay from the three younger women. The front of his shirt was blood-soaked, the crimson stain covering his entire stomach. Using her scissors, Emily cut the material and peeled it away. She sucked in her breath as she stared down at the wound in consternation. "Nicki," she said, "go get the doctor."

"Dr. Calder? But Aunt Emily, he's . . ."

Emily held up her hand. "Unless the man is out of town or dead, I really don't care what the problem is. Just get him."

For the first time Herman Lowell's eyes fluttered open. "Don't . . . want . . . that . . . damn quack . . . Calder . . . touching me."

"But Mr. Lowell," Emily said, "that bullet has got to come out."

Amanda looked at her beseechingly. "Can you do it, Miss Patterson?"

"I don't know. I've assisted before, but I've never actually removed a bullet, especially one in such a delicate area."

Lowell opened his eyes briefly. "Rather . . . have . . . you . . . than . . . Calder," he rasped out.

"What's wrong with Dr. Calder?" Emily asked.

"He's either drunk or hung over all the time," Nicki told her. "Either way, most folks would rather do without."

In the end Emily did perform the surgery. Peter held Lowell down on one side, while Nicki and Amanda took the other. With Liana helping her, Emily managed to remove the lead and close the wound.

As soon as the last stitch was taken, Amanda staggered back from the bedside. "Oh dear, I . . . I . . ." She crumpled to the floor in a heap.

"Aunt Emily!" Nicki dropped to her knees beside Amanda and touched her wrist. "I think she's fainted."

Emily nodded. "I'm just surprised she didn't do it earlier. We'd better get her to the kitchen before we wake her up."

Peter nodded and stooped to pick up the unconscious girl and carried her out of her father's room.

Wringing out a rag in a bowl of cool water, Nicki applied it to Amanda's forehead while Emily opened her vinaigrette.

Waving the pungent smelling salts under Amanda's nose produced the desired result. With a groan, Amanda opened her eyes and looked around in confusion.

Before she could say anything an unexpected voice intruded from outside.

"No sense in hiding anymore, Lowell. We've got you now."

"It's Buck and Shorty," Amanda squeaked, jerking herself upright.

Nicki quickly moved to the window and peeked out. "It's them all right, and they don't look like they're here for a friendly visit."

38

"*You keep their* attention and I'll sneak around behind them." Peter's fingers flashed the message before he grabbed his rifle and headed for the side door. Nicki nodded, then motioned everyone out of the way. She counted to ten before opening the door and stepping out onto the porch.

"What do you want?" she asked, holding her rifle trained on Buck's chest.

"Well, well, if it ain't the little tomboy. We've got several scores to settle with you. First, though, we're going to finish off Herman Lowell."

"Then I suggest you go find Lowell, and leave us alone."

Buck laughed. "We know he's here. We followed the trail of blood down the road right up onto your porch."

Nicki glanced at the dark red stain by the toe of her boot and shrugged. "Doesn't prove it belongs to

Herman Lowell. Anyway, if he were here, I'd give him to you. He's been a thorn in my side for a long time."

Shorty shifted nervously in the saddle. "I told you Lowell wouldn't come here."

"Shut up, Shorty." Buck's eyes narrowed as he watched Nicki. "We'll just check the house. If he isn't here, you have nothing to worry about."

"Forget it. I don't trust you any more than I do your boss."

"All right, if that's the way you want it, you can all die together. I've been trying to get you and Lowell to finish each other off for damn near a year, but that mountain of a man you had working here kept making peace between you. We'd have got rid of him with that fire if you hadn't come along."

Nicki's eyes widened. "You started the prairie fire?"

"Yup, and we done everything else too," Shorty bragged. "Stampeded your cattle, killed Miss Amanda's horse, even snuck in and cut up one of your harnesses."

"Then it wasn't Herman Lowell?"

"Nope, but you thought it was and he thought it was you. You should'a killed each other off like I planned." Buck smiled evilly. "It doesn't matter now. I have everybody right where I want them. The sheriff will think Lowell was killed burning you out."

Nicki gave a short laugh. "It might work if you were man enough to pull it off, but I don't think you are." Out of the corner of her eye Nicki saw Peter come around the side of the house. "Now get off my property while you still can."

Buck laughed aloud. "Are you trying to threaten us? There's nobody here but a bunch of women and a dummy."

"You might be surprised at what we can do," Nicki retorted, trying not to look at Peter as he crept between the horses.

"Hear that, Shorty? I think we're supposed to be sca . . ." Buck's words were lost in the scream of the other man's horse as it reared up and pawed the air. Before Buck had time to do more than blink his eyes, Peter's strong hands were dragging him from his horse. The two men crashed into the porch just as Shorty's horse rid himself of his rider and took off up the road.

By the time Shorty regained consciousness, Nicki was standing over him with her rifle pointed at his nose. "If you're smart, you won't move."

Noting the determined set of her jaw and the angry glitter in her eye, Shorty lay completely still on the ground.

Though several inches shorter than Buck, Peter was younger and stronger. The fight was violent but brief, with Peter soon overpowering the other man. Within minutes Peter and Nicki had both men tied up.

"Good job, Peter. They never knew what hit them." Nicki clapped him on the back as the door opened and Liana dashed outside.

"Thank goodness you're all right. I was scared to death." She rushed into Peter's arms and buried her face on his shoulder.

Emily and Amanda joined the others on the porch. "What did you do to that horse?" Emily asked. "I thought it was going to trample you all into the dirt."

With a quick kiss, Peter released Liana and glanced

around for his hat. He picked it up off the ground and brushed the dust from its surface. Then, with a grin, he pulled a long thin piece of metal from the felt and held it up for them all to see.

"My hat pin!" Liana exclaimed.

Peter returned the hat to his head and the pin to his wife before explaining. "I thought it might be more useful than my rifle," he signed, "so I grabbed it on the way out and stuck it in my hat." Peter walked over and picked up the rifle that was leaning against the wall of the house. "I brought this too, just in case."

Listening to Nicki's interpretation, Amanda was amazed by Peter's quick thinking. "He's rather clever isn't he?" she whispered to her.

Nicki gave her a sharp glance. "You sound surprised."

"It's just that he's . . . well you know."

"Deaf? Look, Amanda, just because he can't hear doesn't mean he can't think."

"I guess not." Amanda was silent for several minutes, and then confessed her feelings in a rush. "Oh, Nicki, I've been so stupid. When you were talking to those men, I suddenly realized you had no reason to help us. Daddy was the reason your mother left, and last summer he was ready to take the land you worked so hard for." She bit her lip and averted her eyes. "I haven't always been very nice either, yet you and Peter saved Daddy and me today. I don't know how to thank you."

"Then don't." Nicki was uncomfortable with Amanda's gratitude. "We didn't necessarily do it for you. Most of the trouble I blamed on your father obviously came from those two." She looked down at the trussed-up cowboys. "They won't bother either of us anymore." She paused. "Now what do we do with them?"

In the end they loaded them in the wagon. Nicki, Peter, and Amanda delivered them to the sheriff in town. After Amanda explained the situation the sheriff promised to send a couple of men to watch the Bar X just in case there were any more rustlers in the gang.

On the way home, they all decided it would be safer for Amanda and her father to stay at the homestead where Emily could keep an eye on Herman Lowell.

"Amanda," Emily said as soon as they arrived home, "your father is awake and asking for you."

"Do you think he'll make it?" Nicki asked her aunt as Amanda hurried into the house.

"I don't know." Emily removed her glasses and rubbed the bridge of her nose. "We'll just have to wait and see."

Sometime later Nicki found Amanda sitting alone on the porch, teardrops sparkling on the dark lashes in the final rays of the setting sun.

"It's all gone, Nicki," she said without looking up. Nicki sat down beside her, wanting to give comfort but not knowing how. "What is?"

"The cattle, the money, everything wiped out. That's what Daddy wanted to tell me. All we have left is the house and a few acres of worthless ground."

Nicki stared at her in astonishment. "But your father is one of the richest men in the territory."

"He said the low cattle prices over the last few years, and a few unwise investments took all the cash. Then the drought hit and we started losing our stock. The bad winter finished the job. We lost over half of the cattle we had left. There aren't even enough now to start over." Amanda sighed and turned to Nicki. "You know what's strange? I don't even care. All I want is for Daddy to get better, to be strong and sure of himself again. Oh, Nicki, what if he dies?"

Unable to answer, Nicki put her arms around Amanda and let her sob out her fears.

For the next three days and nights, the four women took turns sitting with Herman Lowell. He had brief moments of consciousness when they tried to get him to eat and drink, but for the most part he just lay there. They watched helplessly as the once-powerful man seemed to shrink before their eyes.

One night, as Nicki sat next to the bed sewing, his eyes fluttered open. "Samantha?" he asked in a hopeful voice.

"No, it's Nicki." She spoke gently, but he seemed not to hear as he reached out and took her hand.

"My beautiful Samantha." He studied her face in the candle light. "You're as lovely as ever."

"I'm not . . ."

"Shhh. I know. You're a dream just like all the other times." Lowell rubbed the back of her knuckles with his thumb. "I thought I would stop loving you, but I haven't. Every time I see your daughter I think of you and I remember."

"But I'm . . ."

"You didn't understand did you?" He went on as though she hadn't spoken. "I sent you back to Cyrus because I didn't want to destroy your family. It was the hardest thing I've ever done." Lowell closed his eyes and smiled sadly. "And you thought I didn't love you. God, how wrong you were. How very wrong." His grip slackened as he slipped back into unconsciousness once more.

Nicki sat staring at Lowell. It had never occurred to her that there might have been love between this man and her mother. Gently pulling her hand free, she adjusted the blankets around him. Samantha and Herman had betrayed Cyrus but apparently not entirely for lust. Herman, at least, had cared a great deal.

Could Samantha also have been in love with him? Not only was he a handsome man; the aura of power and wealth that surrounded him would have been difficult for her to resist. Suddenly her relationship with Herman Lowell didn't seem quite so sordid.

Herman Lowell lingered for another two days, then died quietly in his sleep. He was buried in the Willow Creek cemetery, not far from Cyrus Chandler. The tiny graveyard was crowded with people, as the entire town was there and much of the territory. Cattlemen had come from miles around to pay their last respects to a contemporary and friend.

Peter and Liana soon grew tired of the glowers and hate-filled glances directed at them because of her race and his deafness. As soon as the funeral was over they went home with Emily.

Nicki would have liked to join her family, but Amanda clung to her as if she was a life-line. Amanda was inconsolable, despite all the rich, influential men and their wives who offered their condolences and showered her with heartfelt regrets.

Later there was a huge gathering at the Bar X. The

local women provided the traditionally monstrous piles of food and everyone gathered to share their memories of Herman Lowell.

For the first time since childhood, Nicki wandered through the graceful rooms and was struck by the beauty of the house. Even filled with a crowd of mourners, it had a quiet dignity that appealed to her. There was a subtle, almost masculine charm in the warm woods and large airy rooms. It was lovely and completely without the modern clutter that was so admired by rich Victorians.

The memory of a conversation with Levi niggled at her mind. He'd said if the Bar X were for sale, Cyrus's gold would be more than enough to buy it. The more Nicki thought about it, the more she liked the idea. The cabin on the homestead was already crowded and soon there would be one more. This house would have plenty of room for her child and all the babies Liana and Peter were bound to have. With the money, Amanda could go anywhere she wanted to. It would solve everyone's problems.

Will it give your baby a father? Nicki pushed the unwelcome thought away along with the sudden realization that this was exactly the sort of house Levi Cantrell would want to live in. Some of the excitement ebbed out of her, but the idea refused to die. In fact, it was difficult to hold her tongue until the guests had left. Then Amanda's wan expression forbade any mention of it.

"Nicki, may I stay with you for awhile?" She glanced around the house and shuddered. "I can't be here without him."

Remembering her own plea for Aunt Emily to move into Cyrus's room, Nicki nodded. "I know,

Amanda, I know." Swallowing past the thickness in her throat, she gave Amanda a hug. "You're welcome at our house as long as you want."

When Nicki broached the idea of buying the Bar X two days later, Amanda was understandably skeptical. "Where would you get that kind of money?"

"I have it, don't worry."

"How could you?"

"It was an inheritance," Emily said, looking up from her mending. "Nicki didn't know about it until after her father passed on."

"Oh."

"Will you sell me the Bar X?" Nicki asked again.

"I don't really want to live there, Nicki, but I'm not sure I can sell it. It was Daddy's whole life." Amanda walked to the window and stared outside. "I'll have to think about it."

"I understand, Amanda," Nicki said quietly. "Take all the time you need."

39

"Now who's that?" Nicki wondered. She stepped away from the clothesline, and shaded her eyes, trying to recognize the rider coming up the road at a high lope. Nervously, she started toward the house. The man was in a terrible hurry, whoever he was. She was nearly there when the horse skidded to a stop next to her. Nicki looked up into the vaguely familiar face of a young man. His hair was disheveled and he was breathing hard from the ride.

"Did Amanda tell you where she was going?"

"Amanda?" Nicki was startled as much by his clipped accent as his words.

"Yes, Amanda Lowell," he said impatiently. "Do you know where I can find her?"

"She's right . . ."

"Charles?"

Nicki glanced over her shoulder. Amanda was

standing on the porch, eyes wide and fingertips pressed to her slightly parted lips.

"Amanda, thank God." He was off his horse with the words. Nicki had barely recognized him as Charles Laughton before he'd bounded up the steps and swept Amanda into a crushing embrace. "I thought I'd lost you. Your house was shut up tight. When I asked in town, they said your father had died and nobody knew where you were."

"But, Charles, I don't underst . . ." Amanda's words were lost in a passionate kiss.

Openmouthed, Nicki stood and watched as Amanda put her arms around his neck and returned the embrace. It took Peter's touch to get Nicki's attention.

"You and I are in the way," he signed.

With a nod, Nicki followed him through the dogtrot and into the kitchen.

It was a full three-quarters of an hour before Amanda and Charles Laughton joined them. By then Amanda was blushing merrily, and he looked even more disheveled than before.

"Do you still want the Bar X, Nicki?" she asked without preamble.

"Yes." Nicki was surprised by the question.

"Then you can have it." Amanda glanced up at Charles, then back to Nicki. "But I should warn you. Charles says the days of the cattle barons are over, and a ranch in Wyoming is going to be worthless within the year."

Nicki swallowed a grin as embarrassed chagrin flooded Charles's face at Amanda's impetuous confession. "We don't want to ranch anyway, Amanda. We're farmers. Is that what made you change your mind?"

"No, Charles did that by coming back for me. Even when he was home in England he said he couldn't stop thinking about us." Amanda blushed and lowered her eyes. "We're getting married as soon as we get to England. Charles wants the wedding to be in his family church in Kent. We'll leave as soon as we can find a chaperone to go with us."

"Well, congratulations!" Nicki's joy for her friend was very real, yet she couldn't deny a certain emptiness inside. She had thrown away her own chance for such happiness. "Let's see how fast we can get our business concluded so you two can be on your way," she said brightly. If her smile was brittle, no one seemed to notice.

It took almost a month for Nicki and Amanda to close the deal. The biggest problem arose when they tried to figure out how many cattle still carried the Bar X brand. They spent days riding the range rounding up cows and calves. Finally they decided Amanda would sell the cattle that had been gathered and Nicki would keep the rest. Both Charles Laughton and Peter were opposed to the idea, each feeling his side was being cheated, but the women ignored them.

Together, Nicki and Amanda went through everything in the ranch house, deciding what would go and what would stay. Since their tastes were so totally opposite, the task proved to be an enjoyable one for both. Amanda kept everything Nicki considered fussy and overdecorated. On the other hand, Nicki was quite pleased with most of the things Amanda thought plain and boring. They decided to sell the few items neither woman liked.

One afternoon they were poking around in a room behind Herman's office when Nicki's muffled voice came from the back of a large closet. "Amanda, come here and help me with this thing."

Together they pulled a blanket-wrapped object from the depths. "It must be eight feet long. What do you suppose it is?"

"I haven't the faintest idea." Amanda was equally mystified. "Why don't we unwrap it and find out?"

Amanda pulled back the blankets to reveal an enormous pair of horns that had once graced the head of a Texas longhorn. "Oh dear, I'd forgotten about these. Daddy won them in a poker game. What shall we do with them?"

Nicki rubbed the gleaming surface thoughtfully. "I'll bet Charles would love these. You could hang them in the drawing room."

Amanda grinned. "Or better yet in the formal dining room." She deepened her voice in a creditable imitation of her fiancé's cultured tones. "Why yes, Lady Agatha, those horns are quite real. Came from the wilds of Wyoming you know. Good heavens! Jeeves, bring us some smelling salts. I do believe Lady Agatha has fainted in her soup."

Their giggles erupted simultaneously, and it felt amazingly good to laugh together. In a relationship founded more on mutual need than on anything they had in common, the two had shared very little over the years. They felt closer that afternoon than in all the time they had known each other.

As their laughter subsided, Nicki relaxed against the wall. "Is he really what you want, Amanda? I mean, he seems kind of . . ."

"Stuffy? I suppose he is a bit, but I love him."

"Are you sure?"

"Very." Amanda sighed dramatically. "The first

time I met Charles, I knew there'd never be another man for me."

"Oh? What about Levi Cantrell?"

"Ah, yes, Mr. Cantrell." Amanda smiled as she settled herself against an ornate pillow on the floor and ran her hand along one of the smooth horns. "Levi was exactly what Daddy wanted for me. I tried very hard to fall in love with him, but the best I could do was a mild infatuation. Of course, I did find him terribly attractive. Who wouldn't?" She brushed a spot of dust from her sleeve and sighed. "Anyway, I knew from the beginning I didn't have a chance."

"Why not?"

She gave Nicki a sly look. "As if you didn't know."

"Didn't know what?"

Amanda stared at her. "You have no idea what I'm talking about, do you?"

Nicki shook her head.

"My God, Nicki, how could you miss it? That man was so crazy in love with you he never even saw me."

Nicki was taken aback. "I never noticed anything of the kind. Are you sure you didn't imagine it?"

"Oh, I'm sure all right. The way he looked at you . . ." Amanda propped herself up on an elbow. "I know a man in love when I see one, and Levi Cantrell was definitely smitten."

The next morning Emily caught Nicki in the middle of her daily morning sickness.

"Nicki . . ." The unexpected retching brought Emily to a halt in the doorway. "My goodness, are you all right?"

"I think so." Nicki lay back on her bed and closed her eyes. "Must be something I ate."

Emily felt Nicki's forehead. "Hmm, no fever. Maybe you're right. Why don't you just lie here until you feel better?"

Willing her stomach to stop roiling, Nicki opened her eyes. "Did you want me for something?"

"Well, yes, but it can wait. Would you like some tea?"

"No, thank you. I'll be all right if I can rest a while."

"Very well, dear." The door closed softly behind her.

Nicki cursed under her breath. She'd been so careful, even learning to stifle the sounds that would give her away, and she'd been caught anyway. Well, if she wanted to keep Aunt Emily from being suspicious, she'd best act sick all day.

Dragging about on such a beautiful day proved to be very difficult until she asked Peter when he thought they should move into the new house.

"Liana and I are not moving."

Nicki stared at him in disbelief. "What do you mean you're not moving?"

"We like this house and have decided to stay here."

"But, Peter, I already promised Amanda the money. We can't back out now."

"You don't understand. I think you should buy the Bar X. It will be a good home for you."

"By myself?" Nicki was aghast. "I don't want to live alone. Besides, I'll need someone to help me turn it into a farm."

He nodded. "I know and I will help you get started."

"And then what?"

"Then your husband will take over."

"Husband! I don't want a husband."

Peter gave her a knowing look. "You will."

"But how can you turn your back on all that money? It's as much yours as it is mine."

He grinned at her. "I didn't say I wouldn't be your partner. I just won't live there."

Nothing she said made the slightest difference to him. Nicki struggled to maintain her optimism about buying the Bar X, but it was rapidly being replaced by a feeling of defeat, especially when they sat down to dinner that night.

"I have something to tell you all," Emily announced. "I've decided to go East with Amanda and Charles." A moment of stunned silence greeted her words.

"Has something happened, Mama?" Liana asked fearfully.

"No. Well . . . yes. Dr. Bailey has been suggesting a partnership for quite some time, and I finally decided to accept."

Nicki felt a horrible sinking sensation in her middle. If Aunt Emily went back to her old job with Dr. Bailey in Massachusetts, she wouldn't be here when the baby was born. "How . . . how nice for you," she stammered.

"Wait a minute," Liana said suspiciously. "Just what kind of partnership did Dr. Bailey offer you?"

Emily blushed like a schoolgirl. "He asked me to marry him."

Liana jumped to her feet and ran around the table to hug her mother. "Oh, Mama, I knew he was sweet on you. This is wonderful!"

As everyone talked at once, Nicki felt more and more out of place. Everyone had a mate except her,

Liana and Peter, Amanda and Charles, and now Aunt Emily and Dr. Bailey. It wasn't long before she truly was feeling ill and went to bed.

Nicki didn't even hear the door open the next morning as she emptied her stomach into the chamber pot. She lay back on the bed with an exhausted sigh.

"Something you ate hmm?" Aunt Emily's voice startled her as much as the blessedly cool cloth laid on her forehead. "Tell me, does Levi know he's going to be a father?"

"What makes you so sure it was Levi?"

"My love, I saw the blood on the blanket last summer."

"Oh God." Nicki tried to roll away. "It's not what you think."

"What I think," said Emily pulling her back, "is that you and Levi expressed your love the way nature intended you to. So you forgot to see to the social conventions beforehand. You weren't the first to do that, and you certainly won't be the last."

Nicki finally opened her eyes. Where she expected to see condemnation and pity, she saw only loving concern. "Oh, Aunt Emily." With a sob she threw herself into Emily's arms.

Pouring out her confusion and fear while Emily gently rocked her, Nicki found release. When she sat up at last, she felt purged. Wiping her eyes, she smiled mistily at her aunt.

"How does it feel to have a watering pot for a niece?"

"It feels wonderful," Emily said, returning her smile. "So what do we do now?"

"Nothing."

"But, Nicki, surely you're going to let Levi know . . ."

Nicki shook her head. "I don't know where he is, and even if I did, I wouldn't tell him. Don't you see? He'd feel like he had to marry me. I can't trap him like that. It wouldn't be fair to either of us."

On that point, Nicki remained adamant. No argument swayed her in the least, and at last Emily gave up.

Nicki was just finishing up the evening chores when Peter came stomping up to her outside the barn. It was obvious he was very angry about something. Fists clenched at his side, he stood looking at her as though he was about to burst.

"Peter, what's wrong?"

"You are what's wrong." Nicki felt scorched by the burning gaze he raked over her as his fingers moved in hard, angry words. "I have always called you my sister, but today I am not so sure."

With a sick feeling, Nicki realized he knew her secret. "Did Aunt Emily tell you?"

"No, Liana, but only because I could see she was troubled." He glowered at her. "But I'm not troubled, I'm angry."

"You're mad because I got pregnant? Well, tough! I don't care what you or anybody . . ."

"It isn't your baby that makes me angry," he interrupted. "It's your selfishness."

"My selfishness! What are you talking about? For two months I've kept my shame to myself. The last thing I've been is selfish."

He gritted his teeth. "You are only one, but you make choices for three. To me that is selfish. It is you who have decided your baby will not have a father, and Levi won't know his child. You have taken something very important from both of them."

"But Peter," she cried, stung by his logic. "What if Levi doesn't really want to marry me? He'd do it anyway, you know."

"So you don't even give him a chance to do what he thinks is right?" Peter rolled his eyes. "You decided they should never know each other because of stupid, empty-headed pride and a need to punish yourself for something you didn't do alone. I'm ashamed of you, Nicki."

Appalled, Nicki stared at him. What he said was true; she was keeping a father and child apart. "I . . . I never thought of it that way." For the second time that day she dissolved into tears.

As she pressed her face against his chest, Nicki didn't see Peter's expression sag with relief. Nor did she see him sign, "It worked," to the two women watching from the house before he folded her into his arms.

40

"*Well, this is Horse Creek,*" Nicki said as they rode down the busy main street. "Where do we go from here?"

Peter pointed to a sign that announced, HORSE CREEK GENERAL STORE, Frank Collins, Prop. "If that's like Adams's Mercantile, they will know where these Cantrells live."

Nicki nodded and they turned their horses toward the hitching post. Dismounting, she wondered again if they were on a wild-goose chase.

Mrs. Adams had been the last to see Levi when he'd stopped for supplies, then headed north. They'd been unable to find any other trace. Then, Nicki had remembered Amanda's chatter about the rich Cantrells of Horse Creek. Perhaps they were relatives, just as Amanda had said. If so, they might know where he was. It wasn't much, but it was all they had to go on.

The bell over the door tinkled cheerfully as they walked in, and the man behind the counter glanced up with a smile. "Good afternoon. What can I do for you folks?"

"Could you tell us where we might find a family named Cantrell?"

"Sure can. They own a big spread about ten miles north of town." He pointed toward the street outside. "You follow that road until you get to the main ranch house. Can't miss it." He looked at them curiously. "Lookin' to buy another Cantrell horse?"

Nicki raised her eyebrows in surprise. "Another?"

Frank Collins nodded toward Wildfire who was tied right in front of the store window. "Just figured you might want another to go with the one you're ridin'."

"Ah, maybe. We haven't decided yet." Nicki had a sinking feeling in the pit of her stomach. If Wildfire really was a Cantrell horse . . . she didn't even want to finish the thought. "Do you happen to know Levi Cantrell?"

"Ever since I've been in Horse Creek. He and his family own the Triple C Bar. That who you're looking for?"

"I'm not sure we're talking about the same man. What does he look like?"

"Big fella. Scare a man half to death except he's always got a grin on his face. Wears a beard in the winter, shaves it off in the summer. Some of the ladies seem to think he's mighty handsome." Frank Collins took his spectacles off and began to polish them with a cloth. "We haven't seen much of him the last few years, but I reckon he's home for good now. Says his roving days are over." When he put his glasses back on, he was startled to find his customer's face had turned a pasty white. "You all right?"

"Fine. I just got a little too much sun." Nicki was relieved when the shaft of anger burned through her shock. It was so much easier to be mad. "Thank you for your help." She turned and strode out of the store.

Nicki was on Wildfire and headed back the way they had come when Peter grabbed her bridle. "Where do you think you're going?" he asked. "Levi's home is the other way."

"The son of a bitch lied to me, Peter."

He didn't even react to her use of profanity. "When?"

"When he didn't tell me who he was and where he was from."

"You didn't ask."

"That's beside the point. Damn it, Peter, he owns a ranch, one of the biggest ranches in the territory."

Peter shrugged. "So do you."

"Don't be dense. I'm not going, and that's final."

"If that's the way you feel, I won't fight you." He untied his horse and swung up into the saddle. "I'll go myself. When I find Levi I will tell him you're pregnant and I have come to see that he does right by you." He patted his rifle. "I'll bring him back to Willow Creek one way or the other."

Nicki was horrified. "You wouldn't!"

He gave her a steady look, then turned his horse and headed out of town toward the Triple C Bar Ranch.

Unable to do anything else, Nicki followed him. For the first half mile she cursed at him, calling him an underhanded traitor and everything else she could think of. Throwing invectives at his back released much of the tension but otherwise had no effect. Peter just rode on, blithely unaware that Nicki was yelling at him. When she finally came up beside him, he gave her a sympathetic look.

"I hate it when you do that," she told him.

He nodded. "I know, but it works."

Her anger spent, Nicki's thoughts turned to the upcoming confrontation. Would Levi be glad to see her? Insecurity battled with assurances from Peter, Amanda, and Levi himself, assurance that he loved her and had for a long time.

Over the last three months she had relived their afternoon in the cave innumerable times, but today the memories were even more poignant. It was those images that had given her the courage to come this far. Before the day was over, she'd know if the magic they had created there had been as lasting as it was unforgettable. The closer they got, the harder her heart pounded and the drier her mouth became.

The ranch buildings had just come into view when Nicki and Peter were intercepted by a boy on a big black horse. Obviously an accomplished horseman already, he reined in and flashed a smile that reminded Nicki strongly of Levi.

"Howdy," he greeted them, eyeing them with friendly curiosity. "What can I do for you?"

"We're looking for Levi Cantrell," Nicki said returning his smile.

"He took a herd to the north range this morning but ought to be back pretty soon."

"Is there some place we could wait for him?"

"Sure, go on up to the house. Probably even some-

body around that can take you up to meet him. I'm
suppose to get this note to the neighbor's or I'd do it.
How do you like Itty Bit?"

"Itty Bit?"

He jerked his head toward Wildfire. "Your mare.
We called her that cause she was such a small filly. I
helped break her," he bragged. "I see she filled out
some."

"I . . . yes she's filled out very well, and I think
she's wonderful. She has the smoothest gait of any
horse I've ever ridden."

He nodded with satisfaction. "Figured she'd turn
out good. Well, best get going. Might see you later."
With a wave he was gone, the huge horse thundering
down the road in a swirl of dust.

Nicki wondered if the boy was Levi's little brother.
Somehow she'd thought Cole would be older, closer
to her own age. At any rate, he had dispelled any
thought that they might have come to the wrong
place.

As they approached the house, she felt a rush of
insecurity. What was she doing here anyway? Nobody
in his right mind would want a twenty-year-old
mother-to-be who looked for all the world like an
adolescent boy. As she swung down from Wildfire,
suddenly, irrationally, she wished that she was wearing her pink dress. Levi hadn't been able to take his
eyes off her when she'd worn it.

With a nervous glance at Peter, she knocked on the
door. Almost immediately a feminine voice called out,
"Just a minute. I'll be right there." It wasn't long
before they could hear the sound of footsteps
approaching, and Nicki nervously wiped the palms of
her hands on her pants legs.

The door was opened by a young woman with a beautiful smile. "Sorry I took so long. I was taking a pie out of the oven. Is there something I can do for you?"

Nicki's voice froze in her throat as she looked up into the face that had haunted her for months. She'd seen the woman only once in South Pass City, but there could be no doubt. It was Stephanie, and she was very pregnant.

She looked back and forth between the two visitors curiously as Nicki stared at her in shock. The silence became uncomfortably long, and still Nicki's tongue refused to move. It took Peter's nudge from behind to get her going.

"Good . . . good afternoon . . ." she said, desperately seeking an excuse, any excuse that could get her away from here without Levi ever knowing she'd come. "We . . . ah . . . we seem to . . . ah . . . that is . . . I think we're . . . um . . . lost . . . and . . ."

"Good heavens!" Stephanie's eyes widened. "I know where I've seen you before. You're Nicki!" Hers eyes sparkled in obvious delight. "And you must be Peter. Oh, this is wonderful. Come in, come in."

Nicki gave Peter a bewildered look. He shrugged and pushed her toward the door. The large kitchen was filled with sunshine and the spicy smell of apple pie.

"Please sit down. I'll get some coffee." Stephanie indicated the chairs around the table with a smile. After pulling three cups from a cupboard, she set them on the table and filled them. "I can't believe you're really here. Just wait until Levi gets home. He'll be so surprised."

Setting the coffeepot back on the stove, she turned

back to them. "Oh dear. What am I thinking of? I'm Stephanie Cantrell."

Nicki nodded, forcing herself to look away from the bulging stomach. "I know."

"You do?"

"When Levi had malaria last summer, I helped nurse him. He talked about you a lot. I . . . I saw you in South Pass City, too." Sickly, Nicki realized Stephanie's baby must have been conceived then.

"You were there? Levi never said a word." She ambled over to the table and sat down. "Well, come to think of it, maybe he did at that. He said something about coming back later with a friend but . . ."

She was interrupted as the door swung open and a man stepped inside. In spite of his black hair and the bluest of blue eyes, his face was achingly familiar. It took less than a heart beat for Nicki to realize this was Levi's little brother, Cole. *Little?* She almost laughed aloud. He filled the doorway. Cole might not be quite as broad as Levi, but he topped him by several inches. Nicki had the uncomfortable feeling that even wearing her boots, she could walk under his outstretched arm and never disturb a hair on her head.

"I saw Itty Bit outside. I hope there's no problem with her," he said as he closed the door behind him and hung his hat on a hook.

"N . . . no, no," Nicki said hastily. "She's just fine."

Stephanie tipped her face up to receive the light kiss he dropped on her forehead before he sat down. "These are Levi's friends, Nicki and Peter, and this is my husband, Cole."

Husband? Nicki felt as though a giant hand had squeezed all the air from her lungs. A kaleidoscope of moments whirled through her mind. Suddenly, odd bits and pieces fell into place. Levi counting on Stephanie being the perfect wife . . . for Cole. Levi going to St. Louis to bring Stephanie back . . . for his brother. Levi kissing Stephanie . . . his sister-in-law.

Nicki was sure no one had ever been a bigger fool than she. Stephanie was married to Cole, not Levi, and she was carrying Cole's baby! Gradually she became aware of three faces staring at her in concern.

"What's wrong?" Peter signed. "You look strange."

"I . . . I'm fine. I just felt a little dizzy for a second there."

Stephanie looked unconvinced. "Are you sure you're all right?"

Nicki nodded, embarrassed to have caused such a stir.

"I was just about to get Cole a piece of pie. I'll bet after your ride, you and Peter could use a bite to eat, too." Without waiting for an answer, Stephanie rose to her feet and cut into the still hot apple pie.

"If you didn't see me in South Pass City, how did you know who I was?" Nicki asked trying to collect her thoughts.

"I saw Levi's carving." Stephanie put three pieces of pie on the table and went back to get forks. "You're older, of course, but the resemblance is remarkable."

"What carving is that?"

Stephanie sat down. "Well let's see. You had braids, I think, and a missing front tooth. I guess I paid more attention to your face than the other details."

Nicki turned to Peter in astonishment. "You gave him your carving? But why?"

"He liked it," Peter signed, then took another bite of pie and chewed with obvious enjoyment.

"Peter, I love your carvings, but you've never given me one."

"You never needed one." He smiled at Stephanie. "Tell Mrs. Cantrell her pie is delicious."

Nicki delivered Peter's message then stared at her own pie in confusion. There seemed to be an unending supply of surprises in store for her today, and there was still the question of how Levi was going to react when he saw her.

"Mr. Cantrell, we met a boy on the road who said we might be able to ride out and meet Levi."

"My son Josh no doubt." Cole grinned. "I'm surprised he didn't offer to take you himself."

"He said he had a message to deliver or he would."

Cole chuckled then swallowed the last of his coffee and stood up. "As it happens I'm headed that way. You're certainly welcome to come along if you like."

"Cole, why don't you and Peter go." Stephanie smiled up at her husband. "I think Nicki needs some time to rest."

"But I'm fine," Nicki protested.

"You're still a little pale," Stephanie told her, "and you've hardly touched your pie. They'll be back within the hour."

"I think you should stay here, too," Peter signed to her. "You say you are all right, but you forget your baby. It needs to rest, not bounce around in the saddle."

Realizing there was a great deal of truth in what he said, Nicki gave him an irritated glare but said nothing.

Nicki was so used to people not understanding Peter's language that she sometimes forgot many of the signs were almost self-explanatory. The sign for baby was one of those. Nicki was too busy watching Cole to notice Stephanie's startled look.

The uneasy expression on Cole's face was one Nicki was very familiar with. He was clearly dismayed by the prospect of being alone with Peter. "You can talk to him, Mr. Cantrell. He'll read your lips. Just make sure you're facing him when you speak and talk normally."

With a relieved nod, he was gone, and Nicki was left alone with Stephanie. To her surprise, the next hour turned out to be very enjoyable. Nicki wasn't even aware of how skillfully she was being drawn out by Stephanie's genuine interest in her. She only knew she'd found someone who liked talking about Levi, for Stephanie was obviously quite fond of him.

"Without Levi, I'd have gone crazy waiting for Cole to come to his senses. He became a very dear friend in a short time."

"But you didn't fall in love with him?"

Stephanie laughed. "No, but Levi said that was only because I was already in love with Cole when I met him."

"Cole is a very attractive man," Nicki said politely.

Stephanie smiled. In spite of the compliment, it was quite apparent that Nicki thought she'd been foolish in choosing Cole over Levi.

With a sigh Stephanie rearranged herself in her chair and put a hand on her protruding stomach. "The little one is active today. I'm glad I've only got a few more weeks."

"Does it hurt?" Nicki asked curiously.

"When it moves?" Stephanie smiled. "No, it feels kind of nice. Still I'll be glad when I can go riding again. I do miss that."

"You had to give up riding?" Nicki was plainly horrified. "Why? Is it dangerous for the baby?"

"Oh no. At least I don't think so. I quit because it got too cumbersome to ride my sidesaddle, and I couldn't fit into my trousers anymore. I think I could have ridden astride a month or two longer if I'd had the proper clothes."

"Well that's a relief. Do you get sick when you wake up in the morning?"

Stephanie grinned. "Not anymore, but I used to, and at night, too. I don't know who was more relieved when it stopped, me or Cole."

"It stops?"

"Thankfully, yes, but it's just about the time your clothes get too small. It's like trading one symptom for another."

When they moved on to another topic, Nicki was still completely unaware of how much she had given away. The time passed quickly, but she kept glancing nervously at the window. Finally the noises that heralded the arrival of someone on a horse could be heard outside.

Stephanie rose and walked to the window.

"Oh good. Here's Levi now. You and Peter are welcome to stay the night if you like. Levi's parents will be home tomorrow, and I know they'll want to meet you both."

"Thank you. You've been very kind," Nicki said breathlessly as she moved to the door. "I've enjoyed our visit."

Then she was outside, running down the steps,

everything else forgotten in the overwhelming flood of longing that surged through her at the sight of Levi tying Lady next to Wildfire at the hitching rack.

What should she say to him? A thousand possibilities tumbled through her mind. "I missed you, I was wrong, I love you, Can you ever forgive me," the list seemed endless. Yet, when she was finally standing next to him, her voice deserted her.

For a timeless moment they stared at each other, their gazes caressing, noting small details they'd thought forgotten. Awareness flowed between them like a current, but both refused to acknowledge it, afraid to hope. Seconds passed, minutes, a thousand years, and still they stood frozen in place. At last, the creak of saddle leather as a horse moved broke the spell.

"Hello, Nicki."

"Hello."

Levi's first impulse was to sweep her into his arms and smother her with kisses. Instead, he waited for her to speak, to tell him what she wanted. The pounding of his heart was nearly strangling him, but her words in the cave were still fresh in his mind. Removing his hat, Levi ran nervous fingers through his hair. *Why don't you say something?*

Why are you just standing there? Aren't you going to kiss me? "Stephanie and I had a nice visit," Nicki said.

"I always figured you two would like each other." *Can't you see I still love you, Nicki?* "Peter says your aunt's getting married."

Aren't you in love with me anymore? "Yes, to her Dr. Bailey. And Amanda is marrying Charles Laughton."

"Cupid has been busy."

"Who?" Nicki gave him a bewildered look.

"Never mind. Peter said you had something important to tell me?"

Oh God, I can't just come out and tell him. I need time to think. "I . . . I'd like you to be my foreman," she said, trying to stall for a few extra moments.

Levi snorted. "A foreman for 160 acres?"

"No, you don't understand. I've bought the Bar X."

"You what?"

Explaining the circumstances only took a short time, but Nicki's heart came close to breaking. Where was her kind and caring Levi? How could he have changed so much? This cold-faced stranger was a travesty of the man she loved. In those few minutes she realized she could never tell him why she had really come nor of the child she carried. ". . . so you see I need somebody who knows ranching to run that part of it for me."

Levi shook his head in disbelief. *You want me for a goddamned foreman! That's all I mean to you?* "And you thought I wouldn't mind just dropping whatever unimportant thing I was doing because you bought a ranch."

"No, it wasn't like that. I . . . ."

"Look around you, Nicki. Everything you see I've struggled for. Twenty-five years of my hard work and sweat have gone into this place. We've turned it into one of the top horse ranches in the country, and I'm not leaving it again. It's my life."

"Well . . . maybe you could keep your part of this and buy into the Bar X. You could be my partner," Nicki said desperately.

"I hardly think I'd have time to work two places."

A hot surge of anger stiffened Nicki's spine. What

was she doing begging him? Who did he think he was anyway? She had just offered him half of one of the biggest cattle ranches in Wyoming Territory, and he acted as though she'd insulted him.

"Well, how the hell was I supposed to know?" she said. "We thought you were a drifter, and you never bothered to tell us any different, did you? I only wanted to share my good fortune with a man who helped my family through a tough year. I certainly didn't mean to offend you!" Her violet eyes flashed with anger as she turned toward her horse. How had Peter and Emily ever talked her into coming here? She didn't need Levi Cantrell, and neither did her baby.

Levi grabbed her arm. Looking down into her stormy eyes, he sighed. "I'm sorry, Nicki, I didn't mean it to sound like that."

One look at the sad expression on his face, and Nicki's anger evaporated. Levi hadn't meant to hurt her. He just didn't love her anymore. She swallowed the lump in her throat and glanced around to hide the tears that threatened. "You . . . you really do have a very nice place. I don't blame you for being proud of it."

"Nicki, I . . ." The love he felt for her threatened to choke him. It would be easy to do as she asked, but he wanted so much more. "I'm sorry, I truly am. I'll help you find a foreman if you'd like."

"No, no that won't be necessary. I had someone else in mind if you weren't interested," she lied. "Well, I see Peter's ready to go. We'd better get going. Amanda and Aunt Emily are planning to leave Friday, and I want be there to see them off."

Nicki untied the reins and swung up onto Wildfire.

"Well, I guess this is good-bye then," she said with a falsely bright smile. "Please tell your sister-in-law thank you."

"I will. Nicki . . . I'm sorry."

"Yeah," she whispered, turning away. "Me, too."

41

Stephanie jumped as the door slammed shut behind Levi. One look at his thunderous expression, and her heart sank. He looked very much like Cole in one of his rages. This was going to take careful handling. "Where's Nicki?" she asked casually, turning back to the bread she was making.

"On her way back to Willow Creek, I imagine."

"Aren't you going to stop her?"

"No, I'm not."

"Then you aren't going to marry her?"

"Marry her? Are you crazy? She's the most obstinate, temperamental, contrary woman I ever met in my life."

"Maybe that's why I liked her so much." Stephanie smiled. "She sounds just like Cole."

"Believe me, she's worse." He kicked the woodbox angrily. "I asked her to marry me three months ago. She wouldn't even consider it."

"Maybe she changed her mind."

"She didn't."

Placing a loaf in the pan, Stephanie looked over her shoulder at him. "Isn't that why she came?"

"Hell no. She came to offer me a job." He pulled his hat off and flopped down into a chair. "Wanted to thank me for all I did. Christ! As though she didn't know why I stayed all that time."

"And why did you?" Stephanie asked gently.

"Because I promised her father I would before he died. And because I love her more than life."

"Then why did you leave?"

"Because it hurt too much to stay. Stephanie, I'm thirty-three years old. I want a wife and children. No matter how much I love her, I'm too old to play her games."

"She didn't act like she was playing. I think she wants you."

"Sure, for her ranch foreman."

Stephanie shook her head. "I don't think so." She sat down in the chair opposite Levi and smiled at him. "Nicki felt sorry for me, you know."

"Sorry for you. Why?"

"Because I married Cole instead of you. She thought I'd settled for second-best."

"Second-best! Every woman who's come in contact with Cole since he was nine years old has fallen for him."

"Well Nicki didn't. In fact, I don't think she was particularly impressed." Stephanie reached across the table and patted his hand. "I doubt she paid much attention to him if you want the truth. She loves you too much to even notice another man."

"Then why didn't she say so?"

"It seems to me somebody like her would have a lot of pride. Maybe offering you a job was the only way she could think of to get you back. If I were you, I'd get on that horse of yours and see if I could catch up to her. Then I'd throw myself at her feet and beg her to marry me,"

"I've already done that. She wasn't interested."

"Maybe if you . . ."

"Drop it, Steph," he said. "It's my life, and I know what I'm doing."

Stephanie shrugged and pulled herself to her feet. Silence reigned in the kitchen while she stoked up the fire and set her bread on the table to rise. She was calmly cleaning the flour from the workspace before she spoke again. "Is the baby she's carrying yours?" When total silence greeted her question, she turned to find Levi staring at her.

"She told you she was going to have a baby?" he whispered hoarsely. It was his worst nightmare.

"Not exactly, but I'm nearly sure Peter said something about being careful of her baby when she wanted to ride out to get you. Nicki insisted she was going until he did this." Stephanie rocked an imaginary baby. "She stayed, but she acted like she thought he'd used unfair tactics."

"Lord."

"Later, when the subject came up, she seemed abnormally interested for an unmarried woman. From what she said, I'd guess she's several months along." She gave him a long look. "Is it yours?"

"Of course it's mine! The day before I left I . . . we . . ." He dropped his head into his hands. "Oh God, what have I done?"

"Good heavens, Levi, it isn't the end of the world. Just

go after her, say you're sorry, tell her you love her. Then kiss her and sweep her off her feet. She'll forgive you."

"No, you don't understand. Damn, why couldn't I keep my hands off her?"

"What is it, Levi?" Stephanie asked gently, coming around the table to massage his big shoulders.

"Didn't you look at her?"

Stephanie nodded. "Of course, I did. She's beautiful."

"She's also tiny."

"I think the word is petite."

"Whatever the word, she's too damn small to have my babies!" He turned to her with anguish-filled eyes. "She'll die just like my mother did, Stephanie, and it's all my fault."

Stephanie's mouth dropped open. "That's why you left isn't it? All this nonsense about her loving you or not is mostly hogwash. You're afraid she'll die in childbirth." She sat down next to him and took one big hand in hers. "Oh, Levi, lots of small women have babies. They don't all die."

"They aren't married to a big ox like me either."

"I'm not sure problems with birthing have as much to do with size as you think. Big women with small husbands can die, too. Besides the baby is half hers too. It could be small."

"I hadn't thought of that."

She smiled. "I didn't think you had. Your father told me your mother's health was fragile long before Cole was born. Nicki may be small, but she's strong too. She's not a hothouse flower that's going to wilt at the first sign of stress."

"You think I'm being stupid?"

"No, but it seems to me if she's already pregnant, the time for worrying about it is past."

"Damn, why didn't she tell me?"

"Maybe she wanted to be sure you still loved her. I don't think she'd be comfortable marrying a man just because he fathered her child."

"God, no. She'd face it all by herself first." He jumped to his feet. "What am I sitting here for? The way she rides when she's mad they're probably halfway to Horse Creek by now."

Stephanie grabbed his hat from the table and put it in his hand as he turned toward the door. "Good for you, Levi. Don't take no for an answer."

She smiled as the door slammed shut behind him. Humming under her breath, she turned back to her work.

Nicki finally slowed Wildfire. She wanted to keep loping on and on, away from Levi, away from her pain, but the horse was lathered, and it was unfair to take it out on her.

"You didn't tell him, did you?" Peter asked accusingly when he finally caught up with her.

"He didn't want me, Peter. That's all I needed to know."

"He has a right to know about his child."

"I'll send a letter after it's born. He can spend as much time with it as he wants."

"I think . . ."

Nicki reached over and stopped his hands. "Peter, please. I can't take any more right now. Just leave me alone."

He gazed at the naked pain on her face for a moment and then nodded. She had a right to grieve.

They headed south toward home. About half a mile

from the town of Horse Creek they crossed a small creek. There they stopped to water their horses and fill their canteens. Nicki was just putting the top back on hers when Wildfire nickered a greeting to another horse.

Alert to the restless movement of the horses, Peter pulled his rifle from the scabbard and waited. Heartfelt relief flickered across his face as Levi rode into the clearing.

"You fight with her. I am tired of it," he signed to Levi. "I'll be back later." Turning back to his horse, Peter slipped his rifle back into the scabbard. Neither Nicki nor Levi even noticed when he rode away.

"What do you want?" she asked.

"I forgot to tell you something."

"Write it in a letter."

"I'd rather tell you in person." He dismounted, grabbed her by the shoulders and turned her to face him. "I love you Nicki. I've never stopped; I never will. Stephanie seems to think you feel the same way."

She stared up at him, stone faced, without so much as blinking an eyelash. They stood there, eyes locked for what seemed an eternity. At last Levi dropped his hands, disappointment etched into his face. "No, I guess you don't. I'm afraid Stephanie has a blind spot where I'm concerned." He gave a bitter laugh. "She was sure wrong this time."

"She wasn't wrong," Nicki said softly, staring at her boots. She glanced up and encountered a pair of blue-gray eyes filled with desperate hope. "I didn't come to offer you a job. I came because I love you." She crossed her arms in front of her body and rubbed her elbows. "God, it's so hard to admit. I've never needed anybody before. I thought I could take whatever came my way, but my life is nothing without you."

"And my life has been pure hell since I left Nowood," he said. "Not an hour has gone by that I don't miss you. I thought it would get better with time but it hasn't."

"No, it hasn't for me either. Even with everything that's happened, I couldn't get you out of my mind."

"And I couldn't get you out of my heart."

Suddenly she was in his arms. As their lips met, all the unanswered questions that lay between them became unimportant.

"Marry me, Nicki," he said when he broke it off at last.

The welcome words flowed over her like spring tonic. "You still want me?"

"I'll still want you a hundred years from now."

"Even when I'm old and wrinkled?"

Levi kissed the bridge of her nose. "Especially then." He gave her a slow, seductive grin. "By that time we'll have long since passed our ranch on to our grandchildren and won't have anything to do but chase each other around." His voice was husky as he kissed the corner of her mouth. "And I'll give every one of those wrinkles very special attention."

"Farm," she murmured, her eyes drifting closed as she felt something warm and wonderful uncoil inside her.

"Hmm?" His lips grazed the sensitive skin below her ear.

"A farm." Nicki was having difficulty concentrating. "We'll leave our grandchildren a farm, not a ranch."

There was a stunned moment of silence, then a

chuckle rumbled from deep inside his chest. "Nothing slips by you, does it?"

"I don't know why you even try." A smile played around her mouth. "You know how I feel about ranching."

"Pretty much the same as I feel about farming." His hand caressed her back lovingly through the thin material of her shirt. "Guess we'll have to figure out a way to do both. Maybe we'll start a whole new era in Wyoming." His grin faded. "But not right now," he murmured against her lips.

For once, Nicki let him have the last word.

Author's Note

During the summer of 1886, ranchers and homesteaders alike were plagued by drought, grasshoppers, prairie fires, and a shortage of grass. The overburdened cattle range was in serious trouble before the fall roundups even began. Then, winter struck, the worst ever recorded in Wyoming. Historical accounts speak of blizzards lasting for weeks, fifty-foot drifts, sixty-mile-an-hour winds, and temperatures far below zero. For the cattle industry it proved disastrous.

Unable to find food or water, cattle died by the thousands. Piling up against fences and in deep gullies, they perished of starvation and thirst. It has been said that the wolves and coyotes grew fat during the winter of '86, but everything else suffered a horror the like of which has never been seen since.

Losses varied greatly. One rancher reported he began the winter with a herd of 5,500 and ended with a mere 100 head. Another, who fed hay all winter, lost less than ten percent. Overall, the cattle loss in Wyoming was estimated to be about fifty percent, though no one really knew for sure.

Historians agree that the winter of 1886–1887, following a decade of falling cattle prices, brought an end to the reign of the cattle barons in Wyoming.

ONE NIGHT by Debbie Macomber

A wild, romantic adventure from bestselling and much-loved author Debbie Macomber. When their boss sends them to a convention in Dallas together, Carrie Jamison, a vibrant and witty radio deejay for KUTE in Kansas City, Kansas, and Kyle Harris, an arrogant, strait-laced KUTE reporter, are in for the ride of their lives, until one night. . . . "Debbie Macomber writes delightful, heartwarming romances that touch the emotions and leave the reader feeling good."—Jayne Ann Krentz

MAIL-ORDER OUTLAW by Millie Criswell

From the award-winning author of *Phantom Lover* and *Diamond in the Rough*, a historical romance filled with passion, fun, and adventure about a beautiful New York socialite who found herself married to a mail-order outlaw. "Excellent! Once you pick it up, you won't put it down."—Dorothy Garlock, bestselling author of *Sins of Summer*

THE SKY LORD by Emma Harrington

When Dallas MacDonald discovered that his ward and betrothed had run off and married his enemy, Ian MacDougall, he was determined to fetch his unfaithful charge even if it meant war. But on entering Inverlocky Castle, Dallas found more pleasure in abducting MacDougall's enchanting sister, Isobel, than in securing his own former betrothed.

WILLOW CREEK by Carolyn Lampman

The final book in the Cheyenne Trilogy. Given her father's ill health during the hot, dry summer of 1886, Nicki Chandler had no choice but to take responsibility for their Wyoming homestead. But when her father hired handsome drifter Levi Cantrell to relieve some of her burdens, the last thing Nicki and Levi ever wanted was to fall in love.

PEGGY SUE GOT MURDERED by Tess Gerritsen

Medical examiner M. J. Novak, M.D., has a problem: Too many bodies are rolling into the local morgue. She teams up with the handsome, aristocratic president of a pharmaceutical company, who has his own agenda. Their search for the truth takes them from glittering ballrooms to perilous back alleys and into a romance that neither ever dreamed would happen.

PIRATE'S PRIZE by Venita Helton

A humorous and heartwarming romance set against the backdrop of the War of 1812. Beautiful Loire Chartier and dashing Dominique Youx were meant for each other. But when Loire learned that Dominique was the half brother of the infamous pirate, Jean Lafitte, and that he once plundered her father's cargo ship, all hell broke loose.

COMING NEXT MONTH

CIRCLE IN THE WATER by Susan Wiggs

When a beautiful gypsy thief crossed the path of King Henry VIII, the king saw a way to exact revenge against his enemy, Stephen de Lacey, by forcing the insolvent nobleman to marry the girl. Stephen wanted nothing to do with his gypsy bride, even when he realized Juliana was a princess from a far-off land. But when Juliana's past returned to threaten her, he realized he would risk everything to protect his wife. "Susan Wiggs creates fresh, unique and exciting tales that will win her a legion of fans."—Jayne Ann Krentz

JUST ONE OF THOSE THINGS by Leigh Riker

Sara Reid, having left her race car driver husband and their glamorous but stormy marriage, returns to Rhode Island in the hope of protecting her five-year-old daughter from further emotional harm. Instead of peace, Sara finds another storm when her husband's cousin Colin McAllister arrives—bringing with him the shameful memory of their one night together six years ago and a life-shattering secret.

DESTINED TO LOVE by Suzanne Elizabeth

In the tradition of her first time travel romance, *When Destiny Calls,* comes another humorous adventure. Josie Reed was a smart, gutsy, twentieth-century doctor, and tired of the futile quest for a husband before she reached thirty. Then she went on the strangest blind date of all—back to the Wild West of 1881 with a fearless, half-Apache, bounty hunter.

A TOUCH OF CAMELOT by Donna Grove

The winner of the 1993 Golden Heart Award for best historical romance. Guinevere Pierce had always dreamed that one day her own Sir Lancelot would rescue her from a life of medicine shows and phony tent revivals. But she never thought he would come in the guise of Cole Shepherd, the Pinkerton detective in charge of watching over Gwin and her younger brother Arthur, the only surviving witnesses to a murder.

SUNFLOWER SKY by Samantha Harte

A poignant historical romance between an innocent small town girl and a wounded man bent on vengeance. Sunny Summerlin had no idea what she was getting into when she rented a room to an ill stranger named Bar Landry. But as she nursed him back to health, she discovered that he was a bounty hunter with an unquenchable thirst for justice, and also the man with whom she was falling in love.

TOO MANY COOKS by Joanne Pence

Somebody is spoiling the broth in this second delightful adventure featuring the spicy romantic duo from *Something's Cooking.* Homicide detective Paavo Smith must find who is killing the owners of popular San Francisco restaurants and, at the same time, come to terms with his feelings for Angelina Amalfi, the gorgeous but infuriating woman who loves to dabble in sleuthing.

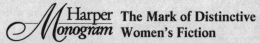

Harper Monogram The Mark of Distinctive Women's Fiction

Harper Monogram By Mail

Looking For Love?
Try HarperMonogram's Bestselling Romance

TAPESTRY
by Maura Seger
An aristocratic Saxon woman loses her heart to
the Norman man who rules her conquered people.

DREAM TIME
by Parris Afton Bonds
In the distant outback of Australia, a mother
and daughter are ready to sacrifice everything
for their dreams of love.

RAIN LILY
by Candace Camp
In the aftermath of the Civil War in Arkansas, a
farmer's wife struggles between duty and passion.

COMING UP ROSES
by Catherine Anderson
Only buried secrets could stop the love
of a young widow and her new beau
from bloomimg.

ONE GOOD MAN
by Terri Herrington
When faced with a lucrative offer to seduce
a billionaire industrialist, a young woman
discovers her true desires.

LORD OF THE NIGHT
by Susan Wiggs
A Venetian lord dedicated to justice suspects a
lucious beauty of being involved in a scandalous plot.

ORCHIDS IN MOONLIGHT
by Patricia Hagan
Caught in a web of intrigue in the dangerous West,
a man and a woman fight to regain their
overpowering dream of love.

A SEASON OF ANGELS
by Debbie Macomber
Three willing but wacky angels must teach their
charges a lesson before granting a Christmas wish.
National Bestseller